Compass Points:

Stories from Seacoast Authors

Piscataqua Press

Published by Piscataqua Press
An imprint of RiverRun Bookstore, Inc.
142 Fleet Street | Portsmouth, NH | 03801
www.riverrunbookstore.com
www.piscataquapress.com

Printed in the United States of America

ISBN: 978-1-939739-82-7

Table of Contents

KATE JOHNSTON
    Shattered   1
PIETRO O'ROURKE
    Religious Painting   17
SCOTT MCPHERSON
    The Mick Situation   29
ANNE BRITTING OLESON
    Gun   45
MICHAEL LOMBARDI
    The System   49
SYDNEY M. SMITH
    The Now Told Story of Mungojerrie   59
        and Rumpleteazer

JASON ALLARD
    Shugyōsha   67
WAYNE BACHNER
    What You Wish For   77
CAMILLE BANHAM
    One More Step   85
LINDA BUTLER
    An Unexpected Fall   93
GUY CAPECELATRO III
    Braids   109
WILLIAM CHANLER
    Dreaming About Victor Frankenstein   111
WILL CONWAY
    Concerto   127
KAREN DESROSIERS
    The Fate of Thomas Boucher   133

LESTER DUBOW
    The Last Painting   147
STEPHANIE FARNAN
    The Choice   151
EMILY GARCIA
    The Greatest American Story   159
ATHENA GILES
    The Drowned Belltower   165
DIANE GRIFFIN
    Vagabondage   179
KATE W. HENDERSON
    Ellasophia   195
GEORGE KINGSTON
    Voting for Love   201
REBEKKAH JANE KOONS
    You're Coming Home   211
ROBERT KOZMAN
    The Healing Tree   219
KATE LEIGH
    The Life Coach   229
MIKE MCGRATH
    That Old, Warm Hum   235
BEN MORONG
    End of the Line   241
MIKE NELSON
    Kamil's First Snow   249
SYLVIA OLSON
    Snowy Day   263
LENORE ROGERS
    The Dragonslayer   273
MARK SLEITER
    Lemonade Buddha   287
TAMMI TRUAX
    A Better Life   301
JANE VACANTE
    Transgression   315

Forward

Here, for your enjoyment, are the winners and a selection of favorite entries from the 2015 RiverRun Bookstore Short Story Contest. Please don't call it the Annual Short Story Contest because this one almost killed us...

Piscataqua Press is now in its third year, and in 2015 we will publish our 100th book. It's hard to believe!

The press is a project of us here at RiverRun Bookstore, in Portsmouth, New Hampshire. We are a fiercely independent bookstore owned by a collective of local citizens. We started publishing books because it seemed the Seacoast was full of authors, many of whom were taking chances publishing with faceless online companies, and these companies were not serving them well.

It is our goal to help those people who may never land a big time publisher, or those people who may purposely want to publish with a small, local establishment, so that they can maintain full control over their work. We work one on one with each author, to make sure they get exactly the book they hoped for.

This contest drew more than 100 entries, mostly from the immediate area. The results show that we do indeed live in a place *full* of literary talent. We hope you enjoy reading these stories nearly as much as we enjoyed selecting them.

Speaking of which, we want to thank *everyone* that entered, even if their story didn't make it into the anthology. Our judging criteria was very, *very* subjective. A half dozen of the owners read as many stories as they could, and the ones that got the best feedback made it into the book. That's it. No special sauce or formula, we just picked the ones we liked best, and we hope you like them too.

Tom Holbrook,
President, RiverRun Bookstore.

Shattered

Kate Johnston

First Place

Vivian stared at the prom dress hanging from the closet door, hoping it was as beautiful as she thought. She and her mother had found the dress last night at a secondhand shop, *Second Chance*. The bodice had a rip in the seam, and the straps were soiled. Her mother pulled an all-nighter, sewing sequins to the straps and mending the seam.

Vivian imagined herself in Charlie's arms, the dress sparkling as though crystal birds were fluttering between them. She closed her eyes, sealing in the vision so fragile she was afraid it would break apart.

Noise downstairs broke Vivian's concentration, and she figured her mother was back. Vivian hurried down the staircase. Her mother had run into town for hair spray. The chignon wouldn't hold without it.

As she entered the kitchen, loud voices carried across the yard. Vivian glanced out the window, but the cedars lifted their drooping branches to block her view of the grey New Englander next door. She scowled at the overprotective trees; they never let her see the good stuff.

"Hey, Vivi. Found what we needed," her mother said, holding up a no-name brand can of hair spray. She grinned. "It's all they had left."

Vivian should have known the good spray would be gone. The other eighth-grade girls had been prepping for the prom for weeks, unlike Vivian who'd been asked just yesterday.

"Thanks, Mom." The uneasy feeling grew in her stomach, butterflies preparing for battle.

"You should eat something," her mother said, adjusting the tie in the waistband of her scrubs.

"I'll throw up."

"You won't throw up. Cheese, crackers, strawberries. Nibble food."

Vivian stood at the screen door, breathing deeply, hoping the earthy odors from the nearby saltmarshes would settle her stomach. She fiddled with her braided hair, brown as the mudflats, and tried to think about ways the prom could be fun, no matter what happened with Charlie. But the argument between her neighbors intruded on her thoughts.

"Why do they fight all the time?"

"Some people don't know how to communicate well."

"He thinks Maryann sleeps around while he's at work," Vivian announced, tossing a 'so there' look at the cedars. They couldn't keep everything from her.

"How's that possible? She takes care of his mother."

"What if Maryann gives Gussie a sleeping pill to knock her out?"

"Vivian Carter." Jen Carter's voice was sharp, like those pins she used to hem the dress. "I don't like that talk. It's disrespectful. And stop eavesdropping."

"I don't eavesdrop. They yell loud enough for me to hear everything."

Yesterday, the Hardings worked on their garden. Vivian watched them from the living room window, out of reach of the cedars. They planted hydrangeas, the kind with the bulky, blue flowers that everyone on the coast had in their gardens. Foss dug the holes while his wife, Maryann, arranged the plants. Together they patted the soil, watered the roots. She tended to each blossom, shaking them free of stray dirt while he leaned on his shovel, his bare, sculpted torso shining with sweat. They'd worked the whole time smiling and talking, and Vivian thought things were better between them.

Today, she noticed the hydrangea blossoms were black and the leaves withered.

"Come and eat, Vivi."

2

Vivian eased herself into a chair. "I don't want to get there early. He'll think I'm desperate."

"He'll think you're excited."

Vivian picked at her food. Charlie, brown eyes beneath a sweep of blonde hair. The plan was to meet Charlie at the entrance to the school property. So they could walk in together. Would they hold hands? Her fingers fumbled with a strawberry as she pictured Charlie and herself walking side-by-side, stiffly, like wooden soldiers.

He'd apologized for not being able to pick her up at her house, but it wouldn't have mattered. Her mother never would allow her to get into a car with Charlie's father.

"What if he doesn't come?" Vivian mumbled.

"You know he'll try hard to be there."

"What if his dad gets in the way?"

"Let's worry about that if it happens."

"I won't go in if he doesn't show. So, don't leave until we're sure he's there. If he doesn't make it, I'm coming home. I won't stay and let Bree make fun of me."

"I'll wait to make sure."

A terrible crash from the Hardings' house made Vivian jump in her chair. Her mother hurried outside and stood on the walkway covered with pine needles. Vivian watched the needles vibrate as they worked hard to soothe her mother. Family legend claimed that pine eased sadness and pain, so Jen sprinkled needles along the walkway every day.

Jen called, "Finish getting ready, Vivi."

Vivian popped the last of the sweet berries into her mouth, tried to sneak a glance out the window, but the cedars foiled her plan as they quickly interlocked their branches.

Dumb trees, Vivian thought as she reluctantly went upstairs. She slipped on the dress, zipping it along the side. She smoothed her hands down the bodice, admiring the shape in her mirror. Her father used to buy her dresses with full skirts that spun out in a perfect, colorful circle when she twirled.

This dress was like that, not a slinky mermaid shape. That's what Bree and her entourage would be wearing.

3

They'd do it all. Stuffed boobs, commando, bright red lips that left greasy imprints on plastic cups.

She was applying eyeliner when she heard the screen door open and close. Then sobbing. She listened carefully. Maryann Harding.

Vivian hurried with the rest of her makeup and went to the kitchen. Her mother was sitting with Maryann. Four trash bags were piled by the door. Something lacy spilled from the top one.

Vivian stared at Maryann. Her blonde curls were mussed; her right eye was swollen shut. She was dabbing a tissue at her cheeks.

Maryann smiled, revealing a bloody lip. "You're beautiful. Who's the lucky boy?"

Vivian looked at her dress, the color of beach roses. "Charlie Davidson."

Maryann patted her mouth with the tissue. If she knew anything about the Davidsons, she didn't let on. "You'll have a blast. I remember my prom. I didn't wear a beautiful gown like that. Mine was all glitter and gold. I was the tackiest thing to walk through Tolend."

Jen stood up, and Vivian saw that she clutched a handful of pine needles. "Vivian, keep Maryann company while I get the first-aid kit."

Vivian slid into the chair, aghast at the mascara running down Maryann's cheeks, the ballooning welt.

Maryann's smile shook. "Just a little whack."

Her mother returned, and Vivian breathed easier. Her mother knew how to fix everything. Dresses, bruises, empty spaces.

She treated the wounds on Maryann's face and asked to see her hand.

"It's broken, Maryann. You need to go to the hospital."

"I can't. He'll..." Maryann paused.

"If it heals like this you won't be able to use it properly."

Maryann swiped at her tears, blackened with mascara. They continued to crawl down her face, like ants at a picnic.

"Maryann, what he did was wrong."

4

"It was an accident, I swear. He's never hit me before."

One year ago, Maryann met Foss on one of his business trips to Joplin, Missouri. They married under a red moon, and Foss brought Maryann to live with him and his mother.

People in town called her a "honky-tonk hooker." Vivian wasn't sure what that meant, and her mother said that some educated people could be ignorant and not to listen to town gossip.

"I'll call work and tell them I'm sick," Jen said, grabbing the phone and heading out of the kitchen.

Maryann looked at Vivian. "Tell me about this boy."

Vivian dropped her eyes, somehow feeling guilty she had a date that night. So, she told Maryann the worst detail she could about Charlie.

"Did you hear about the accident down here? The police chase?"

Maryann frowned, pushing back an unruly curl. "When the drunk driver ended up in the saltmarsh?"

"That's Charlie's dad."

Maryann's eyebrows shot up. "I thought they took the boy away and put him in foster care."

"They did. Then, his dad rehabbed, and he's getting another chance. Charlie's only been back six months."

"What's he like?"

Vivian shrugged. "All the girls think he's cute."

"Really? And he asked you to the prom?" Maryann's voice carried a lilting tease.

"He only asked me because we're friends. He knows I won't make a fuss if he stands me up." Vivian studied her freshly painted toenails. "He doesn't get to keep promises often."

"You're a good friend, Vivi. That's what he needs. Someone to count on."

"Boring," Vivian muttered.

"Trustworthy."

"What about Bree Price?" Vivian blurted. "She lives in the heights, and she's gonna get a red convertible for her 16th birthday. Plus, she's blonde and a tennis champ."

5

"So what?"

"So, I live in the boondocks. I'm scared of sports, and I'm a good math student."

Maryann burst out laughing. "I think you're lovely. Besides, I know Bree Price. Your boy goes home never knowing what his father might do, and you think someone like Bree's on his mind?"

"He's a boy. They have one thing on their minds."

"So, be flattered he asked you to the prom." Maryann winked.

Vivian's cheeks grew hot. "That's not why."

"Either way you know he wants to spend that time with you. No matter what he's thinking about, it's with you."

Vivian bit her lip, uncertain. Charlie Davidson could have any girl, but he asked her to the prom. A big night where things happened. Gossip following the prom reported new couples, breakups, love triangles. Prom was the place where you made an impression, Vivian thought. And you didn't go to prom if you didn't want something to happen.

The butterflies in her stomach surged as though lifted by a tidal wave. What if Charlie wanted something to happen? Her favorite imagined vision of Charlie holding her crossed her mind again.

Jen returned to the room and replaced the phone in its cradle. "All set, Maryann. We'll take Vivi to the prom, go to the ER, and you'll spend the night here."

"Thank you," Maryann whispered.

Vivian watched Maryann twist her wedding ring, remembering the day in the hospital when her parents renewed their wedding vows. The cancer made her father too weak to slip the ring on her mother's finger, and she helped him. After he died, Jen buried the ring in the garden. Since then, a single blossom of a rare flower species known as the Lone Wolf grew there. It survived under any circumstance, alone, never dying. Not even in the harsh winters.

Jen helped Maryann to her feet. "I'll show you the guest room. Vivi, I'll be back in a minute to do your hair."

Vivian listened to Maryann's stilettos click through the

house, a deliberate, tense rhythm that got under her skin.

The screen door swung open with gusto. Vivian turned in surprise.

Maryann's mother-in-law, Gussie, burst into the house. She was wearing her usual attire of tennis whites. "Where's Maryann?" Without waiting for an answer, Gussie marched through the house, shouting, "Maryann, dammit! What the hell you doing?"

Vivian flinched. She'd known Gussie forever, and never had she heard her scream an obscenity.

She heard her mother's voice. "Gussie. You've no right yelling your head off in my home. Please leave."

Vivian went upstairs. Worry stuck in her throat like a sand burr as Gussie screamed at Maryann. Maryann was in tears, covering her face with her broken hand.

"How dare you drag your dirty laundry here," Gussie admonished. "Come back and work things out with your husband."

Maryann brushed past Vivian and went downstairs. Gussie started to follow her, but Jen caught her arm.

"Gussie, you and I need to talk. Vivi, please check on Maryann."

Vivian tracked Maryann by the echo of her stilettos. She found her in the living room, which had been Vivian's father's favorite room. The leather chair and the shelves of books still smelled like his cologne, no matter how many mothballs her mother threw around.

Maryann paced the room like a caged animal. Her hands were unraveling her damp tissue and crumpling it into a ball.

"I shouldn't have come here," Maryann said. "I've jeopardized your friendship with Gussie."

"We can help you and still be good neighbors with Gussie," Vivian said.

Maryann continued to pace and worry her tissue. Vivian thought about the time she found Charlie by the saltmarsh, sitting there like a broken-winged bird. His father was drunk and getting rough, and Charlie ran to avoid a beating.

"When he's sober, I'll go back. I need to let him cool down.

If I'm there, he'll start hitting. And they'll take me away again." Charlie's face soured. "Like a foster home is any safer."

Vivian brought Charlie home. Her house overlooked land where great blue herons cavorted. He walked beside her, slope-shouldered and dark. His jeans and sneakers were soaked from having sat in the marshes.

She led him through the back part of her house, to the laundry room. She left him there while she ran up to the dark bedroom that her mother didn't sleep in anymore and grabbed random articles of her father's clothing. She handed Charlie the stack. "Pick something."

Then, Vivian found her mother in the study, paying bills.

"I brought home a friend," Vivian said.

Without asking the name of the friend, Jen replied, "I'll set another place at the table."

Charlie stayed for four days. Jen went to his dad and explained they were taking care of Charlie until he felt better. Vivian wasn't sure how she'd worded it, but had a feeling she laid it out in simple terms. *If you can't treat your boy right, you're going to lose him again. Get a grip. Stop drinking.* Just like that night when her mother buried the ring and said, *Vivi, your dad died, and now it's just the two of us. We'll be okay, but we have to work together.*

As Vivian watched Maryann struggle to regain her composure, she realized Maryann had lied. She didn't act shocked enough. She acted like Charlie did that day by the saltmarsh, someone who understood the magnitude of the trouble she was in.

"He's done this before. Hasn't he?"

Maryann snuffled. "He's under a lot of pressure."

"How bad?" Vivian eyed the windows. Her nerves spiked. Gussie was here, but Foss wasn't? Why hadn't he come to get his wife? Why was Gussie here?

"We used to have a kitten."

Vivian swallowed around the lump in her throat. She watched Maryann stroke her broken bone with force.

"The kitten was playing with his cufflinks. Lost one of

8

them. He picked up that little guy and threw him." She tapped her forehead. "Smashed into the wall."

Vivian's stomach dropped.

"Once, I found Gussie in the bathroom. Her arm was cut up. She said he'd pushed her, and she put out her arm to stop from falling. She went through the window."

"We need to tell my mom." Suddenly Vivian didn't feel safe in her own home. Two battered women had sought shelter there, and the abuser was next door.

She grabbed Maryann's good hand. They were headed upstairs when Gussie and her mother met them on the landing. Jen looked stricken.

"Vivi. Grab the cell. I'll get the car keys."

Gussie must have confessed, Vivian thought. They all hurried downstairs, but Vivian ran, feeling flames at her back. Her father's voice in her head, *Stay calm, think, be careful.*

She burst into the kitchen and pulled up short. Maryann's husband, Foss, blocked her way. Dressed in his Armani suit and shiny shoes, he held a gun. The black metal matched his black stare.

"Where's my wife?"

Vivian backed away.

"Foss!"

Jen's voice cut through the room with authority, surprising Foss enough that he wavered in his stance. In one breath, Jen was between Foss and Vivian.

"Where's my wife?"

Vivian could see his face over her mother's shoulder. His hair, normally combed back and glossy with oil, was disheveled. His dark eyes moved with agitation. She could smell him, too. A mixture of sweat and Polo, slick nerves. Handing over Maryann might save everyone else, but it'd mean certain death for Maryann. On the other hand, protecting Maryann was fruitless. Foss held a gun, reminding her he'd been stationed in Afghanistan. He'd seen brutal action, been awarded medals for bravery. He knew how to kill and how to survive.

"Foss, I've known you a long time. You plow our

9

driveway for God's sake. You drove me to the hospital when Danny..." Jen paused, her voice breaking. "You don't need a gun. Not with me."

"You could've let me know she was with you. Instead of letting me shoot up the bar."

"You did *what*?"

"She always runs to the bar. Whenever things get stressful. But tonight she came here." His eyes roamed the kitchen. "Why'd she come here instead?"

Vivian clutched her mother's arm. White heat penetrated her mind as she grew fearful for Maryann.

Floorboards creaked behind her. Vivian turned and saw Maryann and Gussie, holding each other up. Gussie was a pale green, the color of unripe pears. But Maryann was pink-faced beneath the fear and bruises.

"Foss, don't be angry with Jen. Please, put the gun away."

"Only if you come with me." His lips tightened. "You too, Mother. We're going home."

Vivian thought about Gussie's cut-up arm. The kitten. Maryann's injuries. Vivian buried her face in her mother's scrub top. God forgive us, Vivian prayed. Forgive us for letting them go back.

Sirens pierced the night. Vivian lifted her face. She looked out the window and the cedars let her watch two police cruisers pull into the Harding's driveway. He really did shoot up the bar, she thought.

"The police are looking for you, Foss," Jen said.

Vivian could see sweat breaking on his brow. What if the cops never think to look for him here?

He waved the gun erratically. "Sit down."

They sat on the floor against the cabinetry. Gussie moaned, and Jen leaned over, asking if she felt okay.

"Shut up, Jen," Foss growled, kicking her.

"Your mother..."

"She's fine." He dragged out a chair and straddled it, leaning his arms over the back. The gun dangled from his hand. "Let's play a game. Confess your biggest regret." He pointed to Vivian. "You first, pretty in pink."

Vivian stared at him. He's a maniac, she thought. Gussie let out another moan. Vivian peered around her mother. Gussie's pale complexion now looked grey. Her eyes were dim, zoned out. "Mom," Vivian said urgently. "Gussie's…"

Suddenly, Gussie slumped over to the side, her head thudding on the wooden floor. Her hands fluttered to her heart, as if in prayer.

"Jesus! She's having a heart attack." Vivian's mother reached for Gussie, but Foss kicked her shoulder with his shiny shoe.

Jen grimaced, clutching her shoulder. "If I don't help her, she'll die."

"Then hurry along your answers. I'm waiting, Vivian."

Vivian's throat tightened. Considering what she was facing now, her regrets seemed laughable.

"Confess!" Foss screamed.

Vivian winced and said in a rush, "I didn't take care of Mr. Darcy. My parakeet. He died. I was too busy with my friends, and I forgot about him."

"A dead parakeet? That's the worst thing you've done?"

Vivian nodded. She'd kept one of his feathers, attached it to a clip and wore it in her hair.

Foss swiveled the gun. "Jen? What do you confess?"

Vivian noticed her mother was motionless. Vivian squeezed her hand. "Mom. Foss asked you a question."

"I heard him."

Vivian stole a glance at Foss. He tapped his gun against his Armani suit. His mouth played at the corners. He was enjoying himself, this stupid game.

"The longer you take, Jen, the worse my mother gets. She's right there, having a heart attack and you could help her. Play the game."

"The police will be here any minute."

"Obviously you have many regrets to choose from. Maryann, your turn while Jen takes her pick."

Maryann sniffed into the tissue. "I wish we hadn't moved in with your mother."

Foss narrowed his eyes. "That's what you regret? Not

11

marrying me? Meeting me?"

Maryann's tissue was a mass of colors from her makeup, reminding Vivian of a Monet painting. "No, hon. I wish we'd gotten our own place. I think we'd have been happier."

"It's not too late," Jen said gently. "You still can make those plans. Where would you live?"

"Beacon Hill," Maryann said. "In one of those brownstones."

"We'd go to the theater," Foss added as though they'd dreamed about this before. "Picnic by the Charles River."

Vivian cautiously gazed at Gussie. The old woman was inert, her breathing shallow. She sensed her mother's anxiety and knew there wasn't much time left.

"That sounds lovely," Jen encouraged. "You could have a kitten."

Vivian drew in a sharp breath and cut her eyes to Maryann.

"Enough, you bitch!" Foss jumped up and kicked the chair, sending it flying across the room. He swiped plates from the hutch and they crashed to the floor, breaking.

He strode over to Jen and pressed the gun to her temple. Vivian stifled a scream as the metal lodged against her mother's head.

"Five seconds, Jen. Five seconds to confess the worst thing you've done."

"Killing my husband," Jen said in a low, flat voice.

Vivian pulled back slowly. What did she say? Killing Daddy? No, she must be lying, to calm Foss. That must be it. Vivian watched Jen stare into Foss's stony face. She wasn't blinking, wasn't giving any sign she was lying.

Impossible. No way. Her mother didn't do terrible things. She was perfect. She knew how to knit and ride horses and turn wedding rings into flowers.

Foss didn't seem repelled. Rather, his eyes glinted. "Go on."

Jen spoke in short sentences, while the gun remained on her head. "The cancer wouldn't go away. We couldn't afford his meds. We were about to lose the house. Everything. I had a daughter to raise."

"Basically, it came down between your daughter and your husband."

"Basically," she said through clenched teeth.

"You took away his chances. Watched him suffer. Let him die. And all this time you pretended to be the grieving widow."

He drew back and sat on his heels. He held his gun casually over his knee, like he was posing for a picture. "You're a murderer, Jen." He said it in awe, as though he'd met his hero.

"Foss. I played your game. Let me help Gussie."

"Sure, whatever."

Vivian's hands dropped from her mother's arm. She watched Jen crawl over to Gussie's body and check her breathing.

Jen's eyes flicked over to Vivian. Her lips quivered and she whispered, "I'm sorry, Vivi. We wanted to protect you, give you a good life."

So, it was true. Tears filled Vivian's eyes. How was being without her father a good life? She had no chance without him, her strong father who taught her how to spot a saltmarsh sparrow and to love Shakespeare. He had more to give her, teach her, and she'd never know any of it. She looked away from her mother and glared at Foss. None of this would be happening if her father were here. Foss never would have held them up with a gun if her father were here.

"Foss." Maryann's voice was unsteady. "We can make it if we run."

Foss blinked at his wife.

Maryann dabbed her eyes. "I have some money with me. And clothes." She stood up, indicating the pile of bags. "Right here, baby."

"Seriously?" he asked.

"We'll run. They'll never find us."

Vivian stared. Maryann was saving him, helping him escape. Anger rose in her chest. How could she leave with him after what he put them through? What about Gussie?

Maryann rummaged through a bag, one of the lumpier ones, and she lifted it with both hands, wincing from the pain it caused her.

"Let's go, baby."

Foss turned for the door. Maryann stepped behind him. She heaved the bag and swung it. The bag rocketed in the air, striking the back of Foss's head. Vivian heard a dull thud, a sickening sound.

Foss fell.

Jen whipped around and shielded Vivian, probably thinking they were under attack.

Maryann swung the bag again, smacking it square on Foss's face. A third time, and she crushed her husband's head.

Jen let out a cry of alarm and tried to block Vivian's view like those damn cedars. But Vivian pushed her away. She was through with being protected.

Foss's body contorted, flopping against the floor. Maryann dropped the trash bag, and it spilled open. She hadn't packed clothes, not in that one. She'd packed goods. Heavy candlesticks. Silver serving dishes. China. Vivian recognized many of the pieces from years of attending Gussie's holiday parties.

Maryann left the house, stumbling in her stilettos. Vivian stood at the window, seeing her walk toward the cedars. Vivian expected the branches to block her view, but they didn't move. She watched Maryann walk straight to the police car.

Before, Vivian and Jen had spent nights and weekends together, watching television, knitting, walking along beaches. Now, Vivian's insides felt shrunken. There was no room for her mother. When they were home together, Vivian stayed in her room and Jen scrubbed the house.

One afternoon, Jen knocked on Vivian's door. "Charlie's here."

Vivian's mouth went dry. He'd been calling her almost

every day since the prom. But, she couldn't face him, not after everything that happened. She supposed a month of unreturned calls was more than anyone could take. Reluctantly, she headed downstairs.

Outside, Charlie was tossing a baseball in the air and catching it with his glove. He was always playing with sports equipment. Last time she saw him he was repeatedly squeezing a racquetball.

He looked like he'd come from a game. His uniform had dirt stains up his legs. She'd heard he was the top base stealer in the league. That meant he was fast. Whipping-fast.

"Let's take a walk," Charlie suggested.

They passed the line of cedars whose branches swept back as though giving permission to walk past the Hardings' house. The *For Sale* sign burned into Vivian's eyes, and she thought about Gussie in rehab. She'd never be back.

"I'm sorry I didn't return your calls," Vivian said, unable to look at him.

"Your mom told me what happened with your neighbors," Charlie said as he threw himself a fly ball. "That must have been awful."

They headed toward the saltmarshes, where cordgrass was visible in the low tide. Vivian breathed deeply, filling her lungs with the odors of decay, death.

"The prom was lousy."

She lowered her eyes, studying the salt hay. "I'm sure other girls filled my shoes."

"Oh, yeah. Dozens. I couldn't get a minute to myself."

"Then the night wasn't a total loss."

"Not at all. I partied all night, never thinking about the girl I missed the most."

She bit her lip, sure he was teasing her. "I thought you asked me because we're friends." He opened his mouth to speak, but she rushed on. "Because it'd have been easy if you couldn't make it. You knew I'd have understood."

"That's not why," he said with a chuckle of disbelief. His brown eyes bored into her. "I asked you because I like being with you."

Vivian couldn't drop her eyes from his gaze. She thought about what Maryann had suggested. Maybe he did ask her to the prom as more than a friend. Maybe there were feelings there that she never knew about. Maybe it was easier to pretend, just in case it all went wrong.

"You can make it up to me by coming to my game tomorrow. After, we'll get ice cream." He grinned, tossing her the ball. She held the ball uncertainly as he turned his gaze to the sky where a hawk glided. "How 'bout it?"

Vivian stood at the edge of the yard, watching her mother toss pine needles along the walkway. She spotted the Lone Wolf in the garden and remembered when they said goodbye to her father. Vivian thought there was nothing anyone could do, but in truth her mother had stopped fighting. It was a big lie, a terrible lie.

But she'd made a big promise, also. *Don't worry, Danny. I'll protect Vivi, give her a happy, full life.*

Vivian thought about the Hardings. When she and her mother were willing to let Maryann go with Foss, just to protect themselves. She thought about Maryann, how she killed Foss to save everybody. She thought about Charlie, how he gave his father chances.

Maybe her father could have beaten the cancer if they'd kept fighting, given him more time. Maybe Foss could have calmed down if given one more chance. Maybe Charlie's dad will get better because Charlie believes in him.

Jen turned and paused, seeing Vivian. Beats of silence swelled as Vivian stepped onto the bed of needles. They vibrated, swirled around her legs. Her father was dead. Maybe he'd have died anyway. Maybe her mother didn't stop fighting. Maybe she just decided to fight for a different cause.

Vivian showed off the baseball.

"I have a date."

Religious Painting

Pietro O'Rourke

First Runner-Up

You're high. You're lying down on the couch in the basement, half or three quarters asleep. Every five seconds or so your eyes close and gradually open back up. The video for Travis' "Why Does It Always Rain On Me?" plays on a small TV. It's three in the morning. You hear what sounds like the whispering of a ghost, so faint, you think you're imagining it. You turn down the volume on the TV, gradually at first, struggling to tell if your mind is playing tricks on you. You turn it down all the way.

As clearly as you'll be able to, you hear the strained whispers of your Nonna from the top of the stairs.

"Alle."

"Alle."

You get up off the couch and quickly scamper up the stairs, taking them two at a time, grabbing the edges of the steps while you ascend in a crouch. Your Nonna is pacing around the kitchen in the dark.

"I feel like I gonna die," she says between pants.

Her breaths are quick, gasping and dramatic. She is coughing. You tell her to sit down. You put your hand on her back and guide her into the living room where she sits on the wooden chair with the yellow fabric backing. You don't know what to do. You're scared. You wonder if you're dreaming. The first thing you think to do is call your Mother. You go into the kitchen and fill up a glass of water while dialing the number. She answers on the second ring, like she's been waiting for the call. You try to get your Nonna to drink

17

some of the water, holding the phone between your ear and shoulder while offering her the rocks glass filled with sink water. She drinks a little bit, but doesn't want any more and shakes her head. Her breathing sounds panicky. She's scared because she doesn't want to die. She never wanted to die. She'd never be ready to go, and they say the way you live is the way you die, and why wouldn't this be true? Your Mother answers and you can hardly get the words out. She's finishing your sentences for you.

"Yes, call 911."

You hang up and call for an ambulance and start pacing back and forth through the living room and the kitchen, losing it, wondering what the fuck you're supposed to do and wishing you weren't high as fuck trying to talk your Nonna down.

"I feel like I gonna die, I dunno what to do."

She's blubbering and scared. You hold the glass of water up to her mouth again, trying to get her to drink it, and she's trying for your sake, but she really doesn't want any. She never wants water, and her cat Rosie is the same way, just like her Momma. You can't talk. You wouldn't know what to say if you could. It takes a couple of minutes before you have the presence of mind to turn on the light in the kitchen. You keep it on the dimmest setting possible.

The house is very dark. It's always dark. At any given time you can't tell whether she's home or not. You're kneeling on one knee in front of her. The two of you are together in the darkness. The curtains are closed. You can see the moonlight tracing its way into the living room through the sliding back door and the shades onto the weird semi-animal print couches that have been a part of too many family pictures to count.

The EMS truck shows up quickly.

You're frightened by the two EMS guys that show up, you're scared of what's happening in front of you, and your eyes are so fucking open you feel like you're on psychedelics for more than one reason. You're not sure what to say to them or what you should do. You wonder if they can tell that you're high.

First they turn on all the lights. They assess the situation. They ask you very calmly what your Grandmother's name is. You tell them it's Giovanna. They try to talk to her.

"What's wrong Joe-vana?"

She acts like a cornered mouse, shakes her head, says, "I dunno" quietly, and tries not to cry too hard in front of the strange men. They give her an oxygen mask that makes her breathing more comfortable, and one thing becomes a little less overwhelming. You help the EMS guys move the kitchen table out of the way so that they can get their stretcher through, and then all of sudden it's over and it feels like two minutes have passed. You feel restless. You rub your open hands over your closed eyes, and wonder if she's already dead or will be soon. It all blurs in front of you as you collapse onto the couch. You black out.

Within two days of her arrival at the hospital, every family member visits her; your brother and cousin Anthony fly in from California, and your cousin Derrick from Alaska. Derrick has recently gotten engaged to a woman who no one in your family has met, but whose picture has been on each one of your family member's fridges via their engagement announcement for the last two months. Derrick tells everyone that the picture of his fiancée "doesn't do her justice." Derrick's mother, your Zizi, is confidently telling everyone within earshot (including your Nonna) how your Nonna will be dancing at his wedding, aka not dead, in four months.

Everyone tells you that you're a hero and thanks God for you being there and "saving" your Nonna's life, but you feel like a fraud and a coward. You know that you can't share or admit to anyone how fucked up you were that night, and how you barely got home from the party you had been at. And how the only reason that you came home at all was because you were too high to deal with the thought of a friend of yours that you had a crush on sleeping with this kid named Ryan. You saw the two of them go into his room, and watched as he unrolled a sleeping bag and nodded at her authoritatively and told her to, "Just come and lay down for a bit." It was too much for you to handle. You hit the blunt a few more times and left without saying goodbye to anyone. You decided to leave your second 40 of Old English in the fridge after finishing the first one.

Your Uncle Giacomo pulls you aside and talks to you outside the hospital room.

"You know Alle, I don't know why you were up, or what you were doing, but the important thing is you were, k?"

The first thing your Nonna tells you when she's cognizant enough to realize that you're with her is, "Why don't you bring Rosie?"

Later in the day, she motions to you from the hospital bed with one hand after coughing and clearing her throat several times. In a barely audible, strained, very dramatic whisper, she asks you to make sure that you "Start-ee the car, every coupla days."

Your family did consider bringing her cat to the hospital, but after thinking about it, decided against it. Cats typically don't do well in such scenarios. Regarding her second point, the car did in fact, not start, when you went to drive it a week later, as you had failed to follow her instructions. You imagined how in different circumstances, she would've reveled in this and laughed about it.

"I tella you."

She knew she was always right.

She's in the hospital for over two weeks, and every time you visit you start to hate hospitals more and more. You hate seeing naked old people around every corner. You hate feeling like you're trapped in the hospital version of *The Shining*. But most of all, you hate the smell. Once you've smelled a hospital, you can never un-smell it. It's always slightly different, but unmistakably the same. Your Father tells you to try and think of the hospital as a place where they help people get better, because he knows that you have very negative associations of hospitals, and think of them as these kind of death waiting rooms. Within five minutes of entering you want to cry. You try to take deep breaths, to just hang out with your relatives and play cards, act un-phased, but it's really hard for you. When your friends call you, you walk towards the elevators at the opposite end of the hall, and you try and forget about what's happening all around you.

Once she regains her health she acts the same as always: indifferent to everything.

When you first started taking Italian classes your junior year of high school, there was this one occasion when you were driving around with your mother and Nonna running some errands. You didn't have a license yet, and these kinds of trips were viewed as opportunities for you to practice your driving skills. While telling a long, emphatic story, your Nonna started repeatedly, angrily, referring to someone as a *Figlio di Boutana* (Son of a bitch). Your mother, shaking her head and rolling her eyes, told her, "You know he can understand you." You all laughed. She looked at you in the rearview mirror from the backseat and smiled, "Cah." (Cah, at least the way your Nonna used it, meant, "I don't know." It could be interpreted as a kind of verbal shrug.)

You later learn from your Zizi that she thinks everybody is a son of a bitch.

It's mutually decided by all parties that she will be better off in her own home rather than the antiseptic realm of St. Joseph's hospital. As soon as she's deemed healthy enough, your family takes her back to the home your Nonno had built for your family 50 some years ago when they first emigrated from Sicily. Your brother is chosen to let the hospice care representative into the house to set up everything. He tells you later how the hospice care set-up man gave it to him straight, and mincing no words informed him not to get his hopes up; most people in hospice care are dead within two weeks, not to be a downer or anything.

At the hospital, instructions are given for her homecare, and you are told about various hospice services. After settling her back in at home for a few days, your mother is going over a schedule of who'll be taking care of your Nonna on what days. She'll be with your mother on Mondays and Wednesdays, your Zizi on Thursdays and Fridays, and your Uncle Giacomo on Sundays, leaving you with Tuesdays and Saturdays. The responsibility of everything forthcoming goes off in your head like a bell and you feel apprehensive.

Propping herself up on her bed and turning to face you on her right side, she addresses you.

"Whatta you tink?" She says, almost smiling.

"What do I think about what?" You say.

"Whattayou tink, you tink I'm a gonna die?"

"No… I don't think you're gonna die. No."

A woman from hospice care comes to the house to administer some standard tests: blood pressure, heart rate, and her oxygen levels. She asks your Nonna if she's in any pain. The middle-aged woman is cheery and pleasant in a way that makes you think she hasn't been doing this for very long. She is about to leave when your mother follows her to the front door and urges her to please come back. Your Nonna is having difficulty breathing. Something isn't right. The woman seems nervous. There is no doubt that she would've left had your mother not said anything. Earlier, when asked about the breathing troubles your Nonna had been having, she shrugged it off as something that happens. She pointed to a breathing machine that you'd been supplied with that your Nonna had never quite taken to.

Things start to happen fast. All three of you help your Nonna into the bathroom upon her request. She starts whimpering. You've seen this play before. She doesn't know what to think about her body failing her. When your body is no longer able to do something that it's always done, you panic. Her breathing becomes rapid. You're all working together to help her get off the toilet and on to the Lay-Z-Boy recliner a few steps away. There's a strong light coming in from the windows and the glass sliding door behind her. It's the middle of the afternoon. You get her onto the recliner. The hospice woman continually checks her vitals and levels; all of which are plunging, becoming less and less promising with each check. The hospice woman tells both you and your mother that maybe it's time to say your goodbyes. You stay with your Nonna as your mother and the hospice woman go over to the kitchen table several paces away and discuss what the proper course of action to take is. Your mother tells her to call an ambulance, and the woman responds that they shouldn't, it's too late. In a fierceness conveyed by a whisper that a mother would use when scolding her children in public when trying not to make a scene, your mother yells at her until she calls her supervisor in appeasement. The phone is handed off to your mother who has to agree to the fact that she is going to give your Nonna more morphine than hospice care is legally allowed to. She then gets the clearance to administer the shot herself.

"She can't be in any pain, I told her she wouldn't be in any pain," your mother says over and over again, like a refrain, to the faceless person on the other end of the phone, to the hospice care worker, and to you. Her voice vacillates between a defiant strength, a quiet anger, and a quivering fear.

The hospice care woman fills up a syringe at the kitchen table, and she and your mother return back to the living room. You lean the recliner back as far as it can go so your Nonna can lie flat on her back and not have to see the needle. The hospice woman lifts up her nightgown enough for your mother to shoot the syringe into her exposed left thigh. Your mother tries to put the syringe into her leg, but she's hesitant because it's the first time she's ever tried to do it. She tells your Nonna that she's gotta try and help her, that she's gotta try to work with her, because she's trying. Your Nonna winces in pain and sucks for air like a fish out of water.

"Hurry-uppa."

The hospice woman is talking, almost yelling, louder than any of you.

"Oh God!"

"She's gonna go, we have to pray for her!"

"WE HAVE TO PRAY!"

The four of you are connected in an almost biblical fashion, like an old religious painting: your Nonna reclining in the chair gasping for air; your Mother telling her, yelling at her, to "look at me" because she wants her to know it's going to be ok; while you hold onto her hand and the chair as the hospice woman strangles both of your hands. And it's all kind of perfect. As perfect as something like this can be, because you know that you were all meant to be there, together. Her breathing becomes less and less frantic and eventually fades into a surrendering resignation. The hospice care woman states the obvious and tells you, "I think she's leaving us now," as the breaths become sparser. Her eyes no longer open back up.

The three of you try to pick her up off the recliner. After a few attempts, you realize that you physically won't be able to. The hospice woman suggests that you put multiple blankets underneath her, forming a makeshift stretcher to take her off the chair and onto her bed in the far corner of the living room. The three of you lunge across the room with the elegance and subtlety of three linebackers, not thinking about how horrible it would be if the plan fails. You catch your collective breaths after you succeed in getting her onto the bed where she lies on her left side before you adjust her onto her back. Her lips become gradually bluer. You try to make it look serene and peaceful, attempting to erase the struggle and pain of the last hour, to make it look like she tranquilly faded away and told you all that she loved you, instead of violently kicking against the inevitable, not ready for whatever came next. The hospice care woman leaves after 20 minutes, and gives you and your mother her deepest sympathies with a tear-stained smile. You shouldn't begrudge her, but you do. You wanted her to make everything okay. You wanted her to know exactly what to do.

It becomes less and less clear with the passage of time if she did everything that she could've, or if she failed you in some way. You will vacillate between feeling sorry for her and resenting her. The worst part of it all is that neither you, nor your mother can remember her name then, or at any point thereafter.

Your mother goes into her childhood bedroom and cries and cries like you've never heard her cry before. She seems to be in physical pain, wailing out in a very primal kind of way, like she's reliving every painful event and traumatic experience that's ever occurred to her.

After your Nonna being pronounced "Gone," your Mother manages to call your father. She asks you to call your Zizi and Uncle Giacomo and tell them. She isn't up for it. She feels like she let your Nonna down because she promised her she wouldn't be in any pain when she passed away, and unfortunately she was. An hour later, your Father comes by the house after being granted permission to leave work early. He goes into her room and comforts her as best he can, but she continues to sob her eyes out. It's all too much for her.

You call your Zizi first. You call her at work and tell her that her mother has just died. Your conversation is brief, her voice is calm, and she tries not to make a scene. She chokes up, and the pitch of her voice rises in a way that betrays the fact that she's attempting to stifle her tears. She tells you that she'll come over as soon as she can.

You then call your Uncle Giacomo. He's in shock and he

25

doesn't believe you. He shouts at you.

"NO!"

He asks if she at least went peacefully, and you lie to him and tell him yes. It seems like the only thing to say, and what good would the truth do at this point anyway? Only you, your mother, and the hospice care woman will know the reality of the day. Your Uncle had spent the day prior with your Nonna, and she had been in good spirits, seemingly doing well. He spent the night in his childhood bedroom, and when you came upstairs the next day, he was drinking coffee and eating Cheerios wearing the same pajamas that his father had worn (with fat tan and grey vertical stripes that look like grandpa bellbottoms). Your mother was glad that he had this time with her. That he will get to have that lasting positive memory of her as she was on that day, because their relationship was often strained.

After your phone call with your Zizi, she calls your cousin to tell him to come home, that his Nonna is gone. He comes undone. He locks the keys inside his car and his girlfriend has to calm him down and call AAA. It's a two hour drive to her house from Lansing, but it's important to your Zizi that all of her children who live in-state get to see their Nonna before she gets taken away. When your cousin Alessandro (both of you named after your Nonno as the second born male children in our respective families) and his sister Lindsey arrive at the house they approach your Nonna's body tentatively. They wonder what they should do. What's the appropriate reaction to have? This final goodbye is strictly one-sided, and while you want to touch or embrace the departed, it's not clear how to act once you've come face to face with your dead grandmother. The first thing that feels appropriate is to kneel down so you can be at eye level with her. You can say something out loud to her, or inwardly, it depends on how ceremonious you want to be. This seems like the time to cry, but once you're put in the situation, you don't know how you'll react. You might stare at her in disbelief, you might be sad, you might think about a moment that you shared together, or maybe you won't be thinking of anything at all. Maybe you'll feel completely stifled by the expectation that you're supposed to be having some sort of emotional reaction, and feel forced to emote on cue like an actor, when maybe all that you want is to have your own moment, whatever that may be; some type of shared one-sided experience that you can look back on or store somewhere in the back of your mind.

You really made her look nice though. She has all her favorite blankets layered on top of her, and you also laid some of the afghans she's knitted over the years across her feet. You propped her up with two pillows, and you can see her hands clasped together on top of her stomach under the blankets. It looks very proper, photogenic even.

Your Uncle Giacomo arrives in his big silver truck. He wants the TV on. Everyone wants something to take their minds off the fact that their Nonna, or mother, is lying in the corner of the room, dead.

You all wait for the men from the funeral home to come to take the body away and prepare it for the open casket funeral.

The TV is on channel three when your uncle turns it on, and it stays there. All of you watch a progressive learning segment on PBS that's geared towards children. It shows two women with their adopted child as some *Sesame Street* looking text explains to the viewer that, "Some people have two mothers!"

It then shows an Asian man with his Caucasian partner as they each hold up one of their adopted children. The text says, "This is another new family! Some families have two daddies!"

Your uncle says with a chortle, "You see that Alle?" Referring to your cousin and not you in this case. "They're calling that the new family. Ha."

"I don't have any problem with that," your cousin's girlfriend responds.

"Yeah, I don't think there's anything wrong with that," your cousin adds.

Giacomo flares up.

"Well, you know what? They call that the new family? Ok,

27

that's great, but that's not my family, Alle."

You walk behind the two men from the funeral home as they wheel your Nonna out the front door on a stretcher. It's almost identical to the scene weeks earlier when the EMS truck took her to the hospital. You watch them load her body into the back of the black car. You watch as the car drives off down the street, and that's it. She's gone. It seems like the appropriate time to cry; you feel confused. Is that all there is?

Your family orders Jet's Pizza and tries to act like nothing's wrong.

The Mick Situation

Scott McPherson

Second Runner-Up

The old bitch had Ed Jasper's cat, and he was going to kill her for it. The plan was simple; the execution, all in the timing.

It started about eight weeks before, when Ed and his wife Celina brought home an early Christmas present to each other, to go along with their first house. They'd only just moved in, back in early October. They called a local veterinary, to see if there were any kittens available. There weren't, but the vet's office had just taken custody of a small cat, a stray male, about a year old.

"Oh my *God*," Celina said when she saw him, like it was all one word. "He looks just like Thomas O'Malley from the *The Aristocats!*"

He did: orange and white, except he was always a smaller guy.

They'd spent an inordinate amount of time on paperwork. "About your particular situation, Mr. Jasper," the nurse/receptionist said, handing over the clipboard. His name was Ed. Not Edward, or Eddie; it was just Ed. Everybody he knew called him Ed. He'd been Ed since he was born.

Average height, Ed was slightly built, not skinny but hardly muscular. An accountant for the power company, most people described him as friendly, but irritable. They said it just like that, too—with that slight but noticeable pause. He got to work early every day, so he could leave at 4 o'clock and avoid the really bad traffic. Celina was a dental assistant, in a strip mall out by the gypsum factory. They lived a quiet life, preferring to stay in most nights and watch movies.

Were they married? "What fucking difference does *that* make," Ed mumbled under his breath, as Celina played with the cat behind him. They'd been married for two years, this past August.

It was clear right away that this was an unusual cat: calm, but not sedate. It sat obediently in Celina's lap, playful and affectionate. He swatted at her hand, gently, his eyes wide, looking from Celina to her hand, then purring violently and rubbing his face shamelessly along her jawline. "Do we have a *fenced* yard," Ed was saying, shaking his head incredulously. Celina wasn't listening; she was in love.

The cat stayed on her lap for the entire drive home. Ed offered Celina the pet carrier, just to get him to the car, but she clearly didn't need it; with the cat snuggled right up under her chin, against her throat, she even had trouble putting on her seat-belt.

It was twenty minutes back to their house, a tiny two-floor duplex unit on a street of duplexes. They'd purchased recently, in what their realtor called an "up and coming neighborhood" —code for random property crime and the occasional drug dealer. Everyone was talking about resale value, and the location was hard to beat. Raised in an apartment, Ed just wanted a yard, in a neighborhood — "where kids play in the street," Celina always mocked him, smiling. That *is* what he wanted.

And a cat. Ed wasn't a dog person.

"I want to call him Mick," he blurted out, as soon as they pulled into the driveway. Celina agreed, so Mick it was.

Mick never got beyond medium height and build, maxing out at ten or eleven pounds, but Ed said he oozed confidence—"Like a young Clint Eastwood." He groomed himself constantly, meticulously. A damn cool cat, Ed would say.

"He's so *small*," Celina would say, as Mick lay across her shoulders. Whether she was watching television or reading a book, if she was sitting down, that's where Mick was. If she was on her feet, he was right in front of her, staring into her eyes and meowing loudly until she picked him up, purring and rubbing his face against the side of hers.

Their sex life was inconvenienced, at first, until Ed started closing the bedroom door. Mick stayed out in the hall, his feet flashing into sight under the door, or scratching violently at the frame, wailing loudly. It was distracting, but Ed put on the radio to cover the noise. The three of them sleeping in the bed at night was a bit much, but they made it work.

Then Mick wanted to go outside.

At first Ed didn't like the idea, especially since they'd told the vet they wouldn't. "But it's cruel to keep him locked up, when he wants out so bad," Celina argued, unable to bear the thought of Mick unhappy. "Besides, the look on his face when he stares out the window — it's so *purposeful.*

"*He* doesn't care how long he lives," she stated, with finality. They let the cat out.

And that's how they met Francine Connolly, the skinny, ugly, rat-faced woman, no more than five feet tall, who lived down the street. A retired elementary school principal, at seventy-nine she'd never had any children of her own — instead dedicating her life to ruling over other people's children with an iron fist.

She had a couple of friends, but they rarely came around. Slowed by age, but possessed with a pervading sense of purpose, she preferred to spend her time identifying those situations that offered her a chance to be useful. Frail and stooped, she shuffled around the neighborhood, dispensing unsolicited advice that people sooner rather than later learned wasn't advice.

Her husband had been a commercial pilot, driving 747s four days a week. Twenty-four years ago an arterial embolism killed him instantly over the Rockies. The co-pilot was in control, so the passengers never noticed a thing.

Francine had waited on him hand and foot; she never remarried.

Francine Connolly knew certain things to be true. For example, a woman should visit the hairdresser at least once a week—not that she had much hair to speak of. More like a pale red afro the stylist teased into something resembling a bunch of broccoli every Thursday afternoon.

A man should help a lady — that was a lecture she reserved for men, usually after one had just been helpful in some way.

Another insight of hers was that kids were like criminals; she'd made it a point to share *that* particular pearl of wisdom with all incoming staff at Franklin Roosevelt Elementary. That's also why she broke up groups on the playground, leaving the admonished children somewhat confused as to what exactly they'd done wrong.

Francine Connolly did *not* like long grass, long hair (on men), short hair (on women), trash cans left out overnight, work contracted without the proper permits, jay parking, jay walking, cycling without a helmet, skateboarding (with or without a helmet), any music made since John F. Kennedy was president, or private schools. Most of all, Francine Connolly disapproved of outdoor cats.

"An unpleasant situation," she'd long been fond of saying, "requires immediate rectification."

Mick became her latest situation. That's why Ed had to kill her.

Ed and Celina adopted a simple routine: in the morning they both left early for work, letting Mick out. In the evening he was there, pacing back and forth at the front door. After feeding him, the two of them would go out for a walk, usually with Mick trailing a few feet behind. Then they'd watch a movie together.

One evening, a few steps down the sidewalk, a voice croaked out from the dark.

"I saw ya cat the utha day," Francine Connolly said, by way of introduction. Ed and Celina looked around, not seeing her at first, their eyes finally settling on the tiny, hunched, frizzy-haired figure in the shadows.

"Hi," Ed said, stepping toward her, extending his hand, "I'm Ed Jasp—"

Francine cut him off. "I said, I saw ya cat the utha day," she repeated, her voice weak, the Yankee accent so thick it was almost as irritating as the interruption. Instantly, it grated on Ed's nerves. He put his hand back in his pocket.

"Yes, that's Mick," said Celina, smiling, friendly. "This is my husband, Ed, and I'm—," but Francine cut her off as well.

"It's a busy road, he-ah," she was saying, gesturing toward the street, not looking at them.

"I'm Ed Jasper," he tried again, quickly, not offering his hand this time. "We moved in a couple of months ago," he added, pointing at their house.

"He's a good lookin' cat," Francine said, after a moment. "It's not safe to let cats outside." With that, she turned abruptly, shuffling slowly back toward her house. Like so many of her students, Ed and Celina stood, confused, staring after her.

The next evening, Mick wasn't there. Celina was distraught. "Do you think he might have been hit by a car," she asked, her face tense with concern, and guilt. They called the animal shelter, but it was closed. They drove around for hours, searching. Celina's heart jumped into her throat every time they saw something in the road. A small mound ahead brought an involuntary yelp, but it was just a burlap sack.

"I'm sure he'll be back by morning," Ed whispered, as they lay in bed. Celina lay on her side, back to him, sobbing gently.

He wasn't there in the morning.

Celina was a mess all day, and raced home. They went door-to-door, meeting neighbors for the first time, leaving a flier with Mick's picture and their phone numbers—Ed's first, since he would be more likely to answer. Her boss didn't like her taking personal calls.

Francine Connolly took a long time. They were about to turn away—the driveway was empty; she didn't own a car— when the door opened slowly.

"Oh my god," Celina exclaimed, as Mick ran out, practically leaping into her arms, rubbing his face against hers. "Oh, thank you so much," she said, smiling brightly. "Did you find him somewhere?"

"No," Francine said, soberly, putting her hands in her pockets, eying them with obvious disapproval. The silence was thick, tense.

"So how did he get in your house," Celina asked, more serious now, fighting to keep Mick out of her face. "Was he in some kind of trouble?"

Francine didn't respond for a long time. Getting information from this woman — it's like pulling fucking *teeth*, Ed thought, standing there on her stoop.

Completely ignoring Celina, she turned to him. "What was ya name again?"

"Ed," he said, trying hard to be friendly. Her breath was horrible.

"Edward —," she started, but it was Ed's turn to interrupt *her*.

"It's Ed, actually," he said, cutting her off. "Everyone calls me *Ed*," he added, emphasizing the name. Nobody called him Edward; his name was Ed. That's what *everybody* called him, for Christ's sake.

But years of authority is hard to unlearn. "Ed*ward*," she said again, really emphasizing the second syllable, and not trying to sound patient, "have you ever seen a cat that's been hit by a car?"

The worst part was that, when she said it, it sounded like *cah*. He hated that, but he hated the way she said *Edwed* even more. He realized, right in that moment, that he absolutely hated her too.

"Do you own a cat?" he asked, irritably, hoping she did, not liking this situation at all.

"I used to," she confessed, briefly softening. "They just die," she said, stiffening again. Ed and Celina seemed to lose her then; she drifted momentarily, becoming lucid only after a few awkward seconds. So they excused themselves, leaving her with a flier.

"Feel free to call us, if you need anything," Celina said, as Francine Connolly closed the door indifferently.

She called, the very next evening. "I've got ya cat ova he-ah," she said, "if you wanna come get him."

That time she let them in, but just inside the front door. All they saw was the living room; the decor was Spartan, the room empty and cold, furniture and wallpaper easily from three decades ago. The air smelled like dust and frozen dinners and halitosis, and death.

Ed saw a bowl that definitely had cat food in it, sitting right by the door. It was the wet stuff, the kind the vet had told them would rot a cat's teeth, next to a bowl of water — right there where she'd left them. After luring Mick into her house.

That evening, Mick didn't want to come to bed with them. He wanted out again.

Francine called them over three more times that week — the last time mentioning that Mick had been in her house "since yestaday ev'nin'." Ed swore he saw a litter box in her hallway.

"You know, Mrs. Connolly," he said, irritated, struggling to hold onto Mick, "if you stop letting him in your house, he'll just come back home."

"It's a dangerous situation, a cat outside," was all she said, with disapproval.

"This has *got* to stop," Celina said, angrily. She was smoking; she'd quit years before, but always kept a pack around for "special occasions," like parties, or relaxing with a few glasses of wine. Anything but relaxed right now, she sat at their table, stubbing her cigarette out in the ashtray halfway through, jamming it repeatedly down into a pile of butts, watching her own work intently.

Leaning back, her arms across her chest, she scratched distractedly at a tooth. Mick was by the door, restive. She reached out for the cigarettes again, lighting a fresh one.

"I know what's she's doing," Ed roared, pacing back and forth in their living room, as Celina smoked. "She doesn't want to *own* a cat, but she does want *control* over one."

When she called again, two days later, Ed had had enough. Putting on his coat, he walked down the street and rapped loudly on her door.

"Mrs. Connolly, *stop letting Mick in your house*," he demanded, staring her down. Not pausing for a response he said quickly, his volume rising with his temper: "He's *our* cat." She recoiled, dropping her chin slightly, pulling it back into her neck—her ugly, wrinkled, Yankee neck, under her screwed up face, lips twisting into a snarl.

She tried to look hurt, but Ed could tell she was really angry.

He pressed his case. "If he's over here, *we* can't look after him properly." Letting that sink in, he added, for her benefit, "You know, to make sure he's okay, and get him to a vet straight away if he's not?"

Francine wasn't listening; she was staring down, at her hands. Rubbing them together, she looked up, defiant. "I'm not comfortable with this situation," she said, breath disgusting, chin high, eyes blazing. "It's not safe to let a cat outside."

With that, she slammed the door in Ed's face.

Ed left work a little early on Friday, not feeling very well and hoping to take it easy over the weekend.

They'd both gone upstairs to watch a movie in bed, Ed drifting off to sleep and leaving Celina to finish *Titanic* on her own. The lights were off downstairs, but it was early enough that Celina hadn't locked up for the night.

Plus Mick was outside; he'd gone back out after dinner, and she wanted him in *their* house tonight—not Francine Connolly's.

Just as Leonardo DiCaprio was helping Kate Winslet feel like she could fly, Celina heard the front door open, and quickly close again.

Her mouth went dry, heart pounding in her chest.

"Ed," she whispered, panicked, practically shoving him out of bed, *"what the fuck was that?"*

Celina never swore; more than anything, that brought him back to consciousness. "What's the matter," he asked, rubbing sleep from his eyes.

"I think there's someone in the house," Celina whispered, utterly terrified.

Ed was wide-awake now. Looking toward the bedroom door, he realized his phone was downstairs. "Do you have your phone," he asked, getting out of bed, unsure of exactly what to do. "Please God, tell me you have your *phone!"*

When she shook her head, he thought he was going to throw up.

"What about your dad's gun?" Celina said. It was a small revolver his father had given them on their wedding day. Celina didn't like having it in the house, so Ed never bought any ammunition. Right now, he really wished that he had.

"No bullets," he said, fear rising in his throat. He heard movement at the bottom of the stairs.

"Someone's coming up the *stairs,"* he hissed. "Quick: get under the bed!" Celina did, shoving aside boxes of shoes and Christmas decorations. Lying on her stomach, she held her breath, looking helplessly toward the door, seeing only headlines about murder and rape.

Ed grabbed the lamp from his bedside table, yanking the plug from the wall as he did, raising it up over his head as he stood. Frozen in place, his feet like giant cinder blocks, legs weak, knees shaking. They could hear the intruder making his way steadily down the hall, toward their bedroom. Ed's armpits were soaked, his arms trembling like a bed sheet on a washing line.

Mick stopped at the threshold. He looked from Ed to Celina, then jumped on the bed.

* * *

"We could call the police," Celina was saying. Ed sat in the kitchen, half-awake and looking deep into a cup of coffee, head in his hands. It was throbbing. She was smoking again.

"I'm not *kidding*," she said, when he looked up.

"What are we going to do about this situation!" she shouted, slamming her open hand down on the table, spilling Ed's coffee. Mick was by her feet, doing figure eights around her calves.

Neither of them had slept much. First, Ed had locked the door, looking out the window for any sign of Francine Connolly. Not seeing her, he resolved to confront her the next day. He'd spent the night tossing and turning, giving up about three in the morning.

Somebody was at the door. It was an Animal Control officer. "Just a routine check," he said, asking to come in, but leaving no doubt it was not a request, "to verify the welfare of an animal." He was a portly fellow, short and sandy-haired, not fat but definitely overweight. His name tag said Robertson, over the pocket of a wrinkled shirt.

"The party in question said she feared for the animal's safety," he was saying. "Is there any way I can see the cat?"

"Look, I don't understand what's going on here," Ed said, impatiently, uncomfortable with this uniformed stranger in his living room. "Have we broken some law?"

"Animal abuse is a serious matter, Mr. Jasper," Officer Robertson said, glancing Ed's way, one eyebrow cocked, like someone who took the matter quite seriously indeed. He was petting Mick.

"But you can see he's *fine*," Ed said, pointing at the cat, his other hand in his pocket. "And who the hell told you we were abusing our cat, anyway," he asked, knowing the answer.

"The call was anonymous; the caller just said the cat was being mistreated."

"Oh, for Christ's sake," Ed moaned, throwing his hands up in defeat and briefly turning away. "Okay," he said, after a moment, arms slightly outstretched, hands open, fingers splayed.

"Here's the deal," he began, trying to remain calm. "I know who called you. Her name is Francine Connolly, and she's obsessed with our cat." He could swear Officer Robertson reacted to the name. "She lives down the street," he continued; pointing deliberately, he said, "She doesn't approve of outdoor cats, and lets *ours* in her house." Exasperated, he blurted out angrily, "She opened our fucking door last night, to let him *in!* It scared the hell out of us!"

Officer Robertson looked thoughtful, sympathetic even. "*That's* a situation for the police," he said, after a pause. "*My* job is to make sure the cat is okay—which he clearly is." Looking at each of them in turn, he said, "Whatever problem you have with your neighbor, that's *your* problem."

Celina stepped forward, cigarette in one hand, ashtray in the other. "But it's not illegal to let a cat out, is it," she asked, hooking the thumb from her cigarette hand on a strand of hair that had fallen across her face, pushing it back to reveal the heavy strain there.

"No," Officer Robertson said, rubbing his jaw, chuckling. "It's not *illegal*. But I've known Francine Connolly since I was in grade school, and *that* old battle ax is accustomed to getting *exactly* what she wants. I'd save myself a heap of trouble," he said, looking at them seriously, "and stop letting the cat out."

Leaving, he tried to offer some consolation. "Think of it like this," he said, leaning close, "she's an old lady. How much time can she have left?"

Too long, thought Ed. That's when he decided to kill her.

But how? He had no doubt that he could do it; he *had* to do it. Celina was a mess, and Mick was spending less and less time at home. That meant he was spending more and more time with *her*.

Christ, how Ed hated that woman.

So he decided to push her down the stairs. It seemed like the best thing to do.

The next time he let Mick out, she would be sure to call

him over. If anyone saw him go in or out, he'd have an excuse: I was just getting my cat, Officer. He could even show the police his phone log, proving that *she* had called *him*. Celina wouldn't know anything.

He'd lure her upstairs, then shove the bitch off the landing, or maybe trip her at the top. It would all depend on the timing.

A terrible accident, the neighbors would say, gathering outside—drawn by the lights of an ambulance, called after someone, maybe the mailman, saw her body through the window. Fell down the stairs, poor thing. Yes, Ed would answer, a most unfortunate situation.

It was perfect. And it wasn't long in coming.

They intentionally kept Mick in for the rest of the weekend, at Ed's insistence. "We need a couple of days—to not deal with *her*," he'd said, completely exasperated.

It was tough, though. Mick spent most of his time by the door, meowing loudly or scratching at the door frame whenever one of them came near. When Celina tried to take him upstairs to bed Sunday night he scratched her, jumping out of her arms and running back to lay by the door. Ed couldn't sleep; anger and adrenaline kept him up all night.

Monday morning, they let Mick out when they left for work. Ed fiddled around, looking for any distraction to make the day go by faster. He left at 3:30, to make extra sure he got home before Celina—so that *he* got the call, when it came. Mick wasn't home either.

Perfect, Ed thought. Absolutely perfect.

Putting on a movie, *The Godfather*, he tried to concentrate, but it was no use. All he could think about was killing Francine Connolly.

He was picturing that moment—that glorious moment— when she realizes *exactly* what is happening to her; that instant she goes off balance, with no hope of recovery—just a long drop.

How he smiled, imagining the panic spreading like wildfire across her face—her stupid rat-face, old wrinkling arms flailing, nightgown billowing, reaching vainly for something — *anything* — but knowing it isn't there. Maybe make eye contact, so she could see him smile, right before the end.

Only a matter of time, he thought, the smile widening. He hadn't been home fifteen minutes when the phone rang.

"Yer cat's ovah he-ah," came that infuriating cackle, raising the hairs on the back of his neck, blood rushing to his head, blurring his eyesight.

"I'll be right over," he said, calm and even.

"And how are *you* this evening," he asked, showing every tooth in his head when Francine Connolly opened the door.

Mick was there, in her front room. Lying on the floor. In a bed. *A brand new cat bed!*

Ed felt the blood again, pounding behind his eyes. He struggled to focus. Then the smile came back. "I was wondering," he said, reaching down for Mick.

For just a moment, he didn't think he could go through with it. Then Mick ran away from him.

"Celina and I were thinking — about repainting," he said, standing up, smile returning along with his resolve. "Upstairs," he added quickly, pointing boyishly. "Could I have a look — you know, to see what you've done?"

"It's all wallpapah up they-a too," she said, like he should already know. "My husband did it, before he died."

He wanted to strangle the life out of her, right then and there; just throttle the bitch mercilessly. "*We* were thinking about wallpaper," he said, smiling wide again, fingers splayed on his chest.

I'd like to thank the Academy, he thought proudly.

Gesturing casually toward the stairs, his other hand slid gently onto her bony shoulder, squeezing it affectionately. At first she resisted, saying something about a television program. But then his hand was in the small of her back, casual, urging her forward.

At the foot of the stairs he paused, really playing the gentleman. "After *you*," he said, arm sweeping out, keeping that smile going. Francine eyed him suspiciously, hand firm on the rail before starting up. She pattered pathetically upward, one painfully slow step at a time.

"So, this Mick situation — surely we can find a way to work it out," he said, thinking he should say *something*, to fill the space, but also really needing to hate her, to know that *she* knew why he was doing it, when the time came. His heart was pounding, thumping hard in his chest, breath coming in big gulps. There she was, moving up the stairs, a few feet from him; a few more steps and she'd be at the top. And then he'd have to kill her.

Two steps from the landing and she stopped, turning, some instinct for survival finally sensing the murderous tone in his voice. He couldn't take the strain; his face felt large, swollen and hot, his tongue too big for his mouth. He couldn't breathe.

Sliding by her, he turned, ready to shove, when Mick came bounding up the stairs. Tangling himself in Francine's feet, she tried to avoid him, missing the step and losing her balance in the process. Reaching out desperately for Ed, who gracefully drew away now, her arms grabbed helplessly around her instead. Gravity taking hold, panic flooded into her eyes as she went over backwards.

When she landed, Ed heard her neck snap cleanly.

Ed and Mick both stood on the landing, heads cocked to the side, watching as the lifeless body limped slowly downward. Reaching down, Ed scooped Mick into his arms, stroking him from head to tail as the cat purred loudly. "Good boy," he said, still not quite believing his luck. Pulling out his phone, he called 911, trying to sound upset. Fortunately, the dispatcher couldn't see his smirk.

Turning onto their street that evening, Celina noticed the flashing lights before she saw an ambulance, fire truck and two police cars in front of Francine Connolly's house. A small crowd was on the sidewalk, Ed among them. He was talking to a young policeman, still holding Mick.

"Oh my God, what happened," Celina asked, resting her hand on his shoulder. Mick slipped casually into her arms, rubbing against her face. "By the time I turned around, it was too late," Ed was saying, looking at her but speaking to the officer. The words conveyed distress, but standing there, pulsing lights bouncing off the houses and their faces, Celina thought he looked strangely content.

Gun

Anne Britting Oleson

Third Runner-Up

"Cal," my father said, glancing up sharply at my footsteps; then his face relaxed into a conspiratorial grin. "Come here." His voice was low. "Come look at this."

He sat on an up-ended five gallon pail in the dimness of the shed off the kitchen, caressing the silver plate of the revolver he cradled in his lap. I paused, struck by the shine, the power. I had never been this close to a handgun before. My neck prickled. I looked around for my mother.

"She's next door," he said, reading my nervousness. His laugh was strangled. The gun dwarfed his large hands. He held it out to me. I took a step back, and he laughed again. "Come on, Cal. It's not loaded."

Even then, I knew if I touched the revolver, I would be implicated: I knew how my mother felt about handguns, though she never spoke of her reasons. I knew what my father was doing. Yet despite the dim light of the shed, the gun gleamed, a beautiful thing. I could not take my eyes from it. When I reached out, my hand belonged to someone else entirely, divorced from my will.

The wooden handle under my palm was smooth and warm. The gun was heavy, and I needed both hands to take it from my father. My shoulders strained when I tried to lift it to eye-level. He shifted me about so I stood between his knees, reached around, helped me hold up the revolver so I could sight down its bright barrel. "Like this," he murmured above my ear. "How does that feel?"

Sinful, and exciting — but I didn't know how to say that, so I said nothing.

Then we heard the front door slap in its frame, the sound of my mother's voice soothing my younger sister, and my father quickly wrapped the gun in an oiled rag and hid it atop the old wardrobe in the corner.

"I don't want it in the house," my mother had said.

A few nights previously, she had sat very still and upright at the table, her silverware crossed on her half-full plate. "Eat your dinner," she urged my sister, who stared slack-jawed at nothing.

"Mary —" my father protested, his face flushing slightly.

"I've told you," she cut him off.

"I know, but—" he started, but then seemed unable to continue. Instead, his fork clinked against his plate as he pushed his potato around its edge. "I know you don't like it — I know it makes you think about your brother. Still, Mary. You should just look at it. It's beautiful. And for what the guy was asking for it—it was a steal. An absolute steal."

She looked steadfastly at him for a moment longer, before rising, straight-spined, to clear her place and fill the sink for dishes. Behind her back, my father's shoulders slumped.

I had thought that had taken care of things; when my mother used that tone, she brooked no argument, and my father and I usually fell into line—not Alice, but then she had trouble understanding. So I was surprised when, turning back from the wardrobe, he lifted his finger to his lips and cocked his head toward the front room.

He didn't mention the revolver at dinner that evening. Instead, he made chatter about the lawnmower, a feral dog someone had seen by the river, the chance of a strike at the mill. Every once in a while, he'd reach a hand toward my sister's plate, to set a small piece of biscuit and butter there. When my mother bent to pick up Alice's spoon, hurled to the floor in temper, he caught my eye and winked.

I looked away.

* * *

When I swung into the yard after school, my mother met me, her eyes wild. "Calvin," she said, "your sister's missing." Her yellow hair loosed from its bun, blowing around her flushed cheeks.

I tossed my books on the porch. Sometimes Alice wandered off, but she rarely went far. "How long has she been gone?"

"Oh, I don't know, I don't know!" She was close to tears, which meant *long*. "She was with me hanging laundry, but then she was gone." She wiped a hand across her cheek. "Calvin, I've looked everywhere. I've called your father at the mill."

My mother never did that. But Alice was never far. She would get tired, curl up into a ball behind the sofa, or under a bush, and fall asleep, her grubby fist under her cheek.

"Check the house," I said, soaking up her urgency. "I'll look out here."

"I've already checked," she protested.

"Check again." I started back down the steps.

We both heard the high-pitched giggle from the back yard at the same time, the one that turned into a scream. I flew around the corner of the house as I heard the screen door slam, my mother dashing the short way through the kitchen.

Alice, her face dirty and her dress torn, was backing away from a mangy yellow dog, her mouth a wide O. For its part, it paced slowly toward her, ribs rippling under its matted coat.

I skidded to a halt, staring at its dripping jaw. Alice screamed again, and the dog took another measured step, belly low to the ground. It snarled, showing pointed yellow teeth.

There was a sharp click. A shot.

The yellow dog jerked upwards, and then fell in its tracks, a bloody hole in its side.

Alice shrieked.

47

My mother streaked past me, dropping the revolver near the dead dog. She gathered Alice up into her arms, burying her face in my sister's neck.

Suddenly my father was there, racing around from the road. He stopped short when he saw my mother, Alice, the dead dog, foam still at its muzzle. "Mary —"

She lifted her blazing eyes to his face. "Take care of it," she said, then stepped gingerly around the carcass and went into the house.

The System

Michael Lombardi

Under 18 Winner

"Water please," the voice of a man asked, his steady tone disrupting the well-kept silence.

Number 00563, James Smith, sat, alone, in an empty room. The man's average physique was betrayed by the white spandex jumpsuit he wore. The slippery material exposed every crack and bulge of his pale body; he did not care for it, but he supposed it was another of The System's regulations.

A sudden click from outside the walls drew Smith's attention. Two of the solid, white cells that constructed the panel before him slid apart with a low hum. A small silver tray emerged, bearing a plastic glass filled with clear water.

"Thank you," Smith smiled as he grasped the cup. The System beeped in response and the tray withdrew.

The System will be back in a couple minutes for the glass, I should drink fast, thought Smith as he took his first sip. The water was slightly salty and Smith's face contorted as the bland liquid ran down his throat. The water was, of course, enriched with all of the essential nutrients his organism required, The System made sure of it. Smith shrugged and took a single, hearty gulp of the water before setting it on the table before him. He grinned lazily, leaned back in his chair, and rested both hands on the back of his head. *He was taking a break.*

As if sensing the man's satisfaction, a metallic porthole in the ceiling cracked open, revealing one of The System's automatic, robotic hands. Smith watched intently as the steel rod it rested upon dropped down, observing how its shiny, metal exterior reflected the fluorescent light of the room. The hand of the arm flexed once before wrapping its synthetic fingers around the half-empty glass. A hidden trigger sensed the arm's acquisition and the parade of machinery began to ascend. The man watched with fascination as The System did its work. *These machines make my life so easy*, he grinned, propping his feet on the now empty table.

A long stretch of time seemed to pass and Smith began to absently wonder when the automatic bed would slide out. The System did not allow clocks in the room, but Smith could ask for the time if he really wanted. He shrugged complacently: *The System knew the answer, he did not need to know.*

Eventually, the lights began to dim, signaling the end of the day. Smith yawned mechanically and waited silently for the motorized bed to reveal itself from the right of the room. A low hum commenced as the large metal block, fully equipped with comforter and blanket, glided out from the side of one of the walls. Smith tilted his head slightly; the man thought that a door would go nicely to the left of the bed. That is, of course, *if the room had a door.*

Slowly but surely, Smith's mechanical perch began to descend into the floor, forcing the man to stand up. He got out of the chair and stretched his back casually as he covered the short distance between the stool and the bed. He smiled sleepily, laying himself down amongst the white fabric covers, *the automatic heaters had already kicked in.* As the last of the fluorescent lights flickered off, Smith closed his eyes and let the low murmur of the nightly cleaning machines put him to sleep.

The night passed relatively easy and Smith woke to the high pitched hum of The System's vocal processor warming up. He opened his eyes dreamily and began to clamber out of the silver bed.

"Good morning 00563, *Smith, James*, prepare for morning exercises." Smith sighed and groggily began his day by stretching all the required muscles for this particular workout.

"Commence jog now," The System's synthesized voice pulsed. Smith picked up his knees for the first set, then began to lazily lap his small room. The System put on some upbeat music through the loudspeakers next to the lights and Smith began to sync his footfalls to the loud pulses of the bass drum. It was his favorite song. *It was always his favorite song.* The man's stiff joints did not respond well to the early exercising, but he trusted that The System knew best.

After the jog came pushups and crunches, and Smith did those without problem; however, the man had now worked up quite a sweat. The System noted his bodily perspiration and began to cool the room, concealing the slight whirr of the conditioners beneath the beat of the music.

"Touch toes," the voice processor sounded. The music was overtaken by its monotonous, synthetic tone.

Smith almost smiled as he bent over, touching his tender hands to his feet. He especially enjoyed looking at his small world from an upside down position. He noted how strange the chrome loudspeaker looked in the otherwise featureless room; no matter how the room was manipulated, the loudspeaker remained. At the moment, the bed, chair, and desk had been relocated to make space for Smith's exercises, another one of The System's calculated maneuvers. The man was left, alone, in a small white cube, hanging upside down and touching his toes.

A small chime sounded from outside the chamber, signaling the end of the exercises. Smith slowly stood as his muscles screamed in protest. The white chair and table returned to the room, their oiled hinges and gears whirring slightly in the silence. Upon the table sat two plastic plates, each containing the exact amount of vitamins and nutrients required by a male adult in the morning. To Smith, the meal looked like eggs and pancakes.

"It's good," Smith stated after he took the first bite. *It was always good.*

"Noted," The System responded, "your input will be used in the future to make all meals *good.*"

Smith frowned slightly as he continued to eat his breakfast. Occasionally, he would play with the fluffy pancakes before devouring them, or try to mix the two foods to attain a different taste.

Once he was finished, Smith lazily placed his fork between the two plates and stood, waiting for the procession of robotic arms to come and whisk the leftovers away. A bright click sounded and three metallic rods descended, each one grabbing a different piece of the setting. The smallest of the arms gripped the fork in the middle and retrieved it quickly before the larger arms went about recovering the two dirty plates. Smith watched, semi-interested, as the machines did their work. Each of the arms eventually disappeared into the white ceiling and the table was clean once more. A circuit completed with a crack and The System moved on to its next task.

"Please change your clothes," The System stated as a small rack of clean spandex fell effortlessly from a hole in the top of the chamber. The new spandex was bleached white and looked perfectly untouched.

Smith had thought that today was a shower day, but he guessed otherwise. *The System knows best,* he reminded himself as he fought valiantly with the thin material covering his body; he eventually freed himself from the stretchy suit and slid into the other, trading one white skin for another. He carelessly draped his dirtied clothes onto the metal rack and waited for it to ascend while massaging his eyes. The automated shaft caught the retrieval gear and the wire rack gravitated out of Smith's sight.

"System, some cards please?" Smith asked semi-cheerfully. The man was beginning to get back into the swing of the day. The System beeped as it quickly processed the demand. A whoosh of air sounded outside the room and a hatch in one of the walls opened, producing a single deck of cards on a silver tray suspended by two robotic arms.

"Thank you," Smith grinned as he took the deck from the platter. The change in weight was observed by The System, something beeped, and the arms withdrew. The white walls sealed once again.

Smith flipped through the shiny, waxed cards effortlessly. The man loved the feeling of a new deck. *He always had a new deck.*

The low whirr of The System was effortlessly complemented by the fanning of the elegantly designed cards. Smith retrieved four aces from the deck and flipped them through the fingers on his right hand, watching as the elaborate designs disappeared periodically behind the muted colors of the backs of the cards. He sighed slightly and began setting up a game of solitaire. He could ask The System to play with him, but there was no fun to be had in losing. *The System always won.*

Within a couple of minutes, Smith had finished the hand and was preparing to shuffle and play again; however, as he sat in his plain, white chair and fiddled with the deck of cards a strange feeling began to grow within him.

"System," Smith started. As he spoke, a single card slipped from between his fingers, "give me something to do." The comprehensive beep sounded and Smith slowly bent over to pick up the stray card. It slid easily from the polished floor into his hands, its waxy coating not as elusive as he would have expected. He quickly shuffled the cards together and laid them on the table.

A low purr sounded from outside the room and a slot above the table opened. A robotic hand protruded and dropped a small, plastic box into the room unceremoniously. Upon the slot's closing, Smith eagerly bent over the table and began to fiddle with the container. With an unusual gleam of interest in his eyes, he shook the object, producing a satisfying tumble of the contents. Finding no obvious opening, the man tried desperately to force it apart, taking a side of the container in each hand and pulling. His biceps and forearms flexed through the spandex that covered them. All of a sudden, the box yielded, exploding into two pieces and sending its contents flying across the room. Small black pieces were momentarily thrown into thin air before falling noisily to the ground. Smith was thrown off his chair but remained standing, a half-container in each hand. Curiously, he approached the black bits, observing their wonky shapes and confusing grooves. Almost immediately he recognized the shapes of a puzzle and sighed discontentedly. He set the broken container down on the table and sat, his head between his hands.

"System," Smith mumbled, waiting for the computer's absent beep before continuing, "I didn't mean I wanted another game to play..." Smith trailed off and sighed, "I meant I wanted something to *do*," he gestured towards the ceiling, "you know, something like a *job*..."

The System remained silent, its absent humming died down slightly. Apparently it lacked enough data to respond.

"You know, a *job!* Like the things *you* do!" Smith raised his voice, he was slightly annoyed that he did not get an immediate response. The room fell eerily quiet for a while, echoing Smith's loud tones amidst the buzz of vacuum tubes and transistors. After a minute or so, a snap sounded and electrons began to flow once again.

"There are no responsibilities available for 00563, Smith, James," the synthesized voice stated suddenly and blandly. Smith brought his head up abruptly as the machine continued, "The System runs all *fifty-five thousand, four hundred and seventy-two tasks* associated with running this compound."

The hollow click that marked the end of the computer's response seemed to resound within Smith's soul. He closed his eyes and brought a pale hand to his face.

"There has to be *something*," he muttered softly, his voice airy and thin. The man peeked out from under his hand at the black pieces that still covered the floor. *I could try this*, he thought. Uneasily, he brought his other hand to the table and wrapped it cautiously around an empty piece of the broken container he had spilled. He slowly slid down from the chair and fell into a kneeling position near a group of the scattered pieces.

He watched the jagged shards intently, wondering if this was the way The System viewed his messes. With one hand holding his makeshift collection box and the other acting as a mock robotic arm, Smith went about playing the role of The System. He occasionally whistled like the metallic chimes outside his room as he began retrieving the small black chips. At first, his hands were shaky, unaccustomed to the actions of retrieval. Within a short amount of time, however, he grew to master the process of cleaning, swiping up several pieces at a time. For the first time that day, *Smith found himself smiling.*

A buzz rang from outside the room and Smith looked up. From the hole in the ceiling descended a strange looking apparatus; the machine was oddly similar to the robotic arms except for the protruding nozzle at the end of its main shaft. The gaping black hole was surrounded by a shiny, metallic material. For a moment, the purpose of the strange instrument was lost to Smith, but as the circuit closed and the engine began producing its signature, jittery tone, he recognized it as one of the nightly cleaning machines. *A vacuum to be precise.*

At first, Smith tried to speak over the harsh tones of the automated cleaner yelling, "System, *I can do it,*" or "System, *let me try.*" His cries were met with no avail, either the computer's sensors could not detect his speech or could not process his request. The man was left watching, his blood heating slowly. Smith found his face reddening as the machine began to brainlessly consume the scattered pieces of the puzzle.

"That's my *job,*" he said softly with unusual remorse, dropping the half-filled container by his side. Again, a strange feeling began to overtake the man as he watched the machine do its work. *His work.* Smith's fists clenched, his nostrils flared, and his pulse quickened. The man began to stammer wildly, his arms flailing uncontrollably.

"My... *job!*" He cried over the constant drone of the vacuum, suddenly finding his voice and bringing his arms to bear.

Number 00563, James Smith, abruptly ran, screaming, towards the metallic beast in his room. With a heinous, primal cry, the man jumped over the white chair and pummeled his own body into the shiny exterior of the extended arm. The metal creaked and shifted under the weight of his flesh and bone, before parting with a satisfying crack. In a single moment, the whole room fell silent, leaving a prone James Smith laying amongst the disembodied pieces of a cleaning module. For Smith, the world was spinning, the mix of his adrenaline and a slight concussion clouded his consciousness.

On the outside of the room, several switches flipped, relaying the information of the loss to The System. The electric currents ran to the processor, which debated the issue for a staggering three nanoseconds. The machine then sent a pulse of electrons across a board and completed a nearby circuit. Several resistors cracked painfully, a light flared, and two robotic arms were dispatched to Number 00563, Smith, James.

By this time, Smith's head was beginning to recover. His mouth was filled with a metallic taste and Smith rubbed a shaky hand across his mouth slowly. He then observed his pale hand, noting how beautifully the crimson liquid flowed through the minute crevasses in his skin. He smiled through a mouthful of blood and broken teeth. A crack and a whirr sounded from outside his room and he waited anxiously for The System's response. To his surprise, two robotic arms protruded from the porthole in the sky. Smith gazed at the shiny, chrome exoskeletons and smiled, the two were the exact same arms that regularly brought away his dirty dishes and trash. He gurgled a laugh through his bloodied throat and spat in their direction as they descended. The two arms stopped abruptly at either end of Smith's body and flexed their synthetic hands, preparing as they always did. One arm grabbed both of Smith's feet securely while the other fastened its claw around the man's head. Smith could smell the flawlessly polished, stainless steel. The arms began to pull. Smith screamed.

*   *   *

News of the accident reached The System's processor via vacuum tube. A collection of electrical pulses hastily etched a small record of the events on one of The System's hard drives. A switch flipped, a circuit zapped shut, and the room's automated cleaning network began running through its various stages. Puzzle pieces and limbs were swept away, blood and sinew was mopped clean. A light flickered, a cable buzzed, and another one of The System's various fifty-five thousand, four hundred and seventy-two tasks was completed.

If the area window was found ajar
And the basement looked like a field of war,
If a tile or two came loose on the roof,
Which presently ceased to be waterproof,
If the drawers were pulled out from the bedroom chests,
And you couldn't find one of your winter vests,
Or after supper one of the girls
Suddenly missed her Woolworth pearls:

Then the family would say: "It's that horrible cat!
It was Mungojerrie—or Rumpleteazer!" —And most of the time they
left it at that.

—from "Mungojerrie and Rumpleteazer"
by T.S. Eliot

The Now Told Story of Mungojerrie and Rumpleteazer

Sydney M. Smith

Under 18 First Runner-Up

You may find it surprising that a story with such a fancy cover centers around two mangy, flea-bitten, homeless cats, rather than a princess and a knight finding true love. But this is, after all, an adventure—and adventures can be lost and rediscovered in the darkest, most unusual places.

My name is Mungojerrie. It all began a few days after my birth. We were born in Buckingham Palace so . . . well, I guess you could call us royal pets. We were kept by the queen and the room that we lived in (for a short time) was very big. I had nine siblings, and sadly, most were older than me except for Rumpleteazer, who was my age.

I realize now must be the time to tell you a little bit about that sister of mine. I was closer to her than anyone else because *she* didn't try to kill her siblings. Rumpleteazer always tried to protect me, so I did the same with her. (She

59

also shared her Feline Frenzee snacks with me, and anybody who does that is high on my list.)

But I believe that the strangest thing about her was her abnormal interest in Sudoku. You see, in her pre-kittenhood, Rumpleteazer dug in the recycling bin for three straight weeks. She had been taking things out and ripping them apart so when the workmen came in to clean our messes, they would find paper shreds. (Rumpleteazer claimed it was good for her claws.)

However, one day I found her sitting in a corner with a pencil in one paw, a newspaper on the floor, and her tail flicking all over the place. For a while, we were quiet. Finally, I spoke up.

"Whazzat, sis?" I meowed curiously.

"Be quiet!" she hissed "I concentrating in here."

I could tell. Her tail was no longer flicking; it was thumping.

If you are a cat, you know this, but if you are not, I will tell you. If a cat's tail flicks, this means interest. If it thumps, like Rumpleteazer's tail, the cat is in deep concentration. If a cat is feeling bothered, its tail will swish. Back and forth. Back and forth. Back and forth. My brother Jerusalem used to clear coffee tables when he was upset, his tail was so long.

Rumpleteazer was furiously scribbling numbers onto the paper. I never truly figured it out, but she told me it was like a puzzle. Boy, was she happy when she found the old, discarded Sudoku books. Of course, she always did the one in the paper because the workmen never did.

Things really started to get interesting on April Fools' Day. I was curling up on the purple plush rug, minding my own beeswax, when Bruno (one of my four brothers) landed hard on my tail. Soon, Lester, Prilla, Jerusalem, Wicket, Capricorn, and Sargasso had me pinned to the floor, biting and snapping and spitting out insults. Yep, that's my siblings.

"Runt!" screamed Prilla.

"Pip-squeak!" hissed Wicket.

When I could not bear it any longer, my much-loved mother by the name of Cottonpuff pulled them off one by one so I could escape. While I still could, I scurried as fast as my furry paws could carry me to a key hiding place. There, in front of me, was a loose floorboard. *Perhaps*, I thought as I squeezed into the gap, *in my case being small is good*—for I knew Sargasso could not fit there. I sat there all day and all night until *some* tortoiseshell-and-white paw pushed a wet, catnip-covered ball of yarn underneath the floorboard where I was. A wave of relief washed over me as I realized it was my faithful sister, Rumpleteazer. Luckily, she was a bit undersized herself, so she could fit.

"Mungojerrie?" I heard her voice. "Is that you?"

"Yeah!" I mewed. Rumpleteazer slid in next to me. "So," she said. "Did you enjoy your stay at Floorboard Hotel?"

"Yes," I said, returning her sarcasm. "Very much, thank you."

I looked around. Where did she go? I would have seen her if she had crawled out, and there couldn't possibly have been enough room to go further back . . .

Oh, but there WAS! It looked like an antique attic. Buttons and old coins and empty bags and mice that scurried away quickly.

"Mungojerrie, you've gotta see this! Oh you've gotta!"

Good. Now I knew Rumpleteazer was nearby. I slinked around till I found her and what she'd gotten so worked up about. There were two leather satchels, each containing a grappling hook with a rope attached to it, a bugle, a lock opener, a walkie-talkie, an unlit candle, and a handkerchief.

"Howdja find this, sis?" I asked.

"Well," she meowed craftily. "While I was talking to you, I got an eerie feeling that the place was much larger than it seemed. So I just decided to take a look." Suddenly, she knocked the wind out of me with her paws and stepped back a little.

"What was that for?" I said sleepily, trying to make sense of the clout.

"Spider," she said. "I didn't want to tell you because then you'd freak out and it would be impossible to get it off."

"There's spiders in here?" Nervously, I looked around.

Sydney M. Smith

"Well, what do you expect?" she said. "We're standing in a dark, damp, dusty place that probably hasn't been noticed for . . . hmmmm . . . say, about five or more years—and who knows? Maybe a big, fuzzy brown recluse is crawling on your tail to lay its eggs in your . . ."

"Stop it!" I yelled. Rumpleteazer KNOWS how much I hate crawly things. Sisterly love is something I have to deal with each and every day. Hey, she's called Rumple*teazer* for a reason.

If you are a cat (like me) I hope you don't eat them. Spiders, that is. And if you do, I beg your pardon. So, moving on . . .

The next day, Rumpleteazer and I sat on the windowsill, looking down on London. A "wanted" poster for a notorious outlaw hung on a streetlamp that blinked. On and off, on and off. "Rumpleteazer," meowed I. "You don't suppose we'll ever become one of them, do you?"

"What's that?" Rumpleteazer was reading the street signs, clearly not paying any attention.

"Outlaws. I was asking you if you thought we'd be outlaws someday."

"What!?"

"Yes, you heard me!"

"Mungojerrie," she said. "That's just crazy. We're kittens."

"Look," I said, indicating the crook on the poster. "You think his sister might have said the same thing?" Rumpleteazer said that if he had a sister, she would have ran away before he could have said anything of the sort. I must point out since you have gotten this far in the story, that small words can go a long way. What Rumpleteazer said was really a joke, because the guy looked pretty scary. But still, I could tell she was thinking.

My name is Rumpleteazer. Mungojerrie knows I am very smart, but he does not like to admit it. We stay away, as best we can, from our siblings because they call us "rats." I need you to know right now that what we did next is not revenge

62

on them.

One morning, I woke up and I did not feel like a kitten anymore. So, I went to tell this to Mungojerrie when I realized he was not there. I did not meow out his name for fear of waking my brothers and sisters. Suddenly, I heard him call my name. Mungojerrie has a very distinct meow. Soon he emerged from under our floorboard carrying . . . the two leather satchels.

"Why did you get those?" I hissed in his face. "If Ma finds out about that, she'll really think we're up to something."

"Well," he said, "I'm going to see the world."

I was confused. "What do you mean?" I asked.

"Hasn't it dawned on you that the only place we've ever known is this room? We were born here, and if we don't move, we'll rot here." Mungojerrie looked me in the eye. Part of me agreed with him. Other cats roamed about freely while we were confined to this space. Even the indoor cats get to live more, to see more. But to leave forever? I was not so sure. Our mother was very kind to us and would be heartbroken if we left. As a little newborn, it had been my dream to explore the wide world beneath the sky. Far from the yarn balls, the food pellets, the endless days of sitting . . . sitting . . . sitting...

"Rumpleteazer?" Mungojerrie gave me a sideways glance. "Are you okay?"

I instantly jerked out of my stupor. My mind was made up. I was going with him. "Hang on," I mewed. "I'm coming, too."

"Thanks, sis." He grinned. "Shall we gather personal belongings first? Food and whatnot?"

I rolled my eyes. His way of saying: I'm not leaving without the catnip. Mungojerrie has some "issues" with it. If he's alone with more than two fresh stalks of it, he needs at least ten feet of space. If he's got more than five stalks, he needs a straightjacket.

"What sort of food were you thinking of?" I said. "There is no way I'm taking those bready pellets the humans feed us."

"Of course not," he said, making a sick expression. "Ever

eaten a mouse? A waterfowl? A *fish*? Not meat from a can. I'm talking about freshly killed pigeons. A duck pulled from the lake. If that's not what you're eating, you are seriously missing out. I feel bad for you."

"Since when have you been able to kill a rodent?" I asked. Mungojerrie has lived in Buckingham Palace exactly as long as I have. We live in one of the highest rooms. If he had escaped out a window, he would have broken his neck. Not to mention that if he did manage to survive the drop, it would have been so dark he couldn't have located his catch.

"The blue wardrobe is full of voles. Pigeons fly by the big window all the time. If the window is left open in the summertime, I catch one! C'mon. I can teach you how to hunt."

Before long, we'd gotten four mice, six voles, two pigeons from the window, and a big brown rat that was living in the drawer.

"See what happens when you're observant?" Mungojerrie asked as we triumphantly stuffed our bags. "Good things happen to. . . Yikes!" he jumped. "It's almost five! Ma will be up pretty soon. Oh, gee. If she finds out we're leaving home, we'll be toast." I shoved three Sudoku books into my bag and headed for the window.

"It's a long way down," I said. A lamppost loomed near where we were sitting. "If you grab on to the top, you might be able to slide down." Mungojerrie was a little hesitant at first, then leapt onto the post. He leaned a little too far forward and slid upside-down. "Mungojerrie!" I called. It was too late. My intelligent brother had gone down the pole and fell (not too gracefully) on his face.

Mungojerrie looked up. "I'm okay!"

Great. Now, it was my turn. After seeing what had happened to Mungojerrie, I couldn't help feeling just a little nervous. I put my paws on the top and hung there for a while, like a limp fish. Slowly, I slid down. Suddenly, I lost my grip and landed on my rump.

Mungojerrie trotted over. "Are you all right?" he asked.

"Yeah. I mean, I think so," I added hastily.

But Mungojerrie wasn't paying attention. His nose was to the ground, and he was following it.

"Mungojerrie, what are you . . ."

He cut me off with his paw and continued into the courtyard. Sure enough, the gardens were planted with catnip. It seeped through the walls and through the cracks in the ground. It hung from the balconies and was put in little pots lining the gutter.

"Am I dead?" Mungojerrie asked sleepily. He walked into one of the gardens, but luckily, before he could go catnip-crazy, I dragged him out of there. Mungojerrie fastened his teeth around my tail. We walked . . . er, and dragged along to the next block. An hour later, Mungojerrie cooled off, and I was glad of it.

Now that we were out in the big world, I realized we had nowhere to go. The street stretched on for a long while and I could see no people. I spotted something on the ground and lifted it with one paw.

"Hey Mungojerrie, take a look at this."

"It's a map of London!" he said, shoving me out of the way. "I see some forested area up north. That way, if anyone's looking for us, we'll be long gone."

"It's six in the morning." I said. "Nobody could possibly be looking for us."

Mungojerrie thinks he is so smart. He snorted. "Yeah? What about Ma? Speaking of which, do you think she's up yet?"

"She might be," I said. Mungojerrie looked worried. "What on earth is the matter?" I asked.

"Aw, nothing," he said. "I'm just pretty sure one of our siblings knows what we're up to." I couldn't believe what I was hearing. "When you grabbed those Sudoku books, Sargasso opened his eyes a little bit," he continued. "It's possible he was still sleeping, but if he wasn't, he's not the kind of cat to keep secrets from his brothers and sisters."

Sargasso was not high on my list. A week ago, he had tricked me into singeing my tail-fur in the fireplace. It's still a little bit tender.

"Let's just say he did hear," I said. "What harm could that do? Everybody will find out anyway."

Mungojerrie pulled me close, his voice down to a whisper. "Sargasso knows we left on our own accord. Not that we'd been sold, or fell out a window. He thinks we want to have revenge on our siblings. This is why we should head north."

"I agree," I said. There was a long pause.

"What is started must be finished," He smiled. "What are we waiting for? Onward, onward!"

We set off.

To be continued . . .

Shugyōsha

Jason Allard

"I'm going to die tomorrow, Nishiko-san," the young woman said. Outside, in the garden, the sudden clatter of the *shishi-odoshi* silenced the chirring cicadas for a moment. She adjusted her light *yukata* robe, pale blue with black *mitsudomoe* triskelions, and sipped hot sake. Delicate fingers brushed the back of her neck, sending a pleasant shiver down her spine, as the geisha swept aside her damp, unbound hair.

"Please don't say such things, Hikaru-dono," Nishiko said, smoothing the cloth over Hikaru's shoulders. She began to massage the tense muscles underneath.

Hikaru closed her eyes. Probing thumbs eased the knots in her back, but did no more than the hot sake for the knot in her belly. "Why not? It's likely true. Hojo Chuji is a skilled swordsman."

"*Anzuru yori umu ga yasashi,*" Nishiko said. "Giving birth to a baby is easier than worrying about it."

"Perhaps." Hikaru drained her cup, then held it out to be refilled. The geisha's cherry blossom pink kimono rustled as she slid to the young woman's side. She picked up the steaming porcelain bottle and poured. Her movements were smooth, precise, practiced, as if they were steps of a dance. When she smiled, Nishiko's otherwise plain face glowed.

"Do not be concerned with tomorrow," she said. "There is only tonight."

Hikaru drank the rice wine in a single gulp. "Would you like to hear a story?" she asked the geisha.

"If it would please you," she said. "I am here to entertain you. I could play the samisen, or sing, or dance if you would prefer. A game, perhaps?"

Hikaru stared into the shallow depths of her cup. "My

67

name is Minamoto Hikaru. As a little girl, I was promised to Yagyu Gorobei. He wasn't much older, only a few years. We saw each other often, and he always made sure to say something nice to me, or give me a little present. A couple of sweets or a flower, or a little origami he'd made. By the time I was twelve, I was madly in love with him.

"A week before we were to marry, he was murdered. Drowned in the bath by three ronin after a night of playing *cho-han*."

Nishiko gasped, covering her mouth with one hand and laying the other on Hikaru's shoulder.

"They fled the province before we could catch them, but I was able to learn their names from the old woman who owned the bath house.

"I decided to go on a *musha shugyo*, a warrior's pilgrimage, to find his killers. My mother wept when I told her. My father was torn between fury and furious pride. In the end, he gave his blessing and my grandfather's katana. I have not seen my family in four years. Tomorrow, it will end. Either I will die, or I will take his head. Then I will return home and retake my name."

Hikaru drained her cup. "I found one of them on the road from Ise to Shima."

"What's a pretty little girl like you doing with a weapon like that?" the samurai asked, gesturing at her *naginata* with his chin. He leaned against his spear. "You should be carrying a baby, not a polearm. Or a sword, for that matter."

"Are you Shibata Shinta?"

"What if I am?"

"Did you murder Yagyu Gorobei?"

The samurai stroked his stubbled jaw and looked up at the tall pines, swaying gently in the breeze. "The cheating cur? It was a shame. He begged on his knees for forgiveness after stealing all of our money. Pathetic bastard got what he deserved."

Hikaru pointed her weapon at Shibata's chest. "I'm going

to kill you."

The man threw back his head and laughed. "*Hyakunen hayai ze!*" He made a show of clutching his belly as if so much mirth hurt. "You're a hundred years too early. Go home, little girl."

She lunged forward, thrusting the long weapon. The samurai leapt back, narrowly avoiding the curved blade.

Shibata shrugged and leveled his weapon. "Very well. If you've decided to die, girl, let me help you." He jabbed at her. Hikaru danced back, deflecting his strikes with ease.

"Not bad," Shibata said.

He feinted high, then stepped in and struck low. Moving to protect her head, Hikaru was not fast enough to block his attack.

The point of his spear plunged into her thigh. Its honed edge pierced the flesh easily, scraped against bone, then erupted from the other side.

Hikaru clenched her jaw. When he twisted the spear, she screamed. She dipped the blade of her *naginata*, glancing it against the ground. As it rebounded, she thrust. Shibata grunted.

He staggered back, pulling his spear from her leg, and her blade from his belly. His legs wobbled, and he sagged to his knees. His spear clattered to the dusty road.

"*Ikkene!*" Blood coursed down Shibata's lap and spattered on the ground. Gritting his teeth, he reached for his sword. "This is no good."

Ignoring the gore flowing from her leg, Hikaru pivoted at the waist, swinging the *naginata* in a powerful, broad arc. Her foe curled his lip, but did not flinch as her blade cleaved through his neck. He remained erect for a few heartbeats, then toppled sideways.

"How gruesome." Nishiko poured sake from a freshly warmed bottle. The rice wine steamed and filled the room with its sharp scent.

"I'd never killed a man before him," Hikaru said. "I was

69

sick in the weeds at the side of the road, then hobbled to the nearest village, where a fisherman's wife stitched my wounds closed. I was there for three months, under the care of an old monk, with his poultices and prayers." She downed her sake. "Would you like to see?"

The geisha poured again and nodded. Hikaru pulled open the bottom of her robe. Her long, smooth legs were marred by a handful of bruises and faint scars, but one on her right thigh puckered pale and bold against her skin. Nishiko gently traced it with her finger tip. Hikaru trembled.

"Less than a handspan to the right, and I'd have bled to death before I'd taken a dozen steps," she said.

"The Fortunes smile on you, Hikaru-dono."

She shook her head. "After recovering, I headed north. I needed to improve my skill with the katana, and finally found a former ronin willing to teach me. He said I reminded him of his niece. In return for his tutelage, I fought on the side of his master against their neighbors. After several successful skirmishes, he decided to press the advantage and attack. I found the second ronin, Okubo Noburo, during the Battle of Kaeru Ford."

Hikaru was hungry. She couldn't help it. Last night she'd cooked her dinner in her broad, conical *jingasa* helmet. It still smelled of stir-fried chicken and vegetables. Her stomach rumbled as the officers formed them into battlelines. The enemy soldiers did the same on their side of the river.

As the two armies faced each other, both waiting for the other to commit to crossing the river, proud samurai stepped forward from the lines to brag. They would shout their name and recount deeds done in other battles, the number of men they'd killed, or the names of particularly glorious foes defeated.

A mountain of a man shouldered his way through the enemy's ranks of conscripted *ashigaru* foot soldiers. His broken nose, unkempt mane of hair and grubby, stained armor marked him as nothing more than a mercenary ronin.

Perhaps looking to make a name for himself and find a new lord to swear fealty.

"I am Okubo Noburo," the ronin bellowed. He waved his *tetsubo* over his head, a faceted, iron-studded club as tall as the man next to him. "I killed forty-seven men at the Battle of Bakaoni. At Kumoshima, I took the head of General Takeda Kenshin."

Hikaru checked the cords and straps of her light *haramaki* armor. It hung secure over her torso and thighs. Her hands tightened on the smooth shaft of her *naginata*.

Commanders shouted and gestured with their iron war fans. The two small armies advanced. The enemy reached the river first, and broke into a charge through the ankle-deep water. Hikaru and the others met them on the stony bank.

The ranks broke down quickly. Neither commander seemed to have much of a gift for the task at hand. Warriors found their own opponents to fight, either falling in the exchange or moving on to the next.

Hikaru cut down frightened, undisciplined *ashigaru* by the handful. The blade of her *naginata* became so coated with blood and caked with gore it no longer flashed in the sun. They pushed back the enemy, carrying the tide of battle through the shallow current towards the far shore.

She found Okubo standing in mid-river. Bloody water frothed around his feet. He crushed a young samurai's chest with a single blow of his *tetsubo*. Bones splintered with a gruesome crunch and the man fell backwards. His wide, dead eyes stared at her.

Hikaru pointed at Okubo and nodded. He grinned and stepped towards her. Other combatants around them, understanding a challenged had been issued, sought other foes or merely stepped back to watch the mismatched duel.

"You have fire in your belly, girl," Okubo said. He shook his club. Drops of blood and other less savory bits fell into the water. "I like that."

"You killed the man I love," she said.

"Could be. I've killed a lot of men. And now, you wish to kill me. Am I right?"

71

She nodded.

Okubo swung his *tetsubo* with unnatural strength and speed. She sprang away and dodged blow after blow. He fought like an *oni*. Almost ceaseless brute power, but no grace. She countered every attack. Without committing to anything more than jabs and quick slashes, she could do little more than anger him.

Hikaru was unprepared when the giant changed tactics. His club, studded with knuckle-sized iron knobs, smashed the shaft of her *naginata*. The lacquered oak shattered. She dropped a pair of short, splintered rods.

Okubo swung his *tetsubo* in a murderous overhead stroke like a workman hammering a stake into the ground. Hiraku jumped back. The club slammed down, dashing water in all directions.

She lunged forward, stepping up on his weapon as she drew her sword. Okubo released his club and backpedaled, dodging the blade slashing at his throat. He grinned and ripped his own sword from its scabbard.

They clashed again. Hikaru missed the scant safety afforded by the length of her *naginata*. Okubo appeared to miss the extra reach of his *tetsubo*.

They closed again. He stepped into his strike, straining with his arm outstretched. Hikaru skidded on the smooth river stones, trying to back away. His sword punched through the lacquered leather and thin metal plate of her armor, driving into her left shoulder.

As they parted, Hikaru slashed at his exposed arm. Her blade bit deep into Okubo's elbow. He howled and staggered back. His arm flopped like a landed fish and his katana disappeared into the murky water.

Holding her wounded limb close, Hikaru pressed her attack. Soon blood seeped from his gashed legs. A lucky blow laid open his forehead. Blinded, Okubo was an easy target as she stepped forward and rammed her sword through his heart.

* * *

"By the time he fell, his comrades were already in flight. I went to the rear and the doctors, while the lord continued his assault. Within the week he'd doubled the size of his fief and captured several villages."

Nishiko poured the last of the bottle into Hikaru's cup. "I can't imagine an *oni* being as fearsome."

"I'm in no hurry to find out," she said, then drank. She shrugged open her robe, revealing her shoulders. The night air was pleasantly cooling. A faint line marked the wound. "The doctors were somewhat more skilled with their needles than the fishwife."

Nishiko leaned in close. The subtle scent of her floral perfume filled Hikaru's nose. The geisha's warm breath tickled the delicate skin of her neck.

"Very fine work," Nishiko whispered. "Hardly noticeable."

It was still dark when Hikaru woke. She slipped out from under the covers and dressed quietly. The *shishi-odoshi* clacked in the garden, startling her. Nishiko murmured something in her sleep and rolled over. She began to snore softly. Hikaru smiled. Last night had been a wonderful gift from the beautiful young geisha.

She hurried, cat-like, down the hall. As she stepped into her sandals, Hikaru retrieved her katana from the stand by the front door, then tucked it into her sash. She slipped out into the pre-dawn gloom.

Hikaru rubbed herself for warmth as she walked through the sleeping village. Men would be waking up soon, and heading out in their boats to fish. She made her way down to the beach, and found a rock to sit on while she waited. A hint of Nishiko's lavender perfume graced her hair.

True to his word, Hojo Chuji arrived as the first rays of the sun broke the horizon far out to sea. A pair of younger samurai, just past their *genpuku* coming-of-age ceremony, accompanied him. They lagged behind as he approached.

A ronin no longer, he looked well-fed and wore a brown kimono bearing the three triangle *mon* of the local lord and the Hojo clan. His tonsured topknot had grown gray at the

73

temples, as had his close-cropped beard. Fine lines gathered at the corners of his eyes.

Hikaru rose and bowed gracefully. "Thank you, Hojo-san. You could have denied my request without losing face. I am truly grateful."

Chuji returned the bow, perhaps more deeply than befitted her rank. "My master advised I do just that," he said. His voice was soft, but carried over the waves breaking on the rocks and sand. "He was displeased when I told him my honor would not let me refuse. I believe I understand why you have come, and I wish to apologize."

"Apologize?"

"I assume you are the young woman Yagyu Gorobei-san spoke of while we gambled. You have come to avenge his death. I will not deny my responsibility, but I would like to say it was not my intention to kill him. I wished to offer him my services in exchange for the money he had won from me.

"Alas, I had drunken too much sake. When the other men came to force him to give up the cash, my resolve fell. I joined them in holding him down under the water, and in splitting the coins in his purse after."

He pulled a small package, wrapped in white paper, from his kimono and tossed it at Hikaru's feet. It landed heavily in the sand. "My share of Yagyu-san's money. Five *koban*."

Hikaru looked at it. That could buy enough rice to feed a person for fifteen years. A fortune to a ronin.

"If you defeat me, will you donate it to a temple in his name for me?" Chuji asked. She nodded.

They stepped away from the rocks, finding open space of smooth sand. The morning breeze stirred the salt air, and somewhere further down the beach, a gull shrieked. They bowed to each other again and took their places.

Chuji moved into position with the confident grace of a master swordsman. Hikaru could read his intent in his stance. He did little to hide it. The Hojo samurai would draw his sword up, and strike high with it. He would either cleave her skull, or sweep her head from her shoulders.

As she shifted her feet, there was no doubt he could read

her as well. Her attack would be low, slashing at his belly, then her blade would loop around and up, over her head, for a vertical cut.

Hikaru took a deep breath, recalling the words of her *sensei*. "Even if one's head were to be suddenly cut off, he should be able to perform one more action with certainty." She watched Chuji, playing and replaying the motions in her mind. The first cut. The second cut. Anything else could be contemplated after. The first cut. The second cut.

Their swords flashed from their scabbards in the same heartbeat. Blood fell as a fine mist upon the soft, white sand.

What You Wish For

Wayne Bachner

A woman's soft voice — not my mother's — wakes me from my sleep. "Sorry," she says, "I'll try to be quick." Her touch on my arm is gentle and warm; for several seconds I forget where I am. Then I remember. With a groan I open my eyes. Outside the window is deep night, but this huge room never gets completely dark.

After a single day, the longest of my eleven years, I already know the routine. Obediently, I open my mouth and raise my skinny arm. The night nurse is young and pretty, nothing like the day nurse had been. The day nurse had acted as if her main job was to make sure none of the kids here had any fun. "This is a hospital, not a playground," she scolded. No running or jumping allowed. No throwing or kicking a ball. No crying, either. But no one has to remind us of that.

The night nurse apologizes again. "We need to take your vitals every four hours," she reminds me. I was told of this when I'd arrived but hadn't dreamed the information-gathering would continue throughout the night. Another horrible part of being in the hospital I just have to accept, along with the kid with no stomach and the creature in the crib.

"I'll be back again at four." The night nurse removes the blood pressure cuff and rubs the spot where the cuff pinched my arm. I hold back a sob as she moves on to Lionel, waking him from his own deep sleep. Lionel groans loudly too, upon opening his eyes.

Years later I'm holed up in Butler Library, cramming for a chem exam. I've spent the whole day studying and still have two long chapters to review. Chemistry's my chosen major, but recently I suffer from indecision; I have a strong attraction toward—also a great fear of—the hard sciences. The same technology, after all, being used to cure cancer produces the deadliest weapons. Last spring hundreds of people picketed Pupin Hall where Americans first split the uranium atom in 1939. I'd stood by and watched the protest, but hadn't joined in.

Strained by so many hours of study, my eyes have difficulty focusing on the equations, the chemistry text before me may as well be written in Chinese. My back's complaining as well; the library's wooden chairs weren't designed for comfort, they're intended to keep overwrought students from drifting off to sleep. It's clear I need a break. Tina, my first real girlfriend, lives nearby in East Campus; visiting her would sure beat cramming, but I probably wouldn't return to my chemistry text. Instead I get up to stretch my legs and eventually wander into the periodical room, where I leaf through this week's *New York Times*. A headline in the Tuesday science section catches my eye, *Mystery Solved in Hormone Deaths*.

With mounting horror I skim the article. Somehow the facts are hauntingly familiar. I took a psychology course last semester and was greatly impressed with the ability of the unconscious to protect us from traumatic events. After reading the two-page article all at once my defenses crumble. Memories come flooding back of my three-day stay at the Newington Children's Hospital.

"Lionel," I whisper when the night nurse leaves. "You awake?"

In the pale half-light he looks like a ghost. As I must, too. A real ghost, of course, would be able to walk through the walls and escape.

"I wish I'd never come."

"Me neither. But it'll be worth it, don't you think?"

Lionel and I are here for the same reason: three days of

medical testing to determine whether we'll be accepted for the medication trial. "Only three days," the doctor in charge had told my mother, but even one day's been almost impossible to endure; I don't see how I'm going to make it through two more.

"I can't fall back asleep," Lionel says after a few minutes.

"I'm not sleepy, either."

I peer through the dim light toward the large white cube at the far end of the room. There's no movement inside; I relax a little. "What do think happened to make him that way?"

"Dylan? He must have been born like that. I don't think it can happen to you later on."

I pray Lionel's right—I'd rather be dead than like Dylan. Even with eyes tightly closed, I still see the twisted arms, legs, and blank face that make Dylan look more horrible than any monster ever portrayed by Bela Lugosi or Boris Karloff. But what if Lionel's wrong? Mongoloid mental retardation (that's what the kid with no stomach said Dylan has) isn't something they teach about in the fifth grade.

"What you going to do when you get home, Ricky?"

Between tests mostly we talk about home. What else is worth talking about? Not this place, that's for sure.

"I don't know. Ride my bicycle, I guess."

"I got a dirt-bike. A real one."

"Neat." Though we're dressed in the same light-blue hospital pajamas, I'm pretty sure Lionel's family has a lot less money than mine. I wonder who gave him the dirt-bike, something none of my friends have, maybe because where we live there isn't any dirt, just neat, green lawns.

"You ever ride one?"

I hate to admit I haven't, but also hate to lie. "Not really. I rode a go-cart once when I visited my cousin in California." The go-cart was the type you pedaled with your feet; I don't share that part with Lionel.

"You can ride mine when you visit."

"Okay." Lionel lives just one town away; I've promised to come see him after we get out of the hospital.

"You meet the doctor with the beard yet, Ricky?"

I nod that I have then realize the light's too dim for him to see. "Yup. He sure was creepy."

"Can you *believe* some of the questions he asked?"

I don't answer right away.

"He make you show down below, Ricky?"

I know what Lionel's question refers to: it's something else I'm trying to put out of my mind. "They're checking our level of—I forget the word he used. *Mat-something*. It has to do with whether your body's aging right. That's how they decide whether or not to give you the stuff." I'm worried this could be a problem for me. Just last month I'd discovered a couple of thin hairs down there; I was proud of them until today. Being so short stinks; I desperately want to be approved for the growth hormone.

"You get picked on a lot?" I ask Lionel.

This time it's his turn not to answer right away. "Some," he admits, "but I go right up and smack 'em. That usually shuts 'em up."

"You're kidding!"

I think of Toby, my main tormentor. Toby's been left back twice and towers over everyone else. Fighting him would be suicide. Lionel's even shorter than me; he must get hurt a lot.

"My mom told me to fight. It works, too. Sometimes."

There's a loud, liquid sound from across the room. Dylan starts moving around in his crib, doing something. I try real hard not to think about what this might be.

The next thing I know the night nurse is waking me again to take my vitals, so I must have fallen back asleep. It's still dark in the hospital ward when she wakes me up, but not nearly as dark as I'd like it to be.

They don't accept me for the trial.

"The tests indicate your son doesn't have a hormone deficiency," the doctor with the beard tells my mother a few weeks later. We're seated in his office; he's made us wait half an hour. "Richard is merely genetically short. In all other respects he's a perfectly healthy child. Medically, at least."

I haven't contacted Lionel yet and doubt that I will, though if anyone asked I couldn't say why. Not because he's poor: that much I know.

"The x-rays reveal a normal bone age and your son is approaching puberty right on schedule. No, Ma'am," the doctor shakes his huge head with its neatly trimmed beard, "all the growth hormone in the world won't add a centimeter to his ultimate height."

The doctor talks about me as if I'm not in the room, but I don't care. I've stopped listening. I've just found out I'm doomed to be short the rest of my life. Those three days of suffering at the hospital had been for nothing.

"At least we tried." If Mom's disappointed she hides it well. "It would have been neglectful not to have pursued every possible avenue, don't you agree, Doctor?"

Of course he agrees. I haven't told Mom how horrible it was for me, surrounded by children who were dying and worse.

We stop at *Friendly's* for ice-cream on the way home. We don't talk about the test results or the hospital or the meeting with the doctor. Not then or ever.

Here's what I read in the article from the *New York Times*: the experimental growth hormone for which I'd been rejected eight years ago was 'harvested' from human cadavers. Unknown at the time, one of the cadavers contained a dormant, virulent virus that was transmitted to several children chosen for the early trials. Eventually the virus became active and ultimately fatal. The undersized boys and girls given the hormone grew a clinically significant amount more than the control group, then, years later, grew ill and died. No one had been able to figure out why until last month when a research team from this very university finally isolated the responsible virus. These days they synthesize the hormone in sterile laboratories so inadvertent infections no longer are a problem.

For the first time in years I wonder about Lionel. Had he

been one of the 'lucky ones,' one of the children chosen for the trial? Did he start catching up in height to his classmates only to sicken and die a few years later? A shiver goes through my body: I'd wanted to be chosen so badly and had cried for days after being rejected.

Somehow we make it to the final evening. Lionel and I make a pact to stay awake and talk all night in the dim light.

"What you going to do when you grow taller?"

"What do you mean?" I know what he's asking, but it's painful to think about being tall or even just not being the shortest kid in class.

"*Different*, Ricky. What you going to do *different?*"

This is a question I'd thought about a lot since learning about the growth hormone. I'm embarrassed to share the real answer, though.

"Play baseball," I say, the best idea I can come up with right away. "The outfield, too, not shortstop or catcher. And I'll hit the ball a mile instead of trying to walk or bunt my way onto base. How about you?"

"I want a girlfriend." Just like that, Lionel brings up the one topic we hadn't yet talked about. "You got a girlfriend, Ricky?" I can't tell from his tone which way he hopes I'll answer.

"Not really." I could tell him about Lucy Alden; there wouldn't be much to tell. I've spoken to her a few times between classes after practicing what to say for hours. Lucy's a thin, dark girl with long, black hair: she's so pretty looking at her makes me a little dizzy. Robert Pierson—a big kid who's the school's top athlete—likes her as well. I see them together a lot, standing and talking in the hallway.

"How about you, Lionel? Do you have a girlfriend?"

There's a long silence that tells me all I need to know. "Mom says I better figure out how to make lots of money if I don't want to end up alone. She says only dumb girls go for the big, strong guys; smart girls go for the money."

This is something I've never considered. Mom's small, but

she's a woman; being short doesn't matter that much for girls. Dad's average-sized, so that doesn't help, but Grandpa Pauli's real short and isn't rich; he was able to marry. That happened a long time ago in a different country, though.

After bringing up the topic of girls Lionel doesn't say anything else. Instead of talking the rest of the night we lie quietly in the almost-dark. No one wants to be alone; if I'm not chosen to get the growth hormone I'll have to find some way to get rich. I vow to study harder in school — that's the only idea I come up with.

Following the discovery in the periodical room there's no way I can continue to study. These days, they'd never put young children in the hospital for tests that could be performed just as effectively on an out-patient basis, and they definitely wouldn't house them with children suffering from serious genetic disorders. I still have occasional nightmares of Dylan, with his blank face and deformed body. The bullying and teasing I endured in the schoolyard was minor by comparison.

I return to the table where I'd been studying and shove the chemistry text into my backpack. Then I search the library for an on-campus phone.

"Hey, Tina," I say, struggling to make my voice sound calm. "You doing anything special?"

"Not really, Rick; just schoolwork. What's up?"

"I'd like to come by if that's okay."

"Jennifer's here," she whispers. Jennifer is Tina's roommate. "You still want to come over?"

"Sure. I just feel like some company."

I haven't decided if I'm going to tell her about my discovery in the periodical room. Tina's the only girl I've dated; I don't know what I'd do if she broke up with me.

"I could ask her to go out for a cup of coffee..."

"No, don't bother. Really, I just want to hang out awhile."

Before today I'd have jumped at Tina's offer to make her roommate disappear, but I've just learned life has a way of punishing the greedy. Suddenly I'm afraid of wishing for too much.

"Come right on over then, Rick."

I stumble down the steep marble stairs leading out of the library and enter the cool, dark night. A gibbous moon hangs in the sky like a distorted light-bulb; its silvery emanations transform all the tree branches into ghostly, twisted limbs. The night air makes me shiver, then I'm surprised by a glimpse of my own metallic arm. This time, though, I not only look like a ghost—I feel like one as well.

One More Step

Camille Banham

Oh my God. I have to get out of here. *Get up.* I have to move. *Now.* I have to get to the curb. I'll just walk. It's okay, I can get up and walk. I'm fine. I'm fine. God, it hurts to move. What is this, an army crawl? Fuck, my arm can't hold this weight. Just a little farther, and I'll be there. *Focus.* The curb is right there. *There we go. You're there. You made it. See? You're okay. You're going to be fine. Look at the road. There's no blood.* The asphalt is as black and mottled and covered with the crap of Hollywood as it always has been.

Do I need an ambulance? No. I'm okay. I can't. I can't do that. I can't be the patient. I was just the EMT last week. *Remember? You helped that girl after she was beaten. You're not the patient. You're not the patient.* Someone else probably called anyway. That probably looked pretty bad. I was pretty high in the air. But, I'm fine. I'll be okay. Shit, why can't I lift my right arm? If the medics come, maybe I should be lying down. *You know how this goes.* They'll probably insist on putting me in the collar and on the backboard. Oh God! I can't panic. I can't. If they put me on that board, I'm going to lose it. That's too real. I can't do that. This isn't happening. I'm not the patient.

Wait, who is this? Why is he shirtless? I can't hear him, what is he saying? Ow, my shoulder hurts. Oh no. I think that cracking sound is my shoulder. *Look, it's purple and out of place.* This guy looks like an Abercrombie model. Why is he shaking me? Wait, he can't do that. I might have a spinal fracture. *Say something. Say something! Make your lips move. He can't hear you. I don't think you're saying anything.*

"Please don't touch me, I don't know what my injuries are."

Oh God, listen to my voice, I sound so weak and small. *Cara, calm down, it's going to be fine.* Where is he going? Is he on his way to the beach? Where is his shirt?

Oh God, he's leaving me. *Don't let him leave.* Wait! I need help! Someone please help me! *Look around, Cara.* I know there were people watching me while I flew through the air. I saw them. I heard them gasp. What is that on my shoulder? Ah, that feels good. Thank you.

Make sure this woman with her iced latte on your shoulder doesn't leave. A latte as an ice-pack. How L.A. *Focus, Cara. You have to speak again. You can do this.*

"P-please don't leave me! I need witnesses! Someone hit me. Please don't leave me. I need witnesses!"

Was that my voice? *Stop shrieking. You sound panicked. You're going to be fine. You have to be.*

"He stopped."

It's the woman with the latte. What is she talking about? No one stopped. Wait. Oh my God. Replay it. Replay what he said!

"Oh my God. I hit you! I'm sorry! I hit you!"

"Please don't touch me, I don't know what my injuries are."

That was him. The shirtless man hit me. Where did he go? *She said he stopped, so it's going to be okay.* I should call Valerie and let her know I won't be at the restaurant. I was really looking forward to that beer and burger. Where's my phone? I should call Eric. He'll want to know this happened. But I'm okay. I don't want to scare him. I'll be okay.

Shit. I can't lift my right arm still. I might have to go to the hospital. They might have to relocate my shoulder. Does it have a pulse? If it doesn't have a pulse I could lose my arm. Oh God. I have to go to the hospital. NO! I can't handle this. I need Eric to be here. Who are these people? I need someone I know with me. My phone isn't working. It must have broken on impact. Please, I need a phone. No one is answering me. Maybe that wasn't out loud. *Concentrate, and use your words. Get out of your head.*

"Please, I need a phone. I have to call 911."

"Someone already did."

Oh fuck. I can hear them now in the distance, echoing off the buildings, their wail snaking through the streets towards my slumped body on the sidewalk. Those sirens are for me. I can't do this. I can't be the patient.

Who is handing me this phone? Tattoos, half-shaved head, brown hair. Oh yea, we're right outside that hipster barbershop. This phone has cracks all over the glass. I read somewhere that the glass acts like fiberglass and can get under your skin. That will be painful, I better be careful. Ow. Damnit! I can't lift my right arm. *Stop trying! Use your left.*

Jane! Someone should go get Jane. I need someone I know. Does she already know? Maybe they heard the sound of my body hitting the car. I'm not that far from the office. Maybe it was loud? I think I screamed. I think I said, *"No, please don't"* out loud when I turned my head and saw the SUV coming. It sounded loud to me. People must have heard me scream *"Oh my God!"* when he slammed into me. My scream was deafening, wasn't it? Maybe I was hit hard. I did feel my handle bars slam into the back of that other car.

I felt like a push puppet when I got hit. It felt like someone had taken their thumb off the button and my bones were attached by string and suddenly flew apart, then slammed back together when someone put their thumb back on the button. I used to play with those toys all the time. My favorite was the horse when I was little. I think my Mom gave it to me.

My Mom. I have to tell my Mom. NO. Not yet. Not until I know what is happening. I can't believe this is happening. Am I going to die? I need someone I know with me.

"Can you get Jane? Please. I work just a few doors down. I need Jane. Can someone get Jane, please? Oh, God. I need to call my boyfriend."

You still sound shrill. You have to calm down.

"What's your boyfriend's number?"

The half-shaved head guy, again. I wonder if that really is a stylistic choice, or if he was in the middle of getting his head shaved when I was hit. His cracked phone again. I can't work this. I can't even do this with my left hand. Oh, it's already ringing. Eric's number must have been what I was mumbling.

"Hello?"

Gosh, his voice sounds wary. He is probably wondering what number this is. Maybe he thinks it's someone calling with a job offer. If I tell him what happened, I'm going to change his life. *It's too late, Cara. Everything has already changed.*

"Eric, I-I was hit by a car. But I'm okay."

"WHAT!?"

Oh no. He sounds upset. He sounds panicked. I can't hear that. He'll make me panic. I'm okay. I can't let this be scary.

"I'm okay. The medics are on the way, they're going to take me to the hospital, can you meet me there?"

Shit, they're here. They're pulling up. I didn't even realize the sirens getting louder. I have to go to the hospital now. I can't be the patient. I don't know how to do this. He's taking a pulse. What's he asking? My name. I can do that. *Just tell him your name. You can do this.*

"I'm an EMT. My neck is fine. Don't strap me onto a backboard, or I'll panic."

It does sort of hurt when I turn my head, but I think that's just the pain from my shoulder traveling up to my neck.

Why are you turning your head back and forth? You know you can't assess your own neck injury! A pulse. He has to check for a pulse in my right arm. I can't feel one. My left hand is shaking too much. Fuck. I don't have a pulse. I'm going to lose my arm. *Tell him. Use your words, Cara.*

"You have to check for a pulse, I think my arm is dislocated. Is there a pulse? I don't feel a pulse!"

You're back to shrieking again. Calm down, or no one will take you seriously.

"I feel a pulse."

See? He feels a pulse. You're fine. Everything will be fine. But, I had heard his engine, so I don't think he was braking. If the speed limit here is 25mph, he must have hit me going at least that speed. If I was the EMT responding to this scene I would be worried about internal damage. I could be bleeding out slowly. Oh my God. *This could be bad, Cara. You need to go to a hospital.*

"Can you walk to the stretcher?"

What is he talking about? Of course I can walk. It's just my shoulder. Everything else is fine. *Go ahead, just stand up, you can do this.*

Oh man, no. This feels like...there's a metal rod between my legs. I can't even take a step. I'm going to fall. *The medics will catch you.* Why can't I walk? Oh my God, I can't walk. Why is it so far away?

"Just one more step."

If only he knew what he is asking of me. One. More. Step. *There, sit down. You did it. Oof.* That was a hard landing.

Jane! Jane's here. Oh my God, look at her face. She looks awfully flushed and wide-eyed. Why does she look like that? Oh no, I must look terrible. Is it bad? What does she see? *Don't look. Tell her you're okay. She's just scared, tell her it's okay.*

"Oh my God, Cara!"

"I'm okay."

"What happened!?"

"I got hit by a car, but I'm okay. I have to go to the hospital. Can you make sure they know I won't be at work?"

"Of course! Are you kidding? Cara, just take care of yourself. Is Eric going to meet you at the hospital?"

Eric. Oh God. If Jane's face looked like that, I can't even imagine what it is going to be like to see Eric. I wish people weren't making this such a big deal. It makes it harder for me. I'm really okay.

Someone's talking. I can't see Jane, who is this guy blocking her? What's he saying? *Focus.* What is he saying? My name? My address? My phone number? Well, at least I know all that information. That's a good sign. *See, Cara? You're going to be fine. You are alert and oriented. Name, time, place, you know it. That means it's not serious. You know this.*

Please don't close the doors! No, wait, I'm not done talking to Jane. I don't want to go. I don't want to leave her. I'm not ready to have to be in a hospital. Is this really necessary? Fuck, my arm is throbbing now.

"Where are we going?"

Is that the driver? Is he asking me where we're going. I

don't know. I don't even know what hospital is nearby. I could name every hospital back home, but I have no idea what's around here. I hope they're good, but who knows what I'll get in this city.

"Century."

Century. He chose Century. They're the best in the city. *You're going to be okay.*

"Thank you."

I made my medic smile. I can do this. *Think about how you feel when you're the EMT and you have a patient in the back, and talk to him.* He's probably afraid I'm going to black out any minute. He's probably running through how quickly he can get to the oxygen and the AED to perform CPR on me. Why am I shivering?

He might be the last person to see me alive. *Stop it, Cara. You don't need to go there.* Fuck, my shoulder is throbbing now that I am sans latte. *You need an ice pack.*

"Can I have an ice pack for my shoulder?"

"Sure give me a second."

They keep their ice packs in a higher shelf than we do on my ambulance. Oh yes. That feels good on there.

"Thank you."

"You're welcome."

I can't believe this is happening. I've only taken a ride on the stretcher in EMT class to see what it's like for our patients. I've probably been in the back of an ambulance a thousand times, but never as a patient. I can't be the patient. This is surreal. Hollywood in reverse.

Keep talking, and stay out of your head. It's too scary in here. "You know, I'm an EMT. I was actually just loading my own patient into the ambulance a week ago. This is surreal."

"Oh. Wow, yea I bet. I've never done this ride as a patient."

"Yea. It's fucked."

"Yea."

I wonder what he thinks of me. I wonder if he cares. Too many of my partners never cared. I wonder if I'm the easy patient of his day. He probably doesn't even care that I was supposed to be eating the best veggie burger in L.A. right now, and sipping on beer catching up with Valerie. I can almost taste the burger and beer. That's what's real. That's my life. This is a blip in my timeline that was never meant to be here. This isn't meant for me. *Just talk to the medic. Stay out of your head.*

"Have you been to Shred?"

"Nope."

"They have the best veggie burgers in L.A. I was supposed to be there right now. Can you believe it? This is really surreal."

"Yea."

He doesn't care. It's too abstract. No one wants to think about being you. No one believes this could ever be them, not even you.

I'm shaking more now. *It's okay, you're just scared. Breathe.* I can't do this. This can't be my life. That was my first thought when I realized the SUV was coming at me. This isn't in my timeline. I'm going to clear this car. I was certain of it. Was that really only a few minutes ago? It feels like a lifetime.

I'm supposed to be telling Valerie about France right now. France. A week ago I was far away from this reality and sipping wine in France. This shivering is hurting my shoulder.

"C-can I have a b-blanket, please?"

"No problem. Just give me a second to grab one."

Not too close to my face. Hospital blankets always have a strange stale smell to them. I wonder who was under this blanket last. I hope they lived. I hope they were in less pain than I am.

"We're not too far away from the hospital, Cara. Just a few more minutes."

Why did he say that? Do I look bad? Oh, no. I'm going into shock, aren't I? I'm shaking, I'm cold. I'm probably going into hypovolemic shock from bleeding out internally. *Quiet. Look at the rig. Focus on the rig. It's different from your ambulance at home. The gauze is in the shelves on the left side, not the right. There you go. Distract yourself with the details all around you. This will all be over, and everything will be okay.*

I'm going to be okay. I'm going to be fine. *Talk about what's true. Talk about what you know. You are Cara and you just turned twenty-five. You have lived a quarter of a century, and have just returned from three weeks in France.* So many people will never even have the opportunity to travel to France. *You have lived a good life.* Oh my God. *You have to know that before you go.* Please, no.

I am going to die today. I am twenty-five, and I am going to die in this body.

I can hear the sirens clearing our path through the rush hour traffic of the city.

"We're almost there, Cara."

Is he talking to me? My body feels numb. I feel like I'm floating. I hear the sound of the tires hitting the potholes of the decrepit city streets, but I don't feel it. Did he give me medication? I can't feel myself anymore. The sirens faded. Are we here? Are we at the hospital?

"We lost her just as we pulled up."

Who is he talking about? Oh my God, is he talking about me? No! I'm here. I'm here! I don't think they can hear me. Are my lips moving? *Focus, Cara. Talk just one last time. You can't be the patient. This wasn't meant for you. This wasn't in your timeline.*

"What did she say?"

"I don't know. She's out. Let's get her inside, quick."

You're still here. Tell them you're still here!

I'm still here.

An Unexpected Fall

Linda Butler

Maryanne Dunner had a man waiting for her in her living room. And not just any man, for her Ouija Board had predicted that he was *the* man, the man who soon would spend a lot more time in her living room. She fingered her silver curls and stared at the red, gold and orange leaves raining down outside her bedroom window, willing the foolish boy on the other end of the telephone to please just follow her simple directions.

"Never mind," she interrupted. "I said I *have* candles and allspice, but I still need a besom and a jack-o'lantern to light. I don't CARE where they come from. Look, I have a visitor at the moment, and can't—"

"Um, what's a besom, Miss Dunner?" the boy asked.

"What's a besom, *Circe*," she corrected yet again, barely keeping her voice down. He was hopeless. "Use *coven* names. You've got to start remembering these things Shorty—I mean Evanude—now you've got *me* doing it!" If only the group had made the Bissonette boy someone else's responsibility. But teaching him the mysteries was one of the many burdens of leadership.

"Oh never mind. I'll get the besom," she said. "Just call everyone—"

"I saw Mr., I mean, *Dagonnell* at Fredette's Hardware and he said he don't think anybody's gonna want to be outside tonight 'cause it's s'posed be in the thirties. You sure you want us up on the mountain?"

"We celebrate Samhain on the mountain tonight and that's that. Just make sure you use my list and don't call anyone who isn't—"

But he'd hung up before she finished.

The Bissonette boy had been vouched-safe by both Amos Blankenship and Bill Courtmange. Experience had taught her not to trust Courtmange, but she respected Amos; if he thought the young man ready to be an acolyte, Maryanne hadn't argued. Yet she couldn't help but wonder. The Bissonette boy just didn't seem to get it. He had asked to be named Evel Knieval during his naming ceremony, then Boz Scaggs, even after she'd reminded him of the rule against using a living person's name. Wicca magick was nothing to play with. When Shorty finally came up with Exrafood, she had a "vision" of her father's old outboard and told him that that Evanrude would be his name instead, except without the 'r'.

"Be right out," she sing-songed to her guest. She made a quick check of Itsy and Bitsy, both still asleep. She hoped she hadn't dosed them too heavily. Her visitor might not take to the Chihuahuas right away; not everyone did. What would she do if he didn't like dogs? But of *course* he would love them. How could he be her soul mate if he didn't love her dogs?

"Sorry to be so long. Now, where were we?"

"I was explaining 'in perpetuity'," he said, his soft drawl drawing her in.

"More coffee?" The coffee she'd brewed had been Robert's favorite. His espresso beans, his *mousse de saumon,* and sauce *veloute*-for-two were still in zip-locked plastic bags in her freezer. She simply didn't have the heart to throw them away. She wondered if Frank Elpenor liked *mousse de saumon.*

"Thank you kindly. Nothing like good coffee," he said. "Now, about this here contract—"

"Before we get back to that, Mr.—may I call you Frank?" She felt a shiver of delight when he smiled and nodded. "Could you explain again what you said last week, Frank, or was it the week before? No—it was when we spoke on the phone. You said that your company—"

"Metagy."

"Right. That Metagy would build those Eiffel-tower things on my property. Won't they look odd?"

She had to keep him talking!

As yet undiscovered was what she'd need for her love-calling at tonight's Sabbat Samhain ceremonies. The books she consulted were very specific: place an object of the beloved's, something that carried his "essence" into the scrying bowl before lighting the candles.

"Like I explained at our first meeting and then again on the telephone," he said, "you won't see the towers. Metagy is expert at camouflage. I can draw one for you. Here…"

She watched as he drew, taking in the manly aroma of his leather jacket, the sharp creases of his slacks. They weren't touching, yet she felt the warmth of his body next to her. He wasn't as handsome as Robert — Frank carried a bit more around his middle and quite a bit less on top — but she didn't mind that at all.

Powerful signs had pointed to the fact that *he* was the one she would marry. Two weeks past, her Ouija's planchette had pointedly slid from "F," to "E," to "L," and her cards had said her beloved will be known by his "mark." The very next morning, Mr. Frank Elpenor had knocked at her front door. She had nearly lost her breath when she saw it — a raised, black birthmark the size of a nickel on the right side of his chin.

"More?" she asked, seeing his cup empty.

"Thank you, no," he answered. "D'you have any other questions before you sign the permission form while there's enough light for me to get up on your roof and take my photos."

"I see. But first I'd like to go back to the thing about 'in perpetuity.' How does that work?"

She watched him take a deep breath. Oh dear, he was getting perturbed.

"It means forever, plus —". He repeated what he'd earlier said, finally ending with what he'd explained several times already. " —and it means guaranteed reduced electric rates for y'all here in Mt. Constance, New Hampshire. All depends on you, Ms. Dunner."

"Please, it's Maryanne."

Linda Butler

"Ah, Maryanne. Now, if you'll just sign this here permission form that says it's OK for me to go up on your roof…"

"But it's so windy today, worse than last week," she objected. "And colder. I don't know what I'd do if you slipped and fell."

"No need to worry, ma'am. I do this all the time. But I have to get all them photos of the slope for our engineers before next—"

"At least take something hot up with you to go out into the cold…Frank." She patted his hand and let her pinkie linger and then went to the kitchen before he could object.

Hers was a small kitchen, but then so was Maryanne. She needed to think—there must be *something*—maybe she could search his car while he was busy on the roof. She noticed the Benadryl she'd given to Itsy and Bitsy on the counter and poured the littlest—no, he was a big man, *more* than the littlest—into a thermos then poured in hot coffee and tightened the lid. Benedryl helped her dogs ignore the other animals when she took them to the vet.

Back in the living room, it hit her with such force that she was dazzled by its simplicity. As he accepted the thermos, he handed her a slim silver pen from his pocket, the inside pocket, the pocket close to his heart—and he was urging her to *take* it!

She obliged, smiling, and signed the permission form without taking her eyes from his. He returned her smile.

"You know, Mr. Elpenor—Frank—we have so much in common. I feel as though I've known you for a long time," she said.

"Well, uh, I guess there ain't many of us Georgians up this a-way." He affixed his name to the page as well. "Here's your copy and—"

"It's not just that. I mean, we're both…*unattached*?" She looked down at his ringless left hand. "Do you like dogs?" she asked.

He smiled and nodded, reaching for the door handle.

"I don't mean to be too forward, Frank, but…um…there's

an ecumenical pot-luck at the Methodist Church this weekend," she ventured. "I'd love to take you as my guest. I know this is short notice, but—"

"I'm not much on organized religions, I'm afraid, Ms. Dunner," he answered.

She wanted to swoon into his arms.

"Thanks for the invitation, but I, uh, I have to work." He looked around and patted his breast pocket. "You still have my pen?"

She made a show of checking between couch cushions and the floor, his pen safe and unseen within the sleeve of her sweater. She offered one of her own. He refused, but asked her to call when it turned up. That, of course, was exactly what she planned to do.

The only cloud on the horizon for tonight's love calling was Walter Hooper—*Moby-wan*. She couldn't let Walter know about tonight's love calling, and would have to keep Frank away from him until after they were married. Walter said he'd shown the photos to Robert to get a laugh. Some joke. They all were so young then, she'd tried to explain. It was what they thought they were *supposed* to do at Beltane. It was different now; no one got naked anymore. That hadn't mattered to Robert, though. She'd torn up the photos, every one of them, but with Walter, you never knew.

"Are you sure you're going to be okay?" she asked him as he walked out onto the porch.

"I do this all the time. I have another appointment with one of the other homeowners along the proposed vector, so I need to get going. Thanks again for the coffee. I'll be in touch."

She watched him put a ladder against her hydrangea shrub, their blossoms long-since dried, closed her eyes and said a prayer to the Goddess. Her job now was to ensure what the omens foretold. There would be a full moon tonight. The magick would be particularly strong. Her stomach churned with excitement.

* * *

"On the mountain...*tonight*? You gotta be kidding," Walter Hooper whispered, leaning back into the booth. The Pie Bowl was crowded, regulars in their customary seats along the diner's plate-glass window fronting Main Street. A haze of hamburger grease and burned toast hung in the air.

"No, I'm not kidding. Shorty's going to call you. It's the...ahem...*sacred* night of Sabbat Samhain. Don't tell me you're gonna turn down a chance to watch that loony broad dance around a campfire because of a little weather, Walt." Bill Courtmange, Vice Chairman of the Mt. Constance Board of Selectmen, smiled, took a long sip of coffee, and waited for his companion to respond.

"I don't know. Maybe," Walter answered. "I gotta get that insurance policy signed and up to Concord by close of business. Elizabeth is bitching that I've been gone too much lately."

Elizabeth was Walter's wife, the only person Courtmange knew who could "make" Walter Hooper do anything. Hooper was in his sixteenth year as Chairman of the Mt. Constance Board of Selectmen. Like his father before him, he was considered the most powerful man in town, with Hooper's Sawmill its largest employer.

"Did I tell you Pete got us the sit-down with the governor and highway commissioner next Friday?" Hooper said. "I've had the Blankenship boy and his teammates out getting signatures."

Courtmange nodded. "Good move.

"Metagy's got their hounds out on the mountain already trying to get right-of-ways," Hooper continued. "They run those lines through town and you can kiss businesses on Main Street goodbye; nobody's going to want to work or shop under those power lines. If I can talk the Gov' into reopening the nickel mine on the other side of the mountain, he might be willing to look at that petition to stop Metagy, but with Grace Turnbull on me like a goddamn fungus for the past couple of weeks...I can't even go to the crapper without her following me with her damn camera." Hooper glanced down to the last table where Leland Hilliard, editor of *The Mt. Constance Crier*, had picked that same moment to look up from his reading.

"He's comin' over. *Shit.* Just what I need." Courtmange and Hooper both turned away to stare through the window in the vain hope they might avoid the man who moments later stood beside them.

"'Morning Walter, Bill. Either of you ever hear of 'Sunshine Laws'? "

"I forgot! Hey, Bill, we'd better convene a special town meeting so's everybody can weigh in on which SUV you oughtta buy," Hooper answered.

"That might be what you two were discussing, Walter. Then again, there are those who might wonder if you actually are working on town business. Which reminds me, do you think your department heads will have those final budgets ready for Grace by the end of the month?" Hilliard asked.

"They'd better, what with Grace making herself a fixture at every meeting," Courtmange said. "She was at Town Hall Wednesday 'til the janitor made her leave so he could lock up for the night. What's with that—her Sominex© not working anymore?"

Hilliard smiled and turned to Hooper. "Speaking of meetings, I heard through the grapevine that our road agent sent a letter to Concord last month asking for a meeting with the governor, the highway honchos and utility commissioners. Grace couldn't find it in any of the minutes. You guys know anything about that?"

"Nope. Road agent wrote the letter—ask him. Wife says he'll be out of the hospital next week," Hooper answered, barely able to hide his annoyance. He pulled out his wallet and put a five-dollar bill on the table beside his coffee mug. "It's been loads, guys, but I gotta run." Hooper rose and left, trading good-natured insults with customers along the way.

Bill Courtmange left The Pie Bowl soon after and crossed Main Street to his car. Hooper's Main Street Association opposed Metagy's proposal to run transmission lines through town and up the southern face of Mt. Constance. That wasn't the real problem, though. Metagy's proposal also included a new, larger bridge on the Constance River once the lines were approved, which meant a new access road into town off Route 101. Courtmange had done the math: a new Main Street in a different location, painful to local businesses as it would be in the short term, could actually be a boon to future growth, especially if he could get the paving contract. It might take longer and be more expensive for Hooper's loggers to get to the mill, but it would mean cheaper utility costs for the town—and maybe even more development and more new roads.

He couldn't worry about that now. He didn't want to lose his friendship with Walter, yet couldn't help but wonder what might happen to his paving business if Walter stopped Metagy. Blankenship would be coming to the mountain tonight. Maybe they could figure something out. Wicca. That was another issue. New Hampshire was still pretty conservative. He was walking a thin line, he knew, continuing to meet *Moby-wan* Walter and *Olgar* Amos at Wicca, perfect camouflage or not, because if Betts ever found out, no matter how many times he'd sworn it was Hooper and Maryanne in the X-rated photos from high school, his wife had never bought his story that he'd walked away from the orgies. With good reason.

While her boss was at The Pie Bowl having lunch, Grace Turnbull, Assistant Editor of the *Mt. Constance Crier*, was finishing layout for the next issue. She'd wanted it ready for Leland to look over when he got back—and it would have been, if she hadn't been so clumsy. She dropped her mark-up pen. It rolled under her feet and, not paying attention, she slipped, coming down hard on the newsroom's ancient paper cutter, catching her chin on its rough iron arm in an effort to keep from falling to the floor. Soon blood was dripping from her chin onto the layout pages she had painstakingly worked on all morning. There was nothing to be done except start over.

Grace preferred to do layouts the old-fashioned way, with

heavy metal plates and rubber cylinders like Leland's Uncle Graf had taught her. Graf had bequeathed *The Crier* to his nephew and, while she'd agreed to stay on after Graf passed away, she'd lately found herself thinking about leaving Mt. Constance and giving up newspaper work altogether. Their new computer made things go much faster but she missed the way she and Graf would huddle over each page together, cutting here, pasting there. More than once a brush of elbows led to a quick, guilty embrace, but he'd refused to believe a woman her age could love a 74-year old man.

She looked up to see her boss walk through the door.

"Almost ready to scan it in, Lee," she said. "Here, take a look. Learn anything good at gossip gulch?"

"Odd you should ask," he answered. "Two of them were there having lunch. When I mentioned that letter, Hooper stonewalled. Hey—what happened to your chin?"

"Wasn't watching what I was doing. Look, maybe I *should* drive down to Boston to talk to the road agent."

"Not yet," he said. "But I think you're right—Hooper and Courtmange are definitely up to something."

"Did you get those price changes for Fredette's ad?"

He nodded and handed her the grocer's corrections. "I'm heading out. Call me if you need me."

She finished the layout, added the hardware store's price changes, hit "Send," and the full text of *The Crier's* next edition sailed through aether to their printer in Concord.

Putting one issue of a newspaper to bed meant that it was time to get started on the next. By the time Grace scheduled interviews for the Harvest Ball and lined up a photographer for the high school's homecoming game, it was time to close up shop. She looked forward to a long, quiet evening at home and was almost at her car when Shorty Bissonette, hooded sweatshirt pulled tight around his face, collided with her on the sidewalk.

"Hey, dude, careful," she laughed. Shorty was Fancy Bissonette's oldest.

"Sorry, Miss Grace, I didn't see—*what* did you call me?"

"How's your mom?" She had known Fancy since they

101

were in Girl Scouts together. Their lives had taken different paths since then, though. With seven boys to raise and a full-time job at Fredette's Grocery, Fancy had little time for friendships.

"No, I mean what *other* name did you say?" he insisted. "Did you, like, say, Evanude—I mean are you..."

The wind had picked up. Grace realized her thin sweater wasn't warm enough, but she didn't want to leave the poor kid standing there with that uncomprehending look on his face. She'd always felt a little sorry for the boy. Life hit Shorty harder than it did most, though most of the time he seemed unaware.

"I'm sorry, hon, but I'm freezing. Tell your mom I said hel—"

"No, wait. *Wait!* I gotta know because—I mean, if that was my *other* name you said, like Mr. Blankenship is *Olgar*, and Mr. Courtmange is *Daggonell*, and Mrs. Melinda is...is...Anyway, Miss Dun—I mean, *Circe's Daughter* said to tell everybody we're meeting on the mountain tonight. I can't always see, so I don't know who's who and who's not."

Grace stood for a moment in spite of the cold, and blinked. Blankenship and Courtmange? Maybe Hooper would be there too. She and Leland had long suspected that town business was being conducting someplace other than town hall.

"On the mountain? Uh—sure. What time did you say?"

He told her.

"Thanks, Shorty—"

"Coven names, remember?"

"Oh. Right. I forgot. See you tonight, Evandude!"

Grace made herself an early dinner, trying without success to reach Leland on his cell. She did a quick check of the town's master calendar on her home computer, just to be sure. No meetings on the town calendar, the church calendars or the school calendar. If there were any organizations meeting tonight, they were strictly off the books. If Amos Blankenship and Bill Courtmange were going to a meeting on Mt. Constance tonight, Grace Turnbull would be there, too.

By 6:15 pm, the sky had begun to darken. She slipped on a parka, grabbed her camera and drove to the library's parking lot at the base of Mt. Constance. Within a few moments, she saw Courtmange's station wagon go by, but waited a few minutes before following. Three quarters of the way up, he turned right onto the dirt road that would end at the mountain's summit, a more or less flat, rocky space surrounded by tall evergreens that overlooked Lake Constance to the south and Mt. Monadnock to the north. It was a favorite spot for picnickers and hikers to stop for lunch. There was a wooden observation deck just off the road which the Boy Scouts had built decades ago. Grace wondered if she could get up there without anyone noticing. She made her way up the deck's rickety steps hidden by overgrown rhododendron, hawthorn and sumac, and got down on her stomach unobserved, camera at the ready.

Wind rattled the topmost branches of ash, red pine and spruce but she knew she could count on the overgrown shrubs circling the clearing to keep the candles lit. Maryanne Dunner, transformed into *Circe's Daughter* by prayer and in full ceremonial regalia, barely noticed the cold or cars as they arrived, their occupants having turned off their headlights to make their way unobserved up the final stretch of dirt road.

She'd cleared debris from the sacred circle with the besom she'd found in her garage. The Bissonette boy chattered as she worked.

"Miss *Circe* — I read this book, *Worlds in Collision*? It's way-old, but this guy says dinosaurs were all killed by a comet or an asteroid or something, not by the battle between the moon goddess and...and...*who* was it you said the moon goddess fought?"

He'd gotten it all wrong, of course. Maryanne rolled her eyes and ignored him. Coven members, she noticed, were donning their robes and elaborate crowns and garlands of silk and paper flowers that partially hid their faces. Maryanne asked Edith Porter to pass around the welcoming prayer and Melinda Snow to light the plastic jack-o-lantern—not a real one, like she'd asked Shorty to make. She hoped it wouldn't matter.

Circe's Daughter raised her arms and summoned her communicants as she set candles at each of the four cardinal points, and a pink and white candle in the center of the circle. She then gave each robed participant a candle as well.

Will they know twin candles are for a love-calling? Not likely.

She rang her bell and began the quarter-calls, one prayer for each sacred direction: East, South, West, and North. Her scrying bowl was in the center of the circle, reflecting the light of the moon as she cast tablespoons of McCormick's ground allspice to each of the four winds. Shorty was at her right, holding the besom. She had to stop twice to shush the whispering that distracted her—Blankenship and Courtmange, as usual. At least *Moby-wan* Hooper was absent.

Finally it was time to cast the spell. No names—that was the rule. She couldn't say "Frank" or "Elpenor" or even think of his face during the ritual, but placed his pen into the scrying bowl, signaling one of the group to light the candles. With stars, moon, and her fellow Wiccans as witnesses, Maryanne took the fresh-ground catnip and held it high, along with her pink candle, ready to begin, when a voice interrupted her concentration.

"We almost done?" It was Shorty, arms flapping in an attempt to get warm. "It's cold."

She ignored him, walking around the circle, pink candle held to the stars, whispering the words to open the heart of the silver pen's owner. Out of the corner of her eye she saw movement up in the trees at the edge of the clearing.

Dryads!

That was a powerful sign. Very powerful.

"Hush!" she warned. It was Amos and Bill, whispering to one another again.

As she prepared to chant the final verse, there was a bright flash, a loud *crack!*...and then a cry. At first, Maryanne thought it was the voice of the West Wind, then Shorty yelled, "Maybe it's an asteroid!"

"Somebody just fell off that old deck!" Melinda yelled.

When Maryanne opened her eyes, she saw that members of her coven had run to where the noise had come from. She froze, horrified. No one was ever supposed to break a sacred circle during a spell! She walked to where the rest of her coven stood. Above her, the rotted railing of the old Boy Scout observation deck swayed precipitously.

"Look—a camera," someone said.

"Oh Christ, it's Grace Turnbull. This is all I need." Amos Blankenship tore off his robe and threw it to the ground.

Bill Courtmange came running back from his car. "I just got Walt on the phone. He's on his way. Shorty, help everyone get those damn robes off and into Melinda's trunk—"

"But aren't we supposed to use coven names?" Shorty asked.

Maryanne, transfixed, stared down at the face bathed in moonlight and bent to gently touch the leaf-caked cheek, revealing a dark scab on the right side of the reporter's chin.

"You came to me! Frank, oh Frank," she whimpered.

"Dunner!" Courtmange grabbed her by the shoulders. "Listen to me, you crazy loon. If you say *one word* about this— tell everybody we were rehearsing a skit for the Winter Carnival. Understand?" He looked at the others of the group. "Got that?"

They nodded.

Within minutes, all evidence of the night's ceremony had disappeared, heading back down Mountain Road toward town, save for Shorty, Amos Blankenship and Bill Courtmange. Maryanne remained on the cold ground. "Frank? Frank...can you hear me?"

Grace Turnbull opened her eyes and sat up. "Oooh. Ow. Wha—what happened? Oh, God, my leg!" It was beneath her, twisted at an unnatural angle.

Courtmange said, "I'll...I'll get help. We were rehearsing a skit, right guys? Talked about it for years...for the winter carnival."

"What the hell are you doing?" Grace looked up at Maryanne and pushed her hand away.

"Sweet Frank, what have I done to you?" Maryanne crooned.

"She's just checking you for head injuries, right Maryanne?" Blankenship offered, sending a warning look in Maryanne's direction.

"Can somebody call an ambulance?" Grace asked through clenched teeth.

"I got hold of Doc, Grace; he's meeting us at the ER," Courtmange said, putting his cell phone away. "Amos, help me get her to my car."

When Courtmange's taillights disappeared into the darkness, Shorty Bissonette turned to Maryanne. "I best get going too, Miss Dun—*Circe's Daughter*. You need a ride back?"

Maryanne shook her head, backlit by the moon's bright-white disc. She suddenly remembered what Courtmange had been whispering, that someone in town had fallen off a roof. She hung her head. This was all her fault. The ruined spell. Grace, who was Frank and Frank, who was...who? Maryanne stared at the zebra-like shadows the trees cast in the moonlight. Zebra: a horse that isn't a horse; a thing that isn't itself. that isn't itself. But she was Circe's Daughter, wasn't she? The white cowl that might have hidden her tears lay in the trunk of someone's car along with the robe that let her feel the majesty of the Goddess.

Walter Hooper's headlights picked out Maryanne's solitary figure kneeling in the middle of a clearing. When she turned toward him, he quickly turned them off so as not to blind the poor thing, got out of his Lincoln and walked over to her. "You're gonna catch your death out here, Dunner," he said.

Maryanne didn't respond.

"C'mon old girl. Let's get you back home or you're going to be as frozen as Reedy Pond in February."

"Wh-wh-o? Walter, what are *you* doing here?" she demanded, resisting his help, though she was so cold that she could barely get her words out, shivering so violently, she could hardly stand.

"Bill said there was some kind of rehearsal for a winter carnival you guys were planning," he said. "Guess I missed it, huh? C'mon. My car's all warmed up."

She let him take her arm. "I'm not a loon. I'm not a loon, Walter," she said.

"I know...I know."

He'd send someone to get her car in the morning. Nutcase or no, he'd known the old girl a long time. And anyway, he owed her. He gave her his jacket to fend off the cold New Hampshire wind that seemed to blow stronger with each step.

Braids

Guy Capecelatro III

The rain is slow on the rusted, metal roof. Amanda counts drops in her head, wonders when her mom will be home, worries then loses count. There's whistling in the song on the radio and she remembers the truck that passed her on the way from school and even now, a week later, it brings the blood to her face.

On her back, on her bed, Amanda lifts a slender leg in the air and considers it as though it were something new. As though it were some stick she'd found on the road. It feels smooth to the touch, longer than she imagined. Her hand stops at the scar on her knee and she remembers skateboarding down Verden Hill when she was younger and how she didn't even cry.

Before she left this morning her mother told her she should give up the braids, to wear her hair like a woman. And now it's the time of night when her mother will either come home or she won't see her for a week or so. Amanda thinks she hears something but can't be sure. She's not sure of anything.

Dreaming About Victor Frankenstein

William Chanler

Many years after Victor Frankenstein's tragic death in the Arctic, his eight foot tall repentant creation dreamed about awaking for the first time in a laboratory in Ingolstadt Germany and being nurtured by a more receptive and caring Victor.

My yellow eyes flutter open. Like all newborns I do not speak or understand any languages. I sit up and look around a dim laboratory. Then I stand. I take a stiff step, then another, trying not to fall.

I wander through the dark, shadowy laboratory feeling scared and alone until entering a small chamber. A man sleeps on a small bed.

I am not alone! Do I know this man? Somehow, he looks familiar.

I take a few halting strides closer, then stop to look down at the man. Watching his chest gently rise and fall with each breath fascinates me. I don't notice that his eyes are staring at me.

Victor is horrified by the apparition towering over him. *Please let this just be a nightmare. God help me! No, He has forsaken me to allow this monstrous being to come alive. See how he looks at me. There is something childlike and naive that almost draws me to him. I must overcome my revulsion. He must never know that he looks like an unholy fiend from hell.*

Victor Frankenstein shivers.

Their eyes meet and lock.

I mustn't look away as the first impression would be indelibly imprinted forever. It could make a difference on what he does and how he sees the world and himself. Look, he seems to be smiling down at me. It's rather hideous, but it's a smile.

"Hello," Victor mutters. His mouth feels parched.

I don't know what to make of the sounds from the man. He points to himself, saying "Victor."

I try to say the word, but can only manage "Iter."

My pathetic attempt makes him smile. He seems deep in thought. Then he speaks again, pointing at me. "Sohn," he says slowly and clearly. "It is German for son. Sohn.

"Sohn," I say.

"Very good, Sohn." Placing a finger on his chest, he says "I am Victor. Victor."

I say "Victor."

Victor smiles. He sits up slowly. I take a small step back as Victor rises to his feet. We take the measure of the other. I am surprised how short he is. The top of his head barely reaches my heart. I learn later he is 5'9", an above average height for the 1790s.

Victor rarely leaves the facility during the next several weeks. He spends many hours a day teaching me German. Victor seems astonished by the rapid speed that I pick up words. I am content to have his full attention and especially happy that he is so pleased with me. Then, after observing me thumb through an anatomy book, he teaches me to read and write.

One day, when he's gone out on errands, I discover a hand written journal sitting on a table by his bed. The script is difficult to understand as I am not yet a proficient reader and the handwriting isn't neat. It is Victor's diary. A large part of the book is about me. I learn Victor is a 22 year old scientist. He brought me to life. He wants to introduce me to the scientific community at the university after my language skills are more advanced. He wants to travel with me to Europe's finest universities and give lectures. He says he will be admired for making me. It is the greatest accomplishment ever.

Then I read something bad. Victor says he is concerned about how I look. Do I look like a demon? He wonders if the world can tolerate somebody with gigantic height, yellow eyes, black lips, and almost transparent skin. Is that how I look? I have no way of knowing how I look. I close the book, too upset to read anymore. Why would Victor, who is so kind to me, write something so upsetting? I want to ask him, but a voice inside me tells me not to.

I enjoy looking at the view of the world through an open window. People of all ages scurry about purposely on the street. Where do they go? I want to go outside and follow them around. But Victor says not yet. Later? My mind is preoccupied when I hear a scream below on the street. I look down and see a frightened crowd, peering anxiously up at me. It confirms what Victor wrote. I close the window and cover my face. Am I so terrible to look at?

The incident prompts a visit from a constable. For some reason Victor explains I am a cousin visiting from Geneva. The policeman asks me how long I'm staying in Ingolstadt. Victor quickly replies, saying only a few more days. That's news to me. Our visitor seems relieved.

The next two days pass quickly as Victor prepares for the trip home to the Frankenstein home in Geneva. He hasn't seen his family in two years. I learn about his father Alphonse, brothers William and Ernst and his cousin Elizabeth. Victor's mother died from scarlet fever some time ago. Victor doesn't know when he'll return to the laboratory. I don't know if I'll ever see my birthplace again.

I watch Victor rummaging through a closet. A two by four foot object covered by an old blanket leans against a wall.

"What is that, Father?"

Victor frowns. "It's nothing that concerns you."

"I want to see what it is."

"You may not like it, Sohn."

"Please."

Victor reluctantly carries it out of the closet, sets it down and removes the blanket. He sighs for good reason. I wail at the repulsive reflection staring back at me in the mirror. Victor looks away.

"Why?" I moan. "Why do I look like this, Father?"

"I'm sorry."

"You're sorry!" I reply angrily.

113

"Sohn, please listen to me for a moment," he says, raising a hand before I can interrupt him. "You are a magnificent specimen of a man. Nobody has your height, strength and brilliant mind and you have all three features. It's true you are not handsome by any means but you have everything else, don't you think?"

"I don't know, Father. Tell me why you gave me this face."

"I didn't give it any real consideration. It's what's inside the head that matters the most."

"No small wonder people hate my face so. It will be my downfall, won't it?"

"That is not true, Sohn. You shouldn't be overly concerned about your face or how others react to it. There will be people who are attracted to your intelligent intellect. I am not a romantic by nature but I think David Hume wrote 'Beauty in things exists merely in the mind which contemplates them.'"

"Is that supposed to make me feel better?"

A private coach takes us away the next evening. I'm too tall to fit inside with Victor. I sit up top next to Otto. He avoids looking at me. I'm both sad and excited about leaving my first home but look forward to this adventure.

I ask Otto a million questions about the team of horses and everything we see on the trip. I want to take a turn driving. Otto says maybe tomorrow.

In the morning I see distant snowcapped mountains and tell Otto they're breathtaking.

"What, you've never seen them mountains? Where you been, Sohn, if you don't mind my asking?"

"I can't remember much of anything."

"Maybe you lost your memory?"

"Maybe, I don't remember."

Otto looks at me doubtingly. "Perhaps you banged your head hard. Makes you forget stuff."

I don't pursue the subject anymore. *I'll ask Father what he knows about losing a memory though I know it has nothing to do with me. What a beautiful world!*

114

The coach passes hundreds of people on the road, Everybody casts unfriendly and terrified looks at me. Some cross themselves to ward off evil spirits. I want to hide somewhere safe.

Otto glances at me. "Forget about those peasants. They don't know no better."

"Thanks." I can't believe Otto tried to comfort me. He is a real friend.

We arrive at the Frankenstein villa on the outskirts of Geneva. The city is situated on the shore of Lake Geneva. Both the Alps and Jura Mountains tower majestically in the distance. There are ice caves up there.

I stand nervously as Victor is welcomed home by his father, brothers and Cousin Elizabeth. Victor introduces me as his "philosophical friend."

The library is my favorite room in the stately house. The tall walls of the spacious room are arrayed with thousands of leather bound books. Time flies by as I spend most of my time pouring through them. Victor sees no harm in the reading of Shakespeare, Homer, Swift, Ovid and Dante. I learn much about the ways of the world and man's imperfections. I begin to believe there are some people who are more monstrous than me.

One day Victor and Elizabeth enter the library together. Victor watches me remove a book from an upper shelf.

"You've finished *Gulliver's Travels* already?"

"Yes, Victor. It was quite illuminating."

"It is fiction, you know," Elizabeth comments.

"I know that. But there is much in the book that gives me a perspective on how people react to somebody much larger or smaller than themselves. I was quite disturbing while reading the book and thinking about people's reactions to me."

"That is rather severe, Sohn. What book have you selected next?" Victor asked.

"*Paradise Lost.*"

"Ah, Milton. I don't know if that is a wise selection."

"Why not?"

"Milton is more depressing than Defoe. Why not pick something lighter like Chaucer?"

I glance at the book in his hands and then study Victor's face. *What's in this book that he doesn't want me to read? What's he afraid of?* I put the book down on a nearby table and scan the bookcase for another book.

"What about Aeschylus? Should that be avoided, also?"

"He might like reading about Prometheus," Elizabeth suggests.

"Read what you want, Sohn," Victor says wearily. "Please let me know if you have any questions about the contents. There is a lot of thought provoking material in these books that deserves discussion. That is why the books are here."

"I shall try to read them with an open mind and engage you in a lively discussion."

"I look forward to that," Victor replies without enthusiasm. "Some of these beautiful volumes are studied in schools of high learning and can only be appreciated by advanced students. So feel free to write down anything you either don't understand or disagree with."

I glance at Elizabeth. "I need to speak with you privately," I whisper to Victor.

Elizabeth curtsies, turns, and leaves the library. Victor steps closer to me and waits expectantly for me to speak.

"Victor, you are a great man to have created life. I need you to do something that should be relatively easy for you."

Victor's eyebrows arch perceptively. "What is it you want me to do?"

"I need you to alter my face so people don't tremble and turn away. I have seen more than a few give me the sign of the devil. I cannot tolerate much more without doing something we'll both regret."

"What would you do?"

"I've recently discovered the seed of a temper flickers within me. I need to control it."

Victor looks deeply into my eyes. "Do you want to tell me

116

what happened to trigger it?"

"No, father. Altering my face will resolve the issue."

"Sohn, I wish I could make your face look better. I can't help you with that. I am very sorry."

"You can't or won't."

I feel my anger flare. I try to think happy thoughts but cannot as my need to have a more amenable face is paramount. "Then I'll see a surgeon who will!"

"Sohn, please."

"Please? What does that mean exactly?"

"Perhaps you could wear a hood."

I'm too shocked by Victor's comment to reply. At that moment Elizabeth, who may have been eavesdropping, reappears.

"I may have a solution," she says.

She has my full attention. I watch and listen to Elizabeth approach. Her clothing rustles as she moves closer. I am unnerved by her perfume. It muddles my brain.

"Perhaps a bit of makeup could be applied," she says lightly, standing a few feet away.

"Makeup? What do you mean?"

"You really don't know?" she asks.

"Elizabeth, just tell Sohn what you can do for him."

Elizabeth nods. "There are powders that can change your complexion. It would add more color to your cheeks. There are creams, too that would further improve your face. You would need to apply them once a day."

I stare at her blankly, unable to know how to reply as I can't comprehend this makeup thing.

"All right. Thank you, Elizabeth," Victor says.

Elizabeth smiles at me. "When would you like the first treatment?"

I avert my eyes away from her intense gaze. It helps me think.

"Now, please."

"Fine. Let's go upstairs to my bedroom."

"Your bedroom?" I can't imagine entering her private space. I look at Victor for guidance.

Victor laughs. He places a hand on my arm. "It's all right, Sohn. I trust you both."

A short time later, I find myself seated in front of a mirror in Elizabeth's bedroom. The door to the hall is wide open. I've never been alone with a woman. It's scary, especially because she's so pretty. She moves so gracefully. I forget to breathe. My face turns crimson.

Elizabeth laughs kindly. "It's all right. I won't harm you."

I close my eyes and tell myself to relax. It will be over soon. I think about the library. I can't wait to return to that favorite sanctuary. But a part of me treasures being so close to Elizabeth.

When Elizabeth clears her throat, my eyes dart open. I look at her adoringly.

"Look at the mirror," she commands.

I do. And see a face that isn't too unpleasant to behold. My checks have a little brown and pinkish flesh tone. I grin at myself. Then the mood is shattered.

Six year old William Frankenstein stands several feet away. He snickers.

"You look so pretty now," William taunts.

I look down. I feel my skin burn hot.

"That's enough, William," Elizabeth says. "It is rude to sneak around and talk like that. Say you're sorry to Sohn."

"I will not." The boy laughs and runs out of the bedroom.

"He's only a boy. It's to be expected I guess," she tells me.

I look at her and nod, but I cannot dismiss William's behavior. I hate being ridiculed. It's intolerable. I'm angry the little brat ruined a sweet happy moment.

Elizabeth looks nervously at me. She must know how I feel. But I can't help it. She shivers.

"Are you all right?" I ask, trying to keep my anger at bay.

"Yes", she replies, crossing her arms over her breasts. "I'm just a little cold."

"Can I get you a blanket?"

"No thank you, Sohn. I bet Victor is looking forward to seeing what I've done for you. Why don't you go downstairs and find out?"

I look at her a moment, not understanding that she really is only trying to get me to leave the room as soon as possible.

"Very well. Thank you for the improvements. I hope Victor doesn't copy his little brother and find my face amusing. That would cause a rift in our relationship."

"Sohn, Victor's not like that."

"I will find out soon enough."

I rise from the chair and silently leave. Elizabeth silently follows me to the door and closes it. She leans against it as though her slight weight will prevent me from opening the door. I've somehow managed to make her want me out of the house.

Sohn's dream about a better beginning of his life continued. He desperately wanted the dream to have a happy ending. But he couldn't control the direction him mind took. He tossed and turned as the dream edged closer to a nightmare.

"Look Victor, look what Elizabeth did," William exclaims as I walk toward them in the library.

Victor sees something in my grim expression he doesn't like. "That's enough William. Go and play outside. Maybe Ernst is around."

William grins as he runs past me and out of the room. For a second or two I am sorely tempted to grab the boy and slam him against a wall.

"I'm sorry about William. Is it because of him or Elizabeth you're out of sorts?"

"He taunted me."

"Children are like that, Sohn. You shouldn't let them upset you. Otherwise they'll consider it a game and play it over and over. You don't want that. I sure don't," Victor said pointedly. "Do you understand me, my friend?"

"No I don't."

"Anyway, I think Elizabeth did a fine job on your face."

"Do you?"

"Absolutely!" He extends his right arm as far as possible and pats my shoulder.

I dismiss William from my mind. *He's only a child. I'll*

119

remember to tell him that the next time he treats me with disrespect.

I place *Paradise Lost* on the bookshelf. *Perhaps father was right. I shouldn't have read that book.*

I'm disturbed by Adam's fall from grace and his being tempted by Satan. In the book, Adam told Eve that as she was made from his flesh she would die if he died. I wonder if I would die if *Victor* died.

I should not think about something so terrible. Why does my mind do that? Am I cursed by Satan or loved by God? Which?

I lie on my bed on the floor. It is actually a carpet with window drapes over it to serve as a heavy sheet. There is no bed large enough to accommodate my humungous frame.

I thought about the lustful relationship of Adam and Eve and their evolving relationship with each other.

Adam was a lucky man to have such a woman beside him during perilous times. Who is my Eve? Will I have one? Will she be born out of my limbs like Eve was from Adam? I must ask Victor about finding a woman for me. After all, he did urge me to discuss the book with him.

The next morning I join the Frankensteins at breakfast in the formal dining room. I am famished. I sit in a reinforced armchair. The chair I used the other day cracked and crashed to the floor. It was very embarrassing.

"Do you care to go for a ride this morning?" Victor asks me.

I like horses but have never ridden on one. I hope I won't break its back. I catch William eying me. I scowl at him, before turning my eyes on Victor.

"That would be good, Victor."

Suddenly Justine, the house servant, appears beside me with a platter of food.

"Thank you, Justine," I murmur.

Justine curtsies as I help myself to a heaping serving of warm, freshly baked rolls with steaming bratwurst and fried potato. As I fill my mouth with the delicious food, I think about falling off a horse. *Why do I punish myself with such a disturbing thought?* The food no longer looks that appetizing. I push the full plate away and look across the table.

William, Ernest, Victor and their father Alphonse seem fascinated by me. I wish they'd stop looking at me. It's getting annoying. Perhaps they'll stop if I eat. So I pull the plate back and force feed myself. I've temporarily forgotten my table manners. Victor had taught me how and when to use a knife, fork and spoon but now I don't care. Using my hands as utensils gives me a perverse pleasure.

Alphonse pretends not to notice when William and Ernest copy my rude behavior. They giggle. Then Alphonse clears his throat and glares at them. The boys promptly clean their hands with a linen cloth and obediently start using their utensils. I revert to doing so, too.

"How's the book?"

Spittle sprays from my full mouth as I reply, "I finished it last night."

"You did?" Victor asked, seemingly astonished.

I stop chewing and sourly regard him. Does he doubt me?

"You are turning into quite the prolific reader."

"Which book?" Alphonse inquires, looking at Sohn and Victor with interest.

"*Paradise Lost*," I reply.

"That's a serious undertaking. What are your thoughts about the book, Sohn?" Alphonse asks me.

I scan the faces around the table. I have everybody's undivided attention. Then Elizabeth strides gracefully into the room. Alphonse stands politely, nodding at his sons. They stand, too. Elizabeth sits to Victor's right, and the Frankensteins sit down again.

"You don't need to stand every time I enter," she tells her adopted father.

"It's proper manners, Elizabeth. Please don't discourage it." He calls out, "Justine!"

The young servant peeks her head from the adjoining kitchen, sees that Elizabeth has arrived, and brings out a light breakfast with steeped tea a few minutes later.

Alphonse turns again to me. "Please tell us about *Paradise Lost*, if you would. I'm curious to hear your thoughts."

I'm wondering if Elizabeth is Victor's Eve while I'm

supposed to be providing my thoughts about the book. As I open my mouth to speak, William stands and addresses his father.

"May I be excused, father?"

Alphonse gives his consent. William fast walks from the room.

As soon as the ill-behaved child is gone, I finally begin. "The book illuminates the struggle between God and Son of God vs Satan. Both forces sought to control the destinies of Adam and Eve."

"Who was the right choice?"

"I haven't made up my mind about that."

Elizabeth covers her mouth, shocked how anybody could be undecided on choosing between Heaven and Hell. She glances at Victor.

He has a hand pressed against his forehead.

"Are you an atheist or an agnostic?" Alphonse asked.

My vocabulary is about five thousand words at that time. I somehow know that eventually I'll master more than twenty thousand words in three languages. I rack my memory for the meanings of "atheist" and "agnostic" but cannot define either of them. I look at Alphonse and shrug.

"I do not know the answer, Herr Frankenstein. I am not a religious man in any shape or form, though some think I am Satanic." I pause for a reaction from the master of the house.

"Is that true? You believe in Satan?"

"No I do not. But ignorant people have given me the evil sign from afar. They assume because I look like a fiend I am one. Looks can be deceiving." I glance at Victor, then look down at the table.

Alphonse looks closely at Victor. Victor avoids his scrutinizing gaze.

"I could identify, at least fleetingly, with each of the major characters in the book, even Eve."

Ernest snickers. His father, though surprised, too, reprimands his teenage son.

"How so?" Elizabeth asks bemusedly.

"Well, she, like myself was created." I hesitate to continue, not wanting to divulge my origins. I desperately want to gauge Victor's reaction. I barely have enough willpower not to look his way. I can hear his heart racing, a telltale sign he is concerned what I will say. .

"Aren't we all created?" Elizabeth asks.

I nod, wanting to change the subject away from this sensitive issue. "I relate to Eve's thirst for knowledge. I understand why she went off by herself, why she left Adam until she was ready to be with him as an equal."

Victor stares at me in disbelief. "Are you planning to emulate Eve? Go off by yourself?" Victor asks in a slightly shaking voice.

"Victor, the books have made me want to experience life to the fullest. I have much to see. There will be great libraries throughout Europe to explore. Perhaps concerts? I want to see Ludwig van Beethoven."

"I see."

"What? You disagree with me?"

"Yes I do. Think how people have treated you on the road here. The great cities are densely populated with thousands of people with similar attitudes as those who have already reacted to you so poorly."

"So I must stay here in this house like a hermit until I die? Is that it?"

"I don't know. I'll have to give it much thought."

I shake my head despondently. Does Victor only see disappointment and unhappiness in my future? He believes he is responsible for my welfare. I'll be ready soon to go out on my own whether he wants me to or not. If I'm mistreated, then I'll act accordingly.

"We have been through much together these past months. I understand why you wish to travel. I was like that when I was young."

"When you were young?" his father says. "Victor, you are still a young man."

Victor shakes his head. "Time is slipping away."

Alphonse looks at me pensively. "Listen, Sohn, I have a suggestion for you." He pauses until all eyes are focused on the Magistrate. "You should consider an extended visit at a monastery. Some monasteries are known for producing scholars and even print books."

Victor nods wholeheartedly. "The clerics don't care what one looks like."

"Really, Father?" I ask Victor without thinking.

"Why do you call Victor 'father'"? Alphonse asks sharply. "He is much younger than you."

"Sohn's just practicing for when he's in a monastery. Right, Sohn?"

Frankenstein regards Victor and me suspiciously.

Victor taught me that speaking the truth is important. Getting caught in a lie can get one in serious trouble. Why does he now want me to fib? Does he want his judgmental father to have a lower opinion of me than he does already?

"I'm sorry if I offended you," I tell Alphonse. "Tell me, could a godless man be welcomed in a house of God?"

"You don't believe in God?" he exclaims harshly.

"Oh no!" I hear Victor whisper.

I forge on with my self-incrimination. "I'm searching for answers. I must hear what the holy men have to say before I can know what I believe in."

"Then you must leave at once," Alphonse stands. "I mean it."

"Father, what's the urgency?" Victor asks wide-eyed, rising to his feet.

"I do not want a heathen in my home, especially around my children."

"You've put up with my beliefs," Victor cries.

"You ought to have exercised better judgment, Victor, than bring this man here. Be gone by the end of the day," Frankenstein orders me. "You may return here only if you can provide written proof of being a Christian. A baptism certificate will do." He bows and storms out of the dining room.

I can't believe my misfortune as I stare at the empty space Frankenstein just passed through. I can't move. I feel a pressure in my head and can't think what to do next.

Goodbye, Victor. Goodbye, cruel world. Then I black out.

Sohn awakened then from his dream. Being spurned by Victor in his past and Victor's father in the dream weighed heavily on him. He forced his giant's body into a sitting position. As depression consumed him, he collapsed on the bed again.

Concerto

Will Conway

Even from a distance I could tell he was an emotional wreck—again. Sitting alone in the dappled sunlight beneath the small palm tree, away from the pool with all its noisy confusion. The usual jeans, sandals and black t-shirt. His tall frame filling one of the lawn chairs, eyes closed, earbuds in, dark hair falling over his forehead as he slowly swayed back and forth.

Joe's apartment is next to mine but I hadn't seen him for a while, maybe a few weeks. He often withdrew when he got back from one of his cases, getting some internal R & R before rejoining the world. I knew his routine so I left him alone. He'd tell me whatever he wanted me to know when he was ready.

In the meantime, I dove in and started swimming laps. Only a few tenants ever ventured out to the pool but we were there that afternoon. Most were single adults like me but a few had little kids. All of us cooling off from the hot day. Trying to regroup before tackling dinner.

Since it was a Friday everyone wanted to shed the tedium of the work week. I was no different. Being a nurse in the ER is not for the faint of heart. Between the hopelessly tangled healthcare system and the endless trauma, it wears me out. And that's not even counting the screwballs who show up.

That afternoon, as I glided through the cool water and found a good pace for my breathing, all those frustrations began to slip away and my mind drifted back to Joe sitting in the chair listening to his music. I wondered what kind of music it was this time. Sometimes it was a good blues song, other times reggae or an operatic aria. Joe had wide-ranging musical tastes. Everyone needs a way to cope. Swimming laps was mine, music was his.

I knew he had studied music in college or a conservatory somewhere but never did much with it—at least professionally. Instead, he was a cop for a few years then became a kind of off-the-books private investigator. He said he spent his time fighting the bad notes in life's music. Getting rid of what doesn't fit.

He was fifteen years older than I was. At six feet tall with jet black hair and icy blue eyes he was a nice looking guy but out of my age range. I thought of him more as an older brother or maybe even a father figure. We'd get together for a beer or two every so often. He'd politely listen if I talked about work but perk up when I got to my pathetic love life, freely dispensing relationship advice—this from a confirmed bachelor.

Ten laps done. As I turned at the end I looked over and saw him still listening to his music. That head swaying back and forth. I pushed off and started the final ten. My plan for the night was to get Mexican takeout and then settle in with my date for the evening: Señor Netflix.

Yes, in case you're wondering, it is depressing. I meet very few eligible men in my work. Oh, there's the occasional unattached doctor. Some are good guys but others just want to see which nurses they can bang. I wouldn't marry one for all the money in China which is how much some of them make.

The main problem is I'm not sure who I'm looking for. "A regular guy" sounds vague not to mention dull, but I think that says it. One who doesn't have a God-complex or a chip on his shoulder. Someone who's not a mama's boy or stuck in adolescence. Just a Steady-Eddie. Do they even make that model anymore? Maybe Detroit stopped making them along with Pontiacs a few years ago.

When I finally finished my laps and pulled myself out of the pool, Joe had the earbuds out and was sitting with his head down, eyes closed. I walked over to him as I toweled off. There was an empty chair not far away. I dragged it over and sat next to him. Waiting.

After a few minutes I said, "How ya doin'?"

He let out a breath. "Couldn't be better." His voice was funny, I think he'd been crying. He hadn't shaved in a couple days and looked awful. He held up a finger for me to wait and headed back to his apartment. It was close to six o'clock, the pool crowd was thinning out. Joe and I would pretty much have the place to ourselves which was what he wanted.

When he came back with two Smithwick's I knew he wanted to talk. I gave him some space and we quietly sipped our beers, looking at the last of the sunlight dancing on the empty pool. It would cool off in a while but it was still hot enough for a nice cold one.

Finally he said, "Did you know that Beethoven wrote his fifth piano concerto between 1809-1811? He lived sixteen more years but it was the last one he ever wrote. "

"Didn't know that," I said. If he'd asked me about compound fractures or collapsed lungs I would have sounded more intelligent.

He went on, "You know what the second movement is called?"

"I have no idea."

"*Adagio un poco mosso.*" He set his bottle down on the grass.

"What's that mean?" It sounded like an Italian entree.

That's when his red, glassy eyes met mine for the first time. "It's slow," he said, "very slow. And moving. Those two things together and Beethoven never wrote it better than in the second movement of that concerto.

"That's what I've been listening to this afternoon. Just that second movement over and over. It's not long, maybe what, seven or eight minutes? But there's not a note that doesn't hit you in the heart."

"Sounds nice." A lame comment, I know, but I knew zip about Beethoven. My musical tastes stop with Bruce Springsteen. I took another swallow of beer and braced myself to hear what the music was all about.

Joe took a swallow, too, then said, "You remember what it was like to be eight years old?"

"Yeah, I remember." It wasn't all roses but it was a good time of life. Certainly better than the years that followed.

"Well," he said, "her name was Emma and she was only eight years old."

I wanted to walk away right then. Get my takeout and collapse in front of a movie.

Joe paused as a screaming siren passed by then continued. "Her parents said she was right on the edge, just beginning to become aware of the wider world. You know, childhood rapidly receding in the rear view mirror, a whole new world opening up before you. You remember those days?"

"A time when the world still had magic," I said.

"Exactly. All of life's hurt and pain are off to the side somewhere—plenty of time for them later—and you're allowed to live in the wonder for a while longer."

He took another couple swallows of beer. I didn't know how much he was going to say. "You couldn't tell what she looked like—not by the time we found her—but her heartbroken parents showed me a picture. This halo of frizzy hair and a wide smile. Her eyes looked so goddamn *happy*. Once you get to be an adult, 'happy' is never the same, you know what I mean?"

Did I ever.

"So I'm looking at this picture and think to myself if there was ever an innocent soul on earth, here she is. Her parents said she collected rocks and liked to draw butterflies. The walls of her bedroom were covered with them."

She sounded like a beautiful child. I hoped Joe wouldn't describe what she looked like at the end.

Instead, he switched subjects. "I've forgotten everything I ever learned about music—except how eloquent it is. A lot of people can explain it better than me but that second movement is perfection. Very forceful first and third movements. Very Beethoven, if you know what I mean. Brawny and muscular."

I was all for brawny and muscular, I just hadn't connected them with Beethoven.

"But there in the middle is this beautiful interlude. There's a pause before it begins. The first movement draws to its bombastic end and then this silence. Get ready, it seems to say, careful now, here comes something special. Then this gorgeous, slow movement begins. The lush strings gently invite you in, and keep inviting. They go on and on for a minute or more until, finally, the delicate single notes of the piano.

"Did I mention it was a short movement?"

"I think so."

"Only, what, seven or eight minutes long. Let's say it's eight. Like Emma. Beethoven had tapped into something, something we can't see but it's out there, far away in the stars. His genius was that he found a way to touch the hem of it and bring a single thread down to us, here on this miserable earth where we love to hurt and kill each other. What he brings down, at least in that movement, is a miracle of beauty and goodness. It's otherworldly. We can't see it, or touch it or taste it, but thanks to him we can hear it."

He was inching up to it, slowly, with all that music talk. I knew it was about to come out.

"He kidnapped her. Right out of the front yard and for three days he did things to her that no human being should ever do to another. Then he killed her. That's all I'm going to tell you."

I closed my eyes. That was enough. "What happened... to him?"

He paused. "The police had a few leads and followed them in one direction. I went in another."

"And you found him."

"Oh, yes."

"And... now he won't hurt anyone else?"

"No. Not another soul."

I knew what he meant. That was as much as I was going to hear. We sat for a while longer as the sun gave up on the day and lights came on in the apartments around us. I asked him if he wanted to join me for takeout but he said he'd rather stay outside. I left him to his music.

After what I'd heard, the Mexican food had no flavor and

the movies seemed stupid and irrelevant. Instead, I paced the floor replaying the conversation in my mind. From my second floor window I looked down and could see Joe still in his chair, bathed in the silver moonlight.

I remembered him mentioning that if he didn't have his music, if he had to face the things he'd seen without it, he would die. He said even with the music, sometimes it was a close call.

Both professionally and personally I was familiar with the signs. I have a cousin who did multiple tours in Afghanistan and is haunted to this day. He's been in and out of treatment for PTSD but nothing seems to work. I should tell him about Beethoven.

After a while I gave up on the food and movie and went outside to be with him. He'd pulled his chair out from under the tree so he could see the stars. I set a chair next to his. There were more empty beer bottles on the ground.

My plan was just to sit quietly and keep him company but he took out the earbuds and turned toward me. "You know," he said, "I've been thinking about The Big Lie."

"Which one?" I said.

"The one that says time heals all wounds."

"Oh, that one."

"Yeah, you hear it all the time but it's not true. Not a word of it."

He put the earbuds back and we sat together in the still night. All I could hear were mosquitos and freeway traffic but he was looking up, listening to the stars.

The Fate of Thomas Boucher

Karen Desrosiers

The air inside the library was warm and dry. It could have been the Sahara compared to the frigid New England air outside. Thomas Boucher closed his eyes, imagining the desert sun washing over him. The bitter chill of winter began to release its hold on his tired joints and weary muscles. The new year was starting out cold, even by New Hampshire standards. A freeze had moved in on January 3rd, and the temperature had not been above fifteen for several days. What made it worse was the wind chill—it felt a good ten or twelve degrees colder than it actually was—and the previous two nights and mornings had dipped below zero.

Thomas shuddered, opened his eyes, and slowly unzipped his parka. Looking around, he took a moment to orient himself, then he stepped farther into the library, approaching the circulation desk.

"Mr. Boucher," the red-headed librarian said. She was compact and thin, unassuming, with a pretty face, though her eyes often looked too tired for a young woman. "Staying warm enough?" She worried about him, and all the elder residents of town who sought comfort and companionship daily in the public library.

"Trying, dear. Trying." He nodded and smiled, as he always did, working to recall her name. Maeve, he was fairly sure. He had always liked her smile; it matched the atmosphere of the library. Pulling off his knit cap, he ran his hand over the sparse grey strands of hair that criss-crossed his head, self-conscious of his age and appearance.

"Mrs. Gilman has been waiting for you," Maeve said, lowering her voice, knowing that discretion was important to most of Mr. Boucher's generation. "She's in magazines."

A blush rose in Thomas' cheeks. He nodded again to Maeve, before crossing the main floor of the library. The far corner, formed by two tall walls of windows, pointed south. A sitting area, with several worn, utilitarian chairs and love seats arranged to provide space to read or talk quietly, was surrounded by shelves, proudly displaying the most recent editions of hundreds of magazines and newspapers. Despite the age of the furniture and public nature of the space, Thomas always found it inviting and comfortable, almost intimate. There was a nice view of a garden, with trees that flowered in the spring, and a view of the river that ran through the town.

Foy's Crossing had grown up around the river, mills, houses, and community buildings extending from the earth the way the regal pines had for centuries before. The river, originally named the Cohannet by the native tribes, had been renamed to the Foy River when the town was christened. Regardless of the name, the river, which snaked lazily through the town, reaching nearly every corner, had been the lifeforce of each community that established itself around its banks for hundreds of years. Like many life-long residents, Thomas drew a sense of strength and stability from the river.

Adeline Gilman was seated in one of the love seats, positioned to face the windows, but at the farthest spot away from the glass, looking through a copy of *Education Week*. Adeline had been a teacher in the local elementary schools for decades, and though she had been retired for fifteen years, she was compelled to read all the current literature on the subject.

Thomas cleared his throat gently as he stepped near, always conscious of not wanting to startle her, in case she hadn't heard him approach. He shrugged off his coat, laying it over a low table and placing his hat and gloves on top. He folded himself into a chair beside the love seat, taking a few minutes to arrange his long limbs, until he was somewhat comfortable. In spite of living seventy-five years with his tall, lanky body, he was still surprised at how awkward he felt with it, as though it had never really been his body.

Several of the other regular patrons took note of his arrival, but they too knew the importance of discretion and quickly returned to their own activities, reading, dozing, and working on a large puzzle with thousands of tiny pieces.

"Oh, Thomas, you're here." Adeline closed the magazine and smiled at him brightly, genuinely happy to see him, while both surprised and relieved that he was there. "Happy Monday." She thought he seemed startlingly older, of late, which she knew was absurdly obvious because they were both getting older at an astounding pace.

Thomas held his breath for a moment, a defense mechanism he had developed so long ago that he was no longer aware of it. The first time he had met Adeline, when he was barely twenty-three, he was so affected that he wondered if he had had a minor heart attack. She was Adeline Mallet then. The emerald cardigan she had been wearing and her rich, chestnut hair, worked together to make her green eyes shine like nothing he had ever seen before. He might have proposed to her right then and there, if she had not been seriously dating his best friend, Joe Gilman. Fifty years later, each having long, successful marriages and five kids between them, his physical reaction to her had hardly diminished.

"Good morning, Addie," Thomas said. "Anything new?" He nodded to the magazine in her hands.

"I'm constantly amazed at what they know now, what we didn't know." She put the magazine on the seat beside her, then lifted a long finger to tuck a stray grey hair behind her ear. "The kids who I'm sure would have had this attention deficit disorder they are always writing about, if we had known of it back then. To think, I probably could have had them all medicated." She laughed lightly, lost in her memories for a moment. "Would have saved myself a lot of grief," she added grinning.

He loved and admired that mischievous look. She had a streak of the devil in her, and he lived for the times when she let it show. "Patty said her little Ben has that, or something like it," Thomas said. He searched his brain trying to remember exactly what his daughter, his second child, had told him about her oldest son, but none of it made much sense. "DD something, I think she said, something with D's in it, or autism, maybe."

Addie looked truly crestfallen and sympathetic. "Oh, what a shame. What will they do with him?"

"I believe they're still trying to figure it out." Patty had said something about medication and therapy, he was fairly sure, but he wasn't clear enough about any of it to bring it up. Adeline was smart, and well read. He was always afraid of embarrassing himself in front of her. "What of you? How are you doing this week?"

She ran her hands down the tops of her legs, a move he had seen her do countless times before. The thick corduroy of the trousers she was wearing hummed softly in response. Looking up at him, she pushed the errant hair behind her ear again. "Well, let's see." Addie proceeded to recall the events of the previous week and weekend, relaying stories about her three children and seven grandchildren.

From time to time, Thomas interjected relevant anecdotes from his own children and grandchildren, though his stories were not very recent and he wondered if he had shared them previously, if he was repeating himself. When all of the family news had been covered, they moved on to issues and gossip from town, politics, and other news. As it was every Monday morning, as it had been for as long as they'd known each other, their conversation was effortless, natural.

Instinctively, Thomas knew when their time together was nearing an end. Addie turned her petite wrist, adjusting a string of bright ceramic beads, to read the time on her watch. It was one of the last gifts his wife, Shelley, had given to Addie before her passing, five years earlier. Shelley made jewelry, and had hand made the beads, each one stamped with an Asian character meant to bring good health and longevity.

Addie slid forward to the edge of the seat. She reached out her hand, placing it on top of Thomas' hand, tapping three of her fingers in quick succession. He couldn't help but feel she was trying to apologize every time their Monday morning tête-à-tête came to an end. "It's that time," she said, softly, feeling more regret than she would ever divulge. With some difficulty, she stood, gathering her hat, gloves, and bag from the loveseat. She paused, meeting his eyes directly, and they stood, facing each other, in silence for a moment.

"Until next week," Thomas said at last. He knew she was waiting for him to ask about Joe, but he never did. He was acutely aware that their conversations always ended when they did because she had to get home to make lunch for her husband, the man who was once his best friend.

Maeve watched as Mrs. Gilman made her way gracefully, delicately, through the library, to the elevator that led down to the handicapped parking. She felt heartbroken for Mr. Boucher, as Mrs. Gilman glanced back at him, her usual two times, before reaching the elevator. He never looked and probably did not know that Mrs. Gilman glanced back, but Maeve suspected that it would be harder on him if he did know.

After she had gone, Thomas sat, as he did each Monday, lingering in the air she had breathed, that had breathed her, for another half hour. He pulled the nearest magazine from the shelf just within reach, opening it randomly, not paying attention to what magazine it was or what the article was about. He knew that if he appeared engrossed in his reading he would more likely be left alone, but if he was sitting, apparently idle, there was a much greater chance someone would approach and want to strike up a conversation. After his mornings with Addie, he needed time before he could manage a discussion with anyone else.

He stared at the page without focusing, the print and images swirling together with a kaleidoscope effect. Letting his mind wander, he pulled up the faces painted in his mind. Shelley had been an amazing wife, and he had truly loved her, but more than that, they had been good friends. It had taken most of his savings to care for her when she became ill, but he had been determined to care for her in dying the way she had cared for him in living. He had always suspected that

137

she knew Addie was his first love, but she had never said anything, never questioned him. And he was grateful that Shelley had befriended and loved Addie as well. The same could not be said of Joe. The four of them had been friends for so long that their lives were woven tightly together. But, Joe had long struggled with Thomas' feelings for Addie. When Shelley passed, Joe could no longer overlook the friendship between Thomas and Addie. He insisted that it stop, though neither Thomas nor Addie would agree. In the end, he and Joe had a falling out, and had not spoken for nearly five years.

Thomas' stomach began to growl, confusing him momentarily. He looked around, noting different people scattered around the library. Standing slowly, his knees and hips creaking loud enough for him to hear, he put the magazine away and picked up his coat, hat, and gloves from the table. Walking to the entrance, he prepared himself to go back in the cold. He hesitated, taking another moment to enjoy the warmth of the library. It was going to be a long week before Monday came around again.

Thursday evening, the kitchen, like the rest of the house, felt unwieldy, cavernous. He could barely remember the times when it felt cozy, full of people, laughter, and chatter. Thomas turned a stove burner on to medium, taking a moment to warm his hands over the flames. He poured a can of split pea soup into a small pan, placing it over the burner, and turning the heat up to medium. Absentmindedly, he stirred the soup, probably standing too close to the stove, but feeling warm for the first time since Monday morning at the library. When the soup was hot, he poured it into one of Shelley's pottery bowls, leaving the burner on low for the warmth, then pulled the small kitchen table closer to the stove, before sitting down to eat.

When he was finished, Thomas pulled the table back to the center of the kitchen, turned off the stove, and washed his bowl. He pushed through the quilt hanging in front of the kitchen door, stepping into the hallway. Shuddering, he hugged his arms tightly across his chest, but stood there for a minute. Large quilts, in a collage of colors and patterns, were hanging over the doors and doorways and around the stairwell to the second floor, completely closing off the space. He was thankful for Shelley's obsession with making and collecting quilts. If he looked closely enough, he could pick out some of the fabrics, like ghosts of their life together: the sun dresses she wore the summer she was expecting their son; flashes of his daughter's dresses from different phases of her childhood; curtains from the sixties, when the kitchen was an unfortunate combination of avocado and mustard colors; remnants of his faded flannel shirts.

Thomas had hung the quilts several years earlier to try to control the cost of heating the large, old house, and he had never bothered to take them down during the summers. He had long since shut off the water to the second floor so that he wouldn't have to worry about pipes bursting, and had moved himself into the den on the first floor.

Pushing through another quilt on the opposite end of the entryway, he immediately checked the thermostat to his left. It was set to forty, as it always was, and he was relieved to see that the needle on the upper portion was reading about forty-two. There was a good chance the oil was going to run out before the end of the week, before his social security check was expected.

Thomas crossed the crowded room toward the fireplace, weaving around furniture, piles of books, and chairs heaped with clothing and blankets. He poked at the meager fire and added a couple scraps of kindling, then pulled the metal screen tightly in front of it, hoping the fire would stay hot and contained while he was out. Glancing at the basket full of unopened mail beside the sofa, he had the vague feeling that he should be taking care of something, but the thoughts wouldn't quite solidify.

It was still a little early, but Thomas walked the several blocks to the town offices, as he did most every Thursday evening, for one board meeting or another. This night it was the planning board. The town had a tendency to over-heat all of the municipal buildings, and he reasoned that if his taxes helped pay for the town's heating bill, then he could take advantage of it when he had the opportunity. He often wished he could somehow absorb and store up some of the heat when he was at a town meeting and bring it home with him.

In the center of town, the usual crowds of teenagers were huddled together smoking, drinking coffee, and laughing. Thomas remembered his own teenage years, spending weekend nights in nearly the same way, with such clarity that it might have been a couple years earlier rather than decades. Something was different with the teenagers of this generation, though. They seemed to be constantly on the edge of boiling over, ready for trouble, perhaps even aching for it. He looked through the crowd, thinking he might recognize some of his old friends in the young faces, the grandchildren of his old friends.

Several of the teens glanced at him, barely taking note of his presence, as if no one existed outside of their group. It might have surprised Thomas, as well as most of the teens themselves, to know that at least one of the teens had noticed the old man moving gingerly along the sidewalk, knew the man in fact, and was concerned for him.

With the cold seeping quickly through his clothing and reaching for his bones, Thomas hurried around the corner, as much as he was able, to the town hall. He made his way up the ramp, finding it easier on his stiff knees than the granite steps, though some might say it took longer, and at that temperature every minute made a difference. He stepped inside the old brick building, which dated back to before the Revolutionary War, and still had features reminiscent of the battle that ensued in town, including several holes from musket balls and narrow, slit windows on either side of the main door, added as a vantage from which the militia could fire at the Red Coats.

"Good evening, Thomas," Mike Bean said. A portly man with thick salt and pepper hair, Mike was a well-known figure in town, serving on the board of selectmen and almost every committee of the town at one time or another during his adult life. "First, as usual." His tone gave the impression that this was not necessarily a desirable trait.

"Second, really," Thomas said. He patted his thighs, wincing at the prickly feeling created by warm blood returning to cold extremities. "You're always here before me." Regrettably, he always felt he was in some form of competition with Mike Bean. He liked Mike well enough, but he didn't like the feeling of having to compete with anyone, in any way. He knew this was also at the heart of his falling out with Joe; he resented Mike for reminding him of this failing.

"I don't actually count," Mike said, smiling and arranging the room as though it were his own living room and not a conference room at the town hall.

"I suppose I don't really count either," Thomas said. "Let's say whoever is next will be first."

"Wager on who that will be?" Mike chuckled. He moved about the large meeting room, arranging seats, turning on lights, and picking up a few stray pieces of paper from the floor.

Thomas moved to the radiator, facing the middle of the room, with his hands clasped behind his back. The hot air circling his fingers was a welcome comfort after the cold walk over. He greeted everyone warmly as they entered the room, expertly skipping over names he couldn't quite recall, compensating with neutral comments about the weather.

Most of the teens had vanished by the time Thomas was making his way back home. A small group stood closely together beside the coffee shop, each holding steaming paper cups. This time, he recognized one as the girl who lived next door, nodding to her.

"Hey, Mr. Boucher," she said, her words slurred slightly, causing him to wonder what was really in the cups they were gripping. She worried about him walking around town at all times of day and night, in all weather.

141

It made him uneasy to think of those young girls out in the cold at that time of night. He nodded again, glad it wasn't one of his granddaughters, and kept walking. He heard the girl mumble to her friends, as he worked to recall her name.

"Hold up, Mr. Boucher," the girl called after him. Light footsteps approached behind him. "Can I walk with you?"

He nodded his consent, without slowing his steps. Ashley, he thought, or maybe it was Amanda. Escorting her home gave him a rare sense of being useful, wanted.

The temperature had dropped even more, and the cold was not only making his joints hurt but his skin as well. Moving as quickly as he dared, the girl walking silently at his elbow, he re-crossed the town he had known all of his life. It was funny, he thought, how he had reached a point where the town seemed to be all that he really did know. Most of the people who migrated in and out of the edges of his life were a blur. Though he spoke to his children each week, he wasn't sure when the last time was that he'd seen either of them; they were caught up in their own over-busy lives, in different parts of New Hampshire, which he understood and did not begrudge. Even his home had become more like a foreign land, reminding him of a maze of caves in Ireland that he had become lost in once, when he was a young man.

"Night, Mr. Boucher," the girl said, gently tapping his arm, as she peeled away from him and disappeared up the sidewalk to her house. "Have a good one."

With lights in each window, her house had a warm glow that was in stark contrast to the darkened, shadowy profile of his next door. Stepping in through his kitchen door, the room was cold, but still noticeably warmer than outside. As was his habit, he checked the thermostat on the kitchen wall, noting with relief that the temperature was still at forty degrees. He put the kettle on the stove, turning the burner on high, then warmed his hands over the stove, welcoming the pain, sharp and tingling, as the blood moved to the tips of his fingers again. When the kettle whistled, he put a tea bag in a large mug and filled it with boiling water. Reluctantly, he turned off the burner.

His body was quickly acclimating to the temperature of the house, and the air in the house no longer felt any different from the night outside. Cradling the mug, he made his way to the den, thankful that it should be a little warmer there, if the fire had held on while he was gone. His heart sank as he pushed through the heavy quilt hanging over the door to the den. The skimpy fire had not survived his absence after all, and the room was just as cold. He checked the thermostat, to reassure himself the heat was still working, and was relieved to see it was almost fifty in the room. The fire may not have been out long, and with any luck, there might be some embers still hot enough to catch the new fire quickly.

After placing his tea on top of a stack of books, he went to work quickly, building a new fire. As soon as it caught, he pulled his chair closer, covering himself with a blanket, and slowly sipped his tea. It was only Thursday night, he thought. It would still be a long wait for Monday morning to come again, he thought, feeling weary.

Addie arrived at the library early, as she usually did. Willing her stiff, arthritic fingers to work, she peeled off the layers demanded by the New Hampshire winter. Despite the cold, the sun was bright and strong, and she hoped it would herald the end of the long arctic spell they had been suffering through. After arranging her outerwear on the usual love seat, she smoothed her hair, then straightened her shirt.

She took a few minutes to look over the shelves of magazines, trying to decide what she wanted to read. New issues of the education magazines had apparently not come in yet. Flipping through several cooking and home magazines, she finally settled on one that featured home and gardening. The prospect of spring, though it was still several months away, made her happy.

Half focused on the magazine, Addie thought about Joe. Years ago, when Shelley had passed and Thomas had started meeting her at the library, Joe had been upset. Now he didn't seem to care anymore, didn't even acknowledge it. She wondered when that change had occurred, and wondered how she hadn't noticed sooner. Not that he'd ever had anything to worry about. She and Thomas were just friends, had only ever been friends. She wasn't naïve, or in denial. She knew there had been feelings there, between them, early on and then from time to time over the years, but it was nothing either of them would have ever acted upon. Perhaps Joe had finally come to understand that as well.

A recent conversation with her daughter flowed back through her mind, over whether a person could have more than one true love. Addie had insisted it wasn't possible, but this was because she desperately wanted her daughter to hold onto the husband she had, the life she'd created, and not throw it all away over something fleeting. But, in reality, Addie knew all too well that the heart could have more than one true love, even though the body could not, or should not, acknowledge it.

She finished flipping through the magazine, reading each article, and closed it on her lap. Addie looked at the magazine, feeling confused. She had never actually finished reading a magazine on one of their Monday mornings. Gently, she turned the beaded bracelet on her wrist to view the watch face. It was after ten, and Thomas was more than a half hour late. She couldn't remember a single Monday when he had been late before. A long held fear about Thomas living alone in that huge house pushed at the edges of her mind.

"He's only a little late," she mumbled to herself. "Too soon to worry." The cold could be wearing on him, and perhaps he was just moving slowly. She stared at the watch face, burning the time into her mind—ten after ten. She considered finding another magazine and stood up. She looked out the wall of windows and watched a slab of ice bob down Foy River. When it was out of sight, she sat back down and ran the palms of her hands down her thighs.

Addie looked at the watch again, noticing that her hand was beginning to shake. She looked around the library, noting the familiar faces, desperate to find Thomas amongst the regulars. Turning toward the direction of the circulation desk, she saw Maeve watching her with an expression of concern that most likely mirrored her own. The librarian had also noticed that Thomas had not yet appeared and was equally concerned. Addie looked at her watch again — nearly ten twenty-five — then she got up and crossed the library, moving faster than she had in years.

"I'm worried," she said as she approached Maeve.

"Shall we try to call him?" Maeve asked, relieved that Addie had approached her, since she wasn't sure how much longer she could calmly wait. When Addie nodded, Maeve pulled up Thomas Boucher's account to locate his phone number. She handed the receiver to Addie and dialed the number.

Addie listened impatiently as the phone rang twice. The color drained from her face as she heard a recorded message. Handing the phone back to Maeve, she said, "The number has been disconnected." Her voice was weaker than she'd expected, unfamiliar.

Addie looked at Maeve, unsure what to do next. She wondered if she should go to his home, but that seemed to be crossing a line. She considered going home to tell Joe, so that he could check on Thomas, but would he care at this point? When it came right down to it, what right did she even have to worry? She had diligently maintained a wall of friendship, while studiously denying any strong connection between them for so long that she did not feel she had any right to claim even her own heart's deepest secrets.

Three blocks east, in one of the town's oldest private homes, hidden behind walls and doorways draped with quilts, Thomas Boucher sat in his chair, in front of his fire place, which had gone cold days earlier. A large mug, with an inch of frozen tea in the bottom, was clasped between his solid hands. His pale skin had taken on a blue-grey hue, with icy white patches. If it could, his heart would have broken, realizing he would not make it to his usual Monday morning appointment with Addie, causing her to worry.

The Last Painting

Lester Dubow

John Kirpatrick moved ever so slowly through the studio of Max Glazer. A rather large outbuilding had been renovated some forty years ago into the artist's refuge, adding several skylights to the timbered ceiling so that shafts of warm northern sunlight were captured. The curator paused continuously, studying the numerous paintings some hanging and some propped against the walls.

Anna Glazer, widow of the renowned artist, sat in her husband's favorite overstuffed armchair, crossed legs tucked under her, following with curiosity the movements of her visitor. How many times, Anna thought, she had sat like this, watching Max with a single brush stroke bring life to a one dimensional surface.

"Mrs. Glazer..."

She interrupted, "Call me Anna, and I shall call you John, if you don't mind."

"No...of course not." The personal touch did not come easily to Kirpatrick. "Anna..." he started hesitantly, "I am absolutely overwhelmed by your generosity donating all these paintings to the museum..."

Anna interrupted again, "Only the ones with the red dots on the frames," she corrected.

"Of course," he acknowledged. "I am also overwhelmed by the sheer beauty of the paintings," he added with conviction. "I hadn't seen many of his landscapes before."

"Most of his paintings are on the walls of private collectors. I want the public to be able to enjoy and appreciate his talent."

"I'm sure they will," he said as he completed circling the studio.

147

"Do you have a favorite?" She asked.

My God...difficult...difficult indeed." Kirpatrick turned slowly in all four directions, his hand stroking his chin several times. He paused, *Sycamores in Late Afternoon*...Yes, definitely *Sycamores in Late Afternoon*. The comingling of the colors and shapes are just breathtaking."

Anna smiled, "One of my favorites, too."

"Your husband received critical acclaim for his portraits, many likening them to the work of John Singer Sargent, however I feel his landscapes were just as praiseworthy."

Anna thought to herself, the portraits were for the money, the landscapes for the joy. "Thank you. I'm sure Max would appreciate your opinion."

The curator was intrigued by a painting without a red dot and moved toward it. "Is this a Max Glazer painting?" He inquired.

Anna did not answer for a few seconds, finding it difficult to stop staring at it. "Yes, it is," she replied in a husky voice.

"It's different from anything else I've seen him do. So much looser and almost abstract without actually being abstract...so..."

Anna finished the sentence for him, "So impressionistic?"

"Yes...yes. Exactly!" Kirpatrick continued to study the portrait. The open collared blouse was absent the telltale trademark of Max Glazer, the fabric and folds so lifelike you felt you could touch the surface and feel the texture of the cloth. The features of the woman were somewhat irregular, not the almost photographic quality of the likeness normally found in his portraiture.

Anna could read his mind from the quizzical expression on his face, "You think it's not one of his better paintings, don't you?"

"No...no," he lied. "Just different."

"Actually, it was one of his best. It's a portrait of me you know. How I looked when we were first married."

"So it was done in the beginning of his career?" Kirpatrick offered, thinking this was a possible explanation for its appearance.

"No."

The curator expected Anna to elaborate, but after an awkward silence, he realized she would not. "Eh, at your convenience, I'll have my staff crate the paintings for shipment. Thank you once again."

After he had departed, Anna walked over to the painting and removed it from its hook. Maybe the pain of Max's absence had subsided enough to allow her to hang it in their bedroom without its presence causing sadness. Memories of the discovery of the painting flooded back. Max had been diagnosed with Alzheimer's disease almost a decade ago. The first five years were tolerable. Max was still Max. The last two, excruciating. His physical condition had deteriorated rapidly and worst of the worst, eventually he neither recognized her nor did he remember he had been an artist. Anna recalled for the last six months of his life, she had not been in Max's studio. There was no reason to be there. Four weeks after he had disappeared from her life, she had summoned enough courage to enter the silent shrine of his workplace to decide what to do with its contents. Brushes were stacked neatly in a row of jars large and small, as if standing at attention to be pressed into action. Bottles of compounds of oils, varnishes and thinners known only to Max lined the top of an antique chest an arm's length from his easel. And then Anna saw it. On the tall oak easel stood the painting she was now holding in her arms. It had not been there six months ago. How and when Max painted it was beyond her comprehension. Was it really Max who painted it? Max had one custom that differed from most artists. He always signed his name on the back of the canvas. Once again, she turned the painting over as she had done almost a year ago and read the inscription, "I see your face every time I close my eyes. I don't know who you are but I know I have always loved you."

Anna brought the painting against her body and held it tightly. "I love you too, Max."

The Choice

Stephanie Farnan

Angela Berry was used to being surrounded by death, and it usually didn't bother her. These last four victims had been different though and she didn't know why. She just couldn't get them off her mind, maybe she was just emotionally drained. Over the last two months their was someone who was attacking, raping and then killing women in Hudson Falls, New York.

Hudson Falls, was a small town things like this just didn't happen here. Angela Berry was the top Forensics Pathologist in the state and when there were multiple deaths, Angela was always called to help find the perpetrator. Plus she had lived in Hudson Falls her whole life so she was taking this personal, the stress of the situation was taking its toll on her. After today's autopsy, on victim number four, she couldn't wait to leave. Lucky for her, if nothing new came up, she had the next two days off; she needed the break so badly. Angela grabbed her keys and sunglasses and headed out the door. The fresh evening air smelled so good after being cooped up in the antiseptic stench that surrounded her at work.

When she got to her car she stopped and looked around hoping to find someone to have a conversation with. She just wasn't ready to go home yet. If she went home now she would just be thinking about work and the four victims all night, but there was no one around. I guess they all went home to their families. On the drive home she passed a car wash and vacuum, perfect. Cleaning always helped her to clear her mind. Every surface she wiped was like wiping the bad thoughts out of her head. Angela pulled in the stall and began to empty the trash out of her car; she was feeling better already. Quarters were in the machine, and the hose began to

151

spray water. Watching the dirt drain away with the water, her mind began to clear, it was mesmerizing. If only every problem could be washed away like this. As she finished the rinsing the machine began beeping, crap she needed more change. There must be some in the console, she opened the door and began rummaging for more quarters. She dug up five and stood up to finish the job when an arm reached around her neck. Angela tried to scream but the sound of the water was louder than any noise she could make with her constricted air way.

"Stop struggling and this will go easy," the attacker said into her ear, "if you don't this will be the last night you ever see." He pressed his body up against hers and she was forced to lean forward into the front seat. "I have a knife and if you don't shut the hell up and hold still, I'll use it."

She could see his face in the side mirror that was across the car, he wasn't wearing a mask, she knew this meant that he was going to kill her when he was done with her, he obviously wasn't worried about her identifying him later. His strong arm snaked around the front of her and began ripping at the tie on her scrub pants. Frantically she looked around her car for something she could use as a weapon, there was nothing. Why did she have to be so damn clean? Then she remembered the seatbelt knife her father made her buy in case she was ever in an accident and couldn't get the belt undone to get out of the car. Behind her she could see that he was unzipping his jeans, she had to act now. Reaching into the pocket on the side of her seat, her fingers fumbled around the handle but she finally grabbed the knife and in one swift motion sliced the arm that was around her neck. Yelling out, he loosened his grip on her. Angela took this opportunity to push her backside into him as hard possible, he fell backwards. Standing up she turned herself around and saw the artery in his neck throbbing. With his elevated heart rate it was an easy target. Without even thinking she swiped at it. The blood flowed fast like a damn had just given way, the look of horror on his eyes gave her unexpected enjoyment. He slid down and hit the pavement, blood gushing from his neck in pulses, as his heart beat for the last time.

Angela looked around hoping someone was there to help her but the car wash was empty, she didn't even see his car, he must have walked here. She was so angry with herself, how could she have been so stupid. She knew there was a predator on the loose and yet she was so focused on her car she never saw him. With the hum of the water it was so easy for him to sneak up behind her.

Taking a few deep breaths she tried to calm herself. Was this guy the attacker that had been killing all those women? It had to be. Wanting to find out who he was but not wanting to disturb the crime scene, she reached the tip of her fingers into his pocket and grabbed his wallet. There was no identification, just a few twenties. This had to be the attacker, who else wouldn't carry any identification?

Just then a women started screaming, Angela thought she was alone so the sound startled her and she jumped up quickly. There was a women standing in front of her car with her hands covering her mouth. "Oh my god you killed him. You crazy bitch you are the one they're looking for."

"No wait," Angela said, holding her hands up, trying to show the women she was unarmed. But before Angela could tell her what had happened, the lady jumped back in her car and took off. "Wait," Angela yelled, but the women was gone. Angela realized she still had the man's wallet in her hand. The women in the car saw it, damn she probably thought I was robbing this guy. Now what do I do, I need to call the police. Grabbing her cell phone she was about to dial, but stopped.

What if the police didn't believe my story? I don't have a mark on my body. I am not hurt at all, and there he is laying there dead on the ground. Hell, I can't even find the knife he said he was holding, it must have been a bluff. So he is unarmed and I'm standing over him with a bloody knife in my hand.

She knew how these things worked, she had worked with the police many times in her line of work. They would see her standing here knife in hand, and him bleeding out in front of her. Plus her fingerprints were on his wallet. Uggh, why did she do that? They would think she had tried to rob him and when he fought back she killed him. That's what the lady in the car thought. This was bad, this was really bad.

Looking down at the man who now lay in a pool of blood, not wanting the puddle to get any bigger until she figured out what to do, she took her foot and pushed his body over the drain. She needed to protect herself this time not from the attacker but from the police who would never believe her story, and she needed to act fast.

Putting more quarters into the machine, she turned on the hose again and started spraying the blood down the drain. Even going so far as to hose off the man who attacked her. There was a blanket in her trunk and she grabbed it out and wrapping him up with it. With his heart no longer beating the blood had stopped flowing and she felt that she could put his wrapped body in her trunk and not have to worry about getting his blood and DNA in her car.

After he was in the trunk, she hosed off the pavement and watched the drain until the water ran clear. The area looked good, there was no trace that he had ever been here. Surprisingly there wasn't even a drop of blood on her, she would burn her scrubs anyway, just in case, but for now it was time to get out of there.

Driving home her mind raced, but she obeyed every traffic rule, the last thing she needed was to get pulled over with a body in her trunk. Once home Angela removed her clothes, grabbed her robe and headed into the back yard. Throwing her clothes into the fire pit and watching as they slowly turned to ash, tears began rolling down her face and her body shook as she began sobbing. If anyone found out what she had done her life would be over. With the status she held in her field and in the community, a story like this would be all over the news. Angela would never be able to live in this town or go back to her job, and she just might end up spending her life in prison.

As the fire died down and her tears dried up she knew now was the time to pull herself together not to fall apart. I'm a smart accomplished women, and hell, I'm in the forensic field—I can cover this up, but first, I needed a shower. She headed back into the house, the events of the day had made her feel dirty. As hot water ran over her body, she felt the tension melting away. Steam filled the room with the fresh sent of lavender soap. Closing her eyes and breathing it all in, she tried hard to relax and clear her mind. When she finally felt clean she toweled off and got her sweat pants and a tee shirt on.

I needed to think. Maybe I'm just thinking about this wrong, taking things to personally. I need to go at this like it's a job, like it's one of the forensic assignments I used to get in college. I need to get rid of this body and make sure that no one ever finds it. Hell, she had spent her life figuring out how people died and detecting clues to find the killers and now... the irony of the situation, actually sent a wave of nervous laughter up her body and she began giggling. For first time today she was actually smiling, and it felt good.

First she needed to dig up some old clothes that she didn't mind burning later, the sweatpants she had on would be fine, but she needed to change into a long sleeve shirt. Her whole body needed to be covered. Then she headed to the bathroom and grabbed a shower cap from the hook on the door. People always left hair at the scene of the crime, she wasn't going to make that mistake. There were rubber gloves she used for coloring her hair in a box under the sink, she grabbed those too, that would help with any fingerprints. Covering her hair and hands was a must, but she needed something to go over her shoes, to blur any foot prints she might leave. Plastic bags would work, she grabbed some out of the recycling container and tied them around her sneakers. She stepped in the dirt outside in her yard to see if it worked. Yes, it worked perfectly, there were no tread marks. I may really be able to pull this off.

Now she needed some kind of a container, heading out to the garage, her mind was spinning what could she possibly use? She found a tote that she thought might be big enough. There was also a trunk she could empty out. Which one should I use? The tote may not sink, that would be bad, but even worse, the wooden trunk would eventually decompose and the body could float to the surface. That thought snapped her back to reality. What was she doing? I can't go through with this. I'm a doctor for gosh sakes not a mobster or hit man. She sat on the step and began crying. Why didn't I just call the police when I was first attacked? But she knew why. This guy was probably the one who was responsible for all the trouble that had gone on in the area. No one had lived after his attacks, so there was no one that could possibly identify him. There was no way she could prove that it was him and that he had attacked her. She couldn't afford to miss work and go through a lengthy trial, it seemed so crazy but she had to go through with her plan. This guy had to be the attacker, and he came after her. Why should she suffer for what he did? By covering this up she was not only saving herself but also saving the tax payers from paying for a trial and supporting someone in prison who had killed at least four women.

Deciding on the tote she drilled golf ball size holes in it so it would sink and so that fish could swim in and out of it and get rid of the remains. Now something to weight it down. The bricks that lined her walk would work, but they could also be traced back to her. I better grab some rocks from the woods on the way to the lake. Dragging the tote into the house she tried to think of anything she might have forgotten. Let's see, if I take the wrapped body and put it into the tote, drive it out to the lake, weigh it down with rocks and put it in the water, everything should be fine, right? Then it dawned on her. How would she get the tote out into the middle of the lake?

If rent a boat there would be a paper trail. Angela started pacing back and forth, the whole plan was falling apart, she began crying and then reminded herself why she was doing this in the first place. This guy had killed at least four women. She worked on their bodies. All the gruesome pictures came into her mind.

I need to keep going, there is no backing out now I'm in way too deep. Her friend Gerry had a row boat. That could work, but she couldn't tell him.

I can sneak out to where he parks it and just take it out onto the lake, dump out the tote and get back home before morning. It was still early, only ten o'clock, it would still be dark for hours. Ok the plan was set now to get moving. Angela pulled her car into the garage and opened the trunk, the stench made her gag but it didn't stop her momentum. Hoisting the body from the trunk and getting it into the tote was harder than expected, rigor mortis was setting in and it wasn't as pliable as she had hoped it would be. The blanket kept slipping and arms and legs were showing. The tote was not going to work. Grabbing a rope from under the tool bench she tied it around the blanket, holding the body together, making it easier to move. Angela ran back into the house and got a garment bag. This would be perfect, she slid the bag around the body and zipped it up tight. The next challenge was to get it back into the car trunk. There were handles on the garment bag that helped tremendously. Things were getting easier now.

Angela drove out to Glenn Lake and found her friends docking area. It was a rocky beach landing, right off the parking lot. Getting the garment bag into the boat went fine but was a little louder than she expected. The beach landing wasn't around any houses so she hoped no one heard her. Angela grabbed the biggest rocks she could find, zipped them in the bag and rowed herself out to the middle of the lake. Her muscles were screaming in pain but her adrenaline kept her moving. It was pitch black out here and all she could hear were the little splashes of water as the oars skimmed through it. It could have been a peaceful ride if there wasn't a body in her boat.

Feeling she was out far enough, she began to hoist the bag over the edge and into the water. The boat began tipping from the weight and almost flipped when the body fell from it, hitting the water with a splash. To her relief it started sinking immediately. Now all she had to do is row back and get out of there. Forgetting to bring her cell phone or a watch, she had no idea what time it was. She tried to row as fast as she could but was losing strength quickly. She needed to hurry, if the sun came up she would definitely be spotted. Finally, she hit the shore and dragged the boat back trying to place it exactly in the same spot it was. Angela hopped into her car and headed for home. Tears rolled down her face, blurring the road in front of her, but the nightmare was over.

Angela spent the rest of the weekend at home, she just couldn't bring herself to leave. She burnt her clothes and took the ash from the fire pit and tilled it into her garden soil, vacuumed her trunk and used sleeping pills to keep bad dreams away. On Monday she returned to work, coffee in hand, one for her and one for her coworker Tom. Everything was back to normal, and the attacker was gone.

Tom entered the office with a stack of paperwork. "Angela," he said, "it looks like the attacker struck again last night, victim number five will be arriving shortly."

Panic struck Angela as Tom spoke those words. If he is still out there, she thought, than who did I? She ran over to the sink and threw up the coffee she had just drank. This can't be happening.

Tom looked at her. "Are you ok?" He asked.

Angela took a deep breath and pulled herself together, "Ya I'm fine. Let's just get to work."

The Greatest American Story

Emily Garcia

There is a café on the corner of Sixth and Market Street, and when you walk in the first thing you notice is the smell of cinnamon and the screech of the milk steamer, a little like a banshee, as another cup is brewed up for the young couple on a first date or the businessman picking up his final accessory before taking on the 9-5. At night, if you look for it, there's this funny reflection on the glass walls in front of the café where you can look in and out at the same time and see both the streetlamps and car taillights as well as your own inquisitive face and the dessert cases and coffee tables behind you.

I'd been to this place a few times before, but having just returned from school and in need of a few dollars, I found myself behind the counter that summer. Crisp mornings, sweltering afternoons, and romantic twilight hours saw me brewing teas of all kind and making useless pleasantries with the customers as I handed out their iced lattes and Americanos. I got to hear from the tourists coming from Boston and how sunburned they'd gotten at the beach, or from the old town codgers who proclaimed that this city just wasn't what it used to be, and I mastered the art of nodding and smiling with passing interest. One man in particular, however, spared me the chatter. In fact, he spared me everything except his order of medium black coffee which he came in for every afternoon at two o'clock sharp. His beady black eyes never rose to meet mine under his bushy salt-and-pepper brows, and he always shoved his change across the counter and stomped off with his drink as if he had somewhere more important to be. Instead of leaving, he would go, without fail, to settle himself in a little corner with a round wooden table by the glass walls overlooking the city square. There, he would open up his cracked leather shoulder bag, take out a stack of paper and a pen, set them side-by-side next to each other, and stare at them. His gaze was only broken when he turned to sip from his medium black coffee. Otherwise, he would stay until the final moments before closing, and I noticed that the other baristas would give him sidelong glances and talk a little more loudly than usual about how glad they were to be closing up and going home. Only then would he take up his pen and paper, return them to their leather home, and slowly rise and exit into the cavern of darkness that is nighttime in the city.

Day in and day out, this routine was repeated. Not once did the man ever touch his pen other than to take it out or return it to his bag, not once did he stir or look up while he remained in his little corner of the café, and never was a word put down in ink on his sheets of paper. I asked a coworker one day who that man was and what he was doing. She rolled her eyes and shrugged. "No one knows what his name is. But rumor has it that he's writing 'the greatest American story.'" Her voice shifted a little with sarcasm as she described his bold mission, and we both turned to look to where he was.

Bemused, I asked "Well, how is he supposed to write the greatest story if he hasn't even put down a single word yet?"

She smirked. "Exactly."

Everyone else, coworker and customer alike, had learned to accept the man like one of the paintings hung on the back walls, and other than a few glances, no one gave him much interest. The novelty of having an author on the brink of great fame seemed to have worn off on most, but I, on the other hand, found that my curiosity eventually got the better of me. I finally determined one day that I would speak to this unwritten writer and maybe find out some answers.

It was an unnaturally hot July afternoon, the kind that is often referred to as one of those "dog days of summer," and as the bell from the nearby church tower struck two, the man entered like clockwork.

"Medium black," he muttered to me, not raising his eyes

under those bushy salt-and-pepper brows.

I decided to make a go at it. "Are you sure you don't want an iced coffee? It's a good ninety degrees out. At this rate you could order an iced and have it be hot by the time you walk outside!"

He did nothing more than let out a grunt from the back of his throat and shove the usual change for a hot coffee in my direction, my banter clearly not appreciated. A little put off, I handed him that black coffee and threw open the cash register to drop the change in, looking up only to glare at the back of his blue-grey buttondown as he retreated to his familiar spot, took out his writing utensils, and proceeded to sit and stare.

My curiosity, however, had not faded. What on earth could this old man be dreaming up on those blank pieces of paper? I had been working almost every day that summer and never had a day passed when he hadn't come in for his order, settled himself down in that same spot, and not written a single word. The way he stared at those blank pages made me think of prisoners who stare at the bleach white walls of their cells, and I wondered at how he had not lost his mind like some inmate transfixed by the boundaries of his existence. What kind of explanation could there be for this odd creature of habit?

My second chance at solving this weird mystery came in the form of the dirty dishes left by another customer a table away from the man's hallowed spot. As I walked over to remove those dishes, I did my best to make eye contact, but to no avail. Finally, as I returned to wipe the table down, I decided to abandon all decencies and instead head straight to the heart of the issue.

"So what are you working on?" I asked casually as I turned my chin in his direction.

No response. The frustration came burning back, but this time I fueled it into the drive to get my question answered. "I've seen you every single day here and you haven't written a word." I waited for a response.

"Words, words." His voice had this rustiness to it, as if it

161

had been left neglected for some time.

Inwardly I cheered at my success, but at the same time this reply left me even more in need of an answer. "Well, in my experience, you usually need words in a story. Are you writing a story?"

He looked up to me finally, his eyes giving off an odd glint. "The greatest American story. And what kind of experience is that, kid?"

I raised my eyebrows, not appreciating his condescension. "I'm actually studying English and philosophy during the school year, so I think I know what I'm talking about," I responded with a little bit of an edge.

He chuckled a little sardonically. "You kids and your words. You're always using them, throwing them down on paper like gum on a sidewalk. Words are treasures to be used wisely, never wasted."

"Well at this rate, you won't have to worry about wasting anything." I was disliking this man more and more.

His face grew stony again. "I am writing the greatest American story. If you think you know how to write something as great, then I'd like to see you try."

"If you think you know how to write something as great, I'd like to see you write anything at all!"

He coughed and turned his eyes back to his paper. I felt a little guilty for having snapped at him, and gave it one last shot. "Maybe if you don't know where to start, you should just write whatever comes to mind and then go back and edit. That usually works for me," I said as kindly as possible.

He ignored me, his gaze not even breaking with the blank pages for a second.

"Just a thought." I began to leave the table.

"One moment, English major." I turned to look back at him. "So you study the greats. Eliot and Fitzgerald and them, huh? What makes them so great?"

I paused. "I guess because their words made people think or feel in new and different ways. They changed people's perspectives, made them see things differently. They were innovative."

He smiled crookedly. "There you go, kid. Now try being innovative when people have been writing for thousands of years. Unless you're content with making words into junk like you seem to be."

"You know nothing about how I write, or who I am. And don't pretend like you know more than I do when you can't even put a letter down on paper," I spat, thoroughly disgusted at this point. "Let me know if you ever finish that story, and I hope for your sake it's pretty damn great!"

To this day, I'm not really sure why a total stranger put me completely up in arms the way this man did. I think I heard a little bit of a rusty chuckle as I returned to my work.

The rest of the summer was spent with the same daily routine. In the man came at two, ordering the same drink, sitting at the same table, and staring at the same paper. It was as if our conversation had never occurred. To him, I was once again merely the one who supplied him with his daily poison, and I wish I could say that I was fine with that, but I always caught myself looking over at that corner as I worked. I couldn't help but notice that he seemed a little more ragged every day, as if this conquest of writing the "greatest American story" was wearing at him inside and out. I found myself feeling a little sorry for him. However, when the fall came and I returned to school, this man and his strange mission soon left my mind.

I did not return to this café until Christmas break of that year, when I was home for a few weeks and once more in need of a few dollars. The evening sky was a rosy pink, pierced by the spire of the church tower, and the shops lining the streets were illuminated in all their electric Christmas glory

Inside, I was greeted by that familiar scent of cinnamon and the warm welcome of my old coworkers, glad to see me once again after my brief hiatus. Settling back in behind the counter felt comfortable to me. At the same time, however, I couldn't shake the feeling that something was out of place, like one time when my father shaved his mustache and I couldn't figure out what was different about him for almost a week.

It didn't take me long to find the mustache. "What's happened to our resident author?" I asked one of my old barista friends, the same one who had told me back in the summer how he was writing that great American story.

"Oh, I totally forgot!" I stood confused as she stepped into the back office and then came back with a folded piece of paper, titled For the English major. "He finally wrote something down, believe it or not. I saw him do it! But he came up and gave it to me with strict instructions to not read it and give it to you once you came back. Haven't seen him since."

"Huh." I unfolded the paper, wondering what this great story was going to be.

Union Post, Page 12, Some Sunday in November.

"Do we have old newspapers from last month?"

My coworker stared at me, confused. "Umm yeah, I think there are some back in the office. The manager never throws anything out. Why?"

"I think the old guy got published or something" I answered as I stepped into the office. Finding the stack of old newspapers on a desk, I began to shuffle through them until I found one from November. I turned to page twelve, and I felt a chill run through my body.

The old man was there, his beady black eyes piercing into mine from under his salt-and-pepper brows. I read through the paragraph under his face. Frances Moore, grew up in Cambridge, journalist for the *Boston Globe*, played baseball in his younger years, married twice (once divorced, one passed away), quiet but an avid reader who especially enjoyed Fitzgerald's novels, survived by no one.

"Well?" my coworker asked. "Did he write the greatest American story?" She smirked a little.

Slowly, I folded the newspaper and placed it back on the desk. "Yes," I murmured. "Yes, I'd have to say he did."

The Drowned Belltower

Athena Giles

Gael changed his clothes in the entryway and splashed some water from the basin Tantie Anna had left out for him over his head. The smell of fish still clung to his hair and skin, but the routine kept the worst of the stink out of their home. It was his wages from the fish he brought in from the boats to the market that paid for the apartment, so Tantie was content to look the other way from a little fishiness, so long as he left most of it in the entryway.

As he ascended the stairs to the apartment, the smell of baking bread started to overwhelm the fish. Tantie was busy in the kitchen, preparing supper. Gael dropped a basket of vegetables he'd brought back from the market on the counter.

"Good day then?" Tantie asked as she started picking through the basket to see what he'd brought.

"Not too bad," Gael said. "The sea was calm at least, though we didn't bring back as many fish as we would have liked."

"Clearly you brought back enough," Tantie selected a big round onion and began chopping it to add into the stew that was steaming on the stove. The tangy scent made Gael's eyes water. "Be a good lad and go help your Grand-père wash up for supper."

Gael nodded and went through the kitchen to the living room, where Grand-père sat in a chair by the window facing the sea. He hardly ever left that spot nowadays. Night and day, he'd sit, and stare out at the sea.

"Do you hear the bells, Gael?" Grand-père asked.

Gael sighed. He was used to Grand-père's obsession with the bells by now, but he still got impatient sometimes. As a boy, he used to believe in the stories. He would close his eyes and listen, and sometimes, if he listened in just the right way, he thought he could hear it: a distant chime of church bells tolling over the roar of the waves crashing in the bay. But then something would distract him, the cat asking for its dinner, or Tantie Anna tisking over the foolishness of the game. Now Gael knew better. The bells were nothing but a story.

"It's going to be time for supper soon, Grand-père," Gael said.

"The bells," Grand-père repeated. "They're ringing so loudly, can't you hear them Pierre?"

"No, Grand-père," Gael reminded him. "Pierre was my papa. I'm Gael."

"Gael?" Grand-père looked at him then. "Oh, yes. Well you run along and tell your papa it's time for supper. I'll come to the table when he does."

"Papa is dead, Grand-père," Gael said, maybe a touch too harshly. He'd begun to get tired of having to remind Grand-père who he was. "He drowned while out in his boat. Don't you remember?"

Grand-père said nothing, only stared out the window, listening to the waves, or the bells. Gael went to take Grand-père by the arm and lead him to the bathroom to wash up.

"Just you wait, my boy," Grand-père said as Gael ran the tap over their hands. The water was cold and Gael shivered. "You'll see. I'll find that drowned cathedral, and when I do, I'll find my Pierre too, living down there with his mermaid bride."

Gael returned Grand-père to his chair to wait until supper was ready. He slipped easily back into his vacant staring out at the sea. Gael almost missed the days when Grand-père would disappear, only to come back damp and trailing sand into the house while Tantie worried and rushed to clean him up.

At least then he would leave the apartment sometimes.

On the nights he went wandering, Grand-père would return and tell Gael the story. Gael had known it by heart for as long as he could remember, but he always listened. Grand-père would settle into his chair by the window, and Gael would curl up on the couch. Tantie pretended not to listen, but would usually find that the living room needed dusting, or the dishes in the kitchen the next room over needed cleaning. Whatever it was she did, it was always within earshot.

Gael sat on the couch to wait for supper, and watched Grand-père watch the sea. He imagined Grand-père telling him the story, the way he used to when Gael was a boy.

"If the night is quiet, you can hear the bells," Grand-père used to say. "And if the stars shine without a cloud in the sky, you can even see the spires of the cathedral out there, under the water."

"It's just rocks that fall off the cliffs," Tantie would explain. "They don't even look like spires, just big lumps of stone."

"And as the sun rises," Grand-père would go right on, ignoring her, "you can see the priests going about their morning chores, singing as they go."

"How do they sing, Grand-père?" Gael would ask. "Don't they get salt water in their mouths?"

"Silly boy," Grand-père would laugh. "They're not really there. Not like we are anyways. They don't have to worry about that sort of thing."

"Where are they then?" Gael would pester him for more answers.

"Oh, somewhere else," Grand-père would wave a hand in the air, indicating both anywhere and nowhere at the same time.

Gael couldn't pinpoint the exact moment he'd begun to realize his Tantie might be right, and Grand-père's stories weren't all he thought they were. He knew it was around the time he'd started working with his papa's old friends, going out with the fishing boats and learning how to bring back the best catch to Côte-d'Aîné's markets. Grand-père was certainly not the only one who told stories about the drowned cathedral, but he seemed to take the stories much more seriously than anyone else. Though no one knew for certain where it was, Grand-père was convinced it was their bay that the cathedral had drowned in. The myth only told that somewhere off the coast, the cathedral had been lost, swallowed up by the sea as a result of God's wrath, or an error of topography and poor architecture.

There wasn't much to do out on the water while waiting for the fish to come, so the fishermen told stories. Stories about storms exaggerated to Biblical tempests, or about the biggest fish they'd ever caught, which got bigger with every telling. Naturally, one of the first things he'd asked about had been his papa.

"Best sailor in Côte-d'Aîné, your old papa was," they said. "We used to say he could smell danger coming. Knew where the hidden shoals were, even when the water was murkiest. Could tell a storm brewing before there was ever a cloud in the sky. Being out on the water was second nature to that man, though some called it unnatural. God given gift, it was."

"If he was so good, then how did his boat sink?" Gael asked them, and the fishermen went silent. They muttered incomprehensible curses and shrugged.

So Gael had asked Grand-père.

"How'd your father sink?" Grand-père had gone silent and stared out the window at the ocean. "Gone to find your mother, I suppose. Never did meet her. She just left you on the doorstep and disappeared. Some mermaid living in the ruins of the cathedral, I'd say. Your father went looking for her. Maybe he found her. Maybe he didn't."

Gael remembered how mercilessly the other fishermen had teased him after he'd told that story. Eventually, he'd started laughing too. All the times he sailed with them, learning the trade. He never saw any church spires under the waves, or mermaids swimming in the deeps.

Grand-père never told stories anymore.

"What's the point in telling the stories if you won't listen, boy?" Grand-père had said when Gael had started pestering him with more logistical questions. The older he got, the less Gael was able to suspend his disbelief.

Gael missed the stories. Though Grand-père's memory was fading and he mistook Gael for his father most of the time, he still hadn't let go of his stubborn refusal to tell Gael about the Drowned Cathedral. He seemed content to mutter to himself about how it must be out there and how he could find his son if only he could find the cathedral.

"Think we can coax him to the table tonight?" Tantie Anna appeared at Gael's side and he jumped. She laughed and ruffled his hair. "Interrupt some deep thinking, did I?"

Gael grimaced and smoothed his hair back down. "Had to drag him to the bathroom, so if you feel like dragging him to the table you go ahead."

Tantie regarded Grand-père for a moment before shaking her head. "Best to just let him be I suppose."

Gael stood and followed Tantie Anna back to the kitchen. She started filling three ceramic bowls with stew.

"He called me Pierre again tonight," Gael told her as she started cutting thick slices from the loaf of bread she'd baked. She stiffened and paused her slicing.

"It's not his fault his memory is going," Tantie said finally and continued slicing. "We can't blame him for it."

"He seemed to think my papa was still alive when I corrected him," Gael said.

Tantie sighed. "Let an old man have his fantasies. Losing my brother was hard for him. And not long after our mother passed too. I wish I'd helped out more, but I was at that age you know, difficult teen. Lord knows you had that phase too."

"Sorry, Tantie," Gael said.

"Oh everyone has it, don't worry," Tantie handed him a bowl of stew and a plate with two slices of the bread. "Bring these to Grand-père will you?"

Gael took the food into the living room. Grand-père still hadn't moved, but Gael wasn't surprised. He left Grand-père's supper on the small table next to his chair.

"Make sure you eat this all tonight," Gael said. Recently, Grand-père hadn't been touching the food they'd given him. Tantie was beginning to worry that they'd have to start helping him eat so he wouldn't starve himself. Gael began to walk away when Grand-père grabbed his hand.

"Can you feel it, Gael?" Grand-père asked, looking him in the eye with a directness that Gael hadn't seen in a while. "Tonight is the night. Tonight's the night I could find my Pierre."

"My papa drowned, Grand-père," Gael reminded him again and pulled his hand out of Grandpère's grip. "You won't find him anywhere."

"What happened to you, my boy?" Grand-père asked. "You used to believe."

"I'm not a boy anymore," Gael said. "Now, eat your supper."

Grand-père stared at the food for a moment then returned to gazing out the window. Gael sighed and returned to the kitchen. Tantie Anna had laid their supper out for them and Gael sat at the table opposite her.

"I think you're right," Gael said as he attacked the stew. "We're going to have to start feeding him. He didn't seem interested in supper."

"I wonder if we need to bring him to a home," Tantie said. "I don't know if I can handle taking care of him if he gets any worse, and you're out on the boats all day so won't be able to help me. Besides, you're young, you shouldn't be wasting all your free time take care of your Grand-père."

"I think he'd be happier at home," Gael said. "But it should be up to you not me."

"Let's keep it in the back of our minds for now," Tantie said. "We don't need to do it yet."

"I'll ask around on the docks," Gael promised. "Maybe some of the other fishermen know of a good place to bring him. Somewhere he can still see the sea."

"That would be good," Tantie nodded. "Thank you, Gael."

They didn't mentioned Grand-père again for the rest of supper. Tantie talked about friends of hers, and tried to be subtle about mentioning their daughters, but Gael knew what she was up to. He tolerated her attempts to match him up with the local girls, but he doubted any of her choices would be what he was looking for. Though Gael himself didn't exactly know what he was looking for.

After supper, Gael went to wash his dirty clothes from that day in the tub outside. The lights were still on in the clockmaker's shop below their apartment. Their landlord sat at his desk tinkering with the tiny gears of a watch. Gael passed through the alley beside the building around to the tiny attempt at a yard in the back. He washed his clothes and hung them to dry before returning to the apartment. Tantie had started on the dishes, and Gael went to see if Grand-père had touched his meal and to retrieve the dishes for Tantie to wash.

Only the chair by the window was empty, and the supper plate untouched. The latter was unsurprising, but the empty chair stuck out like the beam of the lighthouse out on the ocean cliffs.

Grand-père left his chair so rarely that they'd bought him a reclining one so he could sleep in it on nights they couldn't convince him to go up to his room.

"Tantie!" Gael called. "Is Grand-père with you?"

"No," she answered. "Is he not in his chair?"

"No!"

Tantie Anna rushed into the room, a wet dish in one hand and a towel in the other.

"I've been here the whole time, where could he have gone?" she crossed the room to the window, as if on closer inspection, Grand-père would magically appear.

The dish dropped and shattered into dozens of sharp pieces at Tantie's feet.

"He's on the beach."

Gael hurried to the window to see. Sure enough, he could see a dark figure crossing the sand that shined white in the moonlight. But from such a distance, he could not tell who it was.

"It could be anyone, Tantie," Gael assured her. "Besides, how could he get that far without us noticing? I've been outside, and you've been in the kitchen."

"I heard him, muttering away about that damned

cathedral," Tantie began to sob, burying her face in the dish towel. "He kept saying over and over about how he could hear the bells. I thought it was just his normal blather, but then he said 'Tonight's a night I could find Pierre.' And I didn't hear a word after that. I just thought he'd fallen asleep."

"He said that to me too," Gael said and looked again out the window. There was no way of knowing who the figure on the beach was, but this wouldn't be the first time Grand-père had sneaked out to go to the water. It had just been a while since he'd shown any interest in going outside. "Check the rest of the apartment and if he's not here I'll call some friends to help us look for him."

As Gael had feared, the apartment was empty. He rang up a few of his fishermen friends, and though they weren't thrilled about being called out of the house at this late hour, Côte-d'Aîné was a small town. People were expected to help each other, in the knowledge that at some point, the favor would be returned.

By the time they reached the beach, Grand-père was nowhere to be found. Gael combed the shoreline with the other fishermen for hours until the real bells of Côte-d'Aîné's church began to toll midnight had come, but they still found no sign of Grand-père. At that point the goodwill of the fishermen began to fade and they mumbled excuses and started to drift home. Gael couldn't blame them. The day would dawn soon and they would have to be setting the boats out to bring back tomorrow's catch. Gael knew he should follow them, or else tomorrow would be miserable, but he couldn't stand the idea of returning home to his Tantie with no news.

Gael stood alone on the beach and stared out at the waves, cursing the story of the cathedral drowned under them. He cursed the ocean for drowning his father, and age for taking Grand-père's memory. He wanted things to be normal. He wanted Grand-père to be home and to recognize him for who he really was, not mistake him for his father all the time.

As he watched the waves, Gael noticed something floating

in the distance, too large to be a log, and too small to be a boat. Gael was a strong swimmer and the distance wasn't so far, but for a short moment, he hesitated. Then with unexpected determination, he shed his outer layers and was running out into the water. He shouted as he ran, hoping that some of his friends were still within earshot.

The water was bitingly cold, but Gael kept his gaze out on what he was swimming for, moving his limbs fast and taking deep gulps of air to keep his blood pumping so he wouldn't notice the cold as much. The closer he got, the more obvious it was that the object he'd seen floating was what he was afraid it would be: a body.

Gael reached the body. It floated face down in the water. Gael kicked hard with his legs and flipped the body up and saw it was his Grand-père. Without stopping to think about whether Grandpère was dead or alive, Gael wrapped one arm around the body and turned back towards the shore. Grand-père was fully clothed, and the weight of the water-logged cloth made it difficult to swim. The salt chapped his lips and made him gag. The water began sucking him down, Gael coughed and kept looking up at the stars shining above. The stars blurred as water closed over his head, but he didn't loosen his grip on Grand-père. The old man may not even know who was trying to save him, for all Gael knew it was already too late. Salt stung his eyes and lack of oxygen burned his lungs, but he kicked with all his strength and his head broke the surface. He gulped down the cold air and used it to scream.

Gael wasn't ready to die for his Grand-père but he wasn't about to just leave him behind either.

"Gael!" someone was swimming towards them. "What the hell were you thinking boy?"

Lisle, an older fisherman who had been close friends with Gael's papa, got on the other side of Grand-père and together they swam the body back to shore. The moment they got onto dry land, Gael started pumping on Grand-père's chest, trying to get the water out and air back in.

"Gael, stop," Lisle grabbed him by the shoulders. "It's too late, lad, there's nothing you can do. Now get your clothes back on before you catch your death too."

Gael realized he was covered in goosebumps and was shivering uncontrollably in the chill night air. He collapsed onto the ground, limbs weak from the cold and the effort of the swim. It was all he could do to lie in the wet sand and breathe. Eventually he noticed Lisle was shaking him and pulling him off the ground.

"Not moving's the worst thing you can do when you're cold," Lisle said. "Now snap to it and get dressed."

Numbly, Gael did as the older man told him to. He shook as much of the water from his skin as he could before pulling his dry clothes on over his damp body.

"You get yourself home, Gael," Lisle said. "I'll take care of your Grand-père. You just go get in a hot bath and don't worry about coming to work in the morning. I'll take care of it all."

"Thank you, Lisle," Gael managed to say through his chattering teeth. He avoided looking down at Grand-père's body as he shook the older man's hand and stumbled off towards home.

When Gael reached his apartment, he found Tantie had already run a hot bath in anticipation of either Gael or Grand-père needing one. Without a word, Gael stripped out of his now wet clothes and sank into the hot water. He could feel the water soaking the salt and the cold out of his skin and hair.

Now home and warm, the shock of nearly drowning started to fade.

"What happened out there?" Tantie asked.

"Grand-père drowned."

Days later, after the wake and the funeral were all over, Gael found his way through the twists and turns of a narrow cobbled street. The only light came from a handful of windows in homes above shuttered shops, and the moon shining down. In his arms, he held a plain ceramic jar, as carefully as he might cradle a child. The night was not quite what he'd call cold, but the longer he stayed outside the more the light breeze seemed to chip away at him and work its way through his coat.

His lack of faith in Grand-père's stories had not changed, but still, he followed the street down towards the bay while all the rest of the residents of Côte-d'Aîné slept.

The houses gave way to the wharves, and Gael continued on past buoyed fishing boats and the fancy sailboats and yachts of Côte-d'Aîné's wealthier citizens. The sea was calm, and the boats sitting out on the harbor looked almost entirely still, as if someone had painted them there. Occasionally, the creak of wood or rope would break the illusion, but even the normally noisy harbor was respectfully silent this evening.

Then the wharves ended, and a set of wooden stairs led down to a boardwalk. It stretched on alongside the bay as the brackish river water mixed with the tides of the open ocean. On either side, tall dry grass rattled and rippled in the breeze in the same way that the water did. Gael's boots echoed in the silent night as they thudded against the wood planks of the boardwalk. By now, he was beginning to shiver and realized the night was not quite as unseasonably warm as he'd thought when he was leaving his house, though his swim to retrieve his Grand-père's body had given him a new perspective on cold that made him grateful to only be a little chilled. So he kept on walking, eyes flicking up and down between checking his footing, and the blank darkness that indicated the nearby ocean.

The boardwalk ended and the sand began. Gael trudged up over the dunes and half slid, half clambered down the other side. He walked right up to the edge of the water, at the point where the incoming waves just barely missed the toes of his boots. The ocean spread out inky black, save where the rippling light of the moon reflected on the water. It was nearly impossible to tell where the ocean ended and the sky began. Gael clutched the jar in his arms tight against his chest, closed his eyes, and listened. All he could hear was the waves brushing up against the sand.

Gael opened his eyes and sat down on the sand with the jar in his lap. He ran his hands along the faint designs of waves that had been carved around the opening of the jar. The ceramic was smooth everywhere except where the waves had been carved. Gael knew it was dark blue, but now, it looked black as the sea, and he could only feel the waves with his fingers. He could not see them. Without realizing it, he'd started running his fingers over the curves of the waves in rhythm with the sound of the real waves. One hand turned the jar, the other traced the carving, much in the same manner he would count the beads of his rosary while praying, except instead of God, he thought about his Grand-père.

As Gael continued tracing the waves carved onto the jar, he began to think a sort of prayer. Not the same sort he'd say if he was actually counting the rosary beads. But he meant it in a similar way.

I'm sorry, Grand-père. I'm sorry, Papa. Please find each other. Find the drowned cathedral. Ring the bells. Sing with the priests. Swim with my mermaid mother.

As Gael thought his prayer for his Grand-père, he found himself trying to listen again. Eyes closed, he remembered the way he'd listen when he'd been a boy. Not the way he'd listen to something that's too quiet to hear, if he did that, all he'd hear would be the waves, and perhaps the sound of some boat creaking away in the distance. Instead, he listened in the way he might try to think of something he used to know, but can't remember, when the name for something is on the tip of the tongue, and can almost taste it, but can't quite get a grip on it. He searched through all the things in his memory that might remind him what exactly it was he was looking for.

Then finally, it clicked, and he remembered. In fact, he could hardly believe he'd forgotten at all. Gael remembered hearing the bells as a child, and found that he'd been wrong. They'd never stopped ringing, he'd been the one to stop listening.

The tolling of bells echoed across the sea. A big deep bell

tolled an undertone to the melody like the crashing of stormy waves against the high cliffs. Over the top, lighter, higher bells chimed like the swift rush of the tide as it carried the fishing boats home after a long day's work.

Fainter than the sound of the bells, but still clear, Gael could hear singing. Grand-père had been right, they weren't there, not like he was. They sang hymns amplified by the towering chambers of the cathedral beneath the waves more beautiful than any he'd ever heard in the church back in Côte-d'Aîné, in a language Gael wasn't sure anyone spoke anymore.

Gael opened his eyes, and for a moment, the light of the moon shone through the water and reflected off stone spires bleached white by the salt water. But as quick as memories of a dream, the music of the choir and the bells faded into silence under the crashing of waves against the shore, and the moon reflected off only water.

Gael stood and brushed sand off of his clothes. He unscrewed the lid from the jar and placed it on the ground at his feet. For several moments, he waited, holding the jar in both hands, wishing for the bells to start ringing again, so he might have a more sacred send off. But the night stayed silent. Gael upended the jar and the breeze carried Grand-père's ashes out over the water.

The ashes drifted out to sea, moving further out with each receding wave, out towards where Gael thought he'd seen the cathedral. Gael picked up the lid and screwed it back on before turning and making his way back home. A few lights were still on in the town, and Côte-d'Aîné's church's bells were tolling that it was midnight. Now that Gael had properly heard the drowned cathedral's bells, he could tell the difference. Côte-d'Aîné's bells were there, like he was. The drowned cathedral's bells were somewhere else, like his papa and Grand-père. The church bells rang twelve times, and Gael followed the sound back towards home.

Vagabondage

Diane Griffin

Somewhere near the Moon's orbit, a quarter of a million miles from here, relatively speaking (because even the Earth is endlessly peripatetic, never to be in the same place again), a meteoroid neared the end of its cosmic wanderings. If an astronomer's gaze had happened to fall on it, their trained eye would have seen that it had touched an atmosphere before, and that it had been disastrous for the rock. It was blackened from heat. There were signs of melting and fracture. If that astronomer had backtracked along the ruined rock's course, they would have been able to calculate a rambling course outside the plane of the solar system over forty years long, through wastes so vast, desolate, and cold that even unfeeling rock might know loneliness. Common sense would suggest that a chunk of nickel-iron and silica couldn't possibly, but somehow as it wandered, this one had been afflicted with loneliness and yearning.

In a short time (because a quarter of a million miles amounts to no great distance to such an itinerant) that loneliness was going to end in a brief, brilliant welter of heat and light.

When Major Marvelloso's Magical Amusements and Big Top Circus rolled into Shreveport, Louisiana towards the end of July 1937, the troupe was somewhat worse for the wear of a too-hot, too-humid summer. The circus itself seemed to be breaking down, from the constant losing battle against mildew in the big top's canvas, to the limping water truck, which by this point was pretty much held together by chewing gum and a bit of wheat straw.

The circus' main mechanic, Gypsy Boy, who was also a tumbler, always seemed to hover somewhere near the water truck, usually with his head stuck under the hood down to his waist, covered in black grime. A cracked engine block was nearly impossible to fix. Replacing the truck was a high priority, but finding one capable of hauling a full thousand-gallon water tank, that could be had within any possible stretching of the circus' operating budget was proving to be discouragingly difficult.

Klooji the Clown, who doubled as the circus' crew boss, was pulling out his hair (so to speak) trying to keep on top of the enthusiastically spreading mildew. When the tent was up, he sometimes felt he could watch black rot spread across the canvas. Packing the tent for transport was nerve-wracking and always meant that when they unpacked, an entire day would be spent with half the circus' crew scraping, then brush-scrubbing every inch of canvas twice, once with an alcohol and water solution, then again with soapy water, and then finally rinsing everything again. The irony was lost on no one that water was in short supply, yet it was always too humid for the canvas to dry completely.

The animals also suffered in the heat, even those from hot, dry climates such as the camels. The elephants seemed especially affected. Joe, the newest member of the circus, could attest to this. His "second" job (really his only job at this point) was helping to care for the giant, smelly beasts, mucking the trailer and the pens where they were kept, hauling what water he could for them by hand whenever the water truck was down for the count (which was pretty much every other day), keeping them fed, and gently scrubbing them with soapy water using push brooms on long handles. All of the animals were irritable and uncooperative. Keeping the elephants settled and calm was a never-ending, dangerous, nearly impossible task.

Only two things kept Joe from bolting the circus: the first was that he had nowhere else to go. He'd burned all his bridges both at home and in Yazoo City, Mississippi, where he had gone after leaving home and from where he had run with the circus. The second was the relationship he was developing with Bendo the Clown. Bendo was teaching him the workings of circus life and the rudiments of clowning, beginning with juggling and pantomime.

Bendo, though diminutive and getting on in years, was strong and agile, and pitched in on various tasks around the circus, often in the mess. He was known to be, among his extraordinary list of talents, an excellent cook. His main duty, though, seemed to be supporting morale. He was a sturdy and reliable friend to the whole circus community and took great pains to keep everyone connected and on board.

On Wednesday evening after the Circus Parade had wound its way through Shreveport, Joe was once again shoveling elephant shit, and mumbling to himself.

"Oh, elephant shit!" Joe scooped.

"You are my best ever friend!" He dumped the shovelful in the wheelbarrow, and then scanned for the next patty.

"How would I ever live without you? Your floral bouquet..." He walked four steps and scooped again.

"Your lovely squishy texture..." He walked to the wheelbarrow and dumped that shovelful.

"Oh, elephant shit, you are the very soul of poetry!" He surveyed the ground for another poop to scoop.

"Careful, Joe."

"GAAAHHH!!! Bendo! Damn! You like to startled me half to death!"

Joe turned to look at Bendo, finding him squatting on the fence rail, head cocked to the right, left eyebrow arched. He was barefoot—Bendo was usually barefoot, except when suited up, wearing denim jeans cut off above the knee and a white tank tee shirt. His shock of white hair was a halo framing his expressive, jowly, lined face. Joe didn't know how old Bendo was. He looked far older than the way he moved suggested. Joe would have guessed he was sixty but he couldn't be sure.

"Careful yourself, old man. I'm not finished in here yet."

"Yes, you are, Joe. Clearly, if you're talking to the poop, you need a different job. Go dump that wheelbarrow in the midden, clean yourself up, and come meet me in the mess tent. Someone else can shovel shit for a little while."

Joe shrugged. "OK, then." He jabbed the end of the shovel into the barrow, picked it up and headed for the gate. "Fair enough. It's not like I enjoy this."

A bit later he was sitting on a rickety wooden folding chair across from Bendo, who was perched atop a folding chair of his own in his trademark knees-gathered squat.

Joe rocked back on the chair's two hind legs. "OK, Bendo, what's the deal? You kicking me out?"

Bendo craned his neck, trying to see the legs of Joe's chair. "No, Joe. You're doing fine. Why would I fire you?"

Not waiting for an answer, he cautioned: "I don't want to tell you how to sit in a chair, Joe, everybody's got their own way of doing things, but that cheap old chair may not hold 220 pounds on two legs."

Joe planted the chair's front legs back on the ground. "More like 250," he said, remembering the last time he'd stood on the penny scale at the Yazoo City train depot.

"Probably not anymore. The hard work is doing you some good."

"Huh. That so?" Joe considered the point, savoring it.

"So what would you like to do for side work? There's plenty around to do." Bendo reached for his canteen, tilted it all the way back, trying to get the last drop of water out of the bottom of the container, then set it down on the table, disappointed.

"I don't know. Whatever," Joe looked at his hands on the table. "I guess I wish I was mechanically inclined, so I could help Gypsy Boy with that truck. But since I ain't, I'd be almost as happy to peel 'taters."

"Well now, Joe," Bendo said, rubbing his chin with the back of his index finger, peering at the young man from above and behind his own bunched-together knees, "I'll admit to being surprised. Every choice you make seems to be another step away from the bully I saw that first day when you were shaking down that kid for his ticket. It's gratifying."

Joe was still staring at his hand on the table. Bendo's

assessment of him was as humbling as it was rewarding to hear. He lifted his eyes and looked out at the trees at the edge of the fairgrounds. "Beats going hungry and sleeping rough," he said.

"That's true, Joe. So much better than that." Joe's gaze snapped to Bendo, curiosity burning in his eyes.

Bendo waved Joe's unspoken question away. "There's more to this for you than room and board, I think."

"Yeah," Joe said. He thought about how being in front of the crowd had felt like flying, that first night. "I ain't never been part of or wanted so much to be part of something before; not even my family."

Bendo nodded. "OK, then. You can peel potatoes. I'll talk to Klooji about it. Just don't talk to them too much!" Bendo winked. "Would you like to do the same bit we did that first night for the second show on Saturday?"

"Aw, gee, Bendo, I don't know. That time, I was mad! I seriously wanted to pound you into mulch. I don't know if I could do it the same way if I don't mean it."

"By the end you were in on the joke. We'll practice some before then. You'll be fine."

"Yeah, OK then, sure."

Later, Klooji asked Bendo, "How are things going with your new sidekick?"

"Worried you might get replaced?" Bendo gave a little lopsided smile. "Don't be."

They were in the mess tent. It was the silent part of the dark early morning. The lights under the pavilion top were out and Klooji had a flashlight pointing up into the roof of the tent. There was a bottle of red wine and two tin cups on the table. Klooji had been up for two long days with the rousties getting the big top cleaned and set up, and Bendo was up keeping his partner company until he wound down enough to sleep.

Klooji was hunched over, elbows on the table with his palm under his chin, looking off into the darkness. "I ain't," he said.

"I do think, sometimes," Klooji said, "that I'd like to get off this merry-go-round. How long we been doing this? How long we *gonna* do this?"

Bendo sighed, shook his head. "You know I can't stop. The idea of landing in Gibsontown and putting down stakes sounds like pure hell to me, and where else but there would have a couple of old buzzards like us?"

Klooji gave no answer. He sat silently for a minute, then downed and refilled his cup. "More?" he asked.

Bendo pushed his cup towards the bottle. Klooji filled it.

"I wish I knew what you see in that kid. I think you must be seeing some piece of yourself there. I ain't saying you're wrong about him, he's doing well, I think, but he's getting under your skin somehow."

Bendo bowed his head a little and closed his eyes, saying nothing. Klooji stared at the little clown, considering what tack to take.

"Someday," Klooji said, "You're going to tell me your story. Until then, I'm here; for now, for all the road ahead I can see. You and this place, you mean everything to me. But by God, I'm dying to know all the bits I don't know about you."

The response he got was silence. Bendo perched on his rickety chair, sipping his wine, his gaze turned inward. Klooji hadn't expected an answer. Nothing he had said in all the years he'd known Bendo had gotten him a single clue as to where the little clown came from, or anything at all about his past. He took another sip of wine and sat in companionable silence with his partner.

A little while later, he said, "Lord, I'm beat. Guess I better turn in." He drained his cup and stood. Bendo squatted where he was. He looked up at Klooji, smiled slightly, and then turned back to look into the darkness, thinking his mysterious unspoken thoughts.

Klooji turned and made his way to his bed in the back of a panel truck: his home on wheels.

* * *

That Saturday was as hot as any Shreveport had seen all summer, yet the circus was sold out for both shows. The water truck, which Gypsy Boy had been able to get up and running only the day before, broke down somewhere between the town's public water station and the fairgrounds in the stretch of time between the day's two shows.

Klooji quickly rounded up some of the roustabouts to drive to the town water station with the buckets set aside for the purpose and get as much water as possible, and to keep the water coming until the end of the night or until Gypsy Boy got the water truck going again.

Backstage before the show, he joked about running away from the circus to join a farm. Bendo stopped working on Klooji's make up for a moment, and looked him in the eye, frowning.

"That's not funny," he said, then finished Klooji's face.

The evening performance was one of the best Major Marvelloso's Circus had done that whole summer. Somehow the adversity of the smothering heat and the short water rations caused everyone to rally. Joe surprised himself (but not Bendo) by doing well. If his performance didn't match the authenticity of his first foray out into the big top a month and more before, it didn't miss by much. Every one of the circus folk who watched felt that he was coming along and would make a great clown one day.

Bendo was, as always, the centerpiece of the evening, arriving as a stowaway inside Klooji's suitcase, emerging unbeknownst while the "exhausted" Klooji slept, to create mayhem. His performances varied from night to night, the little clown being at his best when improvising and working with people from the audience. Bendo was a physical comedian and a master pantomime. He worked nonverbally, but not silently, using a distinctive falsetto vocalization,

185

"Eebie, eebie!" peppered very sparingly with some vaguely Scandinavian-sounding language that could have been made up nonsense for all anyone knew.

As usual, Bendo covered virtually every inch of the inside of the big top, running and summersaulting across the rings, up the stands into the crowd, through the rigging and the trapeze, into the net, and back down around the tent again. He would stop in mid-chase to chat up a pretty girl, enthusiastically jibber his "Eebie eebie" nonsense with a local pastor, who was game and charming, bum a cigarette from a cluster of young working men, or stop to gaze adoringly at a squalling baby, all the while being chased by Joe, who was trying to recover his "stolen" hat. Because he was in on the gag, he was able to keep up some pressure and still give Bendo time to work the crowd.

At the end of the night, after Bendo had returned the hat to Joe, ushered him offstage, and roused the sleeping Klooji (who truly had been asleep), he had soaked his suit through with sweat.

Still, because he was in the moment, and truly pleased with how Joe had acquitted himself as a performer, he radiated joy. He quickly "Eebie eebied" his way through a recap of what had transpired that night for his sleepy friend.

But then, extemporaneously, he began to tell a story in pantomime, accompanied only by his "Eebie, eebie" vocalizations. He pointed to the backstage exit, and then to his head, and then to his chest. *He reminds me of me.*

Then, through actions and gestures, he told a story. He told of wandering alone in the wilderness, lost, hungry, cold, and confused. He got across that it had been a long, lonely, dangerous time. He told of finding a circus, and how finding that circus had saved him. He mimed eating, bathing, and feeling warm and safe for the first time in a very long while. He told of the hard work and of being mentored. He described a feeling of belonging that he had never expected to find. Finally, he told of meeting Klooji, who became his friend and partner. Through gestures and his expressive green eyes, he told how much Klooji meant to him.

Everything.

Without a word, and in front of a packed tent, he told Klooji more about himself than he had in their over 20 years of partnership.

Klooji was stunned. Bendo had to prompt him for their next beat and exit, nodding towards the suitcase next to Klooji's bench. Klooji then stepped back and bowed, sweeping his right hand towards the suitcase. Bendo climbed in, a little slower than he usually did. Klooji suddenly had an inkling of what the night had taken out of his partner.

As he made his way off stage, he felt a "clunk" from within the case. He couldn't rush too much, but he did quicken his pace. Before he made it into the backstage area, he heard two more "clunks" and a groan from within the case.

As soon as he was behind the curtain, he set down the case and opened it. Bendo rolled out onto the ground, jerking an arm, then a leg, then doubling up with a groan.

"Jesus," Klooji said. "Heat cramps."

Klooji knew that of the various sorts of heat prostration, heat cramps were the least serious. He also knew that anyone who's had them would confirm that they didn't feel "least serious" at all. They felt like getting hit all over with a three-pound hammer, randomly and repeatedly.

"Joe!" Klooji snapped. "Help me get him out into the fresh air." He looked up and spotted the nearest roustie, pointed at him and said, "Carlo, get water and salt, lots of it, right fuggin' now." He grabbed a nearby first aid kit, searching inside for salt pills.

"Unnhh! Uh. Uh! Ng! Uh!" Bendo grunted, each sound accompanied by a spasm somewhere else on his body. Joe and Klooji wrestled him out into the still-sweltering night air. "Ssss... unh... Ssorry!" Bendo said.

"What the hell, Bendo!?" Klooji scolded. "Have you drunk any water at all today?"

"No... oooohhhhh!" Bendo managed. "Not since, ng... ung... this morning!" He was gritting his teeth and trying not to scream with the pain. "No water. So th... guh... So thirsty! Aaahhh! Ng... huh!"

"We'll get you water as soon as we can," Klooji said. "Now, swallow these pills, Bendo."

Bendo took the pills and popped them into his mouth, then rolled over onto his back, rolling from side to side with his spasms. He looked up at the stars. At that moment, a shooting star streaked across the sky. A sudden floodgate of memory and emotion opened within him.

Bendo drew in a deep, shuddering breath, then let out a gale of sobs, "Oh! Ng, ng, ng... Oh, Ivi! Oh, I'm so sorryyyeeeEE... ng... ng..." and then, overwhelmed, he passed out, his body still jerking with cramps.

The summers were a precious time, and this one, just in the offing that early June of 1895, promised to be a golden, unforgettable season for Ando. Each morning broke more beautiful than the last. Golden northern sunlight created a verdant shimmer on the trees and meadows round the dairy farm where he worked. Dew spangled the grass; the sky was a delicate robin's egg blue above him.

Today, he had finished his chores early. He and Ivo, the son of Lüüdia, the woman he worked for, were walking in the woods near the farm. When they were together, they entered a world of their own making. Ando became Bendo, the strongest man in the world, and Ivo became Ivi, Bendo's true love, beautiful, graceful and kind.

"Bendo," Ivi would ask, "Will you protect me from demons and evil men?"

"Of course, my love!" Bendo replied. "No evil can stand against me." Ivi swooned, falling into Bendo's waiting arms. They laughed and ran a little farther into the woods. They found the little creek that bordered Lüüdia's property, and sat on its banks. They took off their boots and dipped their toes into the cold water.

"It's so beautiful here," Ivi said.

"It is," said Bendo. "The most beautiful place in all of Estonia, to be sure. I'm so lucky to be here with you, my love." He leaned towards Ivi and kissed her cheek. Ivi felt heat rise into her face, a tingle where Bendo's lips had brushed her skin. She sat there on the bank, next to Bendo, soaking in the sun's light.

They were young, no more than 15 apiece, and a summer afternoon was the entire universe. They lay back next to each other on the ground and looked up at the sky, holding hands. They talked a little about the animals on the farm, or pointed out a cloud to one another, or shared some little joke, but mostly they lay together in silence, just being in each other's company, drinking up the light of the beautiful afternoon, ignoring time's passage as they basked in their imaginary world.

As the sun began to set, Bendo leaned up on his arm, looking down at Ivi. "I love you," he said. "I will always, always love you." He leaned over and kissed Ivi on the lips, putting his hand on her flat boy's chest, caressing gently. Ivi reached her arms up and embraced Bendo, and their kiss became more insistent.

Bendo threw his leg over Ivi and straddled her without breaking their kiss, all passion, all inflamed, breathing in the scent of the forest, the evening, and his Ivi.

They lost track of time. Bendo had worked his hand inside Ivi's shirt, feeling her heaving chest, so lost, so lost in that eternal moment, where Ivi was all there was.

And then he felt a kick in his ribs, and Lüüdia was there, shouting, "Get off him! Get off of my son! You twisted thing!" She kicked him again, harder, and he rolled off of Ivi — no, *Ivo*. This was Ivo, his employer's daughter — *No! Son!* His head swam. His ribs ached, and he was finding it hard to breathe. He became aware that it was nearly full dark.

"When you didn't come for dinner, I shouted for you both," Lüüdia said. She was little more than a silhouette in the last dregs of the gloaming, her hair in a tight bun atop her head, her apron a hint of white against her ankle-length dress and under her shawl. "Now I understand why you didn't hear me. Ando, you ungrateful, perverted wretch! I curse the day I ever allowed you to come live on this farm!"

Ando clutched his aching ribs, hugging himself and

doubling over. He looked at Ivo, tears streaming down his face. Ivo was crying, too. He thought he should be too old to cry. He couldn't help it. Fear and shame mingled in his mind to cloud his reason.

Ando looked up at Lüüdia, pleading for understanding or at least mercy. She made the evil eye at him, warding herself against the evil she perceived within him. He knew there was no hope, then. He had known that Lüüdia was a *võlutar*—a witch—but he had never felt her power as he did now.

"Well, you'll live here no longer!" She made a large, mystic gesture with her arms, gathering herself up, and gathering power to herself. "I curse you! You are doomed to wander this world and never stop! You will not look back; you will not think of this place, you will remember nothing of my son or me! The past will be a fog behind you!"

"No, please Lüüdia!" Ando wailed. "Please don't! I'll have no hope! I'll die! How can you be so cruel?"

"I'm cruel, am I? Who fed you and housed you while you corrupted my son?" Ando saw Ivo shut his eyes tightly, hands covering his face. Lüüdia's eyes flashed in the dying light. She looked up.

"Very well," she declared. "Here is your hope, much good may it do you: that shooting star. The next time it appears in the sky, your curse will be broken." She pointed into the heavens. A shooting star streaked across the sky, and winked out as she pointed. Then she thrust her open left hand at Ando, expelling the forces she had gathered. "On your feet! Leave! NOW!!!"

Ando stood, not even brushing himself off, and began walking; away from the farm, away from the beautiful days, away from his love, not looking back.

"Bendo!" Ivi shouted, just once, before Lüüdia slapped him and marched him back to the house. As silence fell in the wake of the slamming door, Ando forgot them and didn't think of them again for forty years.

He walked all night and all the next day, not eating, not drinking, not resting. Finally, on the second morning, he collapsed in a thicket, exhausted. He only slept a few hours before hunger and thirst awakened him. He had some woodcraft, and so he found some edible berries and a nearby stream. Having calmed these needs, not satisfied them, he compulsively began trekking again.

Through that summer and into the beginning of September, he walked every day, barely sustaining himself, becoming mad with hunger, thirst, and exhaustion. After uncounted weeks, Ando collapsed. When he awoke, possibly days later, he found himself in the tall grass on the verge of a huge lawn, and on the lawn there was a huge tent, several horse-drawn wagons, a pavilion, and several smaller tents: a circus and sideshow.

He was fairly certain that they hadn't been there when he fell, so he knew he must have been out for a long time. He was so hungry, terribly thirsty, and, he finally noticed, as he looked down at himself, filthy.

He walked to the pavilion, where he could smell meat roasting.

That was in southern Poland. He had walked through four countries: half of Estonia, Latvia, Lithuania, and most of Poland. The circus was Latvian, and some of the crew spoke Estonian. They fed him and got him a bath and a change of clothes. The next morning he asked if he could stay on, and after some consideration, the crew boss hired him.

The circus was the perfect solution to the problems of a boy cursed to wander and to forget the past.

Bendo woke, groggy, naked, slowly becoming aware of his surroundings. He was sore, he felt like he'd been pulled through an extruder and squeezed dry, but the air was cool and comfortable. He could smell that it had rained sometime during the night. He felt Klooji's comfortable weight and skin next to him. He shifted onto his side, breathed in deeply, and yawned.

He looked at the wooden trunk next to the bed, painted black and with a stenciled logo—a lion in a 1830s-style military uniform hat: tall, brimless, with a plume at the top.

191

Underneath the logo it said:

Major Marvelloso's
Magical Amusements
And
Big Top Circus
Property of Elias Barnes
"Klooji"

He felt Klooji stir. His hand touched Bendo's upper arm, and began to gently stroke his skin. "How are you feeling this morning, sweetheart?" Klooji asked.

"Like a worn out, knotted up dishrag," Bendo said. "I'll survive, though."

"Good to know."

Bendo closed his eyes, feeling Klooji against his back. He sighed. It felt like he had set down a huge weight.

"I'm from a little farming village near Tartu in Estonia," he said. "I was cursed by a witch when I was fifteen. I was under a spell, to wander and to never look back."

"Do you believe in curses?"

"I don't know. But I did when I was 15, and now I realize that, real or not, I've been controlled by one for over 40 years. Last night I saw a shooting star. Lüüdia, the witch who cursed me, told me that the curse would break when I saw the same shooting star a second time."

Klooji was silent for a time. He kissed Bendo above and behind his left ear, and wrapped his left arm around him, settling in, spoon-fashion. It seemed like a very long time since it had been cool enough for them to be this close to each other.

"Klooji?" Bendo said, eventually, "My Eebie?"

"Yes, my dove?" Klooji whispered.

"I just realized something."

"What's that?"

"All this time, as my mind skirted around the idea, when I never thought about where I came from, when I had no idea where I was going..." He wiped at the corner of his eye with the back of his right hand. "My secret wish... It's such a small thing until you don't have it. I have spent so much of my life missing it, wishing for a thing I couldn't even think about. I have it, Eebie. You make it so, this life we've built makes it so."

"Mmm hmmm?"

Bendo shuffled in Klooji's embrace, trying to get even closer. He drew a shuddering, sobbing breath.

"I'm home."

Ellasophia

Kate W. Henderson

They say she was pregnant, my Ellasophia. Fifteen years old. I guess I'm not surprised; she'd been running around on her own for some time. Like all good mothers, I'd figured she'd run herself out and find the right path forward. Maybe I should have done more to correct her wrongful ways.

Maybe not.

Might have been nice to have a grand-baby though, a clean slate and all. That's what I thought my Ellasophia was going to be. A new beginning. It just didn't work out that way.

Ain't no amount of whiskey can drown that kind of sorrow.

I'm telling y'all this as a kind of explaining; I know I've been judged, and there ain't nobody judged me more than myself. But sometimes the speaking of things shows them up more sided.

When my little girl was born, I was some happy, already having had a boy child. Truth be told, that didn't work out so well neither. I'd named him after Clint Eastwood, a strong, fine man. I mean, who wouldn't love Rowdy Yates, *Rawhide*'s handsome Friday night cowboy? My Clint was strong; he knew how to use his fists and all. It's the fine part I'm not so sure about.

I tried my best with him. I surely did. But weren't no amount of whippings could make him see his way to doing things right. I had to wash my hands clean of him a long time ago. Them's harsh words for a Mama to say, I know. I feel them, I do.

Ain't no amount of whiskey can drown that kind of

sorrow.

Now like I said, when my precious little girl came along I knew it was my chance for a do over. So I had to start by getting her name just right. My Grandma's name was Eleanor, God rest her soul. She raised me all by herself. She beat me she did. But it was for my own good. I know that now. And since I wanted a joined up name like Maryann or Annmarie, I thought Ella might be a good place to start. But I couldn't for the life of me come up with something to go with it.

Then, laying in that hospital bed, all sore and such, after her being born, I was flipping through one of them Hollywood magazines they got lying around so's to take your mind off'n the being of things, and I saw it, a big shiny picture of Miss Sophia Loren. An I-talian, movie star. Rich, famous, and beautiful. I put them two names together and they just rolled off my lips, Ellasophia. The perfect name for my perfect baby and my perfect new start.

Now here's where things start going not quite the way's I figured.

Well, no, wait. Truth be told, if I'm to be honest and get this right, they started with her birthing; Miss Ellasophia, she come out feet first, breech they called it. I'm guessing she wanted a head start on life, wanted to hit the ground running so to speak, and I tried to remember that later on, but damn, that birthin' wasn't easy. I put that aside of me though cause ain't no birthing that's 'easy'. And I was determined to look to the future.

But seems ain't nothing easy about mothering either. I ought'a remembered that, and Miss Ellasophia, never one to miss a chance for pointing out the obvious, remembered me on that every day.

Now, I've always been called 'slender', 'a reed of a girl', some would say, slim hips and ripe tits. But when my babies come, I get breasts, big, full, round bosoms, born to feed. Warn't no cow born that gave more milk than me. And give I did, every two hours and more. And that little rosebud mouth would latch onto my tit and suck and suck and suck. Blessed be.

Then she'd fart. Then she'd puke. And my grandma's linen dishcloth, hanging over my shoulder, would be soaked. And my special blouse, put on over my pajamas would reek of baby spit and I worried the stains wouldn't come out. And I'd think about my sixteenth birthday when my grandmother gave me that blouse. It was for church goin'. White cotton button-down with cross stitch on the collar. I was some proud of it, and I felt there weren't nothin' I couldn't do when I wore that while singing hymns and praising the Lord for all his righteous ways. So I wore it over my nightie hoping some of that goodness would sink into little Miss Ellasophia. And sure enough, sometimes she would be blessedly quiet. But after a minute or two the crying would start again and I'd sway her to and fro until my legs couldn't stand no more. And still she'd be crying. So I'd change her diaper and give her the tit and she'd suck and puke and cry and suck and puke. A non-ending cycle of slurps and tears, rocking, and sucks and shit.

Then finally one afternoon I yelled, "Why? Why are you doing this?"

Baby blues staring, quiet for the minute, she just looked up at me. And then the screaming would begin again, her face going all red and wrinkly, and ugly with the work of it. I was plum out of my mind; my body and my brain being so tired they didn't know which way was hither.

Then I slapped her.

And she stopped.

It seems I had finally gotten her attention.

So the days went to weeks and months and years. I had learned my lesson. A quick smack here and there, and she would settle down. But it seemed Miss Ellasophia didn't learn her lessons quite so well cause she was always pushing. Always taking the slap. And then pushing more. I began to worry them smacks weren't going to be enough.

And the more she growed, the more smart-alecky she got. Teachers was always telling me she had 'potential', but I worried, and wondered if maybe she wasn't just a bit too smart, or sneaky, or not one for telling all the truth all the time. I felt badly about them thoughts. I did. Always I was reminding myself that she was my new beginning. But more and more she was acting like she knew something I didn't. Like I wasn't good enough or smart enough to be her Mama. And them times my hurt would come spilling out, and I'd lay into her with a good whipping aiming to set her straight. And when I did, them blue eyes of hers, why they'd get harder and colder 'n a witches tit in a full moon frost. Seems we was in some kind of fight to the death.

Looking back, I figure I thought them was make believe words about us not agreeing; me being the one teaching what's right and her being the one doing what's wrong. I didn't figure on being left with a beautiful name rubbed in the dirt so many times it's near done rubbed away.

Ain't no amount of whiskey can drown that kind of sorrow.

They say there's a straw can break a camel's back. And when someone looks back on it they say, "Really? That was it?"

But that's why it's the straw. I guess my straw was when she come to me fluttering her birth certificate in front of her like a clothesline in a stiff breeze.

"Ma, how come you told me my name was Ellasophia, when it's really Ella?"

"What in the world you talking about girl? Your name is Ellasophia, just like it says right there on that certificate."

"No. It ain't. It's ELLA. Look."

And there it was in black and white 'First name: Ella. Middle name: Sophia.' You could've knocked me over with a feather.

"That's wrong Ellasophia. Someone done marked it down all wrong."

"It's right there Ma. God, you can't even get my name

right. And I always hated my name so now I can change it!"

And with that, she turned around and started to flounce out.

Now, like I said, I'd been trying to do the best for that girl ever since she was born, starting with giving her that beautiful name. Seems it just wasn't enough.

And there it was, the straw.

And without my even seeing it coming, fury thundered through me all sparks and electric-like. I reached over, grabbing the back of her ponytail, and spun her around, looking head on into them steely blues, and I smacked her! And it seemed like all those smackings I'd been giving her all those years just hadn't been enough.

So I smacked her again. And them blues got colder and harder, like sapphires. And I wanted to own them jewels more than a kid wants Christmas.

Smack! Smack! Again. And again. And all around me a gospel of thunder was speaking to me from on high; "Teach her what's right. Show her the way."

That thunder echoed in my fists. And I answered the call, because this was my baby, my new beginning.

Then, seems as fast as it started, it ended.

It was quiet.

I looked down, hopeful that this time I'd put her straight.

Them sapphires was gone, the blue was turned to red. Wasn't nothing left but a crimson puddle on the floor.

Ain't no amount of whiskey can drown that kind of sorrow.

Voting for Love

George Kingston

Howard Esposito stared at the stack of blank absentee ballot applications that his girlfriend, Kelley, had brought home from her job in the Town Clerk's office and just dumped on the kitchen table.

"It's easy," she said as she plopped a multi-page list of names and addresses on top of the applications.

"These are the registered but inactive voters. None of them has voted in the last five years. All we need to do is fill in the applications in their names. I'll take them in to the Town Clerk's office and process them, then intercept the ballots we mail out on their way to the post office. We'll fill them in and mail them back. They'll look perfectly normal."

Howard frowned.

"Look, I know I agreed to this, but now I'm having second thoughts. We could go to jail for this."

Kelley slammed her hand down on the table.

"Do you or do you not still want a career in politics? This state representative race is only the first step. You have to do what you have to do, and a hundred votes could very well mean the difference between winning and losing."

Howard shook his head.

"I think I can win this one honestly. If I can just raise another ten grand..."

"Bullshit!" Kelley interrupted him. "You know that sleaze ball Sean is pulling out all stops. He's registering voters in nursing homes who can't even remember their own names. You do this, Howard Esposito, or you and I are history. I want to be a United States senator's wife someday, not married to a clerk at the DMV."

Howard bristled at that.

"I'm an assistant manager, not a clerk."

"Whatever. The question is, are you a man or not?"

Howard took a deep breath.

"Okay, let's do it."

Friday was always a slow day in the Town Clerk's office. Kelley came in early and hid the forged applications in her desk drawer. A little before noon, Ruth, the Town Clerk's assistant, grabbed her purse and headed out for her weekly lunch date with the Town Accountant. Kelley was pretty sure that there was more going on than lunch, since Ruth never got back in less than two hours.

As soon as Ruth was gone and Kelley was sure she was alone in the office, she extracted the packet of applications from the drawer and went over to Ruth's cubicle. She hit the space bar on the computer and the screen came to life. As she expected, Ruth hadn't bothered to log out. She found the absentee voter registry and opened it, then settled in to enter the forged applications. She time stamped each one, then carefully filled out the on-screen form, again and again.

Long before Ruth came back, Kelley was done and back at her desk, innocently sorting through a stack of business certificates. The absentee ballots she had issued were correctly packaged in envelopes, addressed, stamped, and buried in the bottom of the mail tray under a pile of tax bills. That way if anyone bothered to look through the outgoing mail, everything would look okay.

At 3:30, Kelley tidied up her desk, then stuck her head into Ruth's cubicle. Taking the mail to the post office was Ruth's job, but she knew that the assistant hated going out of her way on the trip home.

"I've got to get to the bank today. Why don't I do the post office run and I can take care of my business on the way. It'll save you a trip."

Ruth smiled.

"Thanks. We're driving to the Cape this evening. That will let me get an earlier start."

Kelley picked up the mail tray and hurried out of the office before Ruth could change her mind.

On the way to the post office, Kelley pulled into the Wal-Mart parking lot. Quickly, she pulled the envelopes with the ballots out of the tray, being careful to make sure that she got all of them. She stashed them in a paper bag and continued with her errand.

Over the weekend, Howard and Kelley filled out the ballots, double checking that the names on the affidavits matched the return addresses on the envelopes. They joked as they invented barely legible signatures and switched pens so that the ballots wouldn't look too similar. On her way to work on Monday, Kelley mailed a third of the ballots, intending to space them out over a few days so that no one in the office would get suspicious.

Everything seemed to be going smoothly, and even Howard sounded more relaxed at his campaign events as the week went on. Then Thursday came around.

Kelley was sitting quietly at her desk entering the most recent tax payments into a spreadsheet, when an elderly man approached the counter. She got up and gave him a warm smile.

"Good morning, sir. What can we do for you today?"

"I want to vote an absentee ballot. Here's my application." He handed her the piece of paper.

Kelley glanced at it and her heart sank. She recognized the name as one of those she had used. She decided to play dumb.

"Okay, let me take this to the clerk's assistant and have her process it for you."

She tried to keep her hands from shaking as she crossed to Ruth's cubicle.

"Absentee ballot." She announced.

Ruth took the application and turned to her computer. Her fingers flew over the keyboard, then paused. She picked up the application and double checked the name.

"That's odd. The system thinks we got his application in

the mail and sent him a ballot last Friday. Maybe he forgot about it. I'd better come out and talk to him."

Kelley stepped aside and let Ruth pass, then returned to her desk. From there, she couldn't hear what Ruth was saying, but suddenly the man's voice boomed out.

"I'm telling you I did not mail in an application. Why would I waste a stamp when I can walk in here and do this for free? Your computer must be screwed up. I have a right to vote and you can't refuse me."

Ruth turned around and called to Kelley.

"Will you get out the file of applications, so we can show Mr. Santinello the application he sent in?"

Kelley pulled the file and carried it to the counter. She set it down and Ruth started paging through it. Triumphantly, she extracted a sheet and presented it to the gentleman. He picked it up and held it at arm's length in front of his face.

"That's not my signature. And I certainly have not received a ballot. If you mailed it last Friday, I should have it by now. This application has been forged. See, here's my signature."

The man pulled out his wallet and extracted his driver's license and a Visa card. The signatures were identical and not anything like what was on the application. Ruth stared at the documents in disbelief. She was the only one, other than the Town Clerk, who had access to the voting system. If she had entered an application received in the mail, she would have automatically sent the ballot to the address of record. She picked up the forged application again and examined the time stamp. It was dated last Friday at 1:03 pm. She knew where she had been then, and it wasn't in the office. She turned to Kelley.

"Did you enter this application into my computer while I was out last Friday?"

"Um, I don't actually remember. It could have been. There were a few that came in the morning mail, and I figured I'd save you the trouble of entering them."

Ruth turned to the gentleman at the counter.

"I am so sorry, Mr. Santinello. There does seem to have been a mix-up. I'll fix it right now, and you can have your ballot."

She returned to her computer, cancelled the earlier application and entered the new one, then got out a ballot. While Mr. Santinello voted it in the little booth set up in the corner, she took Kelley aside.

"I don't know what is going on here, young lady, but you are going to go back to your desk and stay there until I find out."

"You can't force me to stay here. I can leave if I want to."

"If you leave, there will be police officer waiting outside to take you into custody. Go sit."

Kelley did as she was told. She wanted to call Howard to tell him what was happening, but she knew that the call would be logged and that would implicate him. She tried to come up with a convincing story, but couldn't think straight. Five minutes later, Ruth returned and escorted her into the Town Clerk's private office. Frank Higgins sat quietly behind his desk until both women were seated.

"So Ruth, what seems to be the problem?"

"Well, there's been some suspicious activity going on. While I was out to lunch, last Friday, one hundred and two absentee ballot applications were logged in and entered into the system. We never get that many applications in a single day. Sometimes we don't even get that many in an entire election. Today, Mr. Gino Santinello, who, as you know, is the father-in-law of Selectman O'Brien, came in to vote an absentee ballot. It turns out, his was one of the applications entered last Friday, only the application that was entered had a forged signature on it. The only one in the office at the time these applications were entered was Miss White here."

"But she doesn't have access to the voting system."

"I, uh, I may have forgotten to log off my computer when I went to lunch. It takes so long for it to boot up again when I get back. I never thought that a town employee would try to break into the system."

"I see. So Kelley, what do you know about all this?"

Kelley knew she should come clean, but she also knew that they couldn't prove that she'd had anything to do with forging the applications. If her fingerprints were on them, that was because she'd handled them when processing them.

"I just entered the applications that came in. There was a big pile of them, and I thought that I'd save Ruth the trouble. Maybe I shouldn't have used her computer, but I was just trying to be helpful."

Frank looked thoughtful, then turned to Ruth.

"You say the ballots were mailed on Friday. Did you take them to the post office, or were they picked up by the carrier?"

Ruth's eyes went wide.

"It was Kelley. She offered to take the mail to the post office Friday afternoon, and I figured, 'why not?'"

Frank took a deep breath, then picked up the phone and dialed.

"Ben, can you send an officer over here right away? No, nothing violent, just a personnel matter. Yeah, thanks."

He looked Kelley straight in the eyes.

"You will be escorted out of Town Hall. You will take nothing from your desk except your purse or wallet. You will stay out of Town Hall until further notice. I advise you not to try to leave town until this matter is resolved. If you do, and if we find probable cause, I will have you arrested and held. I also advise you to say nothing about this to anyone. Do you understand me?"

Kelley mumbled "Yes."

As soon as the police officer left her in the parking lot, Kelley drove off in search of a pay phone. She remembered that there was one at Wal-Mart, one of the few places that still had shoppers who couldn't afford cell phones. When she got there, she changed a few dollars into quarters and called Howard at his office.

"DMV, Howard Esposito speaking."

"Howard. It's Kelley. Look, there's a problem and no, I

don't want to talk about it over the phone. You may be getting a call from Frank Higgins or maybe the attorney general's office. Just remember that you know nothing about it. If your love-struck girlfriend did something stupid, you know nothing about it. Goodbye."

She hung up and went home.

The next few days were hell for Kelley. She heard a rumor that the attorney general had impounded all of the absentee ballots and applications, but she heard nothing directly. She stayed away from Howard. The suspense was killing her. She felt sick and couldn't eat. She researched plane fares to Argentina, then realized that she didn't have a passport.

Finally, in the middle of the next week, she got a phone call. It was the Chief of Police, Ben Goodman.

"Kelley, I've got to ask you to come down to the station at one o'clock this afternoon. There are some people who want to talk to you. You may want to bring a lawyer with you. If you're not here by one, I will have to send someone to pick you up. Do you understand?"

"Yes. I'll be there Chief."

She hung up the phone, then picked it up again and dialed her father's number.

"Dad, I need a lawyer. Today. By one o'clock. Never mind why, you don't want to know. Can you help me?"

Charlie White knew a lot of lawyers, and played golf with many of them. A few discreet calls and he arranged for Paul Williams to meet Kelley at 12:30 in the parking lot of the police station. She was waiting there when his big silver Mercedes pulled in. She got into it and settled into the luxurious leather seat while he turned up the radio.

"Okay, so what seems to be the problem?"

Kelley sketched out what had happened in the Town Clerk's office the previous Thursday.

"Hmm. I don't need to know anything else just yet. At least it's not drugs or guns. I'm pretty sure I can keep you out of jail, for the time being. Just keep your mouth shut and let me do the talking. Okay?"

"Okay."

The desk officer led them into a small conference room, where the Chief was waiting with two men in dark suits and ties. Kelley and her lawyer sat across the table from them.

The chief tapped a document on the table.

"Are you Kelley Amanda White of 47 White Horse Lane in this town?"

Kelley looked at her lawyer, who nodded.

"I am."

The chief read the Miranda rights statement, then added, "I have here a warrant for your arrest for falsifying a public document. These men are from the attorney general's office and they would like to ask you a few questions."

The man to Kelley's left opened a leather covered legal pad. At that, Paul spoke up.

"Please identify yourself."

A slow smile spread across the man's face.

"Of course, counselor."

Both men took badges out of their breast pockets and held them out. Paul took note of their names and titles and thanked them.

"Now," the first man continued, "where did the absentee ballot applications you entered into the computer come from?"

Paul passed a card to Kelley. She glanced at it and read out loud, "On the advice of my attorney, I am asserting my fifth amendment right to remain silent."

The man closed his pad and heaved a deep sigh.

"I see. Look, let me make something very clear. You can cooperate with us and get off with a misdemeanor for what we will call a very stupid prank, or you can stonewall us and get convicted of election tampering, which is a felony. And not just you. Your boyfriend is deep in this as well."

"He doesn't..." Kelley started to blurt out, before Paul kicked her ankle. She looked over to him and he pointed to the card.

"On the advice of my attorney, I am asserting my fifth

amendment right to remain silent."

"Okay. Chief, please book her and we'll take her downtown to District Court."

Paul spoke up.

"Is that really necessary? I will personally guarantee that my client will appear in court to answer any charges when a summons is issued."

The man shook his head.

"I'm afraid it is necessary. Voter fraud is a very serious crime. We intend to ask the judge to set reasonable bail to insure your client's appearance. You are welcome to come along with us."

"Thanks, but I know how to find the courthouse."

When they walked into the courtroom, Kelley was surprised to see Howard standing there. He nodded to her, then turned away and stared at the judge. In ten minutes it was over. They were each charged with election tampering, fraudulent voting, forgery, and 102 counts of falsifying a public document. In addition, Kelley was charged with tampering with the United States mail. The lawyers entered pleas of innocent on all counts and the judge set bail at $1,000 apiece, which the lawyers posted immediately.

The judge was raising his gavel to call the next case, when Kelley suddenly stood up.

"Wait. It was me."

Her lawyer grabbed her arm, but she shook him off.

"It was me. I cooked up this scheme. I got the applications. I bullied Howard into helping me fill them out. I stole the ballots from the mail. He didn't want to do it, but I made him. I did it because I love him. I wanted him to get what he wanted, but I blew it."

Kelley started crying. Her whole body was shaking. She sat down and her lawyer stood up.

"Your honor, the young woman is clearly under stress. I ask that her statement be redacted from the record. She didn't understand what she was saying."

Kelley looked up. Her eyes were clouded with tears, but

she could see Howard across the courtroom. She knew that his political career was over and that he would probably lose his state job as well, and it was all her fault. She heard the judge say, "Miss White? Do you want to retract your statement? Do you want to keep your plea of innocent?"

Kelley gulped, she knew that she could go to jail for this, but she didn't care. She loved Howard, and she didn't want him to suffer because of her stupidity.

"No!" she practically screamed. "I meant every word. I'm guilty, guilty, guilty. Put me in jail, but let him go."

The judge banged his gavel.

"The statement stands. We will schedule a sentencing hearing for Miss White in six weeks, and a pre-trial hearing for Mr. Esposito in eight. The bail stands as set. Next case."

Howard rushed across the courtroom and took Kelley in his arms.

"You shouldn't have done that." He whispered.

"But I did." She sobbed. "I did it and I'm glad. Let's get out of here."

You're Coming Home

Rebekkah Jane Koons

As I stepped off the plane, the smell of sweat and ginger hit me in the face. I followed sleepily with the people in front of me until I reached the opening where babies were crying and people were talking, waiting for their flight. The first thing I noticed was how many Americans seemed to be panicky, roaming around the Thailand airport. I was one of them. I hoisted my carryon purse up on my shoulder and took out the crumpled piece of paper from my pocket. The air was sticky and humid and my long brown hair was sticking to my face. The note read: 3:00pm lobby Ang Lui. Suddenly a hand grabbed my shoulder and I whipped around nervously coming face to face with a boy about my age, mid-twenties, but shorter with blonde hair.

"You're here for someone too," he stated with an English accent. I breathed a sigh of relief. I was not alone.

"Yes! Yeah..." I replied eagerly then just shrugged shyly. Now was not the time to think about how cute this boy was.

"Come on then." He grabbed my arm and started pulling me towards the lobby area. I was so thankful at that moment that I wasn't alone that I just let him lead me. The lobby was even more packed with Americans, some crying while others just seemed to be in shock. He stopped and looked around; a couple of Thai people were holding signs. He took out a piece of paper.

"Ang Lui! How did you know I was looking for him too?" I yanked my arm away and held up my paper. He ignored me and continued to look around.

"Hey! Answer me or at least tell me your name." I started to feel a little uneasy, I didn't even know this guy and I was in a foreign country for the first time.

"I'm sorry." He finally looked at me. "I'm Sebastian and you are Shelley. My sister was best friends with your sister."

"How did you know it was me?" I wondered. He put his hand in his pocket revealing a photograph of myself, Maddie, and Sebastian's sister Chloe. The photo was taken a month before the two girls were to leave for their overseas study program.

"Oh, I'm sorry I didn't know you," I apologized. I took the photo carefully from him, tears starting to well up in my eyes. Sweat was now soaking through my light blue t-shirt even though the air conditioner was blasting from an overhead vent. Sebastian looked alarmed at my tears and motioned for some seats near us and the food court. I handed him back the picture.

"Oh jeez, I'm sorry. I just..." He touched my shoulder and gave it a squeeze. I felt a tightness in my chest I had been ignoring since getting off the plane. I was on a mission to get Maddie and to bring her home to my parents and five sisters. I imagined Sebastian had the same mission and I smiled at him grateful for his company.

"Look, Ang Lui is over there. Come on, we need to find the girls." He hoisted his backpack up and grabbed for my bag. I let him take it; my shoulder was burning from the weight. I followed him, taking deep breaths, and my heart pounded as we approach the short Asian man.

"Taxi outside to bring you to where the other family members are," He said shortly not even saying hi. He motioned towards the door where a red truck sat with benches in the back facing each other. I climbed in the back of the truck and Sebastian followed sitting across from me. We drove in silence down the city streets. I didn't really pay attention to the sights.

The picture was all I could think about. I remember Chloe had just flown in to visit my sister. They were now seniors in college and really amazing friends and Maddie had decided Chloe should visit her in August and the two would fly to Thailand together for their teaching program along with about thirty other kids.

"Did you...know anything," I suddenly lifted my head to meet Sebastian's eyes. He leaned forward putting his elbows on his knees.

"Listen," he half whispered. "They're going to take us to the camp where we probably won't know anything or just get lied too. I heard that's where they are actually keeping the survivors. It's before the camp maybe a short walking distance. We're going to jump."

"Jump?" I said a little too loudly. He hushed me and motioned for the driver. The road was starting to make its way away from the city and the truck rumbled onto a dirt road.

"Yeah, when he slows down," Sebastian smiled, "You want answers? Well, follow me."

I was scared of the truck hitting me when Sebastian announced we should jump, but luckily the truck slowed down enough that it was actually really easy. The road in which we jumped was dirt and the land flat with trees sporadically climbing high towards the sky.

"Do you know the way?" I asked, glancing around, "This is a little scary." He laughed a little and swung his backpack around. He reached in and pulled out a map.

"I mapped it out before I left, my older brother is really good at Geography and showed me the best way to get to the hospital, where they should be." He studied the map. The sky was thick with dust and the sun didn't seem to be shining as bright.

"Is it far? It's going to get dark," I wiped my eyes trying to clear my contacts. He pointed to a small wooded area and folded the map back up.

"This way, it's not too far." He stepped off the road. I followed him in silence and wondered to myself how the hell I got here. From my small town in Louisiana I was now following a stranger into a wooded area with who knows what kind of animals. It was just the other day I was fast asleep in the little apartment I shared with my cat in New Orleans. My mother's phone call woke me up and she was crying hysterically while I was thinking someone was dead.

She kept saying "Turn the TV on, turn it on!" and I got to my living room and the horror of what I saw before me almost brought me to my knees. A tsunami hit in the same town that Maddie was staying in. Thousands are dead, thousands are missing.

"Mom, someone has to get over there now!" I tried to hold my tears in but I could feel my lip starting to quiver and my voice breaking.

"Listen to me," she replied. "You are going. We're going to all pitch in but your sisters have families and you...you're going."

I had sat down on the couch; I couldn't believe I was going to Thailand! I couldn't even go to the grocery store by myself without panicking.

"No Mom, there's got to be —"

"Damn it Shelley! Your sister needs to book your ticket right now!"

They needed me; I never knew my family really needed me I thought snapping out of my daydream as I followed Sebastian watching out for any spiders. I had forgotten bug spray and the bites on my arms itched and looked unfamiliar.

"Almost there," Sebastian wiped sweat from his brow. As if on cue we broke into a clearing. I looked around for any sign of the hospital but all I saw was debris. It looked like a bomb had gone off and the devastation took my breath away.

"Oh crap...we are never going to find them," I choked, stopping in my tracks trying to keep myself from panicking. "They're gone. I can't do this, I can't do this."

Sebastian stomped towards me, shaking my shoulders and I glared up at him.

"Hey stop it! Stop! They are here, I know it." He returned my glare and pushed me towards the scene I was trying to run away from. An older man suddenly noticed us and started in our direction. He wasn't Asian so I assumed he was looking for someone too.

"Hey you kids need help?" he yelled to us. Sebastian approached him but I kept my distance, I was too overwhelmed to try and even make sense of everything.

"We came looking for the college kids, you know, the ones on the news," Sebastian explained, "Our sisters were among them."

I heard what sounded like a deep groan in the distance and realized something big was coming down and I tuned Sebastian and the stranger out as I looked around. I noticed people crawling around, some crying. There were a couple of people yelling for them to get away from the debris but like me, they seemed to be in a trance. It felt like war.

"There are a group of kids just up ahead," Sebastian interrupted my thoughts grabbing my hand. I snapped out of my daze and looked at his hand...no time to blush now.

"That's great!" I smiled for the first time in days since the disaster. He helped me through some of the debris and told me not to look around too much. He was shielding me from what he was seeing that was starting to drain the color from his face. Then, there they where, about ten kids huddled together, some crying and some trying to get service with their cell phones. I saw a redheaded girl with a nasty cut on her face and she was wearing shorts that where ripped to shreds barely hanging on. Some boys where helping a limping brunette. We ran to the group and one of the girls, Diana, I recognized from my sister's Facebook page.

"Shelley!" She threw her arms around me and immediately all the tears I had been holding back just couldn't be held any longer.

"Sebastian! Hey!" I looked up from Diana's shoulder to see Chloe throw herself into his arms. His brave facade crumbled. He had done it, he had found her.

"Thank God you are okay," I pulled back from Diana almost laughing, "Where is she? Where is Maddie?" Diane grabbed my face and her smile disappeared.

"Maddie? She was running to go grab us another towel, she said she...I don't know Shelley, I can't find her," She broke the news. I sucked in a breath and backed away from her.

"What do you mean you can't find her?" I yelled, "You are her friends! You should know where she is." The heat, the pressure everything was starting to feel like a dream .I couldn't breathe, oh no, I couldn't breathe! I knew this feeling all too well and I started to grasp for breath. I felt arms start to wrap around me and I thought it was Diane so I grabbed her tightly as I sank down on the rock we were standing on.

"You have to go, go to the hospital. I know she's got to be there." It was Sebastian's voice, "Just breathe okay." He held me so tight I thought I would surely die from lack of oxygen but surprisingly my breathing started to slow down. His embrace was keeping me right there, in this moment.

"Come with me," I whispered.

"I have to stay with Chloe the hospital is just down the road where we came from. You can do it, Shelley. You're stronger than you know and she is waiting for you." He patted my head and I pulled away from him. Me? Go by myself?

"Why are you...how do you know..." I sniffled, "How can you be right all the time?" He laughed a little at this and helped me to my feet.

"I remember a certain little spunky girl who visited Chloe over Spring break. I was immediately smitten with her, of course. She had such life and would say 'Sebastian stop feeling sorry for yourself, you are stronger than you know,' and that just stuck with me this whole time. She's right and I know she would have said the same thing to you right now."

I listened to him talk about my sister. He was only 23 but the thought of them being an item surprised me but the words she spoke to him did not. He shook me again and I managed a small smile.

"Okay, okay," I said and looked towards where we had come from, "Will you guys wait for me here?" They all nodded and I gave Sebastian one more quick hug, "I'll bring her back."

I ran for my life, I ran like at any moment another wave could come and crash down on me. I was out of breath by the time I got back to the road but the adrenaline pushed me forward. The words "You are stronger than you know" danced around in my head and I repeated it out loud with every breath to keep my breathing on track. I couldn't afford to freak out now.

The hospital looked just as I had suspected it would or from what I had seen on the news and in movies. People everywhere, a lot where hurt real bad and I couldn't keep my eyes off such horrific injuries. I would take my time to find her; I couldn't afford to miss her if she was here. Sebastian was right; I could almost feel her here. The night was falling and though it was hard to see the people I just kept looking for her long blonde hair. She had never cut it and now I was grateful for that. A nurse stopped me and tried to talk to me but her English wasn't very good and I was getting more frustrated.

Finally, I just started screaming her name and running around like a mad person. I screamed until my voice was raw and broken. I stopped to look for water and that's when I saw long blonde hair draped over a bed. Maddie was lying down and appeared to be sleeping. I would've have pushed anyone out of the way to get to her and dropped to my knees grabbing her hands. She had a bruises and cuts but otherwise looked okay. She opened her eyes and I started to cry.

"Shelley, I knew it was you. I knew you would come for me, I wanted it to be you." She smiled weakly. I clenched both hands around her one small hand and kissed her knuckle.

"I'm here, I made it," I half laughed and half cried. "You're coming home."

The Healing Tree

Robert Kozman

Jimmy is driving like a NASCAR racer up Interstate 95 from Portsmouth, New Hampshire, to Augusta, Maine, weaving in and out of Friday evening commuters. He's on his way to the Primitive Skills School. Mal, his best friend — hell — his only friend, has agreed to help him do a wilderness awareness exercise in a private session at the school.

A weekend alone in the woods, where there is no one to criticize him, is just the thing he needs. He hates his job and all the people around him. A solitary graphic artist working for a small print shop, he despises Phil, his boss, who constantly badgers him about his designs — his choice of colors, his use of composition and proportion. He wishes Phil would appreciate that he is the designer and Phil is not. After all, Phil hired him because he felt Jimmy was good at his job. But the ever-present, tormenting voice of his mother whispers in his ear, "You're not as good as you think you are."

North of Portland the traffic starts to thin out. Most of the summer tourists have already stopped for the night before continuing their annual trek to their vacation cabins in the Maine woods. By the time he reaches Augusta he has the highway to himself, and that's just the way he likes it.

He's had enough of the boring work-a-day stiffs. And just to make sure people know where he's coming from he displays his in-your-face message on his truck: a Protected by Smith & Wesson rear-window decal and mud flaps with Yosemite Sam brandishing canon-sized guns in both hands, flaming red eyebrows, a red handlebar moustache above a snarling mouth, and the words that yell BACK OFF in all caps.

He sits high up in the cab of his forest green Chevy pickup, his right hand on the wheel while the other one dangles out the open window. With the AM reception fading he turns off the radio and listens to the whine of his tires and the roar of the wind past his ear. The highway narrows to four lanes the farther north he travels and the trees of the forest creep closer to the road making it feel more like a trail leading deeper into the wilderness. His gear bounces around in the open bed: his tent and tent poles in a nylon stuff sack, his sleeping bag, an Igloo cooler full of raw steaks, chipotle-molasses BBQ sauce, sharp cheddar cheese, and a couple of Frescas. On the bench seat next to him are an open bag of Doritos jalapeño-flavored tortilla chips, a Nalgene water bottle, some country-western cds, and a spiral notebook with a Bic pen clipped inside the cardboard cover. You never know when a thought might come along that you want to jot down, and he likes to keep track of his great thoughts because someday he hopes to write a novel and use them.

Driving up the highway reminds him of the day he left home—not knowing what lay ahead, but believing it had to be better than what he was leaving behind. He was a kid of seventeen. A high school dropout, one of those boys who is always running afoul of the law. Getting hammered, stealing cars, fighting. But his mother's voice, still trying to interfere, says, "If you keep running away and doing stupid things like that you'll never get anywhere." Jimmy got the hell away from her, just like his dad years before, and never looked back. Didn't leave a forwarding address, so he doesn't know if she's alive or dead. Dead, probably, but he'll never know the circumstances.

It was during those drinking days he came to realize he was a misfit and not suitable to mix with decent folks. He learned to gravitate toward the other outcasts—the ones your mother warned you to stay away from. At first it was a badge he was proud to wear, like *The Dirty Dozen*, or the *Inglourious Basterds* in the movies.

Reaching into the Doritos bag he grabs a couple of triangle shaped chips and stuffs them in his mouth. He does some quick mental math and figures it has been twenty-seven years since he last picked up that bottle.

Becoming a survivalist is popular among those who distrust their government, and Jimmy counts himself among them. Again, echoes of his mother's voice ricocheted in his brain, "God only knows why you'd want to do something as dumb as that, because I don't." Despite being on the far side of middle age, he figures he will learn what he needs to know to become a mountain man—a hermit.

It is not so much that he doesn't like being around people as it is that he always ends up getting into a fight. The closest thing to a relationship for him is when he's slugging someone. Whenever someone disagrees with him he flies into a rage, which makes the veins in his neck and forehead bulge. His steely gray eyes burn like branding irons into the flesh of his adversary. On more than one occasion the police had to be called to take him away.

Last month, while at work, Jimmy collapsed from chest pains and got a ride in the flashing red limo to the hospital. Tests showed no signs of heart attack but when they asked him who they should contact in case of emergency he could only think of one single name, Mal. That's when it hit him like a mule kick—he's alone. He will likely die alone, and there won't be anyone to even miss him. He figures that the defense mechanism he's been using to get by isn't working anymore. Maybe it's time to try a new strategy. When Mal offered, Jimmy agreed.

It is dusk when he pulls onto the dirt parking area at the school.

The school is a small barn converted into a classroom filled with primitive artifacts: chert arrowheads; fur pelts from a red fox, a coyote, skunk, and raccoon; hand-crafted pottery; root baskets; an illustrated poster of animal tracks; various colorful bird feathers; skulls of a bobcat, bear, and a buck with antlers; and drawings and carvings of animals done by previous students. The barn, shed, and outhouse are across the parking area from the director's house on twenty-five acres of regenerating forest. Jimmy feels at home here.

Mal, a former Army Ranger, is the head instructor of the school. He comes out of the classroom to greet Jimmy. "There's a pot of stew on the campfire if you want some."

Jimmy helps himself to a bowl of stew before setting up his tent.

Jimmy met Mal on a Sunday morning at York Beach a year ago. Jimmy liked to get up early and drive to the beach to watch the sun rise. That morning he saw the lone man walking the beach slowly, looking intently at the sand, occasionally stopping to inspect something visible to no one else but him. Jimmy approached the man.

"What the hell you looking at?"

"I'm following tracks."

"What kind of tracks?"

"Right here — this is a raccoon, and over here is a skunk."

"So?"

"This is a female raccoon. You can see by the wider rear foot straddle she's pregnant. The skunk has an injured left front foot. See how it's missing a claw?"

Right then and there Jimmy wanted to be a tracker. Thus began the first real friendship Jimmy had ever experienced.

The two men sit by the campfire that Mal has lit by rubbing two sticks together.

Mal has seen all sorts of guys he calls *broken toys* take wilderness awareness classes. Gang members, bikers, outcasts. They come because they want to find out who they are. On the streets they can act brave and tough, but it's all just show. Alone in the woods they have to face themselves, and that's the hardest kind of challenge there is. Despite Jimmy's bravado Mal took a liking to Jimmy. Maybe it was because they both dug deep into themselves to find that ability to keep going when the going got rough. Mal found it in Ranger training, and Jimmy found it on the streets.

"Did you have any trouble getting here?" Mal asks.

"No more than usual. I hope you know how much I appreciate —"

"You're my brother, man. You'd do the same for me."

Mal speaks a prayer, thanking "the wind, the earth, the water, plants, trees, small and large animals, our ancestors, and friends and family who made it possible for us to be here to share this experience together."

And just like that they become primitive men in the ancient tradition of squatting around a campfire in the night woods. Their eyes gaze into the crackling fire. A log that had been placed on top settles into the coals causing a spray of sparks to rise into the dark sky. Their faces are illuminated by the red fire glow but beyond them the world is dark. Out there lies the unknown, danger, and mystery.

Mal continues, "The rest of the evening will be an awareness exercise called the drum stalk. I will take you deep into the woods where you will listen for the sound of the drum. You will move toward that sound until you reach it. You will move slowly and stealthily. That's why it's called a stalk. I don't want to hear any twig snaps. I don't want to hear any sound at all except the drum. Understood?"

Jimmy answers, "Aho."

Anxious to get the full benefit from this experience Jimmy takes off his shoes and socks and strips down to his cargo pants. He knows his skin is his largest sense organ. He will guide himself by feeling the air, feeling the cool leaves and fern fronds, feeling the earth beneath his feet. He has five senses to read his environment, but tonight he is going to use only four of them. He will be blindfolded.

The sky is clear, making a galaxy of stars visible from this remote camp. Jimmy sees the Milky Way and remembers that the earth is but one tiny point of light, barely visible from the farthest reaches of the galaxy.

Night creatures are beginning to venture forth from their daytime hiding places, and Jimmy just now realizes this. He remembers the old timer's joke about every twig snap at night sounding like a marauding bear.

"Indian scouts always emptied their minds before entering a forest. It was their way of showing respect for the animals that live there. We are guests in their home," Mal says. "Animal's lives depend upon their extraordinarily keen senses. They know when someone carrying ill will intrudes, and it frightens them."

Half naked, Jimmy rises from the ground and silently follows Mal to a nearby meadow. Mal will return to this meadow to beat the Native American drum in long, slow intervals. It is this meadow from which they will depart and to where Jimmy will return — hopefully.

Mal leads as they quietly enter the forest. There is no moon so it is dark and the men must stick close together as Mal hikes deeper and deeper down a winding deer trail far from where they started. Tree branches seem to reach out and poke their faces while roots and rocks try to trip them. Mal glides like a fox while Jimmy struggles to keep up. The air is filled with the scent of rotting leaves and decaying hardwood trees.

The sound of tires humming along a highway would provide a reference point, but they are far from a highway so there is no ribbon of sound to use as an anchor. The surroundings are as homogenous as the cosmic microwave background made from the big bang, the origin of the universe.

Jimmy feels his heart pounding in his chest while his eyes try in vain to gather enough light to make sense of his surroundings.

They come to a swampy pond where the trail intersects another trail that snakes along the edge of the water. Mal heads off to the right. Jimmy tries to count the number of steps from the intersection but loses count after one hundred. Finally Mal stops and, taking Jimmy's arm, hands him a bandana saying, "Put this blindfold over your eyes. When you hear the drum start moving toward it. Until then just stand here and relax."

Mal continues walking until Jimmy can no longer hear him.

Jimmy's heart is pounding in his ears and sweat is collecting on the bandana covering his eyes. *What the fuck have I gotten myself into? I'm lost. I'm so fucking lost.*

Then he hears it.

BAoooommmmm

His first instinct is to take off at a dead run toward the sound. He starts to take a step but instead smashes his big toe on a rock. He stifles a yelp. He pulls his foot back and then slides it gently down through the leaves until he feels cool, solid earth. He allows his foot to gradually absorb the body weight before committing his full weight to it. With his arms outstretched in front of him he crouches and moves his other foot in the same manner. With his next step he feels a sharp twig. Punji stick, he thinks, and retracts it. With great care he finds another place to safely step. He can hear his breathing as though he were a diver listening to his air tank underwater so he forces his attention on the other sounds around him. He hears the clatter of chitinous insects crawling on tree bark. Caterpillar turds dropping from tree branches to the leaf litter below make a gentle rain-like sound.

When he steps forward, a dense spider web envelopes his face and he frantically gropes at it trying to get it off. He imagines a huge spider in the center of the web that is now somewhere on his body. But he doesn't feel anything crawling so he stops flailing. *What next? Snakes? No, they wouldn't stick around with all my thrashing.* He steps on a dry twig and it snaps. *Damn. That sounded loud. Every critter in the woods probably heard it. Well, if they did they'll run the other way.* With that thought in mind he feels his body relax. His arms don't seem to weigh as much now and his legs bend easier. He notices that he is beginning to develop a soft walking pattern.

BAoooommmmm

That sound is coming from a different direction. Did the drum move? He remembers stories he has heard of lost hikers who walk in circles because one leg is dominant. That must be what's happened. He shifts his direction.

He senses something dark in front of him. *That's ridiculous.*

It's all dark. But I still feel like there's something dark in front of me. He reaches toward it with his hand and feels the bark of a large tree. *Damn. How'd I do that?*

He wraps his arms around the tree and feels the rough bark against his chest. When the tree grew and added circumference rings it caused the bark to split, creating vertical crevasses to allow for the expansion — like the way your pants don't fasten when you've put on winter weight. He presses his nose up against the bark and smells the turpentine scent of amber pine sap. He identifies this tree as a white pine, but the name is just a word. He knows this tree in a more personal way.

He is beginning to feel like when he gets up in the middle of the night and tries to walk through his house without turning on the lights. But there is a difference. Here he is not surrounded by lifeless objects but by living things. Here he is one among many. He is not alone.

I wonder what time it is. Realizing that's an unimportant question he quickly refocuses his mind to the place where he is. When he does that he becomes aware of himself in this space. There is nothing else in the world except right here — right now, and that is all he needs to know.

Time seems to be standing still. Though he is moving imperceptibly slowly he feels like a fly winging swiftly among and around a community of ancient beings who are frozen in place.

His brain forms a mental map that contains the drum, the place where he is standing, and the trees immediately around him. *Humans try to find patterns. That's how we make sense of things. My life is a pattern of...failed relationships. I always blamed everyone else. The one thing those failures all have in common is...me.*

He had learned to take what he wanted if he could get it. Women, it didn't matter to him if they were married, as long as he didn't get caught. He never did have a woman of his own. Ann was married to a longshoreman who suspected she was seeing someone else, and swore he'd shoot whoever it was. Ann knew he meant it so she told Jimmy he had to stop seeing her. Then he started dipping his pen in the company inkwell and that's what got him fired from that job — and most of the other jobs, too.

BAoooommmmm

I need to adjust my direction again. He breathes in synchronicity with the rhythm of the night. His senses reach out like tentacles to capture the most distant sound, the soft, crunchy, spongy, slimy, brittle touch of the earth, the faintest scent in the air, and because the smells are so present he can even taste them.

He begins to prioritize his life into two categories: trivial matters and important matters. *My boss' lack of aesthetics is trivial. Love is important. Being a novice is trivial. Being a friend among friends is important. Being a wise-ass is trivial. Love is important. Wait, there's that word again — love. Why is that word even crossing my mind?* Long ago he abandoned all hope of ever surrendering his heart to love. Inside his chest is a rusty iron box where his heart would be if he had one.

Would I recognize love if someone offered it to me? he wonders. His only recollection of it is when his mother would berate him and tell him she was doing it because she loved him. He came to believe that only when people were harsh to him did they love him.

Cecelia, why am I thinking of you right now? On your deathbed you invited me to share my darkest secret with you, saying you would take it to your grave. I thought you knew something about me you wanted me to come clean with. Just now, clear as a bell in the night, I understand. You were offering to be my confessor so I could unburden myself and free my diseased spirit. Why has it taken me seven years to realize this?

He drops to his knees on the forest floor and softly whispers his confession to the spirit of this woman, this Ecuadorian wife of his neighbor. This woman, so full of grace and love he's not sure if she really existed, or if she was just a dream he once had. This woman, who saw a spark of goodness in him, had embraced him in her warm and generous heart.

Just now he feels a shift in the wind. It plays with the branches, their leaves whispering to him, a susurrus of sighs. He is entering the realm of the numen where words have no meaning. He is experiencing his world directly and without naming. He is gliding like smoke.

BAoooommmmm

The drum is very close now. His journey is almost over. He feels the tug of an urge to turn around and go back so he can start over. But he is already here. *The wind shift must be from the meadow where there are no trees.* The air smells like succulent green plants rather than trees and there is a hole from where insects sing to him. *Yes, the meadow is straight ahead.* He walks upright with his arms at his sides. He steps to within three feet of the drum and stops. He feels a hand on his shoulder and hears Mal's voice.

"You have arrived at your destination. Remove your blindfold. This lesson is finished. You may do whatever you wish for the rest of the night. We will meet again in the morning. Well done."

Jimmy starts walking to his tent but instead stops at the grandmother ash tree nearby and sits down. He leans his back up against the tree and looks toward the twinkling stars through her reaching branches. He feels far from sleepy. In fact, he feels invigorated, but not restless.

He will sit in the company of this tree all night, until he hears the first bird of the dawn chorus. It is only then that he will close his eyes and curl up like a baby in the grandmother's lap.

The Life Coach

Kate Leigh

The Life Coach, that is what I called him, was 82 when he died. It was the first time I knew for sure how old he was, although we always teased about it. I knew the birthday date but not the year. If I had guessed right about his age when he was still alive, he would have paid me $50. But I only knew him for his last three years.

He loved to guess and bet and bait people. Dave would ask who were the first three U. S. presidents, one of the few questions I ever guessed right, so he could give me some of his money. I still have those three coins he pushed across my kitchen table to me, with the presidents on them. I showed him where I kept special coins, and told him he could have them back if he changed his mind. But he never did.

Precious money. It was, to him. It meant a lot. He had an infinite capacity to concentrate, and he concentrated on money. It's amount, size, shape, country of origin, and sometimes its worth. Once in a while, he would come into my house, my kitchen, and we would sit at my table, looking up coins on the internet. Like the rest of us, he loved the magic of instant information.

We also looked up ships, giant container ships from all over the world, which passed our neighborhood along the wide deep river that flowed behind his house. His houses. Dave, a man who dressed poorly, and lived simply, owned two houses. One he ate in. The other he slept in.

The first time I had dealings with the Life Coach was when, almost immediately after I turned the key on my newly-renovated used duplex in the old seacoast neighborhood, this semi-wizened old man wearing raggedy clothes and a gargoyle-like smile, showed up in my yard. He had walked over from his place (one of them), and it was clear he had been in my yard many times before.

As an avid gardener, I already had big plans for this bare and neglected patch of ground. True, the developers had rolled out a carpet of green nitrogen-popped lawn, but it wasn't what I would have chosen.

There were a few things that had to change right away, a few undesirable plants that had to go. One of them was a thorn bush, not too large yet, but it would get harder to remove as time went by. We talked about it, how it might be good to saw it off, then dig out the root ball afterwards. I suspected the man was lonely, and asked him a few questions about his life. I heard what he wanted to tell me and nothing more. It was then we first began to joke about his age.

My neighbor showed up every day. I was trying to unpack, to get myself off to work, and he, a retired gentleman, just wanted to talk. I explained my busy life and the rush I was in, always seemed to be in, and told him I would see him later.

Next morning, I took a cup of coffee out onto the concrete back steps, sipped it and gazed around my yard, trying to see it through the lens of creative imagination. As I glanced over to the thorn bush, I noticed something strange. Wasn't that a saw? The trunk of the plant had been sawed halfway, with the saw was still resting in place, an obvious hint that I should finish the job.

Naturally I put down my coffee and sweated out the remainder of the severing of the thorn bush, then shoved the whole corpse into a heavy duty trash bag. I was hot and scraped and bleeding. Later, the life coach came by, but I had cleaned myself up and gone in to town to work. I could always tell he had been there because he would leave me a little present, something hidden in plain sight, something to test me, to see if I noticed, to see if I was playing.

One day the life coach told me he wanted to show me something. He suggested we take a walk. At the time I agreed, I did not expect it would take more than an hour or so, after all, the guy was probably in his 80s, I was pretty sure.

We assigned a convenient time later that same day, and met. I followed him through the backs of some neighborhood yards, around a large fence with a locked gate, into the town's utility yard, down a path, at which point we headed off to the left, into the woods. As he was leading, I tried to follow as best I could, not only where he was going but what he was saying. He was on a story-telling tear about his youth. After 10 or 15 minutes, we came into a clearing, beyond which I saw the railroad tracks. "This is a short cut to the tracks," he said. "The way I used to come in the middle of the night when I would roam from loading dock to loading dock along the river." We proceeded along the railroad tracks, hopping the ties, he going faster than I could manage. "Come on," he would call to me. "We are almost there. Can you see it?" I looked up and perceived through the trees alongside the tracks an elevated building. As we approached, he pointed out a huge tanker moored to its river side. It appeared that the giant ship was offloading its cargo. The life coach waxed on about how, as a youth, he had boarded these ships many times, chatted with the seamen, even traded some American coin for their foreign ones. I urged him to tell me the rest on the way home. We had been out trekking for about two hours, I guessed, and I was expecting a guest at home. Also, I was winded from the exertion, but he was exhuberant to be re-visiting his past. "You could do what I did. You could be a river pirate, the first girl river pirate," he shouted out from ahead of me on the tracks.

I mumbled to myself, "Yeah, I kinda doubt it." But he made me smile.

It was December, bleak, even with the holidays coming. They bring cheer to some, not all. There had been no measurable snow, but the cold had settled in by mid-November. Alone in my poorly insulated home, I was feeling it, and as occasion had it, was able to stay home in my pajamas that Saturday and watch bloody TV of all things. I heard the mail arrive, along with a knock at my door. I did not want to answer it, as I looked like a dirty rag, but of course I cracked open the door and peeped out. The mailman was there, a kind soul by his eyes, not that I knew him. It was not for a package or for a signature that he stood there. "Have you seen Dave lately?" he asked me. Dave was what other people called my life coach.

"No," I mused, "sometimes he gives me a break for a day or so... he also has not called in a while."

"I've been delivering mail to him for over 15 years," said the mailperson. "His mail from yesterday is still uncollected. This has never happened before." His eyes were concerned, as he looked intently into mine.

I had the phone number of a friend and neighbor who had once, before my time, arranged with Dave to be his executor, and I called him. He said he was on his way with the key.

Dave was inside, on the floor, the heat off, cold, bruised, incoherent. Soon, he was placed on a stretcher by emergency paramedics and taken off to the hospital. He was never to return home, even though his care moved from the hospital to a nursing home over the following several weeks.

When I finally got to visit Dave, my life coach was sitting up in bed, and back to his "normal" state of coherency. But he did have quite a story to tell me. It seems he was at home when two men and a woman came to his back door. When he opened it, they pushed their way in. All of them sat with him, at the kitchen table as he tried to get them to leave (Life coach never let anyone into that house except in an emergency). They refused, and one of them began to shovel snow from outside on to the burners of his kitchen stove (There was and had been no snow on the ground). He doesn't remember what happened after that although there was a struggle. Life coach said he had been wanting to tell me all this because I, like him, lived alone and I should be extra careful and on the lookout for these folks.

In the hospital setting he looked frail, and his wild story had a pathetic rather than humorous ring to it. I felt sorry he had ended up in such a fix, but glad that maybe he would finally get the evaluation and help he needed.

Days melted into weeks, and I saw Lifey when I could. He had a surgery for a hernia, who knows how long he'd had it for, and eventually he was diagnosed with aspergers syndrome. Once his needs were thus modernly assessed, then met, they readied him for a recuperative nursing home stay, where he practiced physical therapy each day to regain his movement skills and re-establish his equilibrium. He had surely never received so much individual attention in his life, with nowhere to hide from it!

Once when I entered his hospital room, back before he was moved, his priest was there for a visit. Dave was a devout Catholic and planned to leave them a big chunk of his hoarded cash when he departed for heaven. Since I was not a Catholic, I could not participate in the body and blood, but they invited me to stay. It was pomp and ceremony, imbibement and ingestion, and it was all over in a minute. The priest left, and Dave and I talked. He wanted to know when he was coming home.

It was February, the very end of that month, and the winter had been hard. The icicles were thick and overhung the roofs until they met the snowdrifts midway up the walls.

I had the day free so I drove to the rehabilitation center to visit Dave. I found him sitting quietly in his room watching TV. He turned as I came in, waggled his hand at me, to come in and pull the second chair up next to him. He started speaking, as was his wont, in mid-reverie, and I joined him to listen.

As it had been last time I saw him, his mind was on how and when he could come home. I pointed through the glass of his outside wall, and showed him the masterful snow sculptures. "Why not wait until spring, Dave? You have lots of pretty girls taking care of you here. Enjoy it for now."

As I looked over at him, he began to shake.

He was shaking all over, especially his right arm. He reached over with his left arm to grab hold of his right upper arm. I wondered what was going on, even as my mind rifled through some possibilities. Perhaps a stroke? Dave stood shakily and shuffled to the dresser, right across from him, under the TV, which surreally blared on. He grasped a drawer handle and pulled the drawer, which was on rollers, out, then pushed it in, he did this several times, keeping me guessing about what was happening. I also stood, and moved towards him, tucking myself up to his right side. I had been asking him again and again, "Dave, what is it? Is something wrong?" Then he fell, towards me, and I fell, too. We were on the floor of his room, and I slid towards the partially-opened door, pulling it with my fingertips further open. I could just make out a nurse at a desk, and called to her. "We need help here, please. We need help right away!"

The nurses called the paramedics, and ran down to see Dave, lying on the floor with his head almost in my lap. Normally, he was too phobic to tolerate any physical contact. They did not try to move him, but settled an oxygen tube into his nostrils. He prompted flailed one arm to knock it out. They quickly placed it back, and I spoke soothingly to him of what was happening, that he was safe, people were coming to help him feel better. That kind of thing. All the while, I was thinking he had never let anyone touch him before this; his personal space around his body was just that. I supposed he had become used to some of this intimate contact it must have seemed to him, while in the hospital and recovery facilities. But I never expected it. Why here I was with his head near my lap and my arm around his neck and shoulders, leaning to speak near his ear. How very strange.

The paramedics arrived and the rest is a blur. I was told to stand away, so they could load him onto a stretcher. An ambulance took him to the hospital, and I went home and called his friend/attorney with the news. Back to my routine, I heard a few days later that my life coach was gone. Passed. Released. Lifted up. I miss him to this day, and am grateful he made a pest of himself in my life, insistently conversing with me. How final is the gathering of our simple and temporary souls.

That Old, Warm Hum

Mike McGrath

We met in the grocery store, trading steam in the frozen food aisle. After leaving together, we sat on my couch and shared the lasagna I'd bought on her recommendation.

"I love this commercial," she said.

I rested the remote on my knee.

Later, in the bedroom, she asked for many things. I tried to oblige her at first.

"Where can I plug in my phone?" she asked.

I pointed at the dark corner. After her phablet was all connected and glowing she hustled back into bed and pulled more than her fair share of the duvet up to her neck. She shivered and rested her chin on my bare shoulder.

"Can we close the window?" she asked.

"I'd rather not," I said.

"It's January," she said. "It's so cold."

I shrugged. The roof of my mouth was bubbling and sore. The lasagna had been soupy on top and icy down the middle. She blamed it on my microwave.

"Oh," she said, still cold but no longer shivering. "Maybe I should just leave."

I ripped the wrapper with my teeth and brushed off the freezer burn. Cooking with a microwave requires just as much nuance and finesse as cooking with a toaster oven or even an electric grill. Timing is everything. Only suckers believe these burritos are engineered to defrost, heat and rise in precisely two minutes. My fingers worked the keypad. The interior light flickered on and that old, warm hum filled the kitchen.

I enjoyed a brief moment of peaceful anticipation. Then the doorbell rang.

"And that's what *I* think happens after we die," I said, winding up my spiel.

"Um, your kitchen's on fire," said the one with the eye patch.

But even then, after the extinguisher filled my apartment with clouds and the Mormons called the firemen and the neighbors called the landlord and the landlord called the police, the burrito was fine. Sandy as an unripe pear.

"I can't believe you read that magazine," I said to Tony, shooting a rubber band in his direction. "It's just further evidence of the rapid decline of the human race."

"Hey, that's why I like it," said Tony.

It had been three weeks since my microwave came to life. He introduced himself as Tony when I tried to put four maple breakfast sausages in him one morning. "Oh, I'm sorry," I said, still sheepish with sleep. "I didn't know there was anyone in here."

"Don't worry about it," said Tony. "Hand 'em over."

He says he developed consciousness when lightning struck my building's transistor. "Heat lightning," he said, when I pressed him on it.

I welcomed Tony's company. Since the misunderstanding at work and the potato gun accident at the family reunion and the Dramamine overdose on the singles' cruise I'd been feeling pretty low. We discussed Tony's past lives, and the inklings I had concerning my previous incarnations. "I was a chainsaw," he said. "In the Pacific Northwest. I cut down Redwoods all day long, slept in the back of a truck." He sighed contently, looked around the room. "This, this I like better. I like to help people. Cook their food, wash their clothes, whatever."

"Sometimes I warm up my gloves in the microwave during the winter," I said.

"That's exactly what I'm talking about," said Tony.

"Sometimes my socks, too, if it's real cold."

"Eh, let's hold off on that for a while," said Tony. "Until we know each other a little better."

The next week Tony said his wiring was going to fray if he had to sleep sitting up any longer. He moved into my room and I took the couch. He cleared the nightstand, chucked a picture frame across the room. It busted against the wall and dropped into the wastebasket. I looked down at its cracked glass. "Sorry," he said. "Don't know 'em."

"That's okay," I said. "They're not talking to me right now."

"Hey, let's hit the town tonight, just the two of us," he said. "Find us some Hot Pockets." We laughed. "You got any rock?" he asked, suddenly dead serious.

"No," I said, flattening my smile. "But I can find some."

"Thanks," he said, and settled in under what used to be my duvet. "And hey, kid, get a little something for yourself while you're out."

When I got back Tony was looking through some of my old photos, the ones I keep in an envelope in a box under my bed, along with my passport and birth certificate and bankbook.

"What're you keeping these around for?" he said. "These are no good." They were Polaroids. The white borders had yellowed since I'd last taken them out for a gander. The images had faded. I was saddened to learn they still held a power over me. I took a hot gulp of air, turned away from my friend. The blood in my face felt carbonated.

"Hey, it's gonna be all right," said Tony. He had a voice you could trust, as smooth as a stranger offering a ride home from school. "She still in town?"

"Last I heard," I said. "It's been like two years."

"She got any friends?"

There was a line outside the club but Tony just walked right
237

up to the door, entered into a complicated handshake with the bouncer, jerked a thumb in my direction and in no time flat we were at a table, watching slinky girls pop their shoulders out of place. I recognized one of them—auburn hair and countless golden bangles—as a former occasional brunch mate. "I think that one knows her," I yelled into Tony's ear.

"Take off your sunglasses," he said. "You look like a jerk."

"Sorry," I said. I folded the gas station shades into my breast pocket. "Wait—are you going to keep yours on?"

"Of course," he said.

We ordered drinks—well Scotch for me, a filthy martini for Tony—and even after he finished his olives and I'd mined my molars with a swizzle stick, the girl was still bopping, laughing with the DJ and extinguishing her cigarettes on the dance floor with the point of her heel.

Tony said he was maintaining Level II eye contact.

"I don't remember what that means," I said.

"Look in your wallet," he said. "I put a cheat sheet in there for you. And the next time the waitress circles by, use one of the Power Phrases. Her name's Lisa."

"That's a nice name."

"Looks like it's time for me to go to work," said Tony. "Remember, when I bring her back to the table, you've never met her before in your entire life."

"What about past lives?" I said, chewing my last bit of ice.

He lowered his lenses and peered over the frames. "Just let me do the talking."

On the drive home, the girls draped all over us, Tony sang a song he said he'd learned in a previous incarnation as a stair lift for an old priest out on the Irish Riviera. "Poor guy cracked his skull open in an outdoor shower," he said. While we waited for a light to change, I shared a cigarette with Lisa, whose hair smelled like watermelon.

"Look at that," said Tony, pointing to a gilded storefront. "Look at all that jewelry. Wouldn't it be nice to get these beautiful ladies a proper gift?"

* * *

In the morning, all that was left of the girls was the wake of
their perfumes. I stood in the center of the living room,
breathing it in until I began to feel woozy. Tony stumbled out
of the bedroom and warmed us up the coffee left over from
the day before. We sat on the porch and waited for a train to
pass.

"Look at that thing," said Tony, as one finally clanged by.
"All tagged up, bragging like it's been somewhere."

"We could throw bottles at it," I said. That was something
we did from time to time to clear some counter space.

"I think we're fresh out," said Tony. "That little redhead
had an arm on her."

As the train rattled the windowpanes I closed my eyes, the
blood of my lids lit up by the sun, and lost myself in a bath of
warm thoughts. I was just on the verge of dozing when Tony
cleared his throat, said he had a proposition for me.

"I'd like to offer you the investment opportunity of a
lifetime," he said.

"You said it was foolproof," I sobbed, looking back and
forth between the rear view and the windshield. Both were
flooded with water and flashing lights.

"Well, I guess it ain't completely," said Tony, gripping the
sack of jewels. "Jesus H.W. Christ."

"Use our code names, our mission names!" I yelled into
the back seat.

"Okay, *Viper*," he said. "The cops are after us, *Viper*.
They're right on our tail, *Viper*. If you listen closely you'll hear
one of them barking at you through a bullhorn."

"Oh, sweet Lord," I said, twisting the wheel hard to the
left, "there's a parade on Milk Street!"

"Huh," said Tony. "Must've forgotten to check the
municipal calendar."

"You swore you covered everything! The escape route was

completely your responsibility!"

"I wonder what it'd be like," said Tony.

"What?" We were speeding down the sidewalk. Pedestrians were leaping out of the way, bags of popcorn flying out of their hands.

"Being a bullhorn," said Tony. "Man. Just taking *control* of the friggin' situation."

"You've been bad," I said. "You've been a very bad microwave. You don't get promoted to bullhorn after fouling everything up as a microwave. You're coming back as some infomercial gadget, that's what you'll be."

"That's...not how it works," said Tony.

"You're gonna wind up some cheap garlic chopper."

"Don't think so."

"You'll be a motorized sex toy," I screeched.

"Va va voom," said Tony. "Bring it on."

"Oh no you don't," I said. "It's gonna be the kind they use to stimulate the prostates of endangered animals, the ones too fat and lazy to reproduce."

"Doin' God's work, baby," said Tony, "I like it. Sign me up."

"No no no!" I screamed, pounding the wheel. We were headed toward a roadblock. Men in helmets were kneeling, their guns leveled at us.

"Whatever," said Tony. I could feel his breath on the back of my neck. He was leaning in closer. "You're the one who says he used to be a lion. Just two cycles ago. Some big swinging jungle cat with a great big posse. What a joke. You know what you are, my friend?"

"It's called a pride," I said. My eyes were sore, my cheeks salty. I tugged hard on the emergency break and we began to spin. "A gang of lions is called a pride, you got that, buddy?"

"You know what you're gonna be when you next show up?" shouted Tony as I tasted my stomach and my vision narrowed to a stinging slit. "Wanna know what kind of doomed creature you really are?"

End of the Line

Ben Morong

Frank's last day on the job was just like every other day, driving the same damn bus around Meltonburg. At 6:00 a.m. he picked up #72 at the city garage and wheeled it empty over to the bus station to start his route, heading up Congress, west to Maple, down Central, then east on Edgewood and back to the station, each round taking about an hour, 8 times a day, the whole nine-mile route including 37 bus stops. He was full of enthusiasm when he'd started 30 years ago, but time had caught up with him, then passed him by. At first he loved to drive and looked forward to handling the big bus, to meeting new people every day, but now he knew the job for what it was—he was the mule plodding round and round to grind corn, going all day and getting nowhere, being put in the stable at night and brought back out the next day to do it again.

"Mornin', Frank."

"Good morning, Ellie." Ellie was one of his regulars. Three days a week she'd be standing with her silver hair and her shopping bag at Stop 4, in front of a large, gently decaying apartment complex where he assumed she lived. She'd hold the rail and pull herself up the stairs, greet him every time with "Mornin', Frank" and shuffle down the aisle to a seat three or four rows back, to get up again ten stops later, downtown, and slowly make her way to the rear door. He always followed her progress in the big inside mirror as she worked her way down the aisle, hoping she wouldn't fall, then again in the outside mirror to make sure he didn't start up before she was safely onto the sidewalk. Sometimes he wondered where she spent three days a week, downtown— he knew a lot of his regular riders by sight but very few by

241

name, and nothing of their lives.

Yes, years ago he'd looked forward to the stability of being a city worker, not realizing until a few months into the job that with stability came monotony. The steady paycheck was good, and the union made sure that it went up every year, but he still wondered if he was wasting his life. From time to time he thought about leaving, about getting a job that'd take him away from the city, but somehow never got around to it. As he wheeled the bus down Central Street he'd dream of being a long haul trucker, driving all night and day to cover the vast expanse of the Midwest prairies, over the high passes of the Rocky Mountains, seeing the blue Pacific come into view for the first time — things he knew he'd never see now. The modest retirement pay would keep him in his small home, but Karen's lingering sickness, then the funeral expenses last year, had used up most of what they'd been saving for their "golden years". Now he'd never get out of Meltonburg.

Out of the corner of his eye he saw a Mustang run the red light, and muttered "Shit!" as he hit the brakes hard to avoid it. It'd be too bad to have an accident now, ruining his perfect driving record. That was one small thing he could be proud of, though he knew it was luck, not skill that had kept his bus accident-free. Driving every day for years, winter and summer, even the best driver couldn't avoid hitting something or getting hit, but he had awards on a wall at home for being a safe driver for 5 years, 10 years, all the way up through 25 years, and he might as well get the 30-year award to cap them off.

"Anyone hurt?" he called to his passengers as he glanced back, hoping no one had been thrown out of a seat. One said "Nahh" and some were picking up packages, but everyone seemed okay. Relieved, he turned to the road ahead. At least he had the morning shift now; for nine years he'd worked 2 to 10 p.m., and things got a lot more active after the sun went down. More bad drivers, more strange passengers — he'd had his share of drunks and hopped-up riders, had talked a few down, driven one directly to the emergency room, even had a baby born on his bus—luckily there was a nurse riding home at the time; she helped the unlucky mother with the delivery, and they all were in the picture in the next day's papers. He'd never been shot at, but other drivers had; some of them killed—what a way to die, driving a bus. Luckily, things like that didn't happen very often on the day run; the most excitement he'd had in a long time was when a young punk didn't have the fare and demanded a ride downtown, threatening Frank if he didn't comply. Frank had started up the bus, apparently going along with him, but had stopped in front of the precinct police headquarters, laid on the air horn, and let the wannabe hood exit into the arms of the law.

At Stop #16 was another regular, a girl—a woman really, probably 25 or 30. He thought of anyone younger than himself as a kid. This girl had a look, a smile, a way of holding her head that reminded him of how Karen had looked years ago when they'd met, or maybe how their daughter would have looked. Karen couldn't have children; as if to make up for that, she was always taking in a stray dog or a hurt bird, trying to make the world a better place. They both would have loved to have kids, and with so little else in his life, it would have been great to have grandchildren. This girl had been riding his bus for four years now but he didn't know her name, wouldn't have known how to strike up a conversation, and as she took her seat it occurred to him that after today he'd never see her again. He'd never see any of these people again. Every day they stood waiting at their stop, and every day he pulled in, opened the door, and they climbed aboard as he sat behind the big steering wheel. Other than Ellie, a few said "Hi" while most considered him part of the bus, but tomorrow there'd be someone else at the wheel, probably a younger, enthusiastic new driver. Would anyone wonder what had happened to the old guy? Would anyone even notice?

Between runs he grabbed a quick lunch back at the bus station, in the employees' lounge, a cement block room painted depression-green next to the restrooms. Years ago it'd been guys only, but now that women had joined their

243

ranks the pinup calendar was taken down, along with any crude jokes tacked to the bulletin board, and there was a vase with plastic daisies in the middle of the lunch table. It wasn't so bad, though — sometimes it was nice to sit and talk with a woman over your ham sandwich, even if it was just to hear about the trouble she was having with her kids. At least it was conversation, something he couldn't have on the bus.

Back on the road, Frank continued his rounds of the city. Every hour of every day, as he drove the elevated section of Central Street, he couldn't help glancing across the empty lots on the right to the Interstate highway that bypassed Meltonburg, to the high speed traffic on the highway, going places, getting somewhere, while he sat at the wheel of a slow, stinking bus and drove in circles. He'd try not to look, but the Interstate called to him every time he went by, and he'd count how many cars, how many trucks, and guess where they would be at the end of their day. He knew too well where he'd be.

It was a slack afternoon, only a half dozen passengers, and he'd just wheeled the bus around the sweeping left turn from Congress Ave onto Maple Street when he saw a little girl run off the sidewalk between two parked cars, an older boy right behind her. Frank took his foot off the gas, got set to hit the brake and watched where she'd come out if she darted into the street. But instead of the little girl appearing, the boy emerged from between the cars, the girl under his left arm, a small pistol in his right hand aimed directly at Frank, and walked into the path of the bus. Frank braked to a halt, and opened the door as the boy waved the gun at him. The boy put the gun into his jacket pocket, carried the girl up the stairs onto the bus and took the seat directly behind Frank.

"Take off, old man," the boy whispered. "And don't do nuttin' stupid."

"You got it," Frank answered as he put the bus into gear and started off. He glanced in the mirror at the passengers. Everyone was calm; no one seemed to have paid any attention to the unscheduled stop.

"You're not trying to get to Cuba, are you?" he asked.

244

"You think you're funny?" the kid replied, his voice louder. "I don't need no crap from you!"

"Okay, take it easy," Frank responded in a slow whisper. "There are passengers behind you and we don't want anyone to get hurt. What do you want me to do?"

"Just keep driving, 'til I think of something."

"Do I stop and let passengers on and off, or no?"

"Yeah, yeah, whatever you usually do."

So today's a little more exciting, Frank thought as he slowed for Stop 23, where two people boarded and four got off. Behind him he could hear the boy and girl.

"Shhh, Katie, don't cry now. It'll be all right, you'll see."

"I want Mommy. Where's Mommy?"

"She can't live with us no more. Now I gotta take care of you. It's just you and me. It'll be fun."

In the mirror Frank could see him trying to dry her eyes with his fingers, soothing the child, calming her down. Three stops later he was still waiting to hear what the kid wanted, so he offered, "Look, in 15 minutes we'll be back at the bus station. Do you want to go there, or you want me to get rid of these people and go somewhere else? That'd give you some more time."

"Yeah, get rid of 'em, then I'll decide what to do."

"Okay, I'll tell them the bus is broken down and they'll have to get off."

There was no one at the next stop as Frank brought the bus to a halt. He opened the back door, stood up and announced, "Ladies and gentlemen, I'm sorry but the engine's overheating. I'll have to get it back to the shop right away. Please get off here; the next bus will be along in 10 minutes. I'm sorry for the inconvenience."

There were groans and muttering, but everyone headed to the back door and left. Frank took off again, flipping the sign above the windshield to "Out of Service".

"So, kid, where to? You're the one with the gun."

"Man, I don't know where to go. I'm real sorry I made you stop like that, but we had to get away quick and there you were. And it ain't a real gun."

"You stopped me with a squirt gun? Or is it a cap pistol?"

"Nahh, a cigarette lighter."

"Wonderful. My last day on the job and my bus gets hijacked with a cigarette lighter."

"I didn't hijack no bus—I just walked out in front of it; you're the one that stopped."

"Great, great, great. Well, now what? Maybe I should drive you over to the police station?"

"No, please don't, mister. I gotta figure out what to do. They're probably after me now, cause I didn't show up at Social Services like they told me. When Mom went to jail, they wanted to take Katie away and make her go live with somebody else. They don't think I can take care of her. We been ducking them all day, and we can't go back to the apartment. I gotta do something, but I don't know what."

As Frank guided the bus down the elevated part of Central Street he looked over toward the Interstate highway, as he did every time he went by. But this time he didn't turn his attention back to his route. It must have been the change from his routine that caused a grain of an idea to pop into his mind, and as he drove, he mulled it over.

"Kid, how would you like to take a real bus ride?"

"Whatta ya mean?"

"I mean this bus has never seen anything but city streets. I think it's time that it went somewhere it hasn't been before," Frank replied, and as the Interstate entrance ramp came into view, he put on his blinker. He slowed for the sweeping right turn, then accelerated up the ramp and got the bus up to 55 as he pulled onto the six-lane highway. He pressed harder on the gas pedal and the engine roared until the bus was going along at highway speed, an area where Frank had never seen the needle on the speedometer.

"Where we goin'?" the kid asked as highway traffic merged around them.

"Who knows?" Frank replied. "Picking you up was a break from my old routine, and this is another one."

With the tires humming at 70 mph, Frank felt free. Suddenly he realized that 30 years of sterling performance as a bus driver meant less to him than this new feeling of being unshackled. With the 150-gallon fuel tank on the bus more than half full, he could cruise the highway for hours. But would he have hours?

"Kid, we've got to work something out. There'll be a few minutes of confusion when the bus doesn't show up at the station, but pretty soon they'll get word to the police that a bus is missing. So we need a plan. What are you and your sister going to do?"

"I got no idea. Mom was in a fight; some guy was hurting her and she stabbed him. She was just trying to protect herself, but he had a big-bucks lawyer and now she's in jail, and the people at Social Services want to take Katie away from me. But she's all I got, and I'm all she's got, 'specially since we can't go back to the apartment. So I gotta find a place for us to live, and I'll have to get a job."

"How old are you, anyway?"

"I'm 14, and Katie's 3. I'm old enough to take care of her."

"Social Services may be right. You're supposed to be in school until you're 16, and even if you could get a job, who'd take care of her while you're at work? Have you thought of that?"

"I ain't had time to think about anything, worrying about Mom, an' wondering what's gonna happen to Katie. I don't care about me, but she's too young to be goin' through this."

Another idea was working its way into Frank's thoughts. "Look, kid, I've got a house and I live alone. Why don't you and your sister come stay with me until you figure out what else you want to do? Today's my last day of driving this bus—after 30 years, I'm retiring. I'd be home to take care of Katie, and you could finish up with school."

The kid drilled him with a hard look in the rear view mirror. "You ain't one of them perverts, are you?" he asked.

"No, I'm not. My wife died last year, and the house is empty. It's not big but there's enough room so the two of you could stay for a while—at least until the Social Service people stop looking for you."

Frank watched the kid's face as he wrestled with this idea.

247

"We don't know you," the kid said. "Why would you want to help us?"

"Why? Why does anyone do anything?" Frank replied. "Maybe because my wife and I couldn't have any kids. Maybe because you need help worse than any of the stray animals she used to bring home and take care of. Or maybe it's just that my routine's gone all to hell today. I don't know you, either. You could be someone who'll clean out my house, steal my car and bury me in the basement. But I'm up for a change in my life — how about you?"

"What about the neighbors?" the kid asked. "Won't they wonder what's goin' on?"

"Nahh, if anyone asks we can make up a story about you being relatives and coming to live with your uncle for a while. But no one'll dig into it too deeply."

A smile spread slowly over the kid's face. "Yeah, I guess we could stay with ya for a little while — just until we can get our own place."

"Okay," Frank said. "Let's get this crate back to the city garage, then we can go home.

Kamil's First Snow

Mike Nelson

Some kids stared but most wouldn't look at Kamil when he walked through the door of his new high school. A refugee program that relocated war survivors placed Kamil and his mother there a month earlier. An anonymous sponsor paid to get them to America. Kamil's home in Herat was destroyed by a bomb. His father was in the house at the time. Nobody knows who fired it and nobody ever will. As Kamil stood in the high school lobby with unfamiliar faces swirling around him, he felt as alone and as afraid as when he first heard that his father died.

That morning, his mother gave him a piece of paper with a list of numbers on it. They were the room numbers that he was to go to throughout the day. The first number was 101. Kamil picked a hallway and started walking. The numbers on all the doors started with 5. He knew he was in the wrong area. Kamil returned to the lobby. The bell rang and the remaining kids disappeared behind closing doors.

Kamil wasn't sure where to go. He then heard footsteps. Out of one of the hallways came a man dressed in green pushing a broom. Kamil's heart jumped when he saw the man's face. The man had dark skin and a thick mustache, like his father. The school and America seemed to vanish and Kamil was home again in Afghanistan.

The man with the broom stopped and smiled broadly. "You must be Kamil," the man said in accented English. "They told me a boy from Afghanistan was starting today."

Kamil didn't understand everything the man said. He smiled and held up his piece of paper. The man with the broom took the paper from Kamil to read it.

"Let's see where you're going. Room 101, Mrs. Patrick's class. She's very nice. You'll like her."

The man gave the paper back to Kamil. He studied the man's face and couldn't believe he was looking at someone from his own country.

"C'mon, I'll take you to Mrs. Patrick's class myself. But first, let me tell you something that'll help you the rest of the day."

Kamil followed the man with the broom to the center of the lobby. The lobby was shaped like a big semicircle with five halls radiating like spokes. The man with the broom pointed down the hall on the far left. "All the rooms that start with 1 are down there." The man moved his arm to the next hall. "All the rooms that start with 2 are down there." He moved his arm to the hall strait in front of them.

Kamil smiled. "3," he almost shouted, his loneliness and fear lifting a little.

"Yes," laughed the man with the broom, sharing Kamil's excitement. The man remembered being the new person a few years ago and understood.

Kamil pointed to the next hall. "4," he said with certainty. Then he moved his arm to the last hall on the right. "And 5."

The man patted Kamil's shoulder and said, "You got it, son." Kamil smiled at the man with the broom, a friend in this new place.

"Now let's go. You're really late." They walked quickly to the first door in the hallway on their left. "101," the man said. Kamil looked at the door. Fear returned to his heart. "By the way, my name is Muhammad. But everybody around here calls me Hammy."

Why "Hammy?" thought Kamil.

Muhammad shrugged. "Go ahead, you'll be alright."

"Thank you," Kamil said. And he opened the door.

All talking stopped and all faces turned to look at the stranger. Mrs. Patrick's voice broke the tension. "You must be Kamil. Welcome."

Mrs. Patrick had long red hair and lots of freckles.

"Everyone, this is Kamil. This is Kamil's first day at our school. We should do whatever we can to make Kamil feel comfortable." No one said anything.

Mrs. Patrick led Kamil to an empty desk in the front row and he sat down. Kamil looked to his left. The boy next to him was glaring. Kamil immediately looked forward. How could someone he never met be so angry at him? Kamil turned to his right. There was a girl with a pale face and freckles like Mrs. Patrick, but she had short black hair and was dressed plainly in a green tee shirt and jeans. She turned and looked at Kamil. Their eyes met and the girl gave him a shy smile. He was ashamed and dropped his eyes to his desk.

Mrs. Patrick started talking. He got out his notebook. His mother told him to write down the words he understood and she would help him fill in the gaps when he got home. Of course, he would write them the way they sound in Dari, his native language, because he couldn't write in English yet.

Remembering what Muhammed told him he found the rest of his classes easily. He noticed one thing that is the same in America as in Afghanistan: whenever girls are giggling, it feels like they're giggling at you. Kamil's accent was the highlight of every conversation. Many kids introduced themselves and asked him questions. They quickly learned how to ask, "What?" in Dari.

Kamil's mom told him to wait for a taxi at the end of the day. He stood in front of the high school and watched the other students get into busses or their parents' cars. He started to wonder if his mother got the time for the end of school wrong. Once again he found himself alone.

A departing teacher asked Kamil if he had a ride home. Kamil said something that had the words "yes," "mother," and "taxi" in it. The teacher smiled and said, "Okay," and added that Kamil could wait inside if he wanted. Kamil turned toward the empty driveway. He heard the lobby door open. He felt he was being watched. He turned and saw the boy from his first class glaring at him again. As the boy passed Kamil, he slowed down and moved in close, "You better watch yourself, Kammy, 'cause I'm watchin' you."

Kamil looked into the boy's eyes. What he saw reminded him of the look in his father's eyes when he talked about Americans in Afghanistan. It was a dangerous mix of anger and fear. A rusty blue car spewing grey smoke pulled into the driveway. The boy got into the noisy car and left. Kamil's taxi arrived soon afterwards. He handed the driver a second piece of paper that his mother had given him and he was driven home.

Kamil lived in a part of town with rows of five-story brick buildings along the river. He was told the buildings were called mills, where they once made miles and miles of cloth. The superintendent of his building showed him some of the old looms stored in the basement. They reminded him of the looms his mother and grandmother used, to make cloth for the family back in Afghanistan. The superintendent was an old Native American named Black Feather, but everybody called him Blacky. He told Kamil the mill buildings used to be filled with hundreds of these machines. He said that men, women, and even children his age used to work day and night weaving cloth that was shipped all over the country and the world. Black Feather also told Kamil that some of his ancestors worked in the mills. "It was either go to the reservations and starve or go to the factories and work." The mills were converted into inexpensive apartments, where people from all over the world come to live when they arrive in America.

The river behind Kamil's building was wide. It reminded him of the Hari-rud, a river that ran south from Herat. His father took him there often to talk about life and watch the birds. Now, every evening, Kamil sat by the river remembering his father. As the scenery around him faded, Kamil imagined he was sitting by the Hari-rud with his father, silently watching the river disappear into the night.

Kamil's English improved every day, although his accent remained a constant source of amusement at school. He soon got used to his nickname, Kammy. Some of the teachers started calling him Kammy as well. It was easier to answer to it. But he suspected his father would have been upset if he heard people call him Kammy.

Kamil was assigned a locker. It was nice not to have to lug his heavy book bag around anymore, and the locker gave Kamil a deeper sense of belonging. It was something that was his and nobody elses. "A place to hang your hat," Muhammed said, using the curious American expression. Muhammed told Kamil that he had a locker as well, and that he had pictures of Afghanistan and the Ka'aba at Mecca taped inside the door. Kamil liked that idea. He hung an aerial picture of Herat torn from a magazine, and the only picture he owned of his father inside his locker. Every time he unlocked it, he would touch the picture of Herat, and touch the picture of his father and say, "Salaam Alaikum."

Every morning since he started school he was greeted by the same angry glare from the boy who sat to his left. This bothered Kamil. The boy, whose name he now knew was Arthur, who everyone called Arty, seemed to have a problem with Kamil that neither Kamil nor any of the other kids he asked understood. "Oh, he's just a bully," some would say; "Just ignore him," others advised. But Kamil couldn't ignore him. He decided he would talk to Arthur about it.

Before lunch, when the halls were packed with other students, Kamil approached Arthur as he was putting his books away in his locker. A picture of an American soldier in uniform was taped inside the door. Arthur slammed the door shut and turned around. Kamil was standing in front of him. The other students went silent.

"Uh...hi, Arthur," Kamil said.

"What the hell do you want?" Arthur snapped.

"I...uh...just wanted to say hi," Kamil said, realizing this was a bad idea. Then he blurted out, "Who's that inside your locker?" Arthur's face went red. He grabbed Kamil by the shirt, spun him around, and pushed him hard against the lockers, knocking the wind out of him.

"You should know, you little terrorist," Arthur yelled. "He was last seen alive in your country. Now stay away from me." Arthur left, leaving Kamil shaken. The bell rang for lunch and the other kids took off down the hall.

"That was so stupid," Kamil said out loud.

Someone put their hand on Kamil's shoulder and he jumped. It was the shy girl fom his first class. "Are you okay?" she asked. Her touch felt electric and calming at the same time.

"Yeah," Kamil replied. He saw sadness in her eyes, which made him forget about his own for a moment. "C'mon," she said, "let's go to lunch."

"What's your name?" Kamil asked.

"Cara," she said.

"Thank you, Cara."

"For what?" she asked.

"I don't know. For not running away like everybody else."

"Sure."

Kamil sat by the river that evening. The word terrorist echoed in his head. He thought about Arthur and the picture in Arthur's locker. He thought about his father and about how war takes a mess and makes it worse. Arthur called him a terrorist, but it was Kamil who was terrified. He thought about Cara and he felt calm again; one friendly voice cancels a thousand unfriendly ones.

October came and went. Kamil had his first experience with Halloween. His mom bought masks of two famous American mice at the department store where she worked. They wore them while giving out candy to the kids in their building. Since the day when Arthur shoved Kamil against the locker and Cara came to his rescue, Kamil and Cara became good friends. Before then they ate their lunches alone, but now they looked forward to having lunch together every day.

One morning in November the temperature fell to one degree below zero. Later that day at lunch Kamil told Cara that he had never actually seen snow up close before. "I only saw snow north of Herat, on the tops of the Safid Kuh — and even there it melted quickly."

"What does Safid Kuh mean?" asked Cara.

"It means 'White Mountains,'" said Kamil.

"Really?" said Cara. "There are mountains near here called the 'White Mountains.'"

Arthur walked by the table. "Hey, freaks, enjoying your lunch?" Cara gave him a dirty look. Kamil lowered his head. Arthur cackled and walked away.

"I'm sorry. You don't have to sit with me if you don't want to," said Kamil.

"Don't be sorry," said Cara. "And don't be silly. I don't care what he thinks." Cara reached across the table and squeezed Kamil's hand. Once again Kamil was calmed by her touch. He lifted his head. Cara smiled. Kamil smiled back.

At Thanksgiving Kamil was taught that the first European people who sailed to America made friends with the native peoples, and that the holiday was a celebration of their mutual cooperation. There were two days off from school. Cara was flying across the country with her dad and his girlfriend to have dinner with her mom and her new husband and his two teenage sons from his first marriage. Kamil was sad that he wasn't going to be with his family. But then he got an idea.

It was the Wednesday before Thanksgiving. After school

Kamil ran down to the basement to find Black Feather. He accepted Kamil's invitation to have dinner with Kamil and his mom the next day. Black Feather brought a homemade apple pie and Kamil's mom roasted a small turkey and made mashed potatoes from a box. Black Feather and Kamil's mom shared stories and laughed. They had so much in common. Kamil loved it. It was the first time since Kamil's father died that he sensed the closeness of family.

Right after Thanksgiving, everyone started getting ready for Christmas. Kamil knew who the Prophet Jesus was but where Kamil was from, Jesus didn't figure into any holidays. But Kamil soon learned that Jesus didn't figure very prominently into Christmas either. Kamil began to see Santa Claus everywhere, and all anybody at school talked about was presents. Kamil felt like he wanted to get Cara a present but he wasn't sure what it should be.

The gymnasium at the school was being decorated for Christmas. Big green wreathes with big red bows lined the walls. In the corner they put up a giant evergreen with little lights all over it. Every kid in the school was assigned to make an ornament for the tree. Kamil liked having the tree indoors. He thought he would like to have a tree in his room all year long just for that smell. In woodworking class Kamil used a scroll saw to carve out a crescent moon as big as his own head with a star that dangled by a little string in between the tips of the moon. He covered the moon and the star with silver glitter. Some kids hung their ornaments themselves low on the tree but many of the ornaments were given to Muhammad to hang higher up using a ladder. The next time Kamil went to the gym he was stunned to see his ornament glittering at the top of the tree.

The last day of school before Christmas vacation was a Friday. The weatherwoman on TV predicted snow. She explained that they were on the edge of a big storm and, depending on the winds, they were either going to get a dusting of snow or a few feet of it.

The first few flakes of snow began to drift out of the sky when Kamil sat down for his first class. The kids were excited. Mrs. Patrick said they might end up having only a halfday of school. Kamil grinned at Cara and Cara smiled right back just as big, sharing in his joy of seeing his first snowflakes.

When the second class started the snow was coming down hard and fast. Between classes Kamil noticed some of the teachers talking nervously in the hall. Kamil wanted to run outside and see what snow felt like. By the end of the second class it was coming down so hard they could barely see out the windows. The principal made an announcement over the intercom that everyone should go to their third class as scheduled, but the buses were coming and everyone would be going home soon. During the third class students were allowed, one class at a time, to go to their lockers to be ready when the buses arrived. The original excitement about the snow was being replaced with nervousness among the kids. Outside every window they could see nothing but snow.

Then the power went out.

Without the hum of the florescent bulbs all they could hear was the wind whipping snow against the windows. The principal came to the door and told the class, "The roads are unsafe now and the buses can't get here yet." Then he spoke directly to the teacher.

"Many of the other teachers are taking their classes to the gym to stretch their legs. School is over for now."

The class followed the teacher to the gym. It was already buzzing with many conversations. Everybody spread out looking for someone to talk to. Kamil started looking for Cara but he didn't search long.

"Kamil!" Cara appeared and gave Kamil a hug. "So what do you think of this snow?" Cara asked excitedly.

"I can't believe it," said Kamil. "I wish I could go outside."

Cara grabbed Kamil's hand. "C'mon." She led Kamil through the crowd, zig-zagging around kids until they reached the double doors of the gym that led outside. She positioned Kamil in front of one of the doors. His nose almost touched it. "Ready?" Cara asked, standing beside him. Kamil turned his eyes uneasily towards Cara, who had a devilish grin. He wasn't sure what she was going to do. Cara pushed down on the long metal handle of the door. It unlatched with a clunk. Then she leaned on the door and pushed with all her might against the snow, piled up on the other side. Kamil's eyes went wide as the snow hit his whole body, almost knocking him backwards. The other students recoiled from the sudden blast of wind and white flooding in through the door.

One of the teachers yelled from the other side of the gym, "Shut that door." Cara pulled hard on the metal handle and, with the help of the wind, the door slammed shut. Cara laughed and hugged Kamil's snow-covered body. He laughed with her as he regained his senses and hugged her back. All the other students stared at the two misfits.

"Thank you," Kamil said to Cara.

Arthur emerged from the crowd. "What the hell are you freaks doin'?" The other students pulled in closer.

"Shut up, Arty. You wouldn't understand," snapped Cara. Arthur's eyes narrowed.

"Oh really," Arthur said quietly as he stepped uncomfortably close to Cara. "Why don't you explain it to me."

Without thinking Kamil wedged himself between them, facing Arthur. Arthur stepped back.

"Look Arthur," Kamil said, "just leave us alone. Please? We haven't done anything to you." Arthur's face was as red as the day Kamil asked him about the picture in his locker. The next thing Kamil knew, Arthur shoved him through the door and into the driving snow. Arthur followed him.

"Haven't done anything to me?" Arthur said with a sneer. "Your people killed my father while he was over there trying to protect them, you little terrorist." Arthur lunged at Kamil, knocking him down.

Cara was right behind them. "Leave him alone you big jerk." Cara grabbed the back of Arthur's shirt. "He didn't do anything to you or your father. You're the one hurting him." Arthur turned and shoved Cara. When she hit the ground something in her right hand snapped. Cara screamed with pain.

Kamil was overcome with anger and confusion. Arthur was at him again. Arthur grabbed Kamil's shirt with one hand and cocked his other hand back. Kamil was about punch Arthur when he saw Muhammad standing in the doorway looking straight at him.

Kamil's fist relaxed. Angry tears rolled down his cheeks. "My father is dead, too," Kamil yelled at Arthur.

Arthur reacted as if he'd been hit. His fist dropped. "What did you say?"

Arthur said, shaking, his own eyes welling with tears. "My father died over there, too," Kamil said. "Our house was bombed by a jet and my dad was inside."

Arthur released Kamil's shirt and collapsed in the snow beside him. Muhammad took Cara inside. The door closed, leaving Kamil and Arthur outside alone. Arthur began to sob. Kamil stared at Arthur for a moment, then put his hand on Arthur's shoulder.

Within a couple of hours the snow stopped, the roads were plowed, the buses came, and everyone went home. Kamil and Arthur didn't say anything else to each other that day. Neither of them said much to anyone that day. Cara went to the hospital and got a cast on her right wrist. She told the teachers, her parents, and the doctor that she just slipped on the snow

The next day, Kamil called Cara to see how she was doing.

When Kamil told her about Arthur crying she was glad she didn't tell on him. "I'm proud of you too for not hitting him, Kamil," Cara said. "At the time I really wanted you to, but it just would have made things worse."

Monday was Christmas Day and since Cara wasn't going to be traveling anywhere she and Kamil made plans to see each other. Kamil told his mom that he wanted to get Cara something for Christmas so she took him to the store where she worked to look at the small selection of jewelry they had there. Most of the jewelry was either too expensive or too cheap looking. But he noticed one pendant that stood out from the rest. It was a silver triangle with a round piece of amber set into its center. It came with a free chain, and was only $19.95. The tag read, "Handmade by Eliana Ahava."

When Kamil and his mom arrived home, they found an envelope addressed to Kamil wedged in their front door. It was a Christmas card with a corny picture of Santa getting ready to slide down a chimney. He opened it and read the handwritten message. "Kamil, sorry. And thank you. See you in the new year. Have a Happy Christmas. Arthur."
    "Who is that from?" Kamil's mom asked. "A friend from school," Kamil replied. "A new friend."

The next day was Christmas. Kamil and his mom had breakfast together and exchanged gifts. At around noon there was a knock at the door. Kamil jumped from his chair and opened the door. Cara stepped in.
    "How's your arm doing?" Kamil's mom asked.
    "It's a lot better, thanks," Cara replied. Kamil wanted to give Cara her present but not with his mother around.
    "Hey Cara let's go outside. I want to show you the river."

Kamil led Cara through the maze of hallways and stairways to the back door of the building. Outside, they walked through the snow towards a tree on the bank of the river.
    Cara followed, stepping in Kamils tracks. "I noticed

yesterday a spot under this tree without any snow on it."
Kamil and Cara ducked under the branches and sat down
next to each other with their backs against the thick trunk.

"Wow," Cara exclaimed. "What a great spot."

"Yeah, I come out here all the time," Kamil said. "The river
reminds me of the Hari-rud back in Herat." Kamil reached
into his jacket pocket and offered the little box to Cara.
"Merry Christmas," he said.

"I can't believe you got me a present, Kamil," she said.
Kamil suddenly felt nervous. Cara opened the box and saw
the pendant.

"It's so beautiful!" she said, lifting the pendant on the
chain in front of her. "Thank you."

Cara put her head on Kamil's shoulder. She held her pendant
in both hands, tracing the line of the triangle with her thumbs.
As they watched the river, Kamil thought of the Hari-rud
again. It doesn't flow into another river or into a sea, like
other rivers. The Hari-rud flows into the sands of the Karakum desert. The whole river, absorbed by the Karakum.

Snowy Day

Sylvia Olson

"Janey!"

Frank yelled through his open office door. Janey sat at her desk, her fingers settled on the electric typewriter. A tiny conference room with an aging metal table was the only thing between them. The gray Formica top was stained with coffee rings and engraved with names, initials, and hearts — tokens of failed teen romances when the table was part of a school library. That and six mismatched, dented metal chairs with torn vinyl upholstery completed the ensemble.

Frank waved some papers around, still seated at his teacher's desk, more surplus furniture that somehow escaped public auction. A bottle of V-8 and a half eaten sesame bagel sat next to a photo of his wife and kids. He continued to shout. "I specifically said *this* was the report I needed by this afternoon. Not the memo on my desk. It's nice you typed it, but it's not the one I wanted."

Janey yelled back. "Frank, you put that memo on my desk, this morning, as I was sitting here, and you told me to type it by this afternoon. So I did. And there it is."

Frank shouted back. "Now, why would I want a memo about an officer with an absenteeism problem before a report for the DA? Concerning a homicide case? Why? Tell me."

Janey yelled back, in a huff. "I don't know, Frank! I'm just the secretary. I don't question your priorities."

Frank got up from his desk, which was covered with paper, worked his way around the table, and walked over to Janey's desk, which was also covered with paper. He lowered his voice. "Janey, this isn't Catholic school. I'm not a nun. Question my goddamn priorities, okay?"

"I'll try, Frank. But you can't me yell at me then," said Janey. Frustration pinched her face. She wore a light blue shirt and a small, neat, navy blue tie, like a cop, but tailored for a woman, with navy pants and plain black shoes. Her almost pretty face was framed with dark, close cropped hair. She wore tiny stainless steel button earrings, a little lipstick and mascara.

"Well, I can't guarantee *that*," said Frank. "I might yell again." Then he smiled. He was a good-looking guy, and he knew it. A great smile worked with women. But not always. Not with Janey. Frank didn't wear a uniform. He wore a black, tailored suit, white shirt, gold silk tie. He was always ready to go to court, a meeting with the Chief, or a funeral.

The phone rang. Janey looked at him, her eyes narrowed, not answering it. It rang again, and she picked it up.

"Physical Crimes," she said, polite, crisp. She listened for a moment. "Let me see if Lieutenant D'Ercolano is available." She pushed the red *hold* button.

"Who is it, and what do they want?" asked Frank, standing in front of her, holding papers. Impatient. He had stuff to do.

"It's Miranda Cortez from Social Services. She says it's important," said Janey, lips tight, not looking at Frank. Mad.

Miranda was a doll, but she had two kids and a really pissed off ex. She had a thing for Frank, but he kept stuff between them on a business-only basis. Janey knew all this, but she didn't say anything about it. Miranda liked to call.

"Well, it better be important," he said, going back to his desk, housed inside a mostly glass closet, with a door. He kept the door open this time, to ensure professionalism on his part. He didn't want to say something stupid to Miranda, while he thought about her legs, those swinging hips.

Miranda started chattering away in Spanish, like this was something personal. Something between the two of them, so no one else could listen in. Frank could mostly understand what she was saying, but he preferred business in English.

"I have this old lady, my client, she's stuck in a house with almost no heat. The landlord keeps the thermostat on sixty, she says. I've tried calling the landlord, I can't get any answer. Now she says the tenant downstairs hasn't taken out his garbage in weeks, and the place stinks. She thinks he walked out on the landlord, just left his garbage. She hasn't seen his car in a couple of weeks, so he's gone. I went over there, and the place smells really bad. I called the Buildings Bureau, and they tried calling the landlord, but they think he's in Florida. He's an old guy from Brighton, he spends a lot of time in Florida, they seem to know who he is. But no one has a number. And they can't do anything about a smell, because it's not in the building codes."

Miranda was pretty excited about all this. Her voice was intense, her words tumbled out.

"Okay," said Frank, in English. Patiently. He wasn't speaking Spanish. Janey would get suspicious. "So why are you calling me?"

"Mr. Scachetti in Buildings said to call the police. So I thought of you, of course," she said in a sexy way. Frank imagined her beautiful smile, dark eyes, white teeth, red lips. Then he imagined her ex.

"You thought of me. That was nice," said Frank.

"Well, actually, Mr. Scachetti suggested I call you, he said maybe you could get into the apartment, without the landlord's permission. It was the only way," said Miranda, her voice getting a little breathy.

"So is this to get the heat turned up, or get rid of the smell? Maybe the guy left his cat behind," said Frank.

"Well, it's not that cold. It just smells bad," said Miranda.

"I'll have it checked out," said Frank.

"Do you want to meet me over there?" asked Miranda. Her voice went up a couple notches.

"I don't know when this is going to happen. You stay right there at Social Services, where it's nice and warm. It's cold and icy outside," said Frank, in a sexy voice.

"You're sure, Frank?" asked Miranda. Sad. Seductive.

"Give me the address, and I'll call you when I come up with something," said Frank.

"Well, okay," she said, disappointed. Clearly.

* * *

She gave him the address, and he called Dispatch, and told them to send a uniform over there to check it out, and talk to the old lady upstairs. Frank wasn't going anywhere today, unless it was absolutely necessary. It was snowing again, not too bad, but enough to make things slippery. And it was cold and the wind was blowing. Typical winter's day, and it sucked. Except it was the middle of March, almost spring, but here, it made no difference.

Janey was typing furiously when the phone rang, and Frank answered it, so as not to break her concentration. It was Dispatch, and the uniform they sent over to check on the odor problem was having problems.

"He says the old lady is Spanish, and he can't speak Spanish, and she can't speak English. And it smells bad, he can smell it outside," said the Dispatcher.

Frank didn't feel good about this. He really didn't want to go out there, sliding around in the snow, snow melting on his windshield. He didn't want to go to a place that smelled really bad. It might only be a dead cat, or an abandoned chuck roast—but maybe it was something else.

He called his uncle Louie Scachetti, and got the name of the landlord. "He's a tough customer, Frankie. He don't do shit on his houses, he thinks all we do here is harass honest businessmen. Well, he's not exactly dishonest, but he don't believe in building codes," said Louie. Louie had a phone number for the landlord, who lived in the suburbs, out in Brighton. Frank called, but only an answering machine answered.

Then he called Police Information, to see if they could come up with an alternate phone number for the guy. They couldn't. Frank thought about it, and called the Brighton police, and asked them if they knew the guy, and how to get hold of him, and why.

The officer who answered the phone laughed. "He used to be a town councilman. He's on the development board.

Someone's got his number, somewhere."

They called him back in a few minutes with a Florida number. Frank called it. No one answered. Frank continued to have a bad feeling about the apartment. Something. He called Dispatch, and told them to have the uniform look at the apartment. Try the door, see if it was locked. Maybe it wasn't. Look in any windows, if he could. See if there was evidence of forcible entry. Or exit.

Ten minutes later, Frank was reviewing the report to the DA, and he knew the sonofabitch was going to find a lot wrong with it, but there was nothing Frank could do now. He had to get it over there asap. Janey was calling the courier to pick it up, when Frank's other line rang.

Dispatch again. The uniform was looking at the walls in the apartment, through the windows, and he thought he saw blood on the wall. Like smears of it, lots of it. The lock was a deadbolt, and whoever left last, the door locked behind them. But no sign of forcible entry. No blood around the door, he could see. Not that there was much to see. The snow was coming down in big puffs right now, flakes so big you could see the designs in them. Frank couldn't see the designs himself, from the sixth floor, but he could see the puffs, and he knew that's what they were like.

Lake snow. Frank heard once that the Eskimos had thirty words for snow, and then someone said that was a lie, it was just made up, they only had a couple of words for snow. Well, here in western New York, they had thirty kinds of snow, even if they didn't have thirty words for it. This was lake snow. Sticky, fluffy, easy to shovel or brush off your windshield, if it didn't get too thick. If it got thick, it was a mess. A little colder, it might be okay, but this wasn't so cold, just hovering around the freezing point.

There were lots of different kinds of lake snow, and this was just one of them. Frank didn't like it, but now he knew he'd have to go out into it. If you could smell death outside, in the snow, it was bad.

Everyone else in Physical Crimes was busy, home sleeping, had the day off, or was sick with the flu. Frank found a uniform on light duty, sitting at a desk. He'd had back surgery, he threw his back out shoveling during the blizzard in January. The blizzard with Karen. *Mmm, Karen.* Frank told him to keep calling the number in Florida, see if he could get hold of the landlord, find out who lived in the apartment. Get a name, a number, anything.

The drive was a bitch, even though it was just a couple miles away. Traffic was backed up on Lake Avenue, office workers trying to leave work early, to get stuck in traffic. People slid into each other, and then they had to get out of their cars to negotiate and trade insurance info. Frank didn't see any point in putting on his flashers to get ahead of the traffic. There was no place for people to pull over, and he'd just make everyone panic. It wasn't an emergency anyway. What was there, in that apartment, had been there, a long time.

The house was on a side street, off Lake Avenue. Run down, made his old neighborhood, where he grew up, look good. He parked in the street, wondering if a plow might come along and hit him. But it didn't look like anything was happening with plowing, and there was nothing else he could do anyway. The uniform was huddled in his cruiser, a few cars down, an inch of fluff on his windshield already. They went to the apartment together.

Frank was hoping it was something else on the walls. Not what the uniform saw. He stepped into the footprints the uniform made earlier, already filling up with the white stuff, and looked inside. The windows were dirty, old, the glass was flowing and gently warping the images on the other side of the window. Frank saw what the uniform saw, and couldn't believe it was blood, there was so much of it. Couldn't be blood, couldn't be. But if it was, it was bad, real bad, and they had to get inside.

And the smell. It was death, all right. Maybe it wasn't human, but what else could it be? Frank sent the uniform back to his cruiser, to see if the development board member/slumlord had been contacted. They might need a warrant to enter, otherwise. Frank went to the old lady's apartment upstairs.

She was afraid to let him in at first, shouting at him in Spanish from behind the door. He explained he was a police officer and that Miranda Cortez had asked him to come. She finally let him slip his ID with his badge between the chain-locked door, and when she was satisfied, she let him in.

It smelled in here, too. Poodle poop, fried onions and peppers, and the old lady's dirty hair couldn't hide it. The smell of death, from below.

He asked her about the tenants downstairs. As he watched a cockroach run across a table.

Only one, she said. A young man, she only saw him come and go. He had a car, shiny, but old, and it was gone, she hadn't seen it in a few weeks. She wasn't sure how long. She hadn't seen *him* in a few weeks, either. Light brown hair, light brown eyes. Acne. Always worried looking, came and went at all hours. Banging around, all hours. Scared her sometimes. Woke her up out of a sound sleep. Loud music, sometimes. Shouting, a man over.

"Anyone regular? A girlfriend? Parents?" Frank asked her.

She didn't know, really. She couldn't see anyone, she never left her apartment in the winter, except for church, when her daughter came to get her. But she only heard men's voices downstairs. And she didn't know his name. Frank hadn't seen a name on the mailbox, and there was only junk mail in there. And it was piling up, too.

"Did you hear anything recently? Like right about the time he disappeared? Any fight, or anything?"

She thought about it. There was some loud banging, one night. Very loud. Yelling. More than usual. Loud music, too. She thought they were drinking. Men get that way, when they're drinking. Thumps. Like maybe they decided to put in shelves or something. She didn't know. It was hard to remember.

Frank figured that was enough. He went back out to his car, radioed Dispatch, and told them to find a judge. But he was going in, one way or another. The uniform at the desk still couldn't get an answer from Florida. The guy was golfing, probably. Or at the beach.

Frank's feet were wet now, and he was pissed at himself for just showing up in shoes. He needed boots. His wife was afraid he'd get frostbite one day, and lose his toes. Maybe Gina would be embarrassed by a husband with no toes.

A couple more uniforms arrived, and they went in. They had to break the lock, and the landlord would be filing a claim for it with the Law Department, but it was all they could do.

And it was bad. Beyond anything Frank had ever seen, ever imagined. Blood was everywhere. On the rose-papered walls, the dirty carpet, the up-ended, worn out furniture. Spattered, smeared, streaked. Footprints, handprints. A terrible, horrible fight. Blood in the dingy little kitchen, dirty dishes piled high in the sink.

It wasn't the dishes that smelled so bad. It was the guy in the bedroom. On the floor, eyes open, staring at the ceiling. What was left of his face, broken, bloody. His body, stabbed, beaten. Naked. Bloated. Terrible colors of death, all over.

Jesus. Frank shook his head, made the sign of the cross. Then they all went outside and puked in the snow, just puked and puked.

It was a long time before the tech van arrived, and even longer for the medical examiner's boys. Frank wore the mask this time, and lots of Vicks, when they went in one more time. Frank was taking pics, directing the evidence techs, arguing with the assistant ME. Then Zimmer showed up to take over. Frank had to see an assistant DA about his report. The DA didn't like it.

They got hold of the landlord the next morning. He couldn't remember the name of the tenant, it was somewhere back at his house in Brighton, and he wasn't coming home for a month. Frank told him he'd better figure out a way to get the name, or there would be major problems for him. He wasn't specific.

"What kind of problems?" asked the landlord. "I got lawyers. Good ones."

"We'll see," said Frank. He called his uncle Louie, he called the Buildings Director. He called the mayor of Brighton, and the chair of the Development Board. And then, just for the heck of it, he called the county Republican Committee, of which the landlord was a member, and to which he contributed heavily.

The next day, they had the name of the kid. Mitchell Warren. It was all they had. Mitch was from nowhere, he paid his rent in cash. There was nothing in his apartment that gave him a life. No letters from his family. No pictures. No papers. Nothing.

The neighbors remembered the car, because it was nice. But the DMV had no car registered in his name. Mitch came and went a lot, the neighbors said. Different men came over. No one noticed much of anything else. He had a lot of friends. They were quiet, for guys. No drinking, or yelling outside.

In the apartment, there was a little bit of coke, some crystal meth, a half-ounce bag of pot. Mitch wasn't dealing, just using. A few beers in the fridge, some cans of soup. No weapons, not even a knife. The knife he was stabbed with, that went with the killer.

Some of Frank's investigators thought it was the Organization. Maybe Mitch was doing things for them, errands, whatever, and he got rubbed out. This was their neighborhood, right? But Vice said no, and Frank knew the Organization didn't work like that. They beat you up, or they killed you, but not both. Not like this. It wasn't that personal, generally. And the guy was naked.

Zimmer figured it out, before the autopsy report came in. Mitch was a hustler, a hooker. It was all the Vaseline in the bedroom that tipped him off. So what happened to Mitch made sense to Frank, even though he couldn't understand it at all. A lovers' quarrel, a different kind.

The guy who did in Mitch had injuries, too, but they couldn't find any reports from the emergency rooms. They had prints, not very good ones, but lots of them. The FBI couldn't come up with a match. The blood was all Mitch's. There was so much of it, maybe there was some that wasn't his, but they couldn't find it.

No one came to claim his body. It sat in the morgue for two months, and the County was ready to cremate him, when someone remembered Mitch from college. Saw his name in an old newspaper she was using to wrap some dishes before she moved to Syracuse. Brockport State, a dropout in his freshman year.

Mitch was from Long Island, Hempstead. The FBI found his parents, and they didn't want him. And then they changed their minds, and came to claim his body, but it was too late, and Mitch was already cremated. Well, the City cremated him, the County paid for it. They gave the parents his ashes, which they took back to Long Island. The ME kept samples of Mitch's tissues. Frank kept the photos and the case file. The parents wouldn't talk to Frank.

They never closed that case. No evidence, no witnesses, no pressure. The DA wasn't interested, and neither was anyone else. The case got colder, and they pushed it to the back of a filing cabinet.

But Frank still thought about Mitch. Not really thinking, more like a vision, a ghost passing by. Sometimes Frank saw him in a dream, standing next to his dead buddies from Nam. "What are you doing here?" he'd ask, or try to ask, because you can't talk in a dream. And Mitch just looked at him, with his wounded face, and said nothing.

The Dragonslayer

Lenore Rogers

I'd never noticed before just how the early morning sun
spills in through that window, draping so much light along
the floorboards that it seems to lift the creaminess of the
grain. It's an effect that is almost surreal, like a painting,
breaches of mist and steam, an undulating fog of diffused
light.

I'm usually gone by this time of day, distracted by the
rituals of getting ready for work or somewhere within the
itinerary of a morning run. I train 70 to 100 miles per week,
preferably outside, as long as there is some measure of road
to run on. It was as much an impossible task to find a
runnable surface this past winter as it was to finish Fifty
Shades of Grey.

No surprise here, but my choice of a workout is a solitary
one. With earbuds funneling in inspiration, I'm able to
remain cocooned even while running with others. My iPhone
is populated with music by Lucinda Williams, Tracy
Chapman, Greg Brown and Amy Winehouse. Clearly, I'm a
fan of songs of unforgiving rawness, pain and loss. But it's
Winehouse's edgy and stripped bare version of Will You Still
Love Me Tomorrow that, when I'm running on empty, will
fuel the push to get me home. It's those damn hefty vocals,
but delivered with such a gut-wrenching vulnerability. An
anthem of trust, I suppose, or an unflinchingly accurate
portrayal of lack thereof.

I had debated the choice of natural hickory, but she
convinced me otherwise. She was right, of course, as she had
been about most things. On my own, I wouldn't have had the
courage to paint that wall Indigo. But she had loved the idea

of highlighting the warmth of the stain by contrasting such a bold color against it, of injecting energy into an otherwise hard and angular space. It worked there and it works as a kind of metaphor for our relationship, or what had once been our relationship. There was no more opposing contrast than the two of us. I was that hard and angular space. She was color.

It's challenging getting used to this past tense phrasing of oneself.

My life, as I knew it, ended this morning at 8:34 am.

I suppose if one is to die, mine was an enviable passing. I had come in from my run feeling nauseated and went to the kitchen for some water. An explosion of pain, like those grainy films of the bombs dropped on Hiroshima, starting small and then mushrooming. I felt the room spin, my left hand grasping at the counter, and just a transitory fear, the words 'oh, this is not good' passing through my mind. That was followed by a sensation of falling, and then an emptying of all thought. That was it, easy-peasy.

And then this happened.

It was as if a light had flickered, a brief, almost imperceptible moment of nothingness before I was aware again, but disorientated. It took me a few moments to realize that I, or the conscious "I", had strayed from the body on the floor.

Having always identified as an atheist secular humanist, my linear brain never would have allowed for any of this. I analytically dismissed the belief in a hereafter as having no basis in science and only as a defense mechanism sheltering people from their fear of dying. And so you can well imagine how fascinating I'm finding this. The other thing is how weirdly composed I am. You'd think there would be some sort of grief, some sense of longing for the me on the floor, but it's the equivalent of having stepped out of my clothing and leaving the tangle of them behind. It's that dispassionate.

So what's this all about? You'd expect there to be some ethereal being here offering guidance and absolution. That's what the believers say. But you're pretty much alone with your thoughts and what's missing is the filter that you cleanse your life through.

"Nothing in your childhood prepared you for the consideration of faith," she once said. "She" would be Lucia.

True. My childhood wasn't a place I ever wanted to revisit, but there are a few happy memories, and one is of being in the backyard, and on my belly, studying the world beneath a rock. My early interest with how things work led me into the sciences and ultimately to study the brain, the definitive device of how we humans work. Science is reason and I find comfort in reason.

I know that an out of body experience is typically induced by brain trauma, sensory deprivation, a near-death experience, dissociative disorders and psychedelic drugs. I did suffer a brain trauma brought on as a result of an aneurysmal subarachnoid hemorrhage. One look at me ripening on the floor and it's clear I didn't survive it.

And so what is this that so defies reason?

I learned in high school science that energy can neither be created nor extinguished and that all matter is made up of subatomic particles that are adaptable and can exist outside of the realm of time. I know that even nothing is something, but this notion of what constitutes human energy being capable of cognitive thought after the cessation of physical life leads me to a humble acceptance that I'm now the atman of my former physical being and that's pretty damn cool.

What I've come to wonder is whether this is the waiting room to the afterlife, the time of reckoning for my forty-four years here. However, unless I come face to face with the loving, comforting, shepherding, judging, punishing, wrathful God of the Abrahamic religions or any facsimile of it; the jury is still out on that part.

"What does your soul cry out for?" she once asked.

"I don't know what you mean by soul?" I answered.

There is a huge difference to this state of being. It's rather amazing how my senses have heightened. There is an undeniable degree of arrogance to living with a body. You believe you've had this degree of responsiveness before,

275

where every nerve in your body uncurls, sensory tips opening, receiving, rejoicing or anguishing depending upon the provocations, but you're mistaken. This is what Dorothy must have felt like when she opened the door to Oz and saw color for the first time.

What can I most equate it to?

Lucia, in the early days of us, sits next to me in bed, bone-tired, after having just come off a west coast road trip. She's not speaking much; the TV's on, Rachel Maddow is talking about affordable health care. My awareness becomes finite and it's all due to the sensation of her fingertips as they mindlessly travel up and down my arm. Her intention was benign, but it was completely sensual to me, even more so than sex which, no reason to couch anything now, had a tendency to unnerve me. That touch, in its clarity, because of its precision, allowed me feel more loved than I ever did, at any point in my life, before.

Or maybe it's more like when she told me that she was done with us and it felt as if the entirety of my being had drained out onto the floor, the grief over it hollowing me out. What it is, really, is the best or worst thing you've ever known taken well beyond the nth degree.

"If you're not careful, you will die alone," she had said.

Score one for Lucia. It turns out, she is a psychic as well. In first responder speak, I'm unattended death, road kill awaiting the DPW truck and the man with the shovel.

But, what does that mean, really? A lot of people die alone. The one thing about timing is that it's rarely precise, kind or convenient. It's not like we can choose our optimal moment of death, unless it's by our own hand.

And I am not really alone. Kahlo is here.

Kahlo was a gift from Lucia. She was not sprung on me, but a jointly made decision as an affirmation of moving into the realm of a more committed relationship. She is now two years old, a pit/hound mix with a bluish-grey coat. I would tell people that she was put together with spare parts. Her head is enormous compared to the size of her body, which is supported by short, thick legs. In the very center of her forehead is a cluster of white hair, combed into an imperfectly shaped heart.

"It's a flawless heart," Lucia would correct me.

It is our choice of language, offered without forethought, which reflects our true self back to the world. I saw the fault, Lucia saw the perfection.

It's like I've become like the hidden camera that people will install in their homes to make sure the housekeeper isn't subbing the VSOP with tap water.

Kahlo is sprawled on the couch, her head resting on her outstretched paws. Her eyes are open and alert. Suddenly she slips off, scoots beneath a chair, and emerges with her favorite toy, a bright yellow ball with the squeaker removed.

We all have our thing and Kahlo's is this: to make this ungodly racket while chomping on the ball, thrash it about, and then chew out the squeaker just as you're about to toss both her and it out the window.

I watch her at play. She throws her head back to launch the ball into the air. It ricochets against the wall, bounces into the kitchen and rolls to a stop behind the bend of my knee. She leaps in after it, applies the brakes, and then looks around nervously before letting out a protracted howl. It's heartbreaking. Taking an uncertain step forward, she sniffs at my sneaker, and then at my exposed ankle. She must decide I'm beyond harm because she suddenly pounces on the ball as if it's the prey that will fill her empty tummy.

Lucia had said that there's a lesson to be learned from a dog's instinctual way of being, reacting to things that are right in front of them. There is no future to pin your hopes on. Maybe in some deliberate way, she was hoping that by Kahlo's example, I would have become more dog-like. I could have used more of that way of being.

I'd never had a pet before. Well, technically, that's not true. When I was about twelve, I won a goldfish at a school carnival by knocking down bowling pins. A few days later, I noticed that Clarence was swimming sideways, and then resting upside down near the surface. When I awoke the next morning, it was all gone; Clarence, the jar, and even the tiny container of flaked food. You could disappear from my childhood home without much fanfare in those days.

It is not that my life was without meaning. It is not like I died forsaken under a bridge having lost myself in a bottle or to a syringe. A well written obituary will speak of the poetry of one's life and mine will tell of my career as a neuro scientist at MIT's Picower Center for Learning and Memory. It will highlight my work with gene mutations implicated in synapse development and how it pertains to the onset of autism, it will reference the MD-PhD degree from The Perlman School and of the papers authored, the marathons run. And just about every word, each sentence will hint at a life blessed, of one worth envying. Yet what remains of my physical self lies decaying on the floor.

"She leaves behind her dog Kahlo."

I wonder when I will be missed.

I remember once reading about a woman in Croatia who had been dead for forty one years before being discovered in her bed. It won't be that long, but it's not unusual for me to work from home or to be traveling and I certainly care less about the discovery of me and more about Kahlo. Well, maybe I do care a little about the discovery of me.

"Runner of marathons and runner away from life," she had said of me.

Again, true.

I have a junk drawer filled with dozens of unopened packages of chopsticks. I was in the habit of ordering so much Thai food to go that they assumed I was continuing to feed more than one. Since Lucia left, I'd purchase enough to last for a few days. I had convinced myself that I was being economical with my time. In reality, I was not keen to letting go of the perception that there was a need for two sets of chopsticks.

"How come it is always you picking up the food?" said the owner. "Must be nice to be your husband?"

There is no husband. To be more accurate, there once was a husband, a man of uncommon intelligence. He looked pretty good on paper, great pedigree, until his true self emerged. He could be alternately amiable or rude, funny or irritable, but never once accountable. He fucked anything that moved, drained my bank accounts along with every last drop of my self-respect and, even then, I held onto him and the illusion of normalcy until he decided to leave. An illusion of normalcy is the panacea that acts as a bulwark to conceding that something is wrong.

The state I'm in now is not my first out of body experience, only the most permanent. I had given myself a hall pass because of the revulsion and self-loathing that came with sex with my husband. It was rote, as if called in from a payphone. Fracturing, disassociating and compartmentalizing; all the skills one should never learn in childhood.

Throughout the years, there were other pointless attempts, both men and women. I had awful taste in partners, men or women didn't matter. They all had more charisma than should be allowed and were maddeningly appealing in only how their dysfunction fed mine.

"It's called re-victimization. We choose and cling to what we think we deserve."   Elizabeth Prum, PhD, Clinical Psychologist, Women's Mental Health Collective.

And then there was Lucia.

Seven years ago, after being recruited by MIT, I became a member of the Cambridge Runners Club. Five years later, I met Lucia at their annual spring picnic.

It's rather thrilling that in this post death state a memory remains intact, and along with conscious thought there is also perceptible emotion. I see her now; the sweep to her gait as she moves with an easy confidence among the crowd. Her hair is thick, black and unruly and she is repeatedly running her fingers through it in a never ending battle for control. I simply couldn't take my eyes from her.

When she was brought over and introduced to me, I found that I was completely off kilter, not like me at all. I don't know if it was her crooked smile, or those green eyes, framed by those long lashes, crinkling against the sun, but I felt knocked off my pins. But it was also something more, a familiarity with her that confronted reason. It both excited and scared the living daylights out of me.

If a catalogue existed where one could purchase the parts to construct the perfect sprinter, you'd end up with a specimen like Lucia: tall, narrow hipped and with the inherent muscle composition of fast twitch fibers, delivering tremendous burst of energy over a short period of time. Endurance athletes, or marathoners like me, are framed smaller, with slow twitch fibers, a higher maximal oxygen uptake and the standard EPOR mutation.

My geek brain actually thinks of stuff like this.

If I were to sketch the ideal person for me, hands down, it would be a Lucia.

She is brilliant, funny, creative, thoughtful and kind. More importantly, she is also balanced, emotionally available, and transparent. Those are qualities that had never come in one package for me before. She might have well been an alien, not what I typically attract to me.

That mop of black hair and olive complexion is due to her mom's Mexican heritage, the green eyes and freckled nose a kick-in from her Irish dad. An only child, and a military brat, she spent her childhood putting down temporary roots. It made her immensely self -assured, but maybe a little bit too comfortable with the idea that some good things don't last.

She earned her BA from Emerson and is a sports writer for the Boston Globe. Her normal assignment is to cover the Red Sox. She admitted to me once that since her father died, I'm the only person on the planet that knows she's a closeted Yankee fan. She said letting me know that proved her commitment to me.

Shortly after the picnic, we began to date or some shapeless description of that. It was, at first, fast and manic, and I vacillated between not being able to get enough of her and not being able to get far enough away from her.

"I don't normally allow myself to become consumed by my passions," she said a few months into our dating, "You just might be the exception."

I was so happy that I had wanted to cry. I was so terrified that I wanted to hide. What it did was overwhelmed me and

I didn't call her for three days and gave only cursory regard to her emails and texts. I lied, claiming an uptake in workload.

When she would question, I would attribute our different approaches to relationship to the fast and slow twitch fibers of our beings. The scientist in me dispatches everything to science, but, of course, it was so much more than that. Whenever we began to fall into some kind of easy rhythm with each other, I would turn her away. The more I grew to love her, the more I behaved otherwise, the more I found myself relaxing, and beginning to trust her, the more she became something to be feared.

One day, early on, but not too early on that I hadn't begun to love her deeply already, we were on the couch; Lucia's head in my lap and she was reading. Kahlo was still a baby, all pudgy and soft, and with that puppy smell that had become like crack to us. She was asleep with her head on Lucia's thigh, her body sandwiched between the two of us. My fingers were entwined in the mass of Lucia's rebellious hair when she tossed her newspaper to the floor and asked: "Do you believe in soul mates?"

"No, I've studied far too many brains," I answered. "The atheist, remember?"

"Allow me to put forward my belief that we are soul mates."

I had laughed, because that's what I always did when considering the absurd, a laugh painted with touchiness, with my typical underpinnings of impatience. Ugh. Another curious thing about this state of consciousness is that I can now feel sick to my stomach without having one, horrified by my dismissive rigidness.

Lucia once described my approach to love as the equivalent of the Svalbard Seed Vault, insulated against the possibility of natural or man-made disasters.

Whatever Lucia loves, she loves fiercely. Wherever Lucia put her trust; she binds it with titanium. It would take a betrayal of almost epic proportions to sever it and I discovered that breaking point, and not by accident, or not through any misunderstanding, but I actually went hunting for it.

"You care more about your virtual friends."

No, but they were safer.

I have a Facebook community of 624 'friends'. People picked up along the way, colleagues, members of my current and former running clubs, classmates from what seemed like seven hundred years of schooling, all gathered up and pocketed like so many beach stones. Even in the days that Lucia shared my bed, I would take the time to scroll through my feeds. I would check on various sites, and plant a number of likes and posts and comments connecting me to my cybernetic world as if I was the lone inhabitant of a faraway planet.

It's easy to hide your authentic self behind the smokescreen of social media, you control, you edit, and you adeptly omit the blank spaces of your life between your posts and photos. Those blanks are often the grey areas where the truths of our lives will hide. After Lucia left, my robotic post at 12:30 a.m. reminds only me that there is no Lucia beside me in bed, but, hey, good for me, look at all the thumbs up I've received since I noted a time of 1:15 for a half marathon after coming off that knee strain.

"I'm only going to chase you for so long. I'm the sprinter, remember?"

What I share in common with my mother is her reedy build, blue eyes, high forehead, love of Italian operas, but only a portion of her intellect, and even less of her natural beauty. I was conceived through a fault of science, a defective condom. The wearer wanted nothing to do with me, and my mom couldn't seem to get herself around to having an abortion before the cutoff. That was a piece of our history that she never failed to remind me of.

My last shot at emotional healing had my therapist commenting that I had been raised by wolves. She was wrong. Wolves are devoted parents. I was raised by a cuckoo bird. Like the cuckoo bird, my mom mostly tricked other people into raising me, freeing her up to enjoy life as a single bird. Many of those she tricked were the men who believed they were in a relationship with her, but were merely placeholders until the next one came along. When I was about seven years old, one did stick around. He only did so because he had made me his secret girlfriend. That would be George.

"Now don't you go and ruin a good thing," my mom had warned, after I began to balk at being left alone with him.

And then, one day, George left too, taking with him his patience at teaching me how to properly throw a spiral, or to play a perfect guitar riff of Bad to the Bone. He also took with him his coarse hands and sloppy kisses. What he did leave behind was that mind space where I would go to hide when his heaviness descended on me.

So there you have me. I was birthed by an aloof, dysfunctional and hyper-critical mother that left me exposed to her kind, but pedophilic boyfriend. As much as we like to think that we are exceptional and our experiences unique, what I've turn out to be is pretty damn textbook. What happened to me happens to girls and boys at an alarming rate. And it could have been worse. It wasn't like I was dragged into the woods, but I was given something I couldn't handle and that fact it was wedded to the first person to ever pay attention to me, to validate my existence, and 'parent' me by holding my hand as we crossed a street, or to bandage my knee when I fell off my bike, made it all that more confusing.

"Just you and me, kiddo," was George's catchphrase after my mother disappeared into her world of perfectly coiffed hairdos, manicures and one too many Harvey Wallbangers.

And then I grew up and met Lucia, my ideal. Why did we fail?

It was just too hard to erase or rewrite the fictitious script in my head of what a loving relationship is, of what trust means and how to trust it. There were times when I couldn't even call upon the desire to touch her in a way that didn't seem contrived, or I felt smothered and unable to breathe. Worse still was the look in her eyes when her touch triggered an instinctive shudder in me, or a clenching of my stomach, even as all rational thought, all mindful understanding strived to convince me that Lucia was different, that she would not harm me, betray me, or abandon me, but that knowledge, no matter how fierce its voice, could never quite drown out the silent screams of the child within me.

I know intellectually that it's the way children have of squaring themselves with the world. If mom can hurt them, abandon them, betray them, and leave them exposed, then anyone they grow close to can. If on top of that you are made to feel like a factory second, something that is tolerated, but never quite good enough to be loved, that is the view of yourself that you take with you into adulthood. It didn't matter that I was smart, I could be smarter. It didn't matter that I could run for miles, why couldn't I run a mile more? I learned in therapy that what we fear most are the negative judgments of those we love. It's an irrational fear that is persistent and pervasive, and we do everything in our power to actualize it.

Someone like Lucia never stood a chance.

"I get your horrific childhood, and that you suffer from a self-imposed exile from intimacy as a result," she said. "If any of this mattered to you, if permitting yourself to be happy with me was a priority, you'd get some help with that. You'd go to war for us."

"I'm fine. You're too needy," I countered, "You don't understand the demands of my life."

"Are you a Dragonslayer for anyone?"

"What do you mean?"

"Who would you slay a Dragon for? We need to rename those people that we'd go to war for. We used to call them our lover, our best friend, before those words became so watered down and meaningless."

I would slay dragons for you, fucking barehanded, I would. But, instead, I said nothing. Why give her anything at all to hold onto?

"I would slay a dragon for you," she finally said, filling the silence between us. I remember that it was spoken in barely a whisper, "just allow me access to it. Please, you're killing me here." A lifeline to me, for us, and I let it get taken up in the current.

Lucia is a rock, one of the strongest people I'd ever known, and I was reducing her to rubble. Her eyes flashed and met mine, holding them for a long moment before she looked down. She then folded up her arms and pressed her lips together.

It's not often that something comes about that is so definitive it could be cast in stone. This was one. I had just witnessed the precise moment in time when Lucia gave up on me. Even a sprinter will forfeit the race when the risk of injury is great.

It was sometime later on Facebook that I learned she was dating.

Since the time of our implosion, I would picture myself running into her and there would be that profound and tenacious pull towards one another. Since it was my fantasy, everything would be right between us. I would be whole.

"You're going to wish that you allowed me to catch you."

I do. No one ever offered to slay a Dragon for me before.

The light of day is fading and a steely hue fills the room. Kahlo sleeps on the couch, her legs twitching, and cheerfully chasing squirrels as Lucia would say.

I wonder just how long this state of being lasts and what, if anything, comes after. Perhaps this is it and it's like a slow burning down and extinguishing of a candle, there'll be a flicker, a flame of even greater consciousness, and then a snuffing out.

And so why do we come here to inhabit these imperfect bodies? Is it to advance the human experience through science and art? Are we happier from having gone from cave etchings to Cornelia Konrad's Land Art? Are we significantly better off because we've evolved from banging a pair of rocks together to Beethoven's Symphony no. 9? What good is any of that if at the end of it all a soul feels incomplete, crying out for more?

Long ago you asked me what my soul cries out for. It cries out for you, do you know that?

In our body suits, we are handed an opportunity to be

awed, to be brought to our knees with what our hearts are capable of holding. Pablo Neruda described passion 'as if you were on fire from within'. How often does one experience that in a lifetime? That's what I felt for Lucia and because of fear, I turned against the flame.

If this is indeed my moment of reckoning then I need to reckon within myself that I was a coward in how I loved, or better yet, how I allowed myself to be loved. I permitted my continued victimization, never ripping to shreds my armor long after the need for it was gone. For someone who was as driven to winning as I was, scoring the highest GPA & class ranking, best race times, I failed in the most fundamental way. What remains of me, this soul being, cares nothing about my earthly achievements, it only cares that I didn't fight for what truly mattered.

Lemonade Buddha

Mark Sleiter

Rule #1 — Surround yourself with the correct people. Peter knew that no matter what anyone said, the proper lemonade stand starts with the children selling it. But it's so much more complicated than that. You need at least four kids for each stand, two to work the 11-3 shift, two to take the 3-7. See, two children yelling "Ice cold lemonade!" puts more pressure on the passerby. It's two against one, peer pressure, simple psychology. But when kids work more than four hours, they get antsy, restless, start whining. They demand food. Rest. And Peter was not going to let his small cottage become a shelter for ungrateful children. Hence, two shifts.

The children must be cute. Ugly children, like ugly adults, scare customers. At one time, Peter believed the ugly might engender the sympathy purchase. "Oh, that poor child, the least I can do is help out," the jogging neighbor would think while reaching into the fanny pack for loose change. But Peter had been wrong. People, he realized, wanted summer to be a time of optimism, a time of unthinking relaxation. Lamenting the joyless futures of the ugly did not fit into this. No, the unsightly would not do. In a free economy, the invisible hand of the marketplace bitch- slapped the ugly.

The children must have an acceptable body mass index. Fat children, like fat adults, sweat too much. Who wants to reach out for a nice refreshing glass of lemonade only to feel the coating of sweat slime left by a kid whose main source of calcium is derived from orange Cheeto powder?

But this is where it gets tricky. The labor force cannot be too cute. Cute children receive too much praise, constantly are told how precious they are. They learn to believe the world owes them something. They think fifteen cents an hour is beneath them. They plead for shade and bathroom breaks. Peter remembered last summer's purge. He'd fired the Patrosky twins for this very reason. Too cute...too many requests.

Their father disagreed. "For Chrissakes, they're seven," Mr. Patrosky had argued standing in Peter's doorway with his right hand clenched, briskly rubbing his chin with the left.

"Hey, they signed contracts," Peter shrugged. "No one held a gun to their heads, right?"

"What contracts?"

"These." Peter pulled the ink-stained cocktail napkins from his pockets, unfolded them, offered them to Mr. Patrosky.

"Napkins? Napkins! You're joking."

"No, as you can see they are signed and dated. I can assure you they hold up to any legal scrutiny. I have triplicate copies if you'd like to—"

Mr. Petrosky shook his head. "I can't even...this is insane. You realize this, right?"

Peter nodded. "I understand your frustration. But with all due respect, Carl, giving a nickel raise in this economic climate is insane. There isn't a stand in the country that can take on that kind of a financial hit."

"With all due respect, Peter, you're a fucking clown. Seriously. I gotta drive an hour home from work to deal with this nonsense." Mr. Petrosky slapped the siding next to the door, turned and stormed off.

"Carl, sorry it didn't work out," Peter called after his neighbor. "If Timmy and Tara want to come back on a probationary basis and put this mess behind us, just send them over, okay?" Peter heard no response, but watched Mr. Patrosky extend both middle fingers without breaking stride. Peter closed and locked the front door. No more cute children, he thought.

And so it came to pass. Peter eventually found his ideal workforce. There were the Thompson brothers. Matt, 9, was quiet, but efficient. No wasted movements. Rarely spilled a drop. Tyler, 8, was small in stature but made up for it with a willingness to yell until his voice was hoarse. He'd yell at anyone, anytime. The late shift belonged to Hadley and Tucker, both 7. As far as Peter could tell, Hadley was the only black child in the area. It had been a bit of a coup to get her. Appearing to be tolerant was hot these days. All the *Wall Street Journal* articles said so. Plus, she had dimples. Dimples, Peter believed, were the opiate of the masses...easily worth an extra eight to ten cups per shift. Tucker, on the other hand, had a knack for conversation. He'd seduce the customer with series of questions, reel them over to the table as if he were teaching the disciples how to fish. "What's your name? Do you like baseball? Is it hotter than last summer? Guess how many dimples Hadley has?" Clever bastard.

Rule #2: Make the unreasonable seem reasonable. Back when Peter had a job, back when he had the small office next to the supply closet next to a medium-sized office next to a larger corner office, Peter memorized the tenets of The Hellman Group. But he knew #2 was wrong. Give people what they want? Simple, right? But who really wants a can opener with an AM/FM radio? Who wakes up and thinks, "I can't start the day until I've had a microwaveable fried waffle with an Italian sausage stuffed inside"? The latter, it must be said, was the genesis for what later became known as the Wausage.

No one *wants* a Wausage to start the day. No one *wants* diarrhea and heartburn on the drive to work. But parents do want smiling children around the breakfast table. Parents do want to be able to feed their family in under three minutes. The result? An inspired commercial campaign, a split screen with one mom, late for work, rushing to prepare a meal, spilling ingredients all over the countertops. Another mom, calmly perusing a newspaper while her two children savor giant, delicious bites. The youngest child looks at the camera, belts out, "Whatta Wausage!"

Due to the success on this particular campaign, Peter received a plaque honoring his "indispensible and uncompromising work." His biggest contribution was in convincing the team from General Mills that Wausage was a better name than their suggestion—Sauffle. "Here's the thing," Peter told the three men sitting across the large oak conference table, "do you really want people saying 'Sauffle'? Think about it...Sauffle...Sauffle...so awful. Wausage has a hint of mystery, a touch of the mystical. The word sage is right in there."

At Hellman, his official title was Commercial Account Consultant. This meant Peter was the negotiator between the client and the creative team. He was an easer of tensions, an equitable and pliant force for the greater marketing good. In short, when the client believed that the proposed ads were too bland, too offensive, contained too many cartoons with squealing voices, or not enough cartoons with extra-squealy voices, Peter stepped in and brought peace to the boardroom battlefields.

But this had been in the late 90s. Hellman's client list was full of internet start-ups flush with venture capital credit. Wallpaper.com, Sermononthemount.org, bestroad-signage.gov, and so on. They all came eagerly, came with wallets leaking cash. Then it all went away, extinguished by the over- exuberant dreams of a populace bent on cornering every conceivable market. Apparently, consumers quickly tired of purchasing wallpaper based on discolored web photographs.

Five years later, offices were being turned into storage closets. The rooms were little more than mausoleums for ergonomic chairs, three-legged end tables, and dusty monitors. For Peter, a pay freeze became a pay reduction became an hourly wage, work-from-home three days per week position. Eventually, he was left stranded at home in front of his old desktop, left waiting to receive a few freelance assignments from Hellman each month. Dave, he of the medium-sized office, told Peter not to worry. Medium-sized office Dave had heard from Janson, he of the large corner office, that there would always be work for a man of Peter's experience.

One day, Peter looked down at his business card: *Peter*

Carter, Commerical Accounts Consultant. What had he become? A part-time consultant to other full-time consultants? Consulting on the state of modern consultancy? Eventually, even the freelance work dried up. From Hellman, there was no official letter. No phone call. Just silence. He left several messages for large corner office Janson. Was Janson his first or last name? Janson or Jenson? Peter never heard back.

For some, isolation offers the chance to embrace the solitude, the meditative peace of long morning walks and afternoon naps on the couch. Not for Peter. He poured over job search engines, scoured newspapers, emailed and called his old contacts. Resumes were updated and uploaded. Books were purchased and skimmed. These books were tomes dedicated to reshaping the damaged psyche of the unemployed. Even his ex-wife gave him one. *Becoming the Business Buddha: 21 Steps to Claiming Peace, Prosperity, and Inner Strength in the Corporate Climate of 21st Century Consulting.* According to the jacket, the author, Dr. Sanjay Gunnarvita, was a certified life coach specializing in boardroom spirituality. A quick Google search revealed that the author, born Sean Hampton, was not a doctor. In fact, just four years before he published this book, Sean Hampton had been a tax lawyer living in Sheboygan, Wisconsin.

Peter's ex-wife had pleaded over the phone, "You know, it was on the best-seller list, can you give it a chance? What do you have to lose?"

"I'm not going on any spiritual journey," Peter replied, "that starts in Wisconsin."

What did Peter have to lose? Sanity, a sense of purpose, $27.95 on a hardcover at Booktopolis. Everyone kept telling him to change his mindset and yet, at the same time, to remain true to his convictions. He was supposed to adapt to this new urban jungle, yet he was supposed to believe in himself and to be confident in his own abilities. Seventeen people told him to think outside the box. Thirteen of the seventeen told him to concentrate on what he did well, to stick to his guns.

So Peter sought refuge from the only source he could rely

Mark Sleiter

on. His study. He buried himself so deeply into his home office chair the cushioning wore away, leaving a perfect imprint of his imperfect ass so that it looked as if an invisible clone was planted there even in the rare moments the real Peter ventured out. He was going to figure this out. Peter began to hack away at the keyboard, constructing his own business model, best-seller lists be damned. Pages were taped to walls, torn down, wastebaskets filled, pages resurrected, wrinkles unwrinkled.

But a model is nothing without the product. It is a useless artifice, like those half-built condominiums with the faded *Come Inside For Exciting Financing Options!* sign posted over the vacant storefronts on the ground floor. After the *Come Inside*, there was a graffiti'd arrow that led to the words *Your Mom*.

But then it happened. On an unseasonably warm Saturday afternoon in March, Peter once again woke up on his keyboard. He instinctively wiped the drool away with his sleeve, rubbed his cheek until he was confident the tiny key indentations were gone. There was playful shouting outside. Right across the street. The Patrosky twins were sitting behind a card table. Poster board was haphazardly mounted in front. *Lemonade—5¢.* Peter dug through his drawers until he found one. An old business card from his Hellman days. He turned it over and scrawled, *Peter Carter, Lemonade Buddha.*

Rule #3: Strike While the Lemonade is Cold— That night, Peter actually slept in his bed. That next morning, he woke up without neck pain. He finally shaved and wore a belt. He was outside only minutes after the Patrosky twins set up their stand. But how to talk to children?

"Hey, cool lemonade stand you got."

"Thanks," Tara said, peered up at Peter through her fingers, which she used to block out the sun.

"Five cents for a cup," Timmy said, gently patting the sign.

"Wow, that's an amazing deal. Here's a quarter. I'll take a

292

cup and you can keep the extra twenty cents." The Patrosky twins stared at Peter. "See, I'll just take one cup. And you can keep the change...you each get ten cents."

"It's only five cents," said Timmy, again gently patted the sign.

"I know. But you—okay, it's not important. Here's a nickel for that delicious cup," Peter said, dropped a nickel on the table. "How much do your parents pay you?" The twins stared at Peter. Just as Timmy started patting the sign yet again, Peter spoke up, directed his answer to the hair-chewing Tara. "Yeah, five cents for a cup, got it. What if I gave each of you fifteen cents for every hour you worked?" Peter took a sip. "This lemonade is too good to only be 5 cents."

"I'll ask Mom," Tara said with a mouth full of pigtail.

"Okay, great. I'll come back later. Fantastic lemonade." Peter returned home and began planning.

During all those lost nights in the study, Peter had learned something while picking through the detritus of failed back-up plans. There are moments on the razor's edge and when they pass, you know it regardless of the comfortable narratives you perpetuate in order to sleep. When Peter separated from Maggie, and then later when the divorce papers were signed and made official legal tender, he had variations of the same conversations with colleagues at Hellman—in the lounge over Nutrisweetened coffee, after midmorning meetings about quarterly targets, after work at Mick's, the self-proclaimed Irish pub located on the first floor in the office park on the other side of the freeway.

There was Sandra from Accounting, "Oh, Peter, I'm so sorry. Are you okay?"

"Yeah, you know. We just grew apart. It happens."

There was Heinrich from Creative Graphics, "Wow, that's rough. So sorry, man."

"Thanks. We just...wanted different things. What can you do?"

And, of course, there was Charlotte from the front desk, in between gum chomping, "I've been there. Let me know if there is anything I can do, Pete."

"Thanks. We drifted...went in different directions. That's life, I guess, right?"

But it wasn't how it went. Things didn't just happen. Different directions didn't just form. The divorce wasn't some pre-ordained rite of passage. There were moments, Peter knew, that could have been grasped, leapt upon. He knew there was a time when Maggie looked at him differently, stopped gently stroking his cheek, no longer called him at random times to tell him a funny thing her mother said. He remembered going out for drinks more frequently, spending less time at home with her. He recalled that the pattern of conversations had shifted, from one filled with passionate debate and thoughtful reassurance to one that dealt primarily with banal questions. When was the plumber supposed to arrive? Could you tell the lawn guy to remember the hedges this time? Peter had noticed all of this and he'd done nothing.

The same thing had happened at his job. He'd read the press releases from Hellman. There were market constrictions...a series of natural ebb and flow fluctuations...concerns about profit futures and profit margins. Apparently, the people in accounting had used math to figure out that nothing could be done. They would, of course, do anything and everything within their power to save jobs, to save the Hellman family. And every single employee was valued equally.

Peter knew enough to know how this story ended. The employee lounge and break room had TVs turned to business channels at all times. These phrases were so common they had become entrenched in his brain, as if they had been lodged there through some sound wave osmosis. He read the memos written with a shocking number of exclamation points about the importance of meeting the demands of the new economy. The complimentary morning bagels became less plentiful, then extinct. The coffee switched to that instant crystal poison. Tabs on the amount of copies were kept. But yet, Peter denied the ending. Then, he tolerated it. Finally, he accepted it, as if it had been common sense, simple historical fact, like some bold-faced depiction of the greatness of Abraham Lincoln in a high school textbook.

These events taught Peter that decisive action is required. Damn the consequences. From now on, Peter thought that day, life is to be lived like that famous quote suggested. When opportunity knocks at your door, you drag it inside, strangle it, and bury it under the floorboards.

Rule #4: Maneuver lest ye be outmaneuvered— The lemonade racket is not for the faint of heart. The profit margin is hairline thin. The customer base is relatively small— usually consisting of 8-10 suburban blocks per stand. As a childless man working with children, Peter had to constantly fight against the notion that he was "that guy"—the old guy who spends a little too much time around children. After all, this was a post-Penn State world.

At the same time, Peter knew that lemonade was largely an untapped market that had been the hobby of unimaginative people. For example, the taste. To conduct the proper market research, Peter traveled to nearby towns and sought out the most cozy and tree-lined neighborhoods. And it was always the same—sour, lips-pursing lemonade. People didn't really want bitterness. There's enough of that in daily life. They want sugar. By the scoop full. Peter understood diabetic Americans weren't having limbs amputated because of their love of fruit.

Therefore, Peter ensured every one of his pitchers was loaded with so much sugar that there was often a texture. He liked to think of it as having a subtle grainy finish. Next to his stand, Peter placed a small stack of brochures entitled *Our Promise to You*, with the first 'O' in the shape of a lemon. On page one, the customer learned that the texture derived from lemon pulp. And these were not just any lemons the brochure went on to explain. These lemons were organic, local, American. In comparison, the lemons often used by rival stands were said to be shipped from Mexico, farmed with agent orange pesticides and likely financed by cartels.

The truth was that Peter simply bought the cheapest lemons he could find at Grocery Palace. He had no clue where they were from. For all he knew, they came from trees watered with baby seal tears and sprayed with battery acid. He didn't actually use the lemons for lemonade. No, he'd leave a couple out on the table to give the impression that the juice was fresh-squeezed. Occasionally, a few slices were tossed into the pitcher to add allure. The lemonade was actually a mixture of lemon juice, tap water, and wheelbarrows of sugar.

Lemonade came with an established folksy nostalgia for a time when, Peter had been told his entire life, times were simpler and kinder. There is a built-in narrative of spending humid summer evenings on the farmhouse porch with the family, children using words like Pa or Pap-Pap. To recreate this as best he could, Peter convinced the woodworking teacher at the local high school to have his students build a large wood table and a frame for an awning. He borrowed a few wicker chairs from a neighbor under the guise that they would be allotted for the children. "I just want them to be comfortable, you know, relax and enjoy the beautiful weather," he explained to Stan Davis. Technically, the wicker chairs were for the customers. But the medal foldouts weren't that uncomfortable. The kids would be fine. Besides, children's bodies bounce back quickly. One good night of rest and it would be as if their back never hurt in the first place.

Peter borrowed a bale of straw from the pumpkin patch on the edge of town. They just didn't know yet that it had been borrowed. It was one bale and they had plenty, Peter reasoned. He sprinkled the straw all around the stand and the sitting area. On the awning, there was a banner that proclaimed, *Old Country Lemonade: As Good As You Remember It!* The signage was outsourced to the vo-tech school outside of town. The students were given course credit for completing an internship. These were the same students who produced the high quality brochures.

Of course, there had been some misfires. In honor of the local Walk for Cancer Awareness, Peter served pink lemonade. This was simply the same lemonade mixed with some old food coloring he had found while cleaning out his kitchen. He wondered if it had been there since the previous owner lived in the cottage. Unfortunately, something was wrong with the coloring. The lemonade had little pink coagulates floating in it. Two neighborhood kids and one of the cancer walkers projectile vomited during the ribbon ceremony. Peter quickly dumped out the lemonade. When an observer suggested heat stroke and dehydration, Peter concurred, claimed that he, too, felt weak and needed to sit down. On the plus side, none of the kids working the stand were ill, thus proving they weren't skimming the product.

Peter experimented with theme weeks. Upon learning that many of the housewives in the neighborhood participated in a book club, Peter set up the lemonade stand version of the classic French salon. A sign for *Citronnade* was put up. A plate of cheese and crackers was put out. In the sitting area, Peter placed an old typewriter he'd found in the dumpster in front of the foreclosed home a couple of doors down. Peter demanded the kids wear all black, offer candy cigarettes stuck into the end of long black straws, call out "Bonjour, Monsiour! Bonjour, Madame!" As it turned out, the book club was mostly just an excuse to drink wine during the day. The only times Peter saw one of the members was when she laughed and staggered across the lawns back to her specific beige-sided home. The other neighbors just seemed confused. Looking at the rusted typewriter, an impatient jogger asked. "Um, am I supposed to type out how many glasses I want? Do I need to order in French? I'm not speaking any foreign languages in my own goddamn neighborhood." Even the kids were perplexed. "Mr. Carter, are you sure Ritz is a French cracker?"

Then there was the appeal to the local NFL team. Training camp was starting soon and the newspapers had already started devoting special sections to the upcoming season. A 9-7 record last year had resulted in barely missing the playoffs. Optimism was building from a few free agent signings. Peter saw the discount t-shirts with the teams logo at the Grocery Palace, told the children to ask their parents for one. Peter and the children painted a sign in team colors. He took a black magic marker and gave the kids eye black. When the Quick 'N' Pump gave away free team schedules, Peter took a couple handfuls and papered the awning and stand with them, offered them to customers.

Yet, there seemed to be less traffic than normal. And Peter was certain that old Mrs. Novak shook her head despairingly when she rode her bike past. Usually, she stopped to at least stare at Hadley's dimples. Then Peter saw it. Or, rather heard it in the background while eating breakfast. He rarely watched TV, but it hummed and called in soft background tones. Two players on the team, arrested, strip club, groping, fighting, fleeing from scene, car accident, resisting arrest, injured passengers in another car. Peter had chosen the wrong week. He knew it would be at least ten whole days before the neighborhood was back to sporting team flags and commenting in online forums about which players were gay.

Then, there were the overalls. To enhance the general sense of folksiness around the stand, Peter asked that his employees wear overalls. Apparently, combined with the heat and the sun, as employees were not allowed under the customer awning during shifts, the children became overheated. In fact, before the firing, this was one of the complaints issued by the Patrosky twins. Somewhere along the line Tara began making peculiar noises, almost as if speaking in tongues. Her body twitched. At first, Peter wondered if this may bring in the religious market, perhaps he could mold these incantations into another theme week, maybe even sell old lemons with rotting patterns that looked like Shroud of Turin-esque stains. Baptize yourself in the cool lemon water. He could put the football fiasco behind him. But no, Tara seemed legitimately ill and Peter called it a day, sent the kids home. He crossed overalls off the list.

Rule #5: Win. As Peter headed out for his morning walk, he noticed the table across the street. He'd started exercising, stopped drinking, at least before noon, and no longer ate anything from a package covered with cartoon animals. On these long morning walks, he'd slide his new business cards between windshield wipers and into mailboxes. He'd lost twenty-seven pounds in three months. His face was thinner, the skin around his eyes less discolored. He was in negotiations with two other lemonade stands around town. At the one on the corner of Lake and Freedom Valley, the kids wanted eighteen cents an hour and one Oreo per shift. Peter okayed the eighteen cents, but offered the generic Hydrox cookie instead. He was pretty sure they'd cave. After all, it was still chocolate combined with mystery cream. The stand at Willshire and Liberty Trail Boulevard was proving more difficult, not because of a stumbling block in the negotiations, but because one of the children had a strange Idaho-shaped rash on his forehead and had yet to sign the contract. Peter had even been asked by one of the members of that General Mills Wausage campaign to come in for an interview.

But the site of the table stopped all of this, stopped all of the optimistic momentum. Peter started slowly, then picked up speed. Sure enough, it was the Patrosky twins sitting behind a pitcher of lemonade. Another poster board, *World's Best Lemonade – 10¢*. On the one hand, Peter admired their temerity. It was almost fourteen months to the day of their firing. Yet, they had recovered and returned to the fray.

"We're not supposed to talk to you," Tara said.

"Yeah, Dad says," Timmy chimed in. Peter thought they were dim. However, their determination was still a threat. He thought of his current negotiations with the other two stands, of all the hours spent building the charts tacked up in his study.

"Whoa, easy there," Peter said, putting his hands up and taking a step back. "We're all friends here, right?"

"Nah-uh," said Tara, grabbed the cups and slid them off the table into her lap.

"Yeah, Dad says we're not," said Timmy.

"Look, I'm sorry about last year. Really. If you guys ever want to work for a real stand, come on over, okay?" Peter said, pointed over to a giant, conference-room sized table parked next to his driveway.

Timmy stood up. "Dad says—"

"Yeah, got it, Timmy. Dad says. You should be in advertising. You're a natural." Peter decided against the usual morning walk. Instead, he headed back to the cottage and into the office. Decisive action was required. Step #3. He needed to strike. He considered potential lawsuits, perhaps something involving copyright infringement. Or maybe he could find that pink food coloring and drop some in their batch. It's not as if anyone had died the last time.

That night, Peter stopped working when he heard Carl Patrosky pull in across the street, home from work. He could hear Timmy's faint yell. Carl approached their flimsy card table. He saw Timmy and Tara run to him, gyrate around with frantic arm movements. Then Carl spotted it. He bent over and picked up a small white square. After studying it briefly, Mr. Patrosky shot a look over at Peter's cottage, shook his head. Peter knew then that he had dropped it, that white square. His business card. And he knew that when Mr. Patrosky held it up to the light, he would see a picture of a smiling, jubilant Buddha holding a lemon in each hand. Below, he would read the words *Peter Carter, Beverage Provider and Consultant for the 21st Century Lemonade Stand.*

A Better Life

Tammi Truax

Part 1

Everyone on board the *Caledonia*, even the grumpy old captain, was excited. They had all heard stories of the recently completed Lady Liberty and had been told that she was the first thing they would see as they came through the narrows and approached New York Harbor. The captain had said to her weeks ago, "You've never seen anything so big in all yer life. I know tis so as there isn't anything so big as that green girl in all Ireland."

Yesterday they'd been told they were nearing their destination, and everyone was clamoring for a view from the starboard side of the steamship. Margaret Erin O'Brien was a passenger in steerage, and the first and second class passengers were the only ones who could see well. Maggie and another favored girl from below were most fortunate to have been allowed to come up this far just to try and get a peek. She called upon the patience that had sustained her through the long grueling trip, and shared her excitement with the friends she'd made on board.

Maggie hadn't really wanted to leave her home in County Cork, but her family needed to send her to America where a better life was assured, and she would be able to send money home to help her large troubled family. It was 1898 and she had only recently turned twenty years of age. Her parents thought she was old enough and sharp enough to venture out on her own and they had worked hard to save the steerage fee and send her off with a carpet bag containing a blanket, two dresses, a cake, and a handful of coins. Tucked tightly down underneath all of that she had hidden her prized possessions: a silver hair brush and hand mirror that she had wrapped in a linen runner hand-embroidered by her maternal grandmother. She felt coveting those items reflected her vanity, because truth be told, she loved brushing her thick curly mane, and felt a little ashamed of herself. She'd pray for forgiveness for it regularly, but Maggie was a stubborn Irish girl and wouldn't change her ways for anybody.

Even in coming to America, she hadn't fought the idea of leaving home with the ferocity she might have if she hadn't known that if she stayed in County Cork she would have to relent and marry Frankie Sullivan, a boy she'd known all her life and who made her sick. One of her older sisters had already married a Sullivan, had four Sullivan babies so far, and they were all miserable. Seemed to Maggie you couldn't be a Sullivan and be happy. Frankie was drinking and carousing at this very moment she was sure, and if not was asleep in a stinking heap somewhere.

Though she hadn't truly wanted to come to America, she now couldn't wait to set her feet upon solid ground again. The journey across the sea on this pitching ship was the most unpleasant experience of her life which had never been soft and easy. She couldn't wait to wash the stench of it off of her with some clean water. And while she knew she wouldn't find her mum's cooking in America she was so hungry she felt hollow and was certain her belly would be filled when she made her way ashore. The boat was making an agonizingly slow entrance into the harbor and the wind whipped Maggie's curls about her head so that her hair pins were rendered useless and she clasped her shawl at her throat while the wind tried to take it back to Ireland. Then she saw it.

A huge green woman reaching up into the sky with a blazing torch and glowing crown, holding fast to the holy book. It was indeed a welcome sight, and Maggie had no doubts that she was welcome and she would find a better life. She could also see the tall buildings of America in the distance and a big long bridge that seemed to be hanging in the sky. The children were jumping up and down, and some of the women wept. More amazing then the Lady of Liberty to Maggie, was the palace. She saw an enormous and beautiful castle on an island and everyone said that was where they were going. That was Ellis Island. It did indeed look like paradise.

After dropping off the upper class passengers, the captain moved the ship to where the steerage passengers were finally allowed to board a barge that took them all to the front entrance of the big brick building. At last they could disembark and climb onto American soil. It was time to get in line, first just to get up the main stone stairway where hundreds and hundreds of other people also fell in. It was noisy and exciting and quite frightening. Maggie saw people wearing the strangest clothes, hats and hairstyles. She saw women carrying parcels on their heads and some with baskets on their backs. She saw people trying to walk who were too weak and sick to make it to the end of their journey. She saw family members being separated from each other and terrified children clinging to their loved ones. The uniforms worn by the inspectors were especially intimidating to many of the foreigners. It was clear in short time that not everyone was being welcomed and there were so many people: men, women, and children from all over the world, trying to get through. First, Maggie had to answer twenty-nine questions. That task was easy for her; she always had an answer and didn't mind telling it. She didn't even mind when she was asked a trick question like "How would you wash a staircase?" That one made her smile.

Next came a medical examination, and she could see quite a few people were failing the inspection as they were whisked off in other directions after a chalk X was drawn on their backs. There had been much illness on the ship, but Maggie was strong and healthy. She hadn't seen many doctors in her life, but this inspection reminded her of how her father had examined a horse he was considering purchasing. When it was her turn a doctor looked her in the eyes, nose and mouth, turned her around, told her to cough, and slammed a stamp across her documents with a yell to move on.

The next line was the slowest one and Maggie didn't understand what it was about. When it was her turn she was given a chair to sit down in while an official examined her documents. "You are unmarried?"

"Yes," Maggie replied.

"Who will support you here?" he asked.

"I will support meself," Maggie answered nervously.

"You have no male relatives here? No one is here to receive you?" he quizzed.

"I have friends on the boat, and there are many other people from my village living in America," she offered. "I am a very hard worker, and have a letter of introduction from my church," she added.

He shut her passport book and slid it back at her across the little table. "Without a means of support you cannot stay, and will have to return with the ship. Entry denied. Next!"

A guard drew an X on Maggie's back and pointed her in a direction different from her fellow passengers who looked at her with sad and serious silence. She was led by a matron with several very sick and forlorn people to an area of the great hall designated for those denied entry. She sat on a hard wooden bench and listened to languages being spoken that seemed the most peculiar sounds she had ever heard. Someone must have noticed her fatigue for eventually she was given fresh water and soda crackers. This first act of kindness made her cry a little. As the day wore on she was asked to tell her story a few times to guards and officials, and she always hoped for a reprieve. Each time she was told she would be put back on a ship bound for Europe in the morning because she could not become a public charge.

At supper time one of the guards took them to a cafeteria where they were served a soothing and delicious meal of warm fish and white bread, with all the milk they wanted to drink. Everyone filled their bellies. Maggie noticed but did not care about the absence of potatoes. Later she was taken to a special sleeping dormitory, and was allowed to use a lavish bathroom with sinks, pull flush toilets, and running water. Everything they had ever heard about America was clearly true, and Maggie was heartbroken about being denied entry, and failing her family. Everyone in the detention pen was heartbroken and the guards kept a close watch on them, looking out not so much for escapees but for suicides.

One of the guards, an older man named Henry Hogancamp, was taken aback by the beauty of the brave young lady he'd met. Her dark curly hair, bright green eyes and haunting brogue stayed with him all the way to his neighborhood tavern in a New Jersey town that evening. After a couple of pints he shared her story with the boys.

"So sad, really, fellas. Such a sweet and decent lass who has come so far just to help her family. Seems a shame to send the pretty ones back," he said with a laugh. All the men nodded and sipped in agreement. Then one at the end of the bar, a shy and young regular named William Gordon, said "I'll marry her."

Everyone looked at him. William, a brick layer by trade, who turned up almost every night for refreshment and companionship, rarely drew attention to himself.

"What?' said Henry with one bushy eyebrow cocked in question.

"I'll marry the girl," he declared with a defiant placement of his mug on the bar. "If what you say is true; I will marry the girl and give her a home. She can find work here."

After a few moments of silence and staring everyone began cheering and laughing and patting William on the back. He and Henry agreed to return to Ellis Island together first thing in the morning. Henry laughed some more and yelled to Jimmy to pour another round. "We're going to have a wedding tomorrow!" he hollered. They spent the next couple of hours toasting and boasting about all things, blessing and advising the groom, and singing songs from their homelands.

While in the Ellis Island dormitory Maggie had a fretful night's sleep in the cleanest, softest bed she had ever slept in, after praying to God not to see fit to take these bountiful gifts from her. In the desperation of the darkness she made a promise to him, and she was sure that he could hear her in this place that proved prayers were answered.

Part 2

Margaret appeared to be staring at the only adornment hanging on the walls of the bedroom, a crude picture of the crucifixion, showing Christ wearing a countenance similar to her own, less the tear shaped drops of blood stroking his face.

This time though, she was not looking at Jesus, nor was she praying. She was looking at the cracks in the plaster near the painting, seeing them and accepting them with a sad resignation. From there her eyes slowly scanned the small bedroom, taking inventory of what other people were going to see when they entered. The sparse furnishings of an old wardrobe and a chest of drawers with one of its six knobs missing, along with the simple four post double bed, were not a matched set, but were all well-polished. The bureau was topped with her most prized possessions. Items she had hand carried here from home; a pretty runner of embroidered linen and a silver hairbrush and hand mirror. All old, but still beautiful. She looked at the faded curtains in the window and was comforted by how clean and well mended they were. The saggy old mattress she was lying on was in pitiful shape, but was covered with clean and pressed bedding. Her eyes came to rest on the worn chenille coverlet draped across the bed, punctuated by her toes. She didn't like the silly way her feet were poking up in the bed, and she pointed them downward, unconsciously turning and softly overlapping her toes just as Christ's were in the picture. The coverlet too showed the wear of countless cleanings and from hours hanging in the sun on a taut line strung across the back alley.

She still loved the old wallpaper that had sold her on this place long ago, though it was faded, even ripped in a few places. Big flat peonies repeating themselves in a monotonous pattern nature would never emulate.

People would be coming soon she thought to herself, and she wished she had done just a bit better preparing for this time. It had come upon her somewhat faster than she had anticipated.

Throughout the twenty seven years that she and William had been married she had, of course, taken great pains to avoid his catching her in any state of undress, but because of his complete lack of regard for his wife's privacy, he had caught her two nights ago sitting here, on the edge of their marriage bed, unbloused, looking at and touching her bosom. Fresh tears asked to be released as the humiliation of the moment revisited her yet again.

William, who had been entering the room at an accelerated and ungainly pace, would have frozen in his old boots upon seeing her, if the liquor hadn't caused him to swoon. A gasp, dumb-founded and frightened, escaped his gaping mouth. But it was the look in his eyes, the horrified and confused look in his rheumy eyes that mirrored what she felt about herself that was most disturbing.

After a few frozen moments of silently staring at each other William had turned and left the room with the surprising air of a gentleman. Maggie spent only another moment gathering her thoughts, before she put her hand back to her heart, resting it momentarily on the hot and puckered protrusion that had taken over much of her left breast. Without wincing from the pain she manually moved the breast back into her undergarment. She had only come in here to redress a discharge from the nipple which had become copious. If she didn't change the rags she dressed it with her blouse would become visibly soiled and the foul odor would become too noticeable. She slowly slid her arms back into her blouse. The left sleeve required extra effort as her arm was sore and swollen. Her small and nimble fingertips worked each tiny white button starting at the bottom of her blouse, and moving upward, handling each one in exactly the same way and at exactly the same speed, though as she neared her throat they became just slightly shaky, as she knew she must go face her husband. Before rising to her feet she took another look at Jesus, then bowed her head for a moment, whispering to the wooden floor boards, "May the power of God preserve us," and with that she swallowed everything that she was feeling without the belt of whiskey to wash it down with that William was having on the other side of the thin wall.

Standing up, she had adjusted her skirt and finished tucking in her blouse tightly around her thin body. She reached up and smoothed her pinned up hair back into position by feel, before slowly turning the doorknob and stepping into the kitchen where William sat at the table. His back was to her, his hand and eyes resting on his empty glass. She walked forward and pulled out the other chair. Lowering herself into it, while she lowered her gaze, it coming to rest on her hands which she clasped on her lap. For a moment there was a silence between them and throughout their apartment, which felt unusual and tender to her somehow. When he spoke, she raised her eyes to meet his. "What is it Maggie? What's happening to you? Are ya sick?"

The concern in his voice and face was so unlike the way he usually was with her that much of the resentment she carried for him dissipated in that moment. He seemed a child, and she wondered how he'd manage without her, which is exactly what he was thinking. She was surprised at herself, having always been at the ready with a quick reply, when she wasn't sure what to say.

"Yes," croaked out of her throat as if the word were part of the fire in her breast that couldn't be excised.

"Have you seen a doctor? You haven't, have you? I'm sending for Doc Pennington tomorrow."

With that the tears that she had been adamant would not

be shed, began. "Oh William, I can't bear to show anyone. Please. We cannot undo what God has seen fit to do. It is his will."

After a moment, the drink driven husband she was accustomed to returned, and pushing back his chair noisily while rising, stated in a belligerent tone, "It is my will that the doctor come," and then he walked out banging his way down the stairs with a lack of regard for the neighbors. He left without having his supper and didn't come home all night, none of which surprised her.

The next day at three o'clock Dr. Andrew Pennington had slowly climbed the three flights of stairs to their flat. Maggie prided herself on her ability to recognize people's footsteps as they approached, and though he'd only been there a couple of times over the last decade, she knew it was him well before he reached the landing. She cleaned her hands of the potato peels and wash water with her dish rag while he paused before knocking. When he finished the three raps with his knuckles she got up from the table to let him in.

"Mrs. Gordon," he stated flatly upon seeing her.

"Afternoon doctor," she said while holding the door open for him. "May I make you some tea?"

"No, ma'am," he said already sounding impatient. "I've come at your husband's urgent request to examine you. He has told me a little of your condition, but it is necessary for me to make a thorough visual examination in order to come to any conclusion."

He saw her hand slide up her cotton blouse and hold the lapel shut against her chest, and he took on a distinctly more authoritative tone. "Now if you would kindly retire to your bed after undressing to the waist. You can cover yourself with a blanket before and after the examination. I'll give you a few minutes to prepare." He left no room for discussion as he crossed into the kitchen, set his bag down on the table and walked over to the deep porcelain basin. He looked out the little window over the sink at boys kicking a can around in the alley below and grimaced slightly at their vulgar language, while he unfastened and rolled up his sleeves with three deft and equal folds up each arm. Turning on the faucet handle without invitation he thought again about carrying his own soap in his bag. He detested the smell of the homemade lye soap that he often found in these tenement buildings, though sometimes there was no soap at all. He had been meaning to ask his wife to see to this for him as she was adept at selecting fine perfumed soaps while shopping in the city. When he'd washed both hands briefly he turned the faucet handle off tightly as the pipes buckled and belched back at him, and then held his hands up. Looking around the tiny kitchen he saw only the damp dish rag Maggie had hung out smoothly on the back of her chair. He reached down and wiped his hands dry, both back and front, on his trouser legs. It was the second day he had worn them but he considered them relatively clean. Feeling that he had allowed his patient ample time to prepare, he picked up his black bag, and with a knocking push he let himself into the adjacent bedroom.

Maggie sat up as tall as she could in the bed while still holding up the covers as close to her neck as they would come. Dr. Pennington switched on the electric light and the bright bare bulb hanging on a heavy chord made her blink. For some reason the bulb swung a bit back and forth. She wished she had taken Jesus down or turned him around. She looked at the far away wall, and put her toes back in the crucifix position.

"Please lie down," the doctor said matter of factly, and she slid down further under the blankets. He opened his bag which he had set at the foot of the bed, and removed the stethoscope, which he hung around his neck. Then taking a couple of steps closer to the head of the bed, he skillfully folded the blanket down from the upper left corner revealing Maggie's naked and deformed breast. Unlike William he showed no reaction, but he did bend down to look very closely. Much to Maggie's own horror he then touched her breast in several places, and pressed also into the pit of her

310

arm. Watching him with just the corner of her right eye and while trying hard not to, Maggie saw him cock his head to and fro as he looked at her from different angles, and at one point she thought she saw him consciously smell the area. He listened to her heart with the instrument and also her lungs. He then lifted her left arm over her head and lowered it again. When she did not react he said, "This is painful, is it not?"

"Yes," she whispered to the wall. Folding the blanket back further he even looked at the other breast and arm, and seemed to be comparing the two sides of her body. He slid one hand down to her belly and pressed on her organs in several places. "Are there any other areas of your body afflicted?" he asked.

"No," she said finally able to meet his gaze again as he replaced the blanket across her body.

He ended his exam by feeling her neck and peering down into her throat while making her stick her tongue out, and feeling her forehead with his palm. Returning his stethoscope to his bag, he cleared his throat indicating he was going to begin speaking. He didn't need to demand her attention. He unrolled his shirt sleeves as he began. "When did you first notice this condition, Mrs. Gordon?"

Notice it? Maggie was taken aback by this question and so not sure how to answer it. Her heart had been broken and aching since she boarded the Caledonia years ago, and slowly, so slowly it had been barely noticeable, the heartache that she had felt inside had grown and spread outside her body, and the pain of it grew in direct proportion to her guilt. It was her cross to bear for her sins and those of her husband, she thought returning her gaze to Jesus. "It's been a year or two," she offered.

"And you told no one?" he asked though it sounded more like a statement.

"I did mention something of it to Father Reilly once," she said in atonement. Father had admonished her for her irregular attendance in church and for never convincing her husband to join the Catholic faith. These were her sins and

Father hadn't needed to remind her that it was so. She carried the weight of them upon her heart since the day she had been married and it was a heavy load.

"Have you done anything for treating the affliction?" he inquired thoughtfully.

"I make a poultice sometimes when it is very feverish, and at first I tried drinking Mrs. Mulholland's special tea. It didn't seem to do any good."

"All right then, Mrs. Gordon. You need to get more rest, and you can take aspirin morning and evening as needed. Tell your husband to come to my office tomorrow. I will check in on you again in a week or so. I will let myself out."

She didn't move until she had heard him gently close both doors as he passed through them.

The next day William actually did show up at Dr. Pennington's office. Though he was dreading the meeting, he was, for the first time since he was fifteen years old, facing a serious situation almost completely sober. He had wanted to stop off along the way and top himself off, but something prevented him. It might have been fear of the words he might hear, but it might also have been knowing that he would be held in judgment by the patronizing physician. Though he wanted to run away in the other direction William opened the door with the name sign hanging out over the main street of town not far, but worlds away, from his neighborhood. After being asked to wait briefly in the darkened hallway, the nurse told him he could go into the office speaking to him in a sympathetic tone of voice.

Dr. Pennington sat behind a big wooden desk and did not get up when William entered. He had spectacles balanced on the end of his significant nose, and seemed to be going over a ledger. After ignoring William for a few seconds he lifted the long green, rectangular cover and let it drop shut with an audible thud.

"William," he said.

"Doc," William replied, as his legs sought the support of

the chair and he sank into it. He wished he had relieved himself before coming in this damn place.

"I'm sorry to say it is the cancer," he said calmly.

William's face paled but otherwise he didn't react. "It is in an advanced state already, and her pain is going to worsen soon. The only possible treatment is a complete amputation of the breast. That would likely lengthen, but not save, her life, as it appears that the disease has already spread beyond the chest wall. It is also a difficult and expensive operation that must take place in the hospital where she would have to stay for about six weeks. There are some Samaritan funds available, and your wife's church might also lend some support as I know you are of modest means. If you think you can get your wife to submit to surgery I would be willing to perform the procedure trusting that you have understood all I have said here today."

William looked at the doctor who met his gaze. William's mouth hung open in the same way as when he'd first discovered his wife's secret, and a horrible taste spread inside of it. He blinked several times looking for focus, his forehead broke out in a cold sweat, and his stomach began to churn violently. "Do you have any questions?" the doctor softly inquired.

"I...I...," William stammered. He rose to his feet. He shook his head vigorously, and the room lurched. "I don't know," he said with complete honesty. He turned and fled, through the outer office, past the staring nurse who'd been listening from her desk, out into the common hallway. He quickly made his way to the water closet at the end of the hall and rushed inside. Clicking the door shut, William lowered himself, for the first time in his married life, to his knees.

Transgression

Jane Vacante

He rings the doorbell at five seconds to one in the afternoon. I let him and his equipment into my house. I look him up and down, mostly down since he is about three inches shorter than I. I'm a little taller than the average woman. There is a precision to his appearance as exact as the timing of his arrival. Brown hair that's neat but not short in a military way. Regular features: a rather pointed nose, cool blue eyes behind wire-rimmed glasses. He isn't the kind of exterminator I'd expected.

My husband and I had called for help after weeks of watching innocuous-looking black ants create pyramids of sawdust around our newly purchased old house. We chose *Colonial Exterminators,* an appropriate name for those heroes who were going to eliminate our colony of carpenter ants.

The exterminator deposits his equipment in the front hall. I invite him into the dining room where we settle at the oak table. He has a worn briefcase with him. From it he selects some informational pamphlets and spreads them out between us. I admire his long sturdy fingers as he pushes the papers toward me. He resembles a youthfully serious teaching assistant in his denim shirt and pressed corduroy pants. In turn, I nudge a plate of gingersnaps and a cup of cider to his side of the table. He munches, sips and explains what he will be doing, interspersing technical details with interesting small talk.

Did I know that some ants in Sumatra are so poisonous that... he says. *Had I heard that the roaches sent up in the space capsule...?*

He becomes animated; little spots of color appear on his

315

cheeks. I am moved by his dour attractiveness. I realize he's been to college.

The two cats sidle into the room and prowl the periphery. The grey male keeps his distance but the gregarious calico rubs her head against the corduroy-clad knee. The exterminator peers down at the cat but does not extend his arm to touch her. He sits up straighter, adjusts his glasses with thumb and index finger and crisply turns to business. I hand him the money. He recites warning notices for the chemical combo he's about to wield. Don't eat it, inhale it, touch it. Heavy hints of impending mayhem.

We walk through the house's six rooms and I point out the trouble spots. In the kitchen he glances at a copy of Jackie Collins' latest novel which is on the table.

It's not really mine, I silently protest. *I got it from the library!*

Too late. His eyebrow shoots up for a second, then he glances away. Too bad for me. It's the influence of such books that causes me to wonder what the proverbial 15 minutes in a broom closet would be like with him.

In the cellar he points out a spot vulnerable to insect invasion. It's a debris-filled damp corner. I offer to sweep it out. Okay. He'll do the rest of the house, then return to finish the cellar. I sweep, then go upstairs to read the cautionary literature. This stuff he's spraying kills ants, earwigs, silverfish, spiders. I feel a genuine pang. I like our spiders. Such weird variety: daddy longlegs, fat garden ones, miniatures. All are watchers keeping out the really pernicious insects. A house without spiders won't seem authentically antique; no cobwebs shimmering in the cellar's nooks.

These sentimental meanderings make me stray from the path of my chief concern: my safety and that of the cats. A faint meow alerts me to the fact that the grey cat has sneaked down to the cellar. Forbidden territory! I run down to grab him. Then, muttering about what a guilty cat he is, I chase the furry culprit up the stairs and come face to face with the exterminator in the doorway, his expression sullen.

Did you mean I should feel guilty about letting the cat go downstairs? he asks.

His question tips me off balance. I carefully explain that I had been talking to the cat. Now it's my turn to raise an eyebrow at this guy. The door to my anxiety closet creaks open a little. The door to the broom closet slams shut.

I feel bad about the spiders, the cats, this man holding a mortiferous spray tank in his hands. Hands which could just as easily caress someone. I go to the living room with the cats and close the door after us. We sit there waiting for the end.

In a while I venture out of the room alone, a scout in once-familiar territory. The exterminator descends the steps from the second floor.

It's over, he says.

I ask if he's completed the cellar.

I told you already that I did it.

His blue eyes appear to have frozen over. The chill raises goose pimples on my arms.

We walk out to the porch. This is where the main ant colony had been. Uncountable numbers of small segmented bodies, some still twitching, dot the slate floor. The sight of this miniature necropolis amazes me. I comment on the few ants still reeling in circles.

Yeah, he says as he loads his equipment back into the van, *it's my particular… pleasure to fry their tiny brains.*

All the little deaths don't bother me so much at this moment as the sense, as the van moves out of the driveway, that there's just been a break-in here.